Fountain of Secrets

ALSO BY ANITA CLENNEY

Awaken the Highland Warrior

Embrace the Highland Warrior

Faelan: A Highland Warrior Brief

Guardians of Stone (The Relic Seekers)

Fountain of Secrets

The Relic Seekers

ANITA CLENNEY

Printed in the United States of America.

Published by Montlake Romance
PO Box 400818
Las Vegas, NV 89140

ISBN-10: 147780868X
ISBN-13: 9781477808689
Library of Congress Control Number: 2013906196

This book is dedicated to my mom and dad, two of the kindest, gentlest souls I know, whose presence reminds me that in spite of my love of mystery and adventure, nothing is more grand or amazing than real life.

"Never do outrage nor murder, and always flee treason; also, by no means to be cruel, but to give mercy unto him that asketh mercy, upon pain of forfeiture of their worship and lordship of King Arthur forevermore; and always to do ladies, damsels, and gentlewomen succor, upon pain of death. Also, that no man do battle in a wrongful quarrel for no law, nor for the world's goods."

"To ride abroad redressing wrongs, To speak no slander, no, nor listen to it, To honor his own words as if his God's."

"To love one maiden only, cleave to her, and worship her by years of noble deeds, until they won her."

—The Knights of the Round Table

PROLOGUE

WAKE UP!" THE YOUNG GIRL SHOOK HER FRIEND'S SHOULDER. He woke with a gasp, his forehead covered with sweat. "You're dreaming."

"Do you have some water? I'm thirsty."

She brought her cup. "It's almost gone. There's just a little left."

He drained the water, his heart still pounding with visions of swords and battles . . . and the other part that made no sense. The grave.

"Was it the same one again?" the girl asked.

He nodded. "I wish I knew what it meant."

"It means you're special," she said.

Special. How could he be special if no one wanted him?

CHAPTER ONE

IT WAS THE ROAR THAT WOKE HER. KENDALL LAY FOR A moment trying to figure out if it was real or a dream. Her ability to sense things was sometimes a curse. She eased out of bed and walked to the door of her bedroom at Nathan's mansion. He had insisted they stay here when they returned from Italy two days ago. He and Jake were trying to assess the threat level since the Reaper was obviously still out there.

She opened her door and stepped into the hallway. Another door opened near hers and Jake stepped out, disheveled dark hair hugging his neck, a bare chest that would make a nun lust, and, of course, underwear. She darted back into her room, hoping he hadn't seen her. At least he hadn't been naked, which according to him was how he preferred to sleep.

Dismissing the roar as part of her dream, since all the guards hadn't come running, she lay down and tried to go back to sleep, but the image of Jake half naked burned behind her closed lids. She'd been avoiding him for the past two days. She didn't have flings with coworkers, and for now they were both employed by Nathan, whether Jake wanted it or not. But avoiding Jake wasn't easy. He appeared around every corner, tempting her with just a look.

Nathan, on the other hand, was more secretive than ever, which was disappointing since all three of them had bonded over their bizarre experiences in Italy. Those kinds of experiences tended to bring people together or make them steer clear. Nathan appeared to be steering clear.

Giving up on sleep for the moment, she found her bag and pulled out her relics log. For as long as she could remember, she had kept a record of the relics she discovered. Other girls had diaries and boys. She had her log, her relics, and Adam. Kendall opened the log and grabbed a pen from her nightstand.

Relic—The Spear of Destiny . . .

She paused there, letting the words she had written sink in. The Spear of Destiny. Unbelievable. But it was real.

Location—Umbria, Italy, hidden inside a monk's coffin in catacombs.

Nathan recently discovered the existence of a secret order in Italy called the Protettori, a group that protects powerful relics along with vast amounts of treasure. He sent me, along with Jake Stone, a bodyguard/mercenary . . .

Her pen was poised over the paper . . . Hot guy? No, that wouldn't do . . . *to Italy to investigate the claims and search for a mysterious box, which we later discovered held the Spear of Destiny. We found a castle hidden in an isolated area, surrounded by large statues that seemed to function as a sort of electric fence. There was a guard named Raphael who didn't want us there, but who reluctantly played host. He put us in the tower room, which turned out to be our prison. We escaped and found hidden catacombs underneath the castle grounds where the Spear of Destiny was hidden with one of the monks inside his coffin. Three thieves followed us and stole the spear. From what we can determine, the thieves were hired by a man known as the Reaper, as in the Grim Reaper of relics. He steals collections and kills the owners. He appears to be rich* and well connected, not to mention impossible to find. A man named Edward Romano was also working for the Reaper, but he was trying to double-cross his boss and take the spear for himself. He's dead now as well, killed by a ghost. Yet another unbelievable thing, but there were three witnesses, including myself. Ghosts, mystical statues, and creepy guards. Lots of strange things about this place.

And strange people. There was another man at the castle, Marco. He seemed to know me from when I was a child. He said I came to the castle with my father and Adam. I remember only bits and pieces, but I have to wonder at the remarkable coincidence. At first, Jake believed Nathan must have known about the castle and sent me there on purpose, but I don't think so. Although Nathan is hiding things. Something is strange about him. He has these episodes that are brought on by a surge of adrenaline. He's almost inhumanly strong and fast, and, most bizarre, his eyes glow as if on fire. It was terrifying, but impressive, watching him fight the Reaper's men who attacked us at the castle. Fergus and Marco fought as well. Marco was shot trying to protect me and was in a coma until yesterday. He still spends most of his time sleeping but should recover. Nathan has the spear now. He hasn't told us where he's keeping it, and I suspect he won't. We still have to figure out what to do with the treasure hidden at the castle. Too many people know about the place.

One of the threats is a woman named Brandi who's trying to destroy the relics and the Reaper because he killed her family. Her brother was the last to die. He had been working undercover for the Reaper, while trying to find out his true identity. Edward killed her brother, but Brandi still blamed the Reaper. She's more desperate now. I expect we haven't seen the last of her.

I don't know how much longer we can wait for Marco to recover enough to tell us what to do with the treasure. I'm sure the

Reaper still wants it, as well as the Spear of Destiny and the other three relics that the Protettori are protecting. We have to find them before the Reaper does. And I need to find out why Marco keeps mentioning Adam. I have begun to believe that either Nathan or Jake could be him, but I haven't found enough evidence yet.

Kendall closed the log and put it aside. With a yawn, she turned off the light and lay down, staring at the blackness of the room. Was Marco just confused? He remembered Adam coming to the castle with her, but he had mentioned him as if he were still alive. There were other things troubling her. The Protettori's crosses weren't just necklaces; they were keys, but she was certain she was missing something. She tossed and turned well into the night. When morning came, she was gritty eyed and grumpy. She'd slept too long after a night of unrest and dreams. After a late breakfast, which Fergus had thoughtfully kept warm on the sideboard in the breakfast room, she stopped by Nathan's office to ask for a closer look at the crosses. He wasn't in.

She checked the library and the other parts of the mansion, but she couldn't find him. The Mercedes he'd been driving all month was still in the garage. He changed cars like she changed earrings. She hated to disturb him in his private rooms, but she needed to see the crosses. She walked upstairs to the far end of the third floor where his bedroom and study were located. She knew this because Fergus had once asked her to deliver a document to Nathan. He wasn't in the study, but the small velvet bag that held the crosses lay on top of his desk. The moment she picked up the bag, she heard gasping from Nathan's bedroom next door. It sounded like someone was choking. She shoved the bag into her pocket and hurried to his room. She rapped against the heavy wood, but he didn't answer. The gasping continued.

"Nathan? Are you OK?" Worried, Kendall turned the knob and the door opened. Nathan thrashed on the bed, body straining as if he had been chained, eyes closed. Kendall hurried to him, leaned down, and touched his arm. "Nathan, wake up!"

His eyes flew open. This close, the amber looked like a flame. She started to jump back, but he grabbed her arm. Trapped, she stared into his eyes, apprehensive, yet mesmerized by the glow. It was beautiful. His head moved closer, and she wasn't sure if he was going to kiss her or bite her. "Nathan," she whispered, "let me go."

"Kendall?" He dropped her arm and quickly sat up.

There was enough light from the hall to see that he had a tattoo on one shoulder. Nathan with a tattoo? That was almost as shocking as his glowing eyes. And it was obvious that he slept naked. She averted her gaze as he pulled the sheet higher.

"I'm sorry you saw that." He was still breathing hard, but his eyes were normal now.

"I wouldn't have come in, but I thought you were choking. I'll leave."

"Don't go." He reached for her but drew his hand back, clutching the sheet instead.

She didn't leave, but she did take a step away from the bed. "What is it like when it happens? Does it hurt?"

He rubbed his tattooed shoulder as if he were cold. "Some. It feels like an animal is inside, trying to get out."

"You're not an animal."

"Is that one of your hunches?"

The question might have been sarcastic except for the desperate hope in his eyes. She knew Nathan trusted her sixth sense, even more than she did at times. "It's common sense. You're not . . . bad. You've never hurt anyone."

"I did at the castle."

"That was self-defense. You had to."

"I think I hurt someone before, when I was a kid. I can't remember my childhood, but I have this dream. I'm young. There's a

7

man with me. He's injured, bleeding. Dying, then the dream stops. I can't remember anything before or after. But I feel as if it's my fault he died." His British accent wasn't strong, but it was more pronounced when he was tired.

"I'm sure it wasn't, if you were just a kid. You don't know the man?"

"I should, but I don't. It's frustrating."

"You don't remember anything about your childhood? Your mother, your father?"

"No. My mother died when I was a baby."

Just like hers. And Adam's. That might be a clue.

"My father died later," Nathan said. "I don't remember him. Sometimes I get glimpses, not even a face, just a feeling."

She knew that sensation well. "How did he die?" She didn't want to ask if it had been in a plane crash. Her suspicions felt ridiculous, but Marco had looked right at Nathan and Jake when he said he saw Adam.

"He was in some kind of witness protection program, but he was killed."

That didn't sound like Adam. Could Uncle John have been in witness protection? Maybe she should be looking at Jake, not Nathan. "I had no idea." She was stunned that they were actually discussing it now. She had thought he just didn't want to talk about it with her. "Fergus has been with you since you were a boy, hasn't he?"

Nathan nodded. "He's been like a father to me."

"It must be hard to not remember anything." Her memories were wonderful and painful, but they were hers.

The look he gave her was far from the usual serious stare. There was hurt behind his eyes. "It's empty. But maybe it's best. I might be forgetting something I wouldn't want to remember."

"Cozy," a hard voice said. Jake stood in the doorway, hands shoved in his pockets, face tight.

"What're you doing here?" Nathan asked. He started to get up, then looked at his sheet and stopped.

"Not having as much fun as you."

"We weren't doing anything." Nathan scowled. "What do you want?"

"Hank's looking for you. He said it's important. Looked like the veins in his neck might explode."

"Bloody hell. I'm late. I need to get dressed." He slid to the edge of the bed.

"I'm going to my apartment," Kendall said. "I haven't been since we got back."

"Fine," Nathan said, starting to rise.

Jake took Kendall's arm and pulled her from the room. He shut the door firmly behind them. "Now I know why you've been avoiding me. You're in bed with the boss."

Kendall slapped his arm. "Sometimes I want to hit you."

"You just did."

"I want to hit you harder. There's nothing going on between Nathan and me, and if there were, it's none of your business."

"You slept with me. Maybe it's a guy thing, but that feels like it makes it my business."

"You make it sound as if we had sex. I slept in your bed out of necessity, not choice." Kendall stalked off toward her room without looking back. She was going to go home and get away from men for a while. Good-looking ones, mysterious ones, evil ones. She was tired of them all.

She was surprised Nathan hadn't told her not to leave since he'd been so insistent that they stay here until now. After all, as he kept reminding her when they'd first returned from Italy and she insisted she needed to go home, the Reaper was still alive, and he still wanted the Spear of Destiny, and there had been several attempts to kill or kidnap her.

As she drove the winding road toward Charlottesville, she kept thinking about her conversation with Nathan. They'd never talked about their childhoods, and now that they had, she felt even more connected to him. But how could he be Adam if his father was in a witness protection program? Uncle John hadn't been in a program. Had he? She had been just a kid. They wouldn't have told her if he had. But Adam would have told her. Maybe Adam hadn't known. Or maybe she was an idiot and Nathan had absolutely no connection to Adam. Marco was just an old man with a wandering mind.

She stopped at the ATM to get cash and then found a sporting goods store to replace her flashlight and thermal blanket. When she got out of the car to go inside, she felt the bag in her pocket. The crosses. She had forgotten about them. Occasionally, she took objects home to study, but Nathan always knew beforehand. She stuck the crosses in her purse. When she got back to the mansion she would return them. In the meantime, this was a perfect opportunity to see if she could discover the secrets they were hiding.

After fighting traffic and getting stuck behind an accident, she drove toward her apartment, which was in a nice, upscale area. Not as upscale as Nathan's estate in Albemarle County. He was hiding in a place where everyone had money. Old money, new money, inherited money, but money, and lots of it. His mansion and gated entrance didn't stand out so much among all the fancy horse farms and vineyards.

Kendall parked her Volkswagen in front of her brick, Tudor-style building. It was nice and quiet. Most of the tenants were old. Kendall was rarely here except to sleep or pick up a change of clothing. More often than not, she ended up staying at the mansion.

She grabbed her purse, which held the leather pouch, and got out of the car. A large black SUV crept into a parking place farther up the street. She couldn't see the driver through the tinted window, but she'd bet money he was one of Nathan's guards. She had mixed feelings about that. It was nice, but irritating. Especially now. She and Nathan had a deep trust when it came to relics and responsibility. She felt guilty knowing he was watching out for her when she'd just borrowed something valuable without permission. Clutching her purse close to her side, she hurried up the sidewalk. If she was lucky, she could find out what she needed to know and get the bag back before Nathan discovered it missing.

"Hey there."

Kendall looked up, surprised to see her good-looking neighbor standing on the sidewalk in front of her. "Todd. You startled me."

"You look like you're in a hurry."

Kendall pressed her purse closer to her side. "I've got some work I need to catch up on."

"You haven't been around lately."

"I was traveling . . . for work."

"So, no fun?"

Hmmm. Ghosts, killer statues, a deadly race with a madman to find the Spear of Destiny. "Just the usual."

"What'd you say you did again?"

She'd told Todd as little as possible about her job. She hadn't known him long, and Nathan had strict confidentiality clauses for his employees. "I catalog antiques for a private collector." That was the public version.

"Antiques are cool. Maybe I could see his collection sometime."

When hell froze over. "He's not very social. Kind of a recluse."

"Old geezer, huh?"

"Right. What're you doing?"

"Looking for you. How about that rain check? You promised you'd make up for our interrupted date."

"Oh, the date." That seemed like eons ago, not days. "Sure. Let me check my schedule and I'll get back to you."

"Don't take too long. I've missed you." He gave her a sexy smile. He was a handsome devil with dark hair and eyes so dark blue they looked black. She couldn't help the quick mental comparison to Jake and Nathan, and wondered with disgust why all of a sudden she was drowning in handsome men. She'd learned the hard way—romance never worked out for her.

"How about next week?"

Todd gave her a long, promising look. "How about this weekend?"

"This weekend. That might work. I'll check my schedule." She smiled and hurried toward her door. If the SUV was one of Nathan's guards, he would want to know all about Todd. Knowing Nathan, he probably already knew what hospital Todd was born in.

Todd was still watching as she closed her door. She locked up and rushed to the kitchen table. Sliding onto a chair, she opened her bag and pulled out the leather pouch. Carefully, she removed the crosses and laid them on the table. All three were similar, but there were slight differences. She picked up Raphael's and ran her fingers over the worn silver. She felt something building and closed her eyes in anticipation. She wasn't expecting the roar. She jumped, and the cross flew out of her hands. She reached for it, but another hand got there first. A sexy, male hand with a scar at the base of the thumb.

"Stealing from the boss?"

Kendall stood, pulse racing. Jake held the cross in his fingers, the rest of him looking just as sexy, even with that sullen jaw. He was still pissed at her because of this morning. "How did you get in here?"

"It wasn't easy. Nathan has you locked up tighter than some of his treasures." His gaze swept the room. "Cozy place. I could get used to this."

"Don't." She reached for the cross, but he pulled back.

"Does Nathan know you have these?"

"I'm studying them."

"Guess that's a no."

"I didn't mean to take them from the mansion. I forgot they were in my pocket. And I'm going to return them. I just wanted to study them in private," she said, emphasizing the word *private*.

"Who were you talking to?"

"Todd. My neighbor."

"Todd." Jake made a grunting sound. "Where's he live?"

"The apartment across from mine."

Grunt again. "He looked *friendly*."

"He is."

"How friendly?"

Kendall shook her head. "You break into my apartment and you're grilling me about my neighbors?"

"I don't like him."

"You don't know him. Did you make a noise a few minutes ago?"

"Like a burp?"

"Like a roar."

"No."

"I could have sworn . . ."

"What kind of roar? Tarzan? Bigfoot?"

"Bigfoot."

"I've seen ghosts and electric statues, why not a Sasquatch? Next we'll have unicorns and elves."

"I must have imagined it." Had she also imagined it last night?

"Another one of your *feelings*?"

"Maybe. Give me the cross?"

He pulled it back. "What's in it for me?" His expression didn't have that carefree Jake look. Definitely still pissed.

"You get to keep your private parts intact."

He scowled and handed her the cross. "There's really nothing between you and Nathan?"

"I told you no. I went to his study and heard a noise. I thought he was choking. He was dreaming, I guess. His eyes were changing."

"And you went inside? What if he'd hurt you?"

"He's not dangerous."

"Conjure up the guys he's killed and tell them."

"That was self-defense. And he was protecting us."

"So now he's a superhero?" Jake grunted. "Then why have you been avoiding me?"

"I've been busy."

"Busy, my ass."

"I've been sitting with Marco as much as I can." The old man had been unconscious most of the time, only waking for a minute or two at a time.

"You know what I think?" His eyes were steady, maybe even hopeful.

"What do you think?"

"That you're afraid."

"Of you? Ha!"

"Of yourself." Jake moved closer, not stopping until he was so close she could feel his body. "You're afraid you'll lose control and slip into my bed."

She rolled her eyes and backed away so he couldn't sense her pulse quicken.

He closed the gap between them and lowered his head until his face was just inches away. Steel-gray eyes stared into hers, making her stomach flip. "Admit it. You miss having me in your bed."

She took another step back and put her hand on his chest to keep him away. He put his hand over hers, trapping it over his heart. She could feel it beating against her fingertips. "I have no idea why you think I'm avoiding you."

"You run away whenever you see me coming."

"Nonsense."

"Last night you darted into your bedroom the minute you saw me."

"It was late. I was going to bed."

"And when I saw you in the kitchen earlier that evening, you ran off like you'd seen a mouse. Guess you weren't avoiding me then either?"

"I had finished eating."

"You threw a whole slice of cake in the trash."

"I decided I didn't need the calories. I'm watching my weight."

One brow lifted, and his dark gaze raked her head to toe. "Like hell. You're perfect." He looked disgusted with himself and turned away. He walked to the refrigerator and opened the door, critically eyeing the contents. "You need to go shopping. You've got crap for food and you're out of Coke."

"I had three cans when I left."

"Not anymore."

Kendall shut the door. "What are you doing here besides drinking my sodas? Did Nathan send you to spy on me?"

"He doesn't need me. He's watching you twenty-four/seven."

"The black SUV? I figured it was one of his guards."

"I don't know about that, but he has a camera on you."

"A camera? Where?"

"On the building facing you."

Kendall went to the window and looked through her wooden blinds. Todd's curtains were open. She saw a movement at his window, as if someone had stepped out of sight. Had he been watching her apartment? She looked at the box on the corner. "I thought that was some kind of cable box."

"Nope. Camera," Jake said, inspecting her cabinets.

She wasn't really surprised. Nathan kept a tight net on his employees. "So you came to tell me that Nathan's watching me and to find food?"

"I came to tell you we're going back to Italy."

"We just got home two days ago."

"Nathan called me right after we left his bedroom. He has a team at the castle to keep intruders out, but he wants us there to make sure no one gets nosey and finds the treasure. Guess he's afraid someone might decide to take a souvenir."

Considering the objects they'd found hidden underneath the chapel, it would be tempting. "When are we leaving?"

"He said soon. You can follow me. My house is on the way. I need to pick up a couple of things before we leave."

"You have a house?"

"Did you think I lived in a cave?"

"I wouldn't have been surprised." She hadn't realized he lived in Charlottesville. "I can just meet you at the mansion."

"I'd rather keep you in sight."

"Why?"

Jake looked out the window toward Todd's apartment. "Nathan never should have let you come here alone. I don't know where his head is." He started to leave the room.

"Nathan doesn't control me. Where are you going now?" Surely he wasn't planning to help her pack. Having Fergus's help was bad enough. She didn't want more males pawing her underthings.

"I need to use the little boys' room before we leave."

Kendall gave him a quick glance from worn jeans hugging muscular hips and thighs to his soft button-up Levi's shirt with rolled-up sleeves revealing muscular forearms. He'd long since outgrown little boy. "You shouldn't have drunk all my soda."

"It's here or in your yard. I promise I won't take a dump."

Kendall rolled her eyes. "Hurry." While he was in the bathroom, she threw some clothes in a bag. After a few months working with Nathan, Kendall was proficient at packing. She looked at the box holding the camera as they walked outside to her car. Was Nathan concerned for her or just protecting his interests? From the corner of her eye she saw something move in Todd's window again. If he was watching, maybe he would think Jake was a brother. Not likely. No one would look at Jake and think *brother*. He was too hot.

"I'm there," Jake said, pointing to his Jeep parked on a side street. She hadn't noticed it when she pulled in.

Kendall followed him across town to an older section with restored homes. He pulled up in front of a brick colonial with black shutters. It even had the white picket fence. Of course the fence was eight feet tall, so all she could really see was the second floor, but the house was obviously beautiful. She pulled up behind him and waited as he got out of his Jeep. He walked back to her car and opened the door. "You coming in?"

"Uh, sure." She had to admit she was curious to see what the inside looked like. "I didn't see you living in a house like this. It looks like one of those historical homes that would be on a walking tour."

He shrugged as he led Kendall up the sidewalk. "It was my grandmother's."

She hadn't pictured him with a grandmother either. When she was growing up, she'd always wished she had a grandmother. And a mother. She had adored her father, but she'd always wondered about the woman who'd given life to her. Who was she? What was she like? There was only one picture, a small one, not very clear. Her father said the others had been lost in a fire. Kendall hadn't asked many questions since it seemed to trouble her father to talk about it. Her aunt said something once that made Kendall suspect her parents hadn't been married.

"How long have you lived here?"

"A few months. She left it to me last year when she died."

"Sorry." She didn't have a grandmother to lose, but she couldn't imagine losing Aunt Edna.

"I'd planned to rent it out, but after I started working for Nathan, it made sense to have a place nearby."

"The yard is lovely." There were boxwoods and shrubs, very well cared for.

"Can't take credit for that. I'm hardly here."

She knew that feeling. The house was lovely, but she could see signs of Jake. The lock on the gate, the tall fence, the security system.

He opened the door and let her inside. "I just need to grab a few things. Won't be a minute. Make yourself at home."

No invitation to come upstairs? Maybe ignoring him was working. "Take your time." She wondered if his bedroom matched the badass mercenary or the grandson. After he disappeared, she gave herself a tour of the downstairs. It had been carefully restored. Hardwood floors and trim looked old but well maintained. The kitchen was clean, large, and had an island in the middle of the room with copper pots and pans hanging overhead. Did he cook too? The dining room was uncluttered and had a wooden table large enough to fit a big family. On one wall, an antique china cabinet—probably early nineteenth century—held Wedgwood china and Waterford crystal glasses.

The living room looked more like Jake. Oversized leather furniture with a blanket tossed over the back of the couch. Solid wood coffee and side tables. A Coke can sat on one next to a pizza box. Her fingers itched to touch things, to see what she could pick up on him, but it wouldn't be fair. She looked at the bookshelves and noticed that there were no pictures. Not of him or anyone else. She couldn't imagine his grandmother not having pictures. Kendall's aunt had pictures everywhere. Had he put them away? She explored more and found a laundry room, a study, and what appeared to be a guest bedroom. Back in the foyer, she glanced at the stairs. Where was he?

A loud crash sounded upstairs. Kendall raced up the stairs. A door was open in the hall. Kendall looked in and saw Jake's duffel bag open on the bed. The room was neat, but more masculine than the rest of the house. She got there in time to see Jake go out the window and drop down from the rooftop, landing on his feet in the backyard. He ran toward the fence.

Kendall started to go after him, when she felt someone enter the room. She turned and saw a woman standing in the doorway, dressed in a long robe. She was beautiful, blond haired. There was dirt on her face and hands, as if she had been gardening. The woman stared at Kendall, not speaking. Kendall was equally shocked. She knew Jake's flirting was mostly a front to distract her, but she was surprised—and disappointed—that he had tried to get her in bed when he obviously had a . . . what? Wife? Girlfriend? She must be wondering what Kendall was doing in Jake's bedroom.

Before either of them regained their voice, Kendall heard a yell outside. A sense of danger hit her hard. She ran to the window and saw Jake go over the top of the fence. "We have to help him." She raced from the room and down the stairs to the back door she'd seen on her tour. She ran across the yard. "Jake?"

A moment later, Jake's head appeared on the opposite side of the tall white fence. He climbed to the top and dropped over. "Bastard got away."

"Who was it?" Kendall asked, finding her voice. She was still in shock that Jake had a gorgeous woman in his house and hadn't bothered to mention her.

"Don't know. He was watching the house from the trees. He got away before I could get close enough to see his face." Jake looked angry. One sleeve of his T-shirt was torn and there was a rip in his jeans.

"Should you call the police?"

"No. I doubt they'd find anything."

"You think it was a burglar?" Kendall asked.

"I doubt it. More likely someone I've pissed off."

"Have you pissed off a lot of people?"

"In my line of work, you make a few enemies. You go inside," Jake said. "I want to look around for prints, just in case."

"What about . . . Who's the . . . I'll just wait in the car," Kendall said. It would be awkward waiting inside with the woman. The first time Kendall met Jake, when Nathan summoned them to the mansion to tell them they were going to Italy, she was almost certain Jake had been with a woman. The one upstairs?

"No. You're not sitting out in the car alone. Go in the house. I won't be long."

Kendall was too rattled to argue. She went inside but didn't see the woman. She must be showering or getting dressed. She had looked dirty. Kendall sat on a chair, her head spinning with confusion. Jake had come on to her fifteen minutes ago. He was coming on to her constantly. If Nathan hadn't interrupted them at the inn in Italy, she and Jake wouldn't have stopped at a kiss. But she had no claims on him; nor did he have any claims on her. The front door opened and Jake stepped inside. "Did you find anything?" Kendall asked.

"Nothing useful. Let me grab my clothes and we'll go." Still no mention of the woman. A minute later, he appeared in the living room, duffel in hand. He'd changed into a pair of camo pants and a T-shirt, but there was no woman waiting to be introduced. "You live here alone?"

"Yep."

So the woman didn't live here, but it was obnoxious for him to come on to Kendall at her apartment while he had another woman in the house. Even if she was someone he picked up in a bar after sneaking out of the mansion last night. Of course he wouldn't know that Kendall had been upstairs and seen the woman. She was a little peeved that his attraction to her was obviously nothing more than just a thing for blondes.

"Ready?"

"You're just going to leave her here after someone broke into your house?"

He frowned. "Leave who here?"

"The woman?"

His brows did a strange tilt. "What woman?"

"The woman upstairs. Who was she? Girlfriend? Hooker?"

"Hooker? What the hell have you been smoking?"

"Stop playing dumb. I saw her in your bedroom. Did you pick her up in a bar?" Kendall shrugged her shoulders. "Not that it matters. I'm just curious."

"I was starting to think you were sane until now. There's no woman in my house, other than you."

"Yes there is."

He stared at her for several seconds. "You're serious?"

Kendall was the one frowning now. "Yes. She was upstairs."

"Hell." Jake bounded up the stairs. He searched the whole house, but the woman wasn't there. "She must have been working with the guy out back. A lookout." He picked up his phone and made arrangements for someone named Clint to come to his house and handle things.

"Who's Clint?"

"A buddy."

"Is he a mercenary like you?"

"I'm not a mercenary. I contract to the highest bidder just like any business would."

"You carry a lot of muscle and weapons for a business."

Jake's phone rang. He pulled it from his pocket and answered. After a short conversation, he ended the call. "Marco's awake," he told her. "Fergus says if we want to talk to him, we need to hurry."

"Then let's go." She jogged to her car. If it weren't for Marco, she probably wouldn't be alive. It wasn't just gratitude, or guilt. She was fond of the old man, even though she couldn't remember seeing him at the castle when she and Adam were kids. And she had questions for him. If there was a curse that had caused Adam and both their fathers to die, why hadn't she died?

Jake didn't knock on Nathan's door. He went right in. Nathan and Fergus were standing in the atrium. From their dour expressions, they appeared to have been arguing. Since their return from Italy, Fergus seemed as distracted as Nathan. Not such a surprise, Kendall thought since Fergus had been out of his element in the past week. He was a butler, not a fighter, though he'd done a darned good job fighting off bad guys.

Nathan's dark gaze followed Kendall, and she wondered if he was thinking about this morning in his bedroom. Her gaze went to the arm that sported a tattoo, now hidden by an expensive suit. Fergus stepped forward when he saw them. "Kendall, Jake. The nurse says Marco won't be awake for long."

"Has he spoken at all?" Kendall asked.

"We haven't seen him yet. The doctor just left. This way, if you please."

Fergus led them toward the bedrooms on the second floor. Nathan followed, his face dark. Kendall considered prying. She wouldn't get anything from Nathan, verbal or intuitive, but she might pick up something from Fergus. *No fair, Kendall.*

Marco lay in bed, hooked up to tubes. He looked old and weak, not the spry man with bright eyes. He still had his beard. The doctor had wanted to cut it, but Fergus of all people had insisted he keep it.

"We need privacy," Nathan said curtly.

"Don't be long. He's tired," the nurse said. She gave Nathan a sour look and walked to the door. She left and they all approached the bed.

Marco's eyes fluttered open. They weren't bright now. He looked frightened. When he saw Kendall, his gnarled hand reached for hers. "You are alive?"

Kendall touched his hand, careful to avoid the IV. A myriad of pictures flashed through her head. The castle in Italy, the statues, the secret treasure room. Raphael. "Of course I'm alive, thanks to you."

"The spear? Is it safe?" Marco asked, his voice weak.

"It's safe," Nathan said. "The intruders are gone."

Marco let out a relieved sigh that lifted his scrawny chest. "He'll try again. He won't stop."

"The Reaper?" Nathan asked.

Marco nodded.

"We found the treasure at the castle. I think it needs to be moved before someone else finds it."

"Yes, it must be kept safe. Can't let him get it. Raphael knows how to move it."

"Marco, Raphael is dead, remember?" Kendall said gently.

Marco frowned.

Nathan rubbed his chin. He seemed ill at ease. "I'll have Kendall do it. There's no one I trust more than her." He met her gaze and Kendall felt a glimmer of something, as if she'd experienced this moment before. Then the sensation passed, leaving her with guilt at the thought of the crosses in her bag. She would have to tell him she'd accidentally taken them home. Turning, she saw Jake watching her. He was frowning, and so was Fergus. Everyone was frowning.

"I think it's time you tell us about the Reaper and these relics," Jake said.

"Water," Marco said, his voice raspy.

Kendall helped him take a drink from the cup the nurse had left. He shifted in bed, sighed again, and spoke. "There are things in this world that cannot be explained. There are relics so powerful that in the wrong hands the human race could be destroyed."

"More comic book stuff," Jake muttered, too low for Marco to hear.

"Our order was formed many centuries ago to protect those relics, to keep them out of evil hands. We were called the Protettori after we moved to Italy. Once there were many of us, but one of our own turned on us. We were slaughtered and scattered like sheep."

"One of the Protettori did this?" Kendall asked.

"The Reaper. He wasn't always the Reaper. He was one of our trusted brothers, but something happened to him. He changed. He became greedy for power. He wanted the relics for himself. Darkness took root inside him and grew. We didn't realize what he was doing at first. When we did, we cast him out of the order and put up the sentinels to keep him out."

"The statues?" Nathan said.

"Yes. Their duty is to keep him out."

"Duty?" Jake frowned. "They're stone."

Marco nodded. "They are now."

"What the hell is he talking about?" Jake whispered.

Kendall leaned closer. "What were the statues before they were stone?"

"Guardians of the Protettori."

Kendall knew her expression must look as puzzled as the others. "Marco, are you saying the statues were alive?"

"Once upon a time, they were guardians and knights."

"How did they go from being guardians and knights to stone sentinels?" Kendall asked.

"The vow to protect doesn't stop with death. The guardians will always guard."

"Is Raphael a guardian?" Nathan asked.

Marco nodded. "He was one of the first guardians."

"Why isn't he one of those statues?" Jake asked.

"He chose to stay. It's complicated," Marco said.

"Or crazy," Jake muttered.

"Are you a guardian?" Kendall asked.

"No. I am a keeper. I keep the relics and the treasure. The guardians protect it. With force if need be."

"Warriors?" Jake asked.

"Warriors. Soldiers. We each have a function. Different strengths. When the guardians die, they continue to protect as sentinels."

"I think he's had too many painkillers," Jake whispered.

"How did Jake and I get past the statues—sentinels—when we found the castle?" Kendall asked.

"Someone had turned them off," Marco said.

"Raphael?" Nathan asked.

"No. Raphael wouldn't have done such a thing. But someone knew where to find the stone."

"Stone? A stone controls them?" Jake asked.

"I'm not allowed to speak of it. It's in the vow."

"I bet it was Edward," Kendall said. "He knew the spear was there and needed to get inside. His ancestor knew a lot about the castle."

"Who is Edward?" Marco asked.

"He was working for the Reaper," Kendall said. "Or working against him. The Reaper had hired him to find the Spear of Destiny. Edward was going to steal it and sell it."

"This Edward is dead?" Marco asked.

"Yes." Kendall didn't tell Marco that a ghost killed Edward. She offered Marco another sip of water. His hands seemed shakier on the cup.

"The Reaper won't stop," Marco said. "Not until he gets the relics. If he does, I fear for the world."

"If he's that dangerous, why not just kill him?" Jake asked. "He obviously has well-trained men, and if he's stealing all these priceless antiquities, then he has money to back up his scheme."

"There weren't many of us left who could kill him. He's very powerful. He's had hundreds of years to grow stronger and he knows our secrets."

"Hundreds of years?" Jake frowned. "Exactly how old is the Reaper?"

"Very old. No one can remember his birth."

"How is that possible?" Jake glanced at Kendall, and she knew he was thinking of Raphael and the strange vision they had shared when she touched him. They had seen men fighting with swords.

"Was Raphael that old?" Kendall asked. *Before he died?*

"He's very old as well," Marco said.

"And you?" Nathan asked.

"We are all old."

"But how is that possible?" Kendall asked.

"The water. We drink from it once a year. It keeps us strong and young."

"What water?" Kendall asked, hardly daring to breathe.

"The water from the fountain," Marco said. "The Fountain of Youth."

CHAPTER TWO

THERE WAS SILENCE IN THE ROOM AS NATHAN, KENDALL, AND Jake shared a stunned look. "It's real?" Kendall whispered.

"We must keep him away from it," Marco said.

"Where is it?" Nathan asked.

"Only Raphael knows."

"Raphael is dead, remember?" Kendall said.

"Someone else must know." Nathan looked tight enough to snap. He moved closer and knelt beside the old man.

Marco frowned. Was it her imagination or was Marco becoming less lucid whenever Nathan got near? Marco lifted a shaky hand to his beard. "Arthur. Find Arthur."

"Who's Arthur?" Nathan asked. "Is he a keeper?"

Marco's eyes closed.

The nurse stepped inside. "He needs to rest. You can visit later."

They all filed toward the door. They were in the hallway when Marco called for Kendall with a weak voice. He held out his hand.

"I'll catch up with you," she told Nathan and Jake. She approached the bed and touched Marco's arm. "Do you need something?"

Marco looked blank for a moment; then he closed his eyes. "I can't remember."

"You must rest. Don't worry about anything but getting better." She straightened and stepped away from the bed.

"Look out for him," Marco muttered.

"Him?"

"He needs you. You'll have to save him. It must be you."

Kendall frowned. Was he out of his head? "Save who, Marco?"

His voice dropped to a whisper. "Adam."

Kendall's heart leapt. She started back to the bed. *Adam?* "Marco, do you see Adam?"

The old man didn't move or open his eyes. He was asleep.

Kendall turned and saw the nurse watching her. "When he woke up, did he mention someone named Adam?" Kendall asked.

The nurse went over to Marco. "I think he did mention the name once, or maybe it was Arthur. Something that started with an *A*."

"What did he say?"

The nurse shrugged. "I don't recall. He was muttering. Is it important?"

"It might be."

"Should I let Mr. Larraby know if he mentions the name again?"

"Don't bother him. He has a lot on his mind. You can let me know."

"Mr. Larraby does seem troubled. He's been stopping by every hour that you're not sitting with Marco."

Kendall caught up with Nathan and Jake in the hall. They were discussing the trip back to Italy.

"I need you both ready to leave first thing in the morning," Nathan said. "I'm sorry to send you back so soon, but I don't trust anyone else to pack up the treasure. I already have a team on the ground at the castle. The guards don't know about the treasure room. I'll tell them you two are studying some stonework, to keep everyone away so you can work undisturbed. After you get everything crated and out of view, I'll have them load the items up for shipping."

"You aren't coming?" Jake asked, surprised.

"I'll wait for Marco to wake up and try to find out where this fountain is."

Kendall was surprised too that Nathan wouldn't be there. The treasure was incredible. How could he trust anyone to load it properly? To load it without keeping a small souvenir? Especially Jake, as much as they seemed to mistrust each other at times.

"Take care of Kendall," he said to Jake. "I trust you'll follow orders." He gave Jake a loaded look. "All of them."

"Of course, Boss. I live to serve." Jake gave Nathan a slight bow.

"Stop acting like I'm a piece of glass," she said.

"I'll do my best to take care of her," Jake said as if Kendall hadn't spoken. His eyebrows lifted in a smirk, and she knew he was getting ready to say something to piss Nathan off. "But she makes it hard." His hand moved from his waist and hovered for a nanosecond over his groin. "To protect, I mean."

Nathan scowled and walked off, leaving Jake and Kendall in the hall.

"You're trying to make him angry," she said.

"I've gotta do something to liven things up in this place. You're avoiding me. Nathan's no fun. That leaves Fergus, and he's acting as strange as Marco."

"We've all been through a lot this past week." Kendall pulled her hair back and fastened it with a ponytail holder from her wrist. "Do you think he's right about the Fountain of Youth?"

"Sounds crazy to me. And it sure hasn't kept Marco youthful. I like your hair better down."

She pulled it tighter. "The Protettori had the Spear of Destiny. Why not the Fountain of Youth?"

"The spear is real," Jake said. "There's history behind it. The fountain is a myth."

"So we've been told."

"Can't you read Marco or something?" Jake asked.

"I don't like reading people. It's like stealing. And it usually doesn't work anyway." Not when she wanted it to. It worked just fine when she didn't, when she was least expecting it. "But if we can't get anything else from him, I may have to try."

"Where are you off to?" Jake asked.

"I have some things to do." She was going to finish examining the crosses in private before she took them back. She didn't mind prying into the past of an inanimate object. It wasn't the same as rifling through a person's head. "I'm going to do some research on the Fountain of Youth."

She stopped by the library for some reference materials. Nathan's collection of books was extensive. Using the sliding ladder, she climbed to the top shelf and found two books that explored the fabled fountain. She carried them to her bedroom and put them and the crosses on the bed. She made herself comfortable and studied the crosses first. She didn't get any new impressions and after a few minutes, she gave up. Jake was right. Her gift was a pain in the ass sometimes.

Sighing with frustration, she put the necklaces in her purse and walked to the door. She needed to return the crosses. She was surprised to see Nathan leaving Jake's room. They stood in the hallway, speaking in low voices. She didn't want to explain her actions, so she eased her door shut. Later, after everyone was asleep, she would put them back.

Next, she opened her reference materials. The Fountain of Youth was like vampires. Everyone had their own myths and speculations as to the origins and purpose. After her eyes grew blurry, she put the books aside and went to grab dinner. It was informal, usually a buffet allowing each of them to dine at their convenience. Neither Jake nor Nathan was there, which wasn't surprising. Since they had returned from Italy, Nathan usually ate in his room and God knew what Jake was up to. After dinner, Kendall pulled clothing from her restocked closet and packed her duffel bag for the trip. Then she took a long soak in the huge Jacuzzi before turning in early. The jet would leave before sunrise, and packing up the treasure quickly and yet carefully would be a tiring task.

She was glad Nathan was sending them back to the castle. After the treasure was safe, she planned to spend some time exploring the place, letting the sensations and history sink in. If she wasn't chasing ghosts or running from bad guys, maybe she would find answers.

She lay down, anxious for morning. Sometime in the night, she heard the roar again. Her feet hit the floor and she opened her door, almost colliding with a sleep-tousled Jake on the other side. He was dressed in his camos and T-shirt. In fact, he looked as if he'd slept in them.

"Are you OK?" he asked, stepping inside her room.

"Yes."

"Where's Nathan?"

"How should I know? It's the middle of the night."

Jake looked at Kendall's bed and rubbed his eyes. "Sounded like his roar."

"You heard it too?" She'd thought it must be her sixth sense playing tricks.

"Yeah." He gave her a wary look. "You projecting your mumbo jumbo again?"

Another roar sounded, louder than the first, angrier.

"Hell, that was real," Jake said.

"I think Nathan's in trouble." Kendall ran into the hall. "It came from this direction."

"Hold up!" Jake put his hands on her shoulders, stopping her. "I'll go. You wait inside."

"Are you kidding?" She bolted around him. She was quick, but so was Jake, and his stride was longer, so she had to sprint to stay with him. Shouting now accompanied the roars.

"It's coming from the lower level," Jake said.

"What could it be?" Kendall asked, alarmed.

"Maybe he has found Bigfoot. Hell, maybe he *is* Bigfoot."

"If that's Nathan roaring, we need to hurry. Aren't you taking the elevator?" she asked as Jake moved past.

"No. The stairs will be faster." He led her down the steps. She'd never been down here. It was off-limits to the staff, but Jake didn't take well to orders. The lower level was in chaos. Armed guards ran past them, shouting instructions.

Nathan didn't like weapons. Usually only a handful of guards carried guns. Kendall shook her head. "What's going on down here?" She jumped back as a burly guard rushed past them. He stopped and turned around, planting himself in front of Kendall and Jake. It was Hank, one of Nathan's top guards.

He eyed Jake nervously. "You're not supposed to be down here."

"What's that noise?" Kendall asked.

The guard glanced over his shoulder as the roar sounded again. He looked frightened. Nathan's guards never appeared scared. He always hired the best of the best. "An intruder. Now go, before Nathan finds you here." He motioned with the gun.

"Where is Nathan?" Jake asked.

Hank's jaw clenched. "Dammit, just go."

"Jake. Kendall." Fergus hurried toward them, his face tight. "What are you doing here?"

"What's going on, Fergus?" Kendall asked.

Fergus straightened his perfectly straight jacket. "He's gone too far."

"Look out!" Someone yelled, and a wall of guards rushed toward the room.

"Don't hurt him!" someone else called out. It sounded like Hank. "Get the Taser."

"What the hell?" Jake hurried toward the commotion. "Stay here," he told Kendall, and he pushed his way through.

Kendall didn't stay. She followed him. One of the guards flew through the air, knocking down several others.

Jake turned and saw her. "Dammit." He pushed her into a corner where they were out of the way but could still see the guards. They looked frightened, and that made the hair on Kendall's neck stand up. Jake positioned his body in front of hers.

"I'm not leaving," she said. "I want to know what's happening."

"So do I, but I don't want you getting in the middle of it." A streak of light flashed by them.

"What was that?" Kendall asked, peering around Jake. "A flashlight?"

"I don't know."

"Look at that guard. Is he dead?" She pointed to a guard who was lying on his back.

Jake frowned. "I think he's snoring."

Nathan ran up beside her. "Get Kendall out of here now," he yelled to Jake.

"What's going on, Nathan?" Kendall demanded.

"I can't explain now. Just go. Please, Jake. Get her away from here. I'll talk to you both later."

Jake nodded and pulled Kendall back.

"I'm not leaving. Are you OK, Nathan?"

His eyes were dark as he touched Kendall's hand. "I'm fine. Go."

"How did he escape?" Nathan asked. "Did he steal a key to the lock?"

"The lock isn't the issue. Take a look at what the camera caught." Hank pointed to a monitor. "I warn you, you're not going to believe what you see. Look at that. He just appears outside the door to his room. Like he walked through the wall."

No one could walk through walls. "How the hell did he do that? Is the equipment working?"

"Checks out fine," Hank said.

"Slow the speed down," Nathan said.

"That's regular speed," Hank said. "I've never seen a human move that fast."

Maybe he wasn't human. Bloody hell. "The guards didn't stop him?"

"They fell asleep."

"Did he drug them?" He could have stolen meds from the medical room.

"No. He went straight to the garage and took the Mercedes. I'm trying to locate the car now."

Nathan didn't care about the Mercedes. He was worried about Kendall and Jake. He was almost certain Raphael would go back to Italy, to the treasure. He had to warn Kendall and Jake. There was no doubt Raphael could be dangerous. Whether he actually was or not remained to be seen. Raphael hadn't revealed anything during his time here, only sleeping or refusing to talk, watching everything with those strange eyes so similar to Nathan's when he changed. Was he turning into whatever Raphael was? At least Raphael didn't look like a monster.

"Double security and keep looking for him. I'm going to Italy. I have a feeling that's where he's headed."

"I'll get the helicopter here and have the other jet waiting at the airport."

"Keep a watch on the airports and check in with me if anything changes."

"Yes, sir."

He walked toward Marco's room. He needed to talk to him before he left. If necessary, he would wake him. If that nurse tried to keep him out again, he'd fire her. Nathan's head was pounding so hard he stopped in the bathroom first and splashed cold water on his face. Sometimes a distraction could stop the change. He didn't want anyone to witness it. His security team was trusting, but there was no way he could explain that.

Only Fergus had seen him change. And Kendall and Jake. They didn't believe his excuses, but he couldn't tell them the truth. Hell, he didn't know what the truth was, but it had to be connected to his recurring dream of two men whispering about a curse and the relics that would cure it. They must have been talking about his curse, since one of the men was holding the journal that included sketches of the relics he'd dreamed of for as long as he could remember.

He'd tried everything, but even hypnosis didn't help him remember anything. He hoped Marco could tell him where to find this Fountain of Youth. He was running out of time. He could feel whatever was inside him growing stronger. He was afraid he was going to hurt someone. More afraid it was going to be Kendall. It seemed stronger when he was near her, and he couldn't avoid her forever.

Nathan glanced at the worn silver watch on his arm. Kendall and Jake would arrive a few hours ahead of him. He didn't like sending Jake with her, but he could keep her safe. He'd have to warn them about Raphael. They were both going to be pissed that he'd kept another secret.

The nurse wasn't in. Fergus was there, sitting by Marco's bed. His head was bent over and he was whispering. "I must," Fergus said.

Marco's reply was weak. "Not yet. It's not time."

Both men looked up as he entered the room. Fergus looked guilty as a whore in church and hurried out. Nathan watched him go and then sat in the chair he had so quickly vacated.

"Marco, I need to find the fountain. Please, can you tell me where it is?"

"Raphael is the only one left who knows. I don't remember."

And Raphael was gone. Damn. "I have something to tell you." He didn't have time to waste. The helicopter was waiting and that damned nurse could come back anytime. "Raphael isn't dead."

"I know."

Nathan frowned. "Damn Fergus."

"Fergus didn't tell me. I saw Raphael."

"He came here?"

"Yes. He told me to stay here. It would be safer."

"Where did he go?"

"To move the treasure and to find Kendall."

Nathan's pulse quickened dangerously. "Why does he want to find Kendall?"

"She has his cross."

"It's in my study."

"No. She took it. She took mine too. And yours. But it's not yours, is it?"

The blood rushed through Nathan's veins. His eyes burned. Kendall wouldn't stand a chance against Raphael if he thought she'd stolen his cross, and Jake wouldn't be able to stop him alone. Nathan had to get to them before Raphael did. He tried to steady his breathing. He couldn't let it happen here.

"Maybe I should come with you," Marco said. "Raphael isn't happy with either of us. But I couldn't tell him the truth. I couldn't tell any of them. They didn't understand the things I saw, the things I knew."

Knew what? "No. You stay here and rest. I'll find Raphael."

"I am tired," he said. "I don't like getting old. I haven't had a drink for a long time."

"Do you need more water?"

"Not that kind." Marco closed his eyes. "Go to Kendall. She needs you."

Raphael put his foot on the accelerator and the Mercedes shot around a truck. He knew Nathan was sending Kendall and Jake to Italy to move the treasure. He couldn't let that happen. He had to get there first. The only way to do that was by finding the gateway. If it was still there. He was furious with Nathan Larraby, and with Marco. If what he had admitted was true, then Marco had lied to the Protettori. He had betrayed them all.

"We shouldn't have left," Kendall said for the tenth time since the jet had taken off for Italy two hours before. The threats against Nathan had increased in the past few weeks. One intruder might not pose a threat to all those guards, but something wasn't right. Even Fergus was acting weird. Not to mention Marco. Why did he keep talking about Adam? "I think Nathan's in trouble," she said to Jake.

"You have a short memory. I think Nathan can handle anyone he has locked up in his fancy prison."

"Locked up? You think he's holding the intruder?"

"I don't think he had an intruder," Jake said.

"Then who was down there?"

Jake tore off a piece of beef jerky he'd produced from his

backpack. "I think he's experimenting down there, creating some kind of superhuman."

"You really think he's working on people down there? Like some kind of mad scientist?"

"Normal people don't roar. Not even intruders. Not without good reason," he said. "That means one of two things. Torture or sex."

"Speaking of intruders, I wonder who the woman was in your house?"

"I don't know. I can't believe you didn't mention her."

"I thought you were hiding her."

"From you?" He lifted one brow, an expression she was finding far too frustrating and sexy. "She must have been hot."

"Someone broke into your house and you're worried about whether she was hot?"

"I'm just surprised."

"She was . . . beautiful. Probably sent in to distract you. She was wearing a gown or some kind of robe."

"Like a nightgown?"

"I don't know." Kendall frowned. "And she was dirty, like she'd been digging in the dirt. What did the guy look like?"

"Dark hair, not bad looking."

She gave him her best coy look. "Was he hot?"

His look was anything but coy as he picked up the phone to call Clint. The call didn't go well. He slammed the bag of jerky on the table. "Damn it to hell. Someone trashed the place."

"What could they be after?" Kendall asked. "Do you keep anything valuable at the house?"

"Weapons. Some cash."

After a lot of speculation about whether it was a random robbery, something from Jake's past, or this Reaper business, Jake tossed his empty beef jerky bag in the trash and reclined his seat.

"I'm going to take a nap. Wake me when the jet lands." After a minute, he cracked one eyelid. "How hot was she?"

Kendall got up and walked off.

Nathan had a helicopter waiting at the airport in Italy. "At least we won't have to deal with a nosey tourist like last time. I'd rather run past one of those statues than have a conversation with Loretta."

"But you'd like a conversation with Brandi," Kendall said. The redheaded nurse had been part of the tourist group they had stayed with at an inn in Italy. She was after the same thing they were. The relics. But Brandi was as determined to see the artifacts destroyed as Nathan was to save them. And she wanted the Reaper dead. He had stolen her father's collection and killed her parents, leaving her and her brother, Thomas, alone. They had been working ever since to discover the Reaper's identity and the location of the relics.

"I think she has the answers to what happened in Iraq."

"You don't still believe Nathan was involved? I mean, it had to be the Reaper behind it. Thomas was there and he working undercover for the Reaper."

"I think Nathan knows more about it than he's saying, but I don't think he was behind it. Brandi may be the only person besides the Reaper who knows why he requested me for a cover-up mission."

His face clouded, and Kendall knew he was thinking about the young girls he'd discovered at the prince's palace. There weren't any terrorists or weapons, just young sex slaves and a bunch of relics.

"Maybe you were simply hired because of your expertise," Kendall said. "Even Nathan says you're the best."

Jake shrugged. "Maybe."

"I'm surprised Nathan is letting us do this alone," Kendall said.

"I'm not. Nathan cares about two things right now." Jake looked at Kendall and narrowed his eyes. "Make that three. First, he wants what the Protettori are protecting. Second, he wanted us away from the mansion so we wouldn't know what he's up to. Whatever he's got going on in his dungeon is dangerous. Sending us to Italy to get the treasure killed two birds with one stone."

"What's the third thing?"

"You," Jake said, watching Kendall. "He wants you."

"I work for him. That's all."

"Right," he said dryly.

It was getting dark when they arrived, but the castle looked like a different place than it had a few days ago. Nathan had sent a team to the castle as soon as they left. The airstrip had been cleared and guards posted throughout the woods surrounding the castle and along the wall.

The head of the security team met them at the helicopter as soon as it landed and brought them up to date on things. "No sign of trouble. The guards and staff have taken up most of the rooms on the second floor and part of the third."

"We'll find something," Jake said. "We'll sleep in the tower if we have to."

"Dinner's ready in the dining hall," the guard said. He left, and Jake and Kendall walked slowly, taking it all in. Kendall stopped when the castle came into view. It didn't look as imposing now, probably because she knew there were so many armed guards protecting the place.

Jake stopped beside her. "You OK?"

"We're missing something."

"This time you have my permission to explore all you want. A rat couldn't get through all those guards and statues."

"Thank you for your permission, my lord. Any other instructions?"

"My lord, I like that."

"You would." She walked toward the castle without waiting for him. In the distance she saw the statues. She noticed the one with the sword tip she'd broken off on her first trip to the castle. It was watching, almost as if it were alive. And then she thought she saw it move. Marco and his wild ideas. Jake was probably right about the old man being on too many pain meds.

"Should we check on the treasure first?" She looked toward the woods where the chapel was hidden.

"Wait until morning. It might look a little suspicious if the guards see us there in the dark."

"We'll have to work quickly in the morning."

"Won't it take a while to catalog everything?" Jake asked. "I'm not the expert, but there were some amazing things in that room."

"Beyond amazing. I doubt there's a treasure its equal anywhere. We'll have to catalog it quickly for now. We can finish when we unpack it."

"Wherever that is. Nathan will probably do it himself so we don't know where he's hiding it. He doesn't seem inclined to share where he's hidden the Spear of Destiny."

Kendall didn't like that either. Nathan obviously trusted her and Jake, or he wouldn't have sent them to pack up something as valuable as this treasure. But Jake's blatant attempts, and even Kendall's subtle hints, hadn't gotten him to divulge the spear's location. "I'm sure he has his reasons."

Jake shook his head. "If he stabbed you, you'd say he had a good reason."

"You need food. You're getting cranky."

Dozens of people were at the castle. Security guards, cooks to feed the guards, maids to handle laundry and cleaning. Kendall wondered if the castle had once looked like this, bustling with activity. Nathan hadn't wanted to let more people know where the castle was located, but he'd decided that it was more important to have heavy security in place.

They found rooms on the third floor. Kendall expected Jake to make some smart remark about sharing, but he didn't. After they put their things inside, they went down to the dining hall to find something to eat. The security guards had changed shifts and were gathered in small groups eating and talking about the castle. Kendall overheard bits of conversation about statues and the strangeness of the place. Nathan had apparently warned them of the dangers without giving away too much. Jake excused himself and went to talk to the head of security again.

Kendall took the opportunity to explore, hoping something would click. Some message from the stones or something to reveal what she was missing. She found herself wandering the floors and discovered another entrance into the mural room where they'd found the round table and the relics. The treasure room underneath the chapel surpassed this by far, but there were enough relics in here to keep a museum busy for a long time. Suits of armor, chain mail, weapons, scrolls, gold figures . . . There was even a crown.

The round table in the middle of the floor was huge. Thirteen ornate chairs surrounded it. They were old, she suspected. When she touched the back of one, she was certain. They were beyond old. She heard whispers that she couldn't identify. English, she thought. Not as it was spoken in this time. Old English? She heard shouts and a ringing sound like the clash of swords. Both Marco and the Reaper—posing as the historian—had said the Protettori were an ancient order. How ancient?

Kendall moved around the room, touching and feeling until the impressions became too strong. She backed off for a few minutes, letting her senses calm before starting again. A fascinating oak cabinet revealed a hidden catch that opened a door in the top. A golden cup and a vial sat on the shelf. The sensations and whispers began to overwhelm her. If she didn't leave, she'd be useless tomorrow. She trusted Jake, but she didn't know how much he knew about properly packing up artifacts.

Back in her room, she took something for a headache and climbed into bed. After she finished crating up the treasure, she would go back to the mural room and explore some more. That golden cup intrigued her. In the middle of the night she woke up. She'd been dreaming about the tower room and the blood on the bed. The dull throb was still knocking at her head, but there was a sense of urgency so strong she worried that Jake was in trouble. She left her room and climbed the stairs to the tower room. Jake wasn't here. No one was.

She stood at the foot of the bed where she and Jake had slept, unsure what had drawn her here. Was she subconsciously hoping to see the ghost? Or looking for answers about the portion of a letter she'd found underneath the desk the last time she was here? She looked at the faded brown covers and remembered the blood she'd seen. She walked the room, trying to connect with the feeling that had drawn her here. After a few minutes without getting anything, she started to leave, when she heard a cry. Whirling, she saw a woman lying on the bed, her belly large with pregnancy.

A monk sat beside her, holding her hand. His body blocked the woman's face. He leaned over and wiped her forehead. "You should have let me know sooner. I just got your letter."

"I wanted to. But it was a mistake between us, and they would have cast you out."

"It wasn't a mistake. I love you. I would have taken care of you and the baby." He touched the woman's belly. "You should have waited for me to come to you. It's dangerous to travel in your condition."

"It's more dangerous there." She gripped his hand. "He's trying to kill me."

The man's shoulders stiffened. "Kill you? What do you mean?"

"There have been two attempts already, accidents that weren't accidents. And someone is following me. I know it's him."

"Did he follow you here?" The man's voice sounded breathless with fear.

"I don't think so. I didn't know where else to go, and I had to let you know about the baby in case you didn't get my letter. In case he . . . in case he succeeds. You have to take care of her, find a home for her."

"It's a girl?"

"Yes."

He touched the woman's belly. "I'll protect you. You and the baby."

"I don't deserve your help, not after what I did. I'm sorry I betrayed you. He used me to get to you."

"That's what he does. Don't worry about him now. We have to get you to the hospital. You're bleeding."

Red stains were spreading underneath her. She was hemorrhaging. If she didn't get to the hospital soon, she would die.

"Get to the hospital," Kendall said, forgetting that she was talking to the past. She couldn't see their faces. She wanted to move but was afraid the vision would fade.

"There's no time," the woman said.

"No, we can get help."

She cried out in pain and clasped her hands over her stomach. "It's too late." Her hands moved from her stomach to grasp the man's hands. "Please, take care of the baby. Promise me you'll take care of her."

"I promise." His voice was rough as if he were crying. He leaned down and put his face against her stomach. His shoulders were shaking. She cried out again and he lifted his head. "I'm going to get Marco."

He knew Marco? But of course, the scene was happening here, and Marco said there had been a woman here once, but they didn't speak of her. Why? Who was she?

The man stood, turning slightly, and Kendall saw his face for the first time.

Her father.

CHAPTER THREE

T HE SHOCK HAD JUST REGISTERED WHEN THE WOMAN'S FACE came into view. Her features were twisted with pain, but Kendall recognized the woman from the one grainy photo she possessed. Her mother. Kendall's legs shook as she started toward the bed. She stretched out her hand and the vision faded.

"No." She grabbed the footboard, but the bed looked just the same as it had when she and Jake escaped the castle. Messy covers, but no woman giving birth. No mother. No father. "Come back." Kendall crawled on the bed and grabbed fistfuls of covers, trying to reconnect with the vision. Still nothing. She touched every part of the bed, and when that didn't work, she lay on the bed in the same spot her mother had lain twenty-eight years ago. She forced her heartbeat to calm and took slow, steady breaths. Still nothing. "Please come back. Please. I need to know what happened."

"Kendall?"

She sat up and saw Jake in the doorway.

"What are you doing? Are you crying?" Jake strode to the bed and sat, assuming much the same position that her father had when he'd sat by her mother. He brushed a damp cheek. "What happened?"

"I had a vision."

He looked apprehensive. "Want to talk about it?"

"I saw my dad. And my mother."

"Here?"

"The woman who gave birth in here was my mother."

Both eyebrows shot up. "You saw her."

She nodded. "I was born in this bed. My God, I killed my mother."

"What was your mom doing here? Women weren't allowed. What was your father doing here for that matter? You said he was an archaeologist. Was he working here?"

"He was dressed like a monk, and he said he was going to get Marco. I think my father was one of the Protettori."

"Damn."

"The scrap of paper we found underneath the desk was a letter she had written to tell him about the baby." About Kendall. "But she was afraid she would be killed before he got it."

"Killed?"

Kendall told Jake everything she had seen in the vision. "Who would try to kill a pregnant woman?" she asked.

"A jealous husband. Maybe she was married and he found out she was pregnant by someone else."

"I don't know. I guess I'll never know."

"What do you know about your mother?"

"My dad said she died when I was young. He didn't talk about it much. I was curious, but he seemed so bothered when I asked, I stopped asking. I can't believe he hid all this from me."

He slid his hand underneath hers and linked their fingers. "You were a little girl. How could he have told you? We'll ask Marco when we get back. Maybe he'll have some answers." His eyes were dark as they studied her face. "You look wiped out."

She nodded. That was one of the worst things about visions. They sucked the life right out of her. She wanted to lean against him and rest, and after a second's hesitation, she did. She laid her head against his chest and closed her eyes. With each beat of his heart, she felt herself regaining strength. He was strong. Protective. A good man, despite that sarcastic, rebellious armor he wore to keep people at the distance he wanted. His arms moved around her back, his head resting against hers. Sometimes she just wanted to be normal, to know only what everyone else knew, the things normal eyes saw and normal ears heard.

He held her for several minutes, until the shock of her vision faded. His fingers moved lower, rubbing small relaxing circles over her spine, and she wished she could forget about the past and questions without answers. She wanted to feel the things a man and a woman who were hugging on a bed might feel. She wanted to feel him, all of him, outside, inside. Without really thinking it through, she lifted her face and touched her lips to his. "Thank you," she whispered against his mouth.

He put a hand behind her head, holding her close when she would have moved away. "For what?"

"For being a friend."

"What if I want to be more?" he asked, his mouth hovering over hers. Then he lowered his head. His mouth was hot, and she grabbed him and held on. The feel, the smell, the taste of him was almost overwhelming. After a minute, she pushed away to grab a breath and clear her senses, but he didn't let up. One hand ran down her back and moved along her hip to her thigh.

She gave up on breathing and gripped the back of his head, pulling him closer. "Take your clothes off," she said.

He lifted his head and gave her a smoldering look. "You're sure?"

She was tired of being careful. Tired of being alone. "I'm sure."

He let out a possessive growl and kissed her harder. Then he cursed and pulled away. "Damn."

She felt cold after being in his arms. He wasn't getting undressed. He sighed, a sound of disgust.

"You don't want me?"

"Damn straight I want you, but you've had a hell of a shock."

"You're afraid I'm just caught up in my emotions."

"Are you?" He sounded uncertain.

"I don't think so." But her voice sounded as uncertain as his had.

He put a hand on either side of her face and whispered, "You are going to come to my bed, but I want you to know exactly what you're doing when it happens." He pulled her into his arms and held her for a moment. She could feel the indecision and frustration running through him. In that moment, whatever it was that she felt for him grew, and she knew she could easily fall in love with him.

He leaned back and brushed the hair off her face. His fingers weren't soft, but they were surprisingly gentle. "You need rest."

"I know."

"Are you going back to your room now?" He still looked like he half regretted his chivalrous actions.

"I think I'll sleep here and see if I get any more answers."

"Want company?" He said it without a leer, without a smile, and she knew that he would have lain next to her, even held her, and not asked for anything more. Jake Stone was a man of many sides.

"Thank you, but I'll be fine." And Jake was probably right about her being emotional, because suddenly she felt too tired to move, much less make love.

One of the guards appeared at the door with a message from Nathan to call him. They had apparently linked with a satellite that enabled cell phone reception at the castle.

"I'll call him," Jake said. "You rest."

The guard gave Kendall and Jake a strange look before he left. Jake followed him. Kendall slipped off her shoes and lay down on the bed where she had been born. Sleep was impossible. The vision replayed over and over in her head, and when it stopped, she tossed and turned, trying to put together the pieces of her past. Her father had told her that her mother died when she was young. She knew it had been when she was very young. She hadn't realized it had been in childbirth. Why hadn't he told her?

For God's sake, Kendall. She died giving birth to you. He was probably worried that you'd think it was your fault she died. Wasn't it?

Now she was burning to know more . . . who her mother was, where she lived, how she'd met her father, if there was a family out there she didn't know. Why someone had tried to kill her.

When Kendall finally fell asleep, her dreams were just as confusing as her thoughts. Images of the bloody childbirth and her father. Then she dreamed about the plane crash that had killed her father, Adam, and Uncle John. She hadn't been there, but she'd imagined it in her dreams a million times. Or seen it. She didn't know. But it seemed so real, she felt the heat of the flames. When she woke, she felt as if she were on fire.

She sat up, heart thudding so hard the bed seemed to shake. Then she saw that she wasn't alone. Someone stood at the foot of the bed. "Jake?" Had he come to check on her? When her eyes adjusted to the darkness, she saw the robe. The ghost was back. This time he stood looking at the desk where she'd found the hidden letter. His hands were folded in front of him. He looked up and she saw his profile, and she knew why he'd seemed familiar. Why he was attached to this room. Why she had needed to be there in the chapel to protect Jake and Nathan from being killed when Edward died.

The ghost was her father.

"Daddy."

He turned and looked at her. She saw a faint hint of her father's eyes, his strong nose and angled cheekbones, his mouth set tight in concentration as it had been when he studied his latest find. There was an intensity about him when he was focused on his work, but that intensity could just as easily turn to a smile whenever she was near.

He moved closer to the bed, staring at Kendall. But she knew he wasn't looking at her. He was seeing the bloody bed where his lover had died. Her hands reached out for him, but he turned and walked into the same wall he had vanished through the last time.

Kendall threw back the covers and slipped on her Nikes. She grabbed her flashlight and pressed the catch in the wall that opened to the secret passageway. "Wait," she called. She glimpsed his robes and scrambled to keep up. He followed the same path as before, and she wondered if he even knew she was there or was just repeating the same pattern over and over. She stepped out of the tree that connected the secret passageway and the graveyard.

It took her a few seconds to find him. He stood outside the fence near the two square stones where she'd seen him on her first visit to the castle. He stayed longer this time, staring down at the stones. It wasn't until she had stepped within reach of the gravestones that he faded away. Was he trying to tell her something? Was it possible that the Fountain of Youth was hidden here? Hiding treasure in graves and tombs was common in many civilizations. Was her father's spirit still trying to help her find relics, just like the two of them had done when she was a kid? Or was this just a memory she had glimpsed?

Kendall looked at the two lonely graves. She assumed they were graves. There weren't any markings on the stones, but she had sensed a funeral procession when she touched one of the stones the last time she was here. It would make sense if his body had been buried here, but it couldn't be her father's grave. There hadn't been a body to bury. None of the bodies from the crash had been found. Her father, Adam, Uncle John.

The authorities had told Aunt Edna that the flames would have destroyed everything but the bones, which wild animals must have carried off. The crash had occurred on a private airstrip in a wooded, isolated area in Italy, and the wreckage hadn't been discovered for three days. Kendall had searched for the records as an adult, needing to see the place herself, but she couldn't find any mention of a specific location of the crash. Aunt Edna claimed she'd forgotten, but Kendall suspected she was trying to protect her. Her aunt had seen how devastated Kendall had been as a child. The grief she'd suffered. Aunt Edna had put up a memorial in a cemetery within walking distance to her house so that Kendall could visit whenever she missed her father. She had gone there often, leaning against the headstone, knowing he wasn't there, wondering why she had lived when everyone she loved had died.

A few times, Aunt Edna had driven her to the graveyard in Great Falls, where Adam and his father were memorialized. Kendall had sat by Adam's empty grave and talked to him, pretending he could hear her.

Graves, sometimes she hated them. Kendall looked down at the headstones at her feet. They could have been here a thousand years, or a dozen. She slowly put one hand on each of them and waited to see if anything came. She felt a suffocating sense of sadness and loss, and glimpsed a cloudy image of a woman's face ravaged by pain and grief. The same woman in the tower bed. Kendall knew then it wasn't just the woman's sadness and loss she felt. It was her own. This was her mother's grave. Had her father buried her there? He must have. And the other grave, who was buried in it? A thought struck her, so alarming she gasped, but something moved closer to the castle, and she hurried to see if it was her father's ghost or just one of the guards.

She followed the movement and saw the garden with the maze where Jake had first gone with Raphael, scouting out a way to get inside the castle. She'd never had a chance to explore here. The place looked haunted in the moonlight. A perfect place for a ghost. Topiaries stood at the entrance of the garden. A vine-covered wall surrounded it, isolating it from the rest of the castle grounds. There were a variety of trees and bushes, and a fountain stood near the maze, like the one in the entrance of the castle. Fountain? It couldn't be that simple. Moonlight reflected off the water spouting from the fountain and falling into the pond at the base. It was stone, old, like everything here. Kendall dipped her finger in the water and touched the stone.

She felt herself flying through a dark place, then a hard jolt and she was back at the fountain.

What was that?

She heard a noise and thought the whispers had returned. Then she realized the sound came from the rustling leaves of the maze. Turning, Kendall saw the hem of a robe disappear inside. "Wait." She dried her fingers on her pajamas as she hurried after him. Shining her light, she stepped inside the entrance to the maze. It was five feet wide, and even though the top was open and she could see the night sky, she felt spooked. But she wasn't going to give up. She needed to talk to her father. He had all the answers to her past.

The maze continued for several yards before making another turn. The turns came quickly after that, and in minutes, she realized she was lost. She hurried down another narrow passage, her light darting over foliaged walls as she searched for her ghost.

The feel of the maze changed. Kendall felt heavy, as if she were trudging through water. Her head started spinning and memories flashed through her mind. She saw Jake the first time she'd met him, then Nathan, Jake, and herself in the inn after Nathan had broken in. Then she saw Nathan the first day she'd met him. She remembered the unguarded look on his face when she'd found his missing relic at the museum. A look of shock and pain. His expression had haunted her. She'd never understood why.

The memories kept coming, each older than the previous one. She saw herself before she met Nathan, saw her aunt Edna rummaging in her antique shop, and then Kendall was on a cliff in Egypt with Adam. The heaviness lifted and she felt as if she were floating.

She heard a noise behind her and turned, almost expecting to see Adam. A man wearing a dark garment stood behind her. "Daddy?" Then he tilted his head, studying her, and she saw the writing on one side of his face.

She gasped in shock. "You!"

She took a step backward and fell through the air. She reached out but nothing was there.

CHAPTER FOUR

K ENDALL OPENED HER EYES AND SAW NOTHING BUT BLACK-
ness. No moon or stars overhead. She didn't feel injured or
bruised, just shaken and disoriented, as if she'd been taken apart
and put back together again. She rolled over, thinking she must
have fallen facedown, but the moon wasn't there either. She wasn't
in the maze. Her fingers registered a hard cold surface. Stone.
She was lying on some kind of stone. She'd fallen through another hole. Jake would never let her forget this.

She felt a lump underneath her leg and found her flashlight,
still on. Swinging the light around her, she saw that she was in
some kind of tunnel or cave. Her brain felt like thick syrup. It
took a full minute before she could stand, and even then she felt
like her legs would collapse. She must have hit her head. Maybe
she had a concussion.

She raised her light, looking for the hole she'd fallen through.
The ceiling was forty feet above her. If she had fallen that far, she
should be dead. Maybe she was dead. She'd seen Raphael just
before she fell. He was dead. She felt dead. And cold. It was dark.
What about the light? Going toward the light? She'd expected
something far different than this. Would Adam be here?

"Get a grip, Kendall. Dead people don't use flashlights." She examined the wall but couldn't find any openings or secret catches, only some markings that reminded her of cave drawings. But these were etched in stone and were some variation of circles. At least someone had been here before her, and she hadn't seen any bones . . . yet, so there must be a way out. She studied, pressed, and prodded the walls, but she didn't find any secret doors. It must be a one-way door or she needed a key.

A quick look around showed that the cave continued behind her. She searched the wall farther back, but after several minutes, she hadn't found any answers except that she was lost and finding it hard to stay awake. She started calling for help. If she was just under the maze, one of the guards might hear her.

Her head began to buzz, and she heard someone calling her name. "I'm here," she yelled. It must be Jake. She'd rather face his jokes than keep wandering in this damned cave. "Jake?" He didn't answer. She heard the voice calling her name again. It wasn't Jake. Nathan? She closed her eyes and listened closely. No. Not Nathan either. The voice came again. Adam? It was Adam calling her. But his voice sounded older than she remembered. "Adam?" she called, and then felt silly. Her addled brain must be playing tricks, unless she really was dead.

She continued checking the walls for openings or secret catches. The markings were so fascinating she forgot for a few moments where she was and how fatigued she felt. She finally gave up trying to figure them out and started walking. Jake had told her to explore, so it would be morning before anyone discovered she was missing. She would have to rescue herself.

The cave was large in places, narrowing at times, and the floor was remarkably level. She was used to exploring tight areas, but there was always someone with her or close by. She and Adam never went into a cave or tomb without the other.

It wasn't long before she realized she wasn't alone.

"Who's there?" She whirled and looked behind her. "I know you're following me. Daddy? Adam? Is that you?"

There was more than one spirit nearby. Animal. Creature. She didn't know what they were, but she wanted out of here.

"Go away." The whispered voice sounded rusty and old.

She shivered. "Who are you?"

"Get out."

"I'm trying." This time she hoped it was her imagination. She kept walking, goose bumps growing with each step. There was a feeling of anxiety and unrest. Perhaps it was fatigue, or she was picking up something from whatever was in here.

The castle grounds were large, but given the location of the catacombs and the tunnel leading to it, she should run into something soon. She'd walked for several hundred yards when she heard humming sounds like the statues made. They must be near. She didn't have a cross to protect her. Could they kill her underground?

The sound was coming from the inner wall of the cave. She pressed her ear against the stone and the humming grew louder. The statues surrounded the entire castle grounds, but if she had fallen through the maze, only the statue closest to the maze should be nearby. That meant the catacombs should be this way, but there was only a wall. Holding the light steady, she examined the wall for a doorway, when she heard voices yelling and the sound of pounding hooves. Horses? The noise grew louder until it was deafening. She heard metal clashing and flung herself against the wall. A rush of wind brushed past her and the sounds faded.

She felt someone move behind her. Heart racing, she turned and saw a dark shape advancing. She tried to lift her flashlight, but her arm was numb. Two distinct feelings hit her then. Familiarity and darkness. She'd felt the darkness first, then a softening, almost a fondness, before everything went black.

"You can walk faster than that," Adam called over his shoulder. He was ahead of her on the path. He climbed like a goat. She couldn't ever remember seeing him fall.

"I have a blister. It's these stupid shoes." They were new. She'd lost one of her others down a hole yesterday. She'd taken a step when the ground gave way, and her whole foot went inside. Adam had immediately grabbed her and pulled her back. He had taken his T-shirt and wrapped it around her foot so she could walk home without cutting her foot on the sharp rocks or getting bitten by something poisonous. He'd teased her the whole way, calling her Mummy Foot, but she didn't care. She would have laughed at him if he'd lost his shoe down a hole and had to walk home with a T-shirt wadded around his foot too.

Adam scrambled over a pile of stones, dislodging one. "Look out," he yelled.

She darted aside and the stone rolled past her.

He sat down and waited for her. His sun-bleached hair and dusty khakis made him look as much a part of the desert as the dirt and rocks. He belonged here. She'd never known anyone like Adam. It wasn't just because he was her only friend. She felt something for him that she couldn't explain. Not love. Ten-year-old girls didn't fall in love. Maybe it was awe. He was two years older, and she was sure that other than her father and Uncle John, Adam was the smartest person in the world. He scrubbed a hand through his hair. It needed cutting, but there were too many things to explore to waste time getting a haircut, he said.

"Hurry," he called. "We're almost there."

"We'll never get the shoe back," Kendall said when she caught up. "The hole's too deep. Besides, I didn't like those shoes anyway. They were ugly."

"I'm not worried about your shoe."

"Then why are we going back to the hole?"

He put his hand over his heart, their private sign for trust me. She did, so she followed him to the hole.

"I was afraid your dad would be mad. He paid good money for those shoes. So after I took you home, I went back again to see if I could get it, and I saw something when I looked down in the hole."

Her dad hadn't complained about the shoe, a good, sturdy expensive one, which he made her wear since she was always exploring. Her dad didn't notice much anymore. He was always distracted. Always worried.

"What'd you see?" Kendall asked. They'd reached the hole now. It was near the top of the cliff.

"Something shiny." Adam squatted on the other side of the hole.

"Shiny," Kendall said, feeling her heartbeat kick.

Adam gave her one of his wild grins, and his whole face lit up. "Careful," he said. "I think the ground is stable, but lie down flat." He demonstrated, lying down and crawling slowly toward the hole.

Kendall copied his movements, crawling on the opposite side.

"Shine your light down there and tell me what you see."

It was dark inside the hole. The opening was too small to let in much light. Kendall aimed her flashlight. At first it was hard to see, and then she made out a shape. "I see my shoe." She inched closer. "It's a long way down."

"Shine your light a few feet to your left."

"OK." Kendall did and she saw a glint. "I see it. What do you think it is?"

"Treasure." Adam looked up, dark eyes glinting. "I think it's a tomb."

He had been right. It was a tomb. Her father and Uncle John had been shocked, and then excited, but not as excited as they should have been. Something was wrong. The next day, her father

*had taken her and Adam to Italy. An important matter to attend
to, he said, while Uncle John was on a business trip.*

That's where they'd had the fight.

*"You can't," Adam said. "We're supposed to stay put. This is
serious." They were in a small bedroom on the third floor of the
castle they were visiting. Kendall's father had gone to meet with
the owners. Strange men. They looked like monks. Uncle John was
attending to business in Rome. He was getting the jet ready to
move his collection. People were always trying to steal Uncle John's
collection. It was the best in the world. She'd never seen it, but
because she and Adam had never been allowed to see it, they had
decided it must be the best. And they'd seen a lot of treasure over
the years. Adam suspected it was hidden on their estate. He promised to show Kendall the next time they were there.*

*"I've never seen any place like this," Kendall said. "I want to
explore. I'm not going to touch anything."*

"No. You're not going."

"You can't tell me what to do. You're twelve, not twenty."

*"I'm older than you. It's my job . . . ," he broke off. "I don't
want you to get in trouble."*

*"Daddy won't even know we're gone. I've got to look at those
statues. There's something strange about them."*

*"I know," Adam said, frowning. "That's why I don't want you
to go. Something's not right about this place. It feels . . . odd."*

*"Then let's figure out why that is. I want to know what's so im-
portant here that my dad would interrupt the plans to move your
dad's collection. And make them ignore the hidden tomb we found. I
think this place has something to do with why they're both worried."*

*"Your dad's going to be even more worried if we go tramping
around this place."*

*"We worry them all the time. You never let that stop you from
sneaking off before. What's wrong with you? You're never scared."*

"We don't know these people. They might be bad. Your dad locked the door from the outside. I'd say that means he's serious."

Kendall grinned. "We don't need the door. There's a secret entrance in that wall."

"Is that one of your hunches?" He scowled, but he wasn't questioning her claim. Adam was the only person she could be honest with about her gift. He just thought it got her into too much trouble. "You see too much."

"I can't help it. So come on. We'll just go peek at one of the statues."

He scratched his head. He still hadn't cut his hair. "Just to the statues, then back."

Kendall pushed a circle in the wall and a hidden door slid inward. "I told you." They stuck their heads into the dark interior. It was like a tomb, and just as tricky to maneuver. They got lost more than once, and Kendall could feel Adam getting mad. "Stop it," she said when they'd reached their second dead end.

"I'm not doing anything," he muttered.

"I can feel you shouting at me."

"It's not my fault you can read minds."

"It's not mine either. I didn't ask for this stupid gift."

"We should go back," he said.

"No. I want to know what's going on. There's something wrong with my dad. He's scared. I don't like seeing him scared. There's something wrong with your dad too. There has to be a way out of here," she said. "We just haven't found it. You're good at finding hidden entrances. You try."

Adam grumbled under his breath and ran his hands over the wall above her head. He was several inches taller than her. "I feel something." He pushed and a door swung open. Fresh air. They were in a garden with fountains and a maze.

"Let's try the maze," she said.

"No. Just look at the statue and let's go back."

This wasn't like Adam. He was the bravest person she'd ever known. He'd saved her a bunch of times. Once from when she'd fallen in a tomb, and another time from a black mamba. If there were real superheroes, they must be like Adam. But she wasn't letting anyone, not even a superhero, keep her from exploring.

They walked through the garden, and then Adam pointed. "I see a statue over there."

"I'd rather go this way," Kendall said, starting toward the woods. "I feel something."

"You and your stupid hunches," Adam muttered.

"You're just mad because we didn't get to explore the hidden tomb in Egypt." They found an old graveyard, and Kendall heard something calling her. "Shhh," she said, listening. "Do you hear that?"

"I hear the bugs and the trees."

"You don't hear whispering?"

"No."

"I do."

"It's all in your head."

"Maybe." Kendall started walking along an old path that led from the graveyard into the woods. "Look there. It's a church." The church was old and it had stained glass windows. Her dad loved stained glass. He'd given her a piece for her birthday once.

Adam moved ahead of her. He tried the door handle. "It's open."

"Then let's go in."

"I don't want to," he said.

"Come on, you know you want to."

His eyes were narrowed. He was angry with her. "You're going to get us in trouble and expect me to bail you out."

"*Then act like a chicken and stay out here, but I'm going in.*"
She opened the door and went inside. "Where's the seats?" she asked.

"*Doesn't look like a church to me,*" Adam said, sticking his
head inside the door. "*It looks more like a temple.*" He took a few
more steps until he was standing right behind her.

*There was writing on the walls, and in the front of the church
there were three big stones. "This is strange. I've never seen stones
like this in a church. Reminds me of Stonehenge. I wonder what
this means." There was writing on the stones. It wasn't in English.
Didn't look like any language she'd ever seen. She tried sounding
out the words. She reached the end and felt strange inside. Like she
might float to the ceiling.*

"*Kendall, we need to leave. Now!*" Adam's voice came from
behind her. She turned to him. His face was tight and his eyes
looked scared. She'd never seen Adam scared. Not even when he
saved her from the snake. His eyes widened and she looked back at
the stones. The letters were glowing now. She took a step back and
a light burst out of the stone. She felt like a wave had crashed into
her body.

Kendall woke and saw the shadow hovering over her. Her wrist
stung, but she was too weak to move away. She heard heavy footsteps running toward her, and beyond the shadow she saw two
glowing eyes rushing at her. She opened her mouth and
screamed.

CHAPTER FIVE

T WO HOURS EARLIER . . .

"Wake up!"

Jake groaned and rolled over. His skull felt like it had split down the middle. Each breath sent a stabbing pain to his ribs. Several of them were broken. He shook his head and tried to remember where he was. The rattle of keys and the armed guard reminded him.

"You, come with me," the guard said in broken English. An Iraqi.

Jake pulled himself to his feet. His stomach burned from the bullet still festering inside his gut. He'd been shot while helping the girls escape. The girls . . . God, what had happened to the girls?

"Is this him?" the guard asked.

Jake looked at the man standing behind the guard. He'd never seen him before. The stranger wasn't Iraqi. American maybe? Rich. That much was obvious from his clothes.

"That's him," the stranger said. He was British.

"Who are you?" Jake asked. He looked like a GQ model with a bad attitude.

*The man didn't smile, just looked at him with dark, stormy eyes.
"Your savior," the guard said, with an ugly sneer.*

Jake woke from the dream of Iraq to someone pounding on the door. He looked at his watch. Eleven p.m. Must be Kendall. He shouldn't have left her alone. The vision of her parents had been tough on her. No damned wonder, witnessing your own birth. Seeing a mother you'd never met. He got up and opened the door. "Want to sleep in my bed—"

"No, I don't want to sleep in your bed." Nathan pushed past Jake.

"Dream of the devil," Jake said. "You got a good reason for pounding on my door in the middle of the night?"

"Where's Kendall?"

"Not here," Jake said, scratching his chest.

Nathan looked around the room as if Jake might have stashed her somewhere. "Where is she?"

"In the tower room. She was hoping to have a vision."

"Of what?"

"Her parents. Remember the child she said was born in the tower room? It was Kendall. Her mother must have died giving birth to her here."

"Bloody hell."

"Yep."

"I've got to talk to her."

"Can't it wait till morning?"

"No. I have something to say that I want you both to hear."

"Is Kendall in danger?"

"She might be." Nathan dropped his bag on the floor and walked to the door. "You coming?"

"Give me a minute, unless you want me to go like this." Jake pulled on his jeans, shirt, and boots, and then he and Nathan went to the tower room. They knocked on the door, but there was no answer.

"Kendall," Jake called, banging louder. He shouldn't have left her alone. But he had been half afraid he'd take what she was offering. He wanted her, more than he'd ever wanted anyone. But he didn't want her sleeping with him to escape ghosts.

"You're going to wake the whole castle," Nathan said. He tried the door, but it was locked. "You could pick the lock."

"You could rip it off its hinges."

"I don't think she's in there."

"Probably not," Jake said. "She would have come to the door. She's not a sound sleeper."

Nathan gave him a look that made Jake wonder if he had a death wish. If Nathan went into Hulk mode, Jake wouldn't stand a chance. He pulled out his pocketknife and fiddled with the lock. They heard the key hit the floor on the other side. "There." Jake opened the door and walked inside. "Not here."

"Where the hell would she be?" Nathan asked, coming in behind him.

"We're talking about Kendall. She could be anywhere. Let's check her room. Maybe she went back."

"How'd the door get locked?"

"She could've gone out the secret passageway and back to her room through another door. This castle probably has secret doors in every room." They checked, but she wasn't in her room either. The velvet bag holding the crosses lay on a table next to her purse.

"She did take them," Nathan said.

"You knew?"

"Marco did."

"How'd he know?" Jake asked.

"How does Marco know anything? He's a paradox. He knows stuff he shouldn't and can't remember stuff he should. Here." Nathan handed Jake one of the crosses. "We might need these if she's exploring." He put one of the crosses over his head and put the other one in his pocket.

Jake put on the cross. He thought it was Marco's but wasn't sure. They looked alike in the dim light.

They checked the castle, searching the rooms that were open, but she wasn't there. "She must be outside," Jake said. "I did tell her it was fine to explore."

"You're supposed to be watching over her."

"You've got a damned army here. What could go wrong? The way you worry about her makes me wonder if you're in love with her," Jake said.

"She works for me. That's all. I protect my employees."

"Bullshit. It's more than that."

"You're the one who's all over her, trying to get her in bed. Maybe you're in love with her."

"I don't know the meaning of love," Jake said.

"That's why I'm telling you to stay the hell away from her."

"You're the one who keeps putting us together."

"You know what I mean. You're supposed to protect her. That's it. Not that you did this time."

"I didn't know I needed to keep an eye on her in the middle of dozens of guards and all these damned statues. By the way, she knows you're watching her apartment."

Nathan frowned. "How does she know?"

"I told her. I saw the camera."

"There's a damned camera in her apartment?"

"Not inside. On the building facing hers. It's not yours?"

"No. I've got guards keeping an eye on her place, but that's it. I'll have someone check it out."

"Maybe her neighbor is spying on her. He's trying to get in her pants."

"Which neighbor?"

"Dark-haired guy. Looks like one of those cologne models."

"The new one? I'm still checking up on him. She told you he's after her?"

"She didn't need to. I watched him talking to her."

"She needs to stay at the mansion where I can protect her."

"Good luck convincing her of that."

"Someone with her talents isn't safe. If anyone finds out what she can do . . ." Nathan trailed off, his tone worried.

"I can't argue with you there. Speaking of keeping tabs on people, I don't suppose you sent someone to spy on me yesterday? I caught someone outside my window, and Kendall said there was a woman in my bedroom."

"What was Kendall doing in your bedroom?" Nathan growled.

"Trying to save me from the intruder. You've got it so bad for her, it's eating you up inside. I'd fight you for her, but I'm afraid you'd go Hulk on me and win. She probably went to check on the treasure. She wanted to when we first got here. I told her no, but you know how well she listens." They walked outside. The guard at the front door said he hadn't seen her.

"She probably used the secret passageway," Nathan said.

Jake started walking toward the graveyard. "She's the only woman I know who'd go wandering alone in a graveyard in the middle of the night."

"Yeah," Nathan said, but his voice held a hint of pride.

As much as her independent streak irritated Jake, he also admired it. "There's the path," he said, shining his flashlight on the stones leading to the chapel. But when they reached the chapel, the door was locked. "I don't think she's here."

"She's got to be somewhere. Let's look inside to make sure."

Jake put his cross—the secret key—in the opening and heard a click as the door unlocked.

The chapel was dark inside. "Kendall?" When she didn't answer, Nathan said, "We should look underneath the floor in the treasure room to make sure she didn't get locked in."

"How could she be down there? It took all three crosses to open it."

"We don't know that it was necessary," Nathan said.

"That's true. And Kendall does have a tendency to get trapped in strange places."

"She's smart," Nathan said, sounding defensive. "But she's too brave for her own good. Let's try one of the crosses and see what happens. What can it hurt?"

"You forgetting about booby traps?" The beam from Jake's flashlight hit the center stone at the front of the chapel. It had been pushed back, exposing the steps to the secret room. "I guess we won't need the keys after all. Kendall?" Jake hurried down the stairs with Nathan right behind him. He pushed the button on the wall, and the torches flared to life.

The room was empty.

"What the hell?" Nathan looked at Jake.

"Don't look at me. I didn't take it, and there's no way Kendall could have moved it that fast."

"It wasn't Kendall," Nathan said.

"Who could get in here with those statues and your security guards?"

"Someone who knows this place inside out could."

"Marco? He's a strange little man, but I doubt he can move things with his mind."

"Not Marco," Nathan said. "Raphael."

"Raphael's dead."

"No he isn't."

"I saw him," Jake said. "He was dead."

"*Was* is the key word. He was dead when my men found him in the room where the round table is. Then he woke up."

"He woke up? There's no way."

"I'm telling you he's alive."

"How?" Jake asked.

"That's what I wanted to know."

"Did he tell you?"

"He didn't tell me anything."

"Where is he now?"

"I don't know. He escaped."

"Escaped? Hell, is that what all that roaring was about? You had Raphael in Virginia all this time and didn't tell us?"

"I couldn't. You should understand that."

"How'd he get out?" Jake asked.

"We're still trying to figure that out. I wouldn't have believed anyone could get past my security."

"Actually, one of the cameras on the north side of the mansion makes a three-second sweep. If you're fast, you can run behind the storage building and from there hide behind the other buildings until you reach the gate."

"You walked out the front gate? I'll fire all the guards."

"I jumped the fence about two hundred yards north."

"It's got cameras and razor wire," Nathan said.

"That camera has a four-second span, and razor wire doesn't cut through boots and fireplace gloves."

"That's where the bloody gloves went. Fergus accused me of losing them. He builds a fire every night."

"I'll buy him a new pair," Jake said.

"Raphael didn't hide from the cameras. He didn't need to."

"How'd he get past your guards?"

"They fell asleep."

"All of them?"

"They either fell asleep or he tossed them out of his way. You want to know how he got past the locks?" Nathan asked.

"Ripped them off with his bare hands?"

"Walked through the walls."

"No one walks through walls," Jake said.

"Raphael did. Or he made it look like he did. Except he wasn't exactly walking. I've never seen anyone move that fast."

Jake looked at Nathan. "I suspect I have." Outside an inn in Italy. "So he just ran away?"

"No, he drove my Mercedes."

Jake laughed. "Did he take Marco with him?"

"No, but he talked to him. He told Marco he was going to move the treasure and get his cross back from Kendall."

Jake's stomach dropped. "He's going after Kendall?"

"Yeah. Now you know why I pounded on your bedroom door in the middle of the night."

"She just wanted to examine the crosses."

"You knew she took them?" Nathan asked. "Truth, huh?"

"It wasn't my place to tell you. And that's not the same as hiding a man who's supposed to be dead. He'll kill her. You didn't see how he looked at her cross. He doesn't just want his cross. He'll want hers too."

The color drained from Nathan's eyes, leaving them amber. But he took several deep breaths and they returned to normal. "We've got to find her before he does. He's not . . . normal."

"Said the kettle to the pot."

They alerted security that Kendall was missing and there might be an intruder. They reinforced the guards, most of them stationed outside the wall to make sure no one got in, and several around the chapel. They checked with each one, but no one had seen Kendall, except one guard who thought he saw her near the maze on his way to take up his post at the airstrip.

"Jake and I will search there," Nathan said. "The rest of you search the grounds. If she's in the catacombs, the door should still be open. We've got to find her before Raphael does."

There was no sign of Kendall as they hurried toward the maze.

"Did you get the Mercedes back?" Jake asked.

"Turned up abandoned near Great Falls."

"Great Falls, Virginia? Why would he go there, and how the hell did he get from there to Italy in time to move the treasure?"

"I'll ask him when I see him."

"I think I'd stay out of his way if I were you," Jake said. "Although you two have more in common than just your strange eyes. When I followed you from the inn a few days ago, I couldn't even keep up. Nobody runs that fast. Sure you're not related to Raphael?"

"I never met Raphael before the castle."

"Maybe you've blocked it." Like the therapists said he'd done with part of his past. "Or maybe you're the Reaper."

"You're still hung up on that? I saved your ass. The Iraqis believed you killed the prince."

"Do you?"

"If you did, I figure you had a good reason."

"I wish I had as much faith in you, but it's a little too coincidental that some rich guy hires me, insists I'm the only one for the job, and then you show up with all your power and money."

"I pulled you out of hell. You have money, food, clothes, whatever you need."

"I don't have answers. All I have is a constant threat hanging over my head. I need to know what went down in Iraq. Why I was there. Why Thomas was there. Why he shot me. The prince wasn't working with terrorists. My entire team died, and I don't even know why. You have some of the answers, but you're not telling. You never do."

"And you do? What about that wooden doll you carry around? You never talk about that."

"How'd you know about the doll?"

"I know more than you think."

"That's the kind of shit I'm talking about. You know too much. Maybe you are the damned Reaper."

"If I were the Reaper, you'd be dead. Besides, you and Kendall know what he looks like. You saw him at the inn. Remember the man with the ruby ring, and the murderer posing as the historian?"

"Yeah, posing. You're the one who said he's a master of disguises. He could be anyone."

"You're just frustrated because you don't have answers." There was a trace of sympathy in Nathan's voice. "I wasn't the one behind your mission. I found out the prince had a collection of relics that he'd gotten on the black market. I wanted to see them, and I knew the Reaper would be after them too. That's what I was doing there. When I found out about you, I wanted to know how you were involved."

"You thought I was working for the Reaper?" Jake asked.

Nathan shrugged. "You could have been."

"Hell. That's why you hired me?"

"I hire the best. You're the best at what you do."

"And you could keep an eye on me and see if I was working for the Reaper?" Jake gave a harsh laugh.

"Wouldn't you have done the same?"

He would have. In fact, he was doing the same thing by working for Nathan. At first, he'd accepted Nathan's offer because he had no choice. He would have died in prison, but Jake could have disappeared afterward if he wanted. It wouldn't have been easy, not if Nathan had put his money into tracking him down, but there were ways it could have been done. But despite his accusations, after the first few weeks, he'd started to doubt that Nathan was directly involved in his imprisonment in Iraq. Indirectly, possibly, and now Jake knew. Assuming Nathan was telling the truth. It fit what intel he'd collected on Nathan.

"I know about the girls," Nathan said. "How many of them were there?"

'Course he would know. "Ten." He still remembered their terrified eyes and their screams.

"You got them out." It was a statement, not a question.

"Not all of them."

"Most of them. Maybe that was why I rescued you," Nathan said. "You ever think of that?"

"No."

"I'm not a monster. Not yet," he muttered.

"I never said you were a monster."

"What do you think I am?" Nathan sounded oddly unsure.

"I'm hoping you're a mad scientist."

That made Nathan laugh. Jake didn't think he'd ever heard Nathan laugh.

"That's good?" Nathan asked.

"Better than a vampire or a werewolf. You do have the glowing eyes."

"Why a mad scientist?"

"You have some serious adrenaline issues. I know it's adrenaline that controls whatever happens to you. Like when you thought Kendall was dying in that coffin and when she was attacked at the castle. I've seen a rush of adrenaline give a man strength, but I've never seen it change his eyes. You must be experimenting with drugs to create superhuman strength. What'd you do? Use it on yourself?"

"It's a long story," Nathan said. "But I'm not the Reaper, a mad scientist, or a vampire."

"You didn't rule out werewolf."

"I'm not a bloody werewolf."

"I'd feel better if you sounded sure." They hurried toward the garden Raphael had reluctantly shown Jake when he and Kendall first arrived. There was no sign of her here. "Knowing Kendall, she's gone inside the maze." They called her name, but she didn't answer.

"Guess we're going in," Nathan said.

The maze was eerie in the moonlight. Quiet as a mausoleum. Jake didn't like the feeling in his gut. They searched the maze for several minutes, splitting up and going down one turn after another as they called her name. Their voices sounded strange, as if they were in a larger, quieter place than the maze, and the feeling in Jake's gut worsened. They met back in the center. "I don't think she's here," Jake said.

"We didn't try this one," Nathan said, pointing to one of the turns.

They followed it, the sounds of their voices still falling like dampness in a deep forest. Jake's head began to feel heavy, and his whole body felt as if he'd walked through a wall of metal cobwebs and then floated away in pieces. "Damn, I feel strange."

"Me too," Nathan said, but his voice sounded like it was floating above the maze; then the ground disappeared from under Jake's feet.

CHAPTER SIX

THE NEXT THING JAKE KNEW, HE WAS LYING ON HIS BACK. "What the hell?" He tried to stand, but his head and body still felt disconnected. Managing to get to his feet, he saw Nathan was also rising and his eyes were pale. "Whoa." Jake took a step back, but Nathan had bent over and was pulling in long breaths.

"Breathe through it." Jake kept his voice low.

When Nathan straightened, his eyes were normal. "Where the hell are we, and what's wrong with my head? I feel like I'm going to black out."

"Guess we found a booby trap," Jake said. He aimed his light around the space.

"We fell for a good ten seconds. The impact should have killed us."

"What impact?" Jake asked. "I didn't feel anything except this sensation of coming apart. Maybe we're trapped in one of Kendall's visions. They feel kind of like this."

"How do you know what her visions are like?" Nathan asked.

"I shared one with her. Not something I'll forget."

"What were you doing?" Nathan asked.

"Not what you think." It took them both a minute to get oriented. Then they examined the dark space.

"We're underground," Nathan said. "We must be underneath the maze. Looks like a cave."

"Where'd we fall from?" Jake asked, looking at the ceiling above them. "I don't see any holes or doors."

"Look at these markings on the walls."

"Circles, of course. The Protettori love those damned circles." They checked the area thoroughly but couldn't find any sign of where they'd fallen from.

"If it's a hidden door, they've hidden it well," Nathan said.

Jake aimed his light farther into the cave. "We'll have to find another way out. I guess we'd better start walking."

The cave was large in places, smaller in others, but the floor wasn't uneven as might be expected. It was smooth, as if it had been leveled.

"When did you share one of Kendall's visions?" Nathan asked after a few minutes.

"At the castle. She touched Raphael's body to see if she could sense anything, and I was touching her."

"What did you see?"

"Warriors, swords, shields. I think Marco's right about Raphael. He's not as young as he looks. You had a lot of balls to take him prisoner. I sure as hell wouldn't want to keep him locked up in my dungeon. But then I can't do the glowing eyes thing."

"Stop calling it a damned dungeon," Nathan said. "I didn't have a choice. I need answers. Raphael has them."

"You want to know why he's not dead. I'd like to know myself, because he was dead as sure as I'm alive."

"I took him because we need the relics. Raphael must know where they are. Marco's memory isn't reliable."

"*You* need the relics. What you haven't explained is why you're so desperate to find them. And it's not to add to your collection, or even to protect them from the Reaper. You want them for another reason." Jake grabbed his shoulder. "What'd you do that for?"

"Do what?"

"You poked my shoulder."

"Not me," Nathan said. "Must have been a rock falling or bat droppings."

"What does a billionaire know about bat shit?" Jake asked.

"I could write a book on the stuff." Nathan grew quiet, as if his words had surprised him. They walked for a few minutes without talking. "What was that?" Nathan asked, sounding irritated.

"What was what?"

"You hit me."

"Wasn't me," Jake said. "If I had hit you, you wouldn't be standing." He looked up at the ceiling. "Bat shit? Speaking of hitting, what were you and Fergus fighting about at the mansion?"

"What do you mean?" Nathan asked.

"Fergus looked like he wanted to hit you when Kendall and I got there."

"He was afraid I was trying to wake Marco. You'd think Marco was his father. They're both acting weird."

"Marco must be rubbing off on him," Jake said.

"They're up to something. They're always whispering like they're conspiring. It's starting to piss me off."

"Sucks to be out of the loop, doesn't it?" Jake said.

"Shut up and look for Kendall. She could have fallen down this hole too."

"Wouldn't be the first time." The farther they went in the cave, the more tired Jake felt, and more anxious. "I don't like this cave."

Nathan flashed his light behind them and into the encroaching darkness. "You get the feeling we're not alone?"

He hadn't wanted to mention it, thinking it might be his foggy brain. "Yeah. I was hoping it was your lousy company. Probably trolls or giants with one eye." The Fountain of Youth wasn't looking as farfetched now.

"I hear something," Nathan said.

Jake listened, and then he heard a faint humming sound. "That's what the statues sound like. We must be under them."

Nathan touched his head. "Hell, I feel like shit. Maybe it's the statues. You walked past them. Did they make you feel strange?"

"Yes, but not like this. I feel like I could sleep standing up. It almost feels like there's not enough oxygen." Maybe that explained the prickle crawling up Jake's back. But he didn't think so.

Nathan stopped, head tilted. Shadows from the flashlight made him look frightening. He sniffed the air. "I smell blood."

"Blood?" Jake's heart thudded.

"It's Kendall."

Jake was thinking about what Raphael might do when he found Kendall, when they heard the scream. Jake saw the change happen. Nathan's body jerked as if he'd been hit in the stomach. When he straightened, he looked bigger. Jake didn't need to see Nathan's eyes to know they had changed to amber. Nathan took off running with Jake on his heels.

Jake knew from experience that he couldn't keep up, but that didn't stop him from trying. In seconds, Nathan moved ahead. Jake was starting to believe Kendall might be right about otherworldly creatures. Whatever was happening to Nathan didn't feel like an experiment in a lab. Jake's flashlight showed something pale against the blackness of the cave. Clothing. Blond hair. Kendall!

A black shadow hovered over her. It appeared shapeless, just a black mass, but when they got closer, it vanished. Nathan reached her first. When Jake got there, Nathan was checking her pulse.

"She's alive, but unconscious."

Jake knelt beside him. "What the hell was that shadow?"

"I don't know, but we have to get her out of here. Kendall, can you hear me?"

"I'll carry her," Jake said.

"I'll do it. I'm stronger."

"Only in Hulk mode. I'll take her first. You watch out for whatever that black thing was. I have a feeling your talents might be more suited for fighting it."

Jake picked Kendall up in his arms. Her head fell against his chest. "We'll have to keep going ahead." Jake carried her while Nathan kept watch. He was feeling so weak, he was about to see if Nathan wanted to switch, when Kendall roused in his arms. "She's waking up." He stopped and sat down, cradling her on his lap. Nathan bent down in front of them and brushed back her hair.

Kendall woke up with a yell and punched Nathan in the stomach. He grunted and Kendall leapt to her feet. Jake jumped up and grabbed her. "Kendall, it's us. Jake and Nathan."

"Jake? Nathan?" She glanced at Nathan, hunched over, trying to get his breath. "Oh my God." She hurried back to him. "I'm so sorry. I thought you were . . . What are you doing here?"

"Looking for you?" Jake said, since Nathan was still wheezing.

Nathan rubbed his stomach. "Bloody hell. You hit hard."

"I'm so sorry. There was something hovering over me."

"We saw it. It vanished when we got close. One of your ghosts?" Jake asked.

"I think it was something else."

"What?" Jake asked. "Fairies, dragons?"

"I don't know, but it was powerful."

"Did it hurt you?" Nathan asked. His eyes flared but didn't start glowing.

"I don't think so. I blacked out, so I'm not sure. My head feels strange." Like a sponge that had been squeezed dry.

"You're bleeding," Nathan said, shining his light on her wrist.

"I am?" She looked down at her arm and saw a small gash. "I must have cut it when I fell." She didn't recall hitting her arm, but she remembered it stinging.

"It's not deep," Nathan said, examining it. "Just a scratch." The warmth of his hand on her arm made her realize how cold she was.

"Looks like it was cut with a knife," Jake said, squatting beside her.

Nathan nodded. They both gave her a thorough inspection, running their flashlights over her, inquiring about scrapes and even old scars she'd had since she was a kid, until she felt like she'd had a physical. She kept glancing over her shoulder.

"What's that?" Nathan asked, frowning. Her pajamas had a small tear, revealing the ridge of an old scar on her thigh.

She didn't know how her pajamas had torn. It must have also happened when she fell. "I got that in Egypt when I was a kid. I fell into a tomb."

She'd been with Adam. Adam. Now she knew it was her fault he had died, her fault her father and Uncle John had died. Marco said breaching the sacred chamber could cause a curse of death.

She was the one who had trespassed. Adam had tried to stop her, but she hadn't listened. He had looked out for her for years, and she had repaid him with a curse.

The events leading up to the childhood incident in the chapel were vivid, but the events afterward were vague. She recalled several men in robes whispering, their voices angry. Then another man leading them to a tunnel . . . to the railcars. They'd left the castle by the railcars. She remembered being sleepy. Even with all the excitement, it had been hard to stay awake. The events after they left the castle were even cloudier. Adam was there. She remembered him asking for his father, but he hadn't returned from his trip. Her father had been nervous, afraid. That was all she remembered until she woke at Aunt Edna's and was told that they were all dead.

She realized Nathan was still staring at the scar, but he didn't move his hand. "Egypt." He seemed disturbed by the scar. Was that some kind of sign that he could be Adam? They'd spent a lot of time in Egypt.

"A little to the right and you'll be at third base," Jake said.

Nathan jerked his hand back. "Her pajamas look like they've been cut as well."

Now wasn't the time to solve the mystery about Adam. She needed to get out of here, or she was going to embarrass herself and collapse. "Did you find a way back to the maze?"

Jake shook his head. "We couldn't find any openings or hidden catches. We figured there must be another way out. We need to get moving in case that shadow thing comes back."

"Kendall looks pale," Nathan said. "Maybe we should rest."

"We're all pale," Jake said. "It's black as Hades in here."

"I'm fine," Kendall said. "Let's go." She wasn't fine, but there was something hostile about this place, as if it didn't want them here. She was happy to oblige.

"Yeah," Jake said. "I don't like the feel of this place."

Nathan and Jake each linked an arm through Kendall's and they started walking, continuing to keep an eye out for that sinister shadow. Her mind felt a little less foggy as she moved away from the place where she had encountered it. "How did you find me?"

"We followed you through the maze," Jake said. "We must be underneath it. We gotta be getting close to the catacombs. I can hear the statues."

"I hope they don't work underground," Kendall said. "We don't have the crosses."

Nathan let go of her arm and reached into his pocket. "Here." He pulled something out and slipped it over her head. A cross.

"Busted," Jake said. "We found them in your room."

Kendall felt the comforting weight against her chest. "Sorry. I didn't mean to take them without asking. I saw them in your study and picked them up. When I thought you were choking in your bedroom, I shoved them in my pocket and forgot about them."

Jake made a rumbling noise that could have been either a grunt or his stomach complaining.

"It's a good thing you brought them," Nathan said. "I didn't think about it."

"You were *preoccupied* with your guest," Jake said.

Guest? Kendall would have asked what he meant, but she was too focused on staying awake.

It didn't take long until Kendall was slowing down and Nathan and Jake were using more of their own strength to drag her. Her head had cleared some, but her body was still weak. "I'm sorry, but I have to stop. I don't know what's wrong with me."

"We'll carry you," Jake said. "We can't stop if that thing is in here."

They were tired too. Their steps had slowed. "It's gone now," she said. "I can feel that it's not here."

"You're sure?" Nathan asked.

"Yes. It was probably just a ghost."

"Then let's rest," Jake said. "You've had a hell of a night, and I feel like shit."

Using her light, she chose the least dirty spot. "How about here?"

"Dry, no bat droppings," Nathan said. "Looks good to me."

"Turns out our rich boss has a lot of experience with bat shit," Jake said. "Says he could write a book on it."

Nathan might wear suits and have loads of money, but he was no pansy. Still, she hadn't pictured him crawling around places where there were bats, like Adam had. She sat down while Jake and Nathan inspected the area around them. "How long have you been searching for me?"

"A couple of hours," Nathan said.

"Are you sure? I left the castle less than an hour ago."

"You must have blacked out longer than you thought," Jake said.

"It felt like just a few minutes," Kendall said. "I went to the graveyard first, then the maze. What time is it?"

Jake looked at his watch and frowned. "It's not working."

Nathan held up his wrist. "Neither is mine. That's bloody strange."

"Is there anything about this castle that isn't?" Jake murmured.

"Must be something to do with the statues," Nathan added.

But that didn't happen before, Kendall thought with a sense of foreboding.

"Did you sleep at all before you went chasing ghosts?" Jake asked.

"Not much." Kendall felt awkward thinking about what had happened before Jake left the tower room. If he hadn't held back, none of them would be here now. She would probably be lying in bed with him instead of lost in a cave. She should have insisted. She was getting sick of secret caves and tunnels.

Nathan started walking back the way they'd come.

"Where you going?" Jake asked.

"Bathroom."

"I miss the garderobe," she said.

"I miss food and water." Jake squatted beside her and turned over her wrist. "We need to get this fixed. Don't want it getting infected." His touch was warm, and she thought again how close they'd come to making love. Was it always going to be this dance? One of them darting in, the other pulling back? Nathan was back in moments, distracting her train of thought.

"Do you need to go?" Jake asked Kendall.

Was he going to escort her? "No, I'm fine."

"My turn then," he said.

They were babysitting her. As she had so many times in the past week, she felt both grateful and irritated. If she weren't so tired, she'd remind them that she'd probably had more experience in caves than both of them combined, but she was ready to drop from exhaustion. She wondered if the shadow hovering over her had done something to her mind. It was probably just a vision. Intense visions drained her. But even seeing her mother and father hadn't made her feel this bad afterward. And Jake and Nathan were also tired. Was the cave itself draining their energy?

"How's your wrist?" Nathan asked as Jake walked away.

"Stings a little."

He sat down beside her. "If we don't find a way out in the morning, we'll have to go back. There's got to be a way out back there. We didn't just appear here."

"Unless it was a booby trap with no exit designed to trap someone until they slowly died of thirst."

"Thus speaks a girl who's spent her life exploring caves and tombs," Nathan said. "We should save our batteries."

Nathan's flashlight started flickering and he turned it off. "That's not good."

Jake appeared a moment later and sat down on Kendall's other side. "You trying to conserve batteries?"

"Mine's dying," Nathan said. "The batteries were fresh."

"It's this cave," Kendall said. "There's something strange about it. Maybe the statues are draining the batteries and us."

"We'd better turn ours off," Jake said. "Who knows how long we'll be in here." He flipped his light off as a soft rumble sounded in the region of his stomach. "Don't suppose anyone has a candy bar?" His voice sounded strange in the dark.

"I wish," Kendall said. She was getting hungry. And thirsty. "We need water. We might find a spring."

"We'll check after we move on," Jake said. "I don't want to split up and search."

They didn't want to leave her alone. "I think it's safe now."

"We're not taking any chances," Jake said. "Even if it was just a ghost. Hell, a ghost killed Edward."

"That was my father."

Dead silence met her announcement. Then Jake blurted out a word that sounded even more obscene in the silence and darkness of the cave.

"Your father was the ghost in the chapel?" Nathan asked.

"Yes, but I don't know if he's a real ghost or just a . . . memory, a piece of the past replaying itself."

"I thought the ghost was the old guy in the catacombs who was guarding the Spear of Destiny, and he'd seen you at the castle when you were a kid," Jake said.

"No. It was my father. I sensed something familiar about him then, but I didn't see his face clearly until earlier tonight when he came into my room. I think that's why I needed to be there in the chapel with you. So he would recognize me."

"And not kill us along with Edward," Nathan said.

Jake frowned. "How can a memory kill someone?"

"I don't know," Kendall said. "How could a ghost kill someone? None of it seems logical."

"It figures that he'd be haunting that room if that's where you were born," Jake said.

"And where my mother died. Given how much she was bleeding, she couldn't have left the castle alive. There are two graves outside the graveyard. I think my mother is buried in one."

"Outside the graveyard?" Nathan said.

"She probably wasn't put in consecrated ground," she said. "I'm sure she wasn't supposed to be here."

"Makes me wonder who the second unconsecrated grave belongs to," Jake said.

"I think it's mine."

The dark silence grew quieter. "Yours?" Nathan asked.

"My father must have buried my mother there. Maybe he put up another stone to make the Protettori think the baby had died too. He would have been cast out if anyone found out. Maybe he tried to hide it."

"It must not have worked," Jake said. "He wasn't Protettori when you were growing up."

"Where is your father buried?" Nathan asked.

"Aunt Edna put up a stone in his memory, but there wasn't a body," Kendall said. "The authorities told us there wouldn't have been anything left from the crash but bones. They never found them. Wild animals, I suppose."

"Maybe the second grave is a memorial for your father," Nathan said. "If he was part of the Protettori."

"Perhaps," Kendall said.

"Your father never mentioned the castle?" Nathan asked.

"Never. It must have been a bad memory for him. When I saw the vision of the birth—my birth—it seemed as if my mother had hidden the pregnancy to protect my father until she got desperate."

"If he was Protettori, that makes sense," Nathan said. "Who knows what they might have done to him, to all of you, to protect the order's secret."

"There's more," Kendall said. "That piece of paper we found was a letter she wrote telling him about the baby. But then someone was trying to kill her, so she panicked and came to the castle."

"Who was trying to kill her?" Nathan asked.

"They didn't say, but my mother was apologizing for betraying my father. She didn't say what she'd done."

"Obviously your father wasn't part of the order when you were growing up, so either he left or they excommunicated him or whatever they do. Like they did the Reaper . . ." Jake's voice trailed off.

Kendall wondered if his thoughts were headed the same direction as hers. Could the Reaper be her father? Marco hadn't said when he was cast out. A chill rolled over Kendall's already cold skin as she remembered the sense of familiarity she'd felt in the shadow. She recalled the dream she often had where the evil shadow was creeping up behind her father, as if to consume him. "Did you get your situation straightened out at the mansion?"

"Kendall doesn't know about your *situation*," Jake said. "Why don't you tell her who you were keeping in your dungeon?"

Nathan rubbed his chin. "Raphael."

"Raphael's dead," Kendall said.

"Not anymore," Nathan said.

Kendall turned on her light so she could see Nathan. "That's impossible. Jake and I saw him. He was dead."

"He was dead when we found him at the castle," Nathan said, "but he woke up."

"You can't just wake up from being dead."

"Not unless you're Raphael," Jake said. "Or Jesus."

"I saw a vision of him in the maze just before I fell," Kendall said.

"I don't think it was a vision," Jake said. "He escaped. Remember the roaring we heard?"

"That was Raphael?" Just like the roaring she'd heard when she touched Raphael's cross earlier. "What do you mean, escaped?"

"He was Nathan's prisoner. Kind of poetic justice, if you think about it. He did imprison us in that tower."

"You were holding Raphael prisoner?" Kendall asked. "Are you crazy?"

"I had my reasons," Nathan said. "I needed to know how he was still alive, and he must know where the relics are."

"What he really wanted to know was why Raphael's eyes look like his when Nathan goes apeshit," Jake said.

Kendall frowned. "Raphael's are like that all the time, but they don't glow."

"We've never seen Raphael go apeshit. What do you want to bet his glow too? How about it, Nathan? Did they glow when he was roaring like Bigfoot as he escaped your prison?"

Nathan made a noncommittal grunt.

"Maybe the shadow was Raphael," Kendall said.

"Could be," Jake said. "We think he moved the treasure."

"It's gone?" Kendall asked.

"Every last piece of it," Jake said.

"How did he have time to get here and move a room full of treasure?" she asked.

"Only Raphael knows," Jake said.

Kendall was shocked, and also angry. "Nathan, you've been hiding things since the day I met you. I know we all have things we don't want to talk about, but you send us on a search for the Spear of Destiny and don't bother to tell us. And you've got some kind of superhuman thing going on that you never warned us about. I'm surprised Jake hasn't already shot you."

"I thought about it," Jake said.

"You're as bad as he is, Jake." She turned back to Nathan. "Now you've kidnapped someone we thought was dead, and you didn't bother to tell us? If you can't trust us by now, when we get out of here, we need to go our separate ways." Her light flickered and she quickly shut it off. The dark made it feel even colder. And it was already like a freezer.

"You gotta start trusting us sometime," Jake said. "If not, I'm out too. You can *try* to stick me back in prison if you want to."

Nathan rubbed his chin, and Kendall heard the soft rasp of an unshaven beard. "Do you believe in curses?"

CHAPTER SEVEN

N O," Jake said.

"Curses?" Kendall asked, startled because she'd been thinking about that very thing. "Why?"

"I think I'm cursed. I think that's what's wrong with me, why my eyes change."

"Granted it's not normal, but what makes you think it's a curse?" Kendall asked.

"What the hell would you call it?" he asked.

"She has a point," Jake said. "It happens when your adrenaline kicks in, when you're angry or scared."

Kendall felt Nathan balk at Jake's use of the word *scared*.

"So you've been studying me?" Nathan asked.

"I pay attention when there's something next to me that can rip my head off."

"How long has this been happening?" Kendall asked.

"I haven't felt normal for as long as I can remember, but it's just the last few months that the change has been happening. It's getting worse."

"Are you aware of your surroundings when it happens?" Kendall asked.

"You mean, am I going to not recognize someone and rip his head off?" Nathan asked, his voice dry.

Kendall shrugged. "You could hurt someone with that kind of strength, but so far we haven't seen any sign that you're dangerous, just protective."

"I know what's going on," Nathan said. "I just can't control my strength. Something must have happened when I was a kid."

"Like what?" Jake asked.

"I don't know. I can't remember my childhood. Nothing before Fergus."

"That's odd. Damned odd." Jake seemed troubled by the admission.

"I have a dream," Nathan said. "Maybe it's a memory, I don't know. There are two men talking. One of them mentions a curse that must be removed."

A curse. Like the one she might have brought on her father and Adam? "They didn't say where the curse came from?"

"No," Nathan said.

"Did you recognize the men?" she asked. "Was one of them Fergus?"

"I didn't see their faces, but their voices were familiar. If I knew them, I can't remember."

"Did they mention a way to get rid of it?" Jake asked.

"No, but I think it's connected to the Protettori's relics."

"How's that possible?" Jake asked.

"I don't know, but I've dreamed of them all my life." His light came on, and he pulled something from his pocket.

"How do you know it's their relics?" Jake asked. "You don't even know what they are."

Nathan opened a small black book and pulled out a loose page. "These. I've dreamed of these."

It was the paper with the sketches Kendall had seen in Jake's pack.

Jake turned on his light and looked at the paper. "That's mine. You're the one who took it."

Kendall's head was buzzing. Nathan had been dreaming about relics the Protettori were protecting?

"When did you take it?" Jake asked.

"When I left the inn."

"Where did you get this?" she asked Jake.

"I found it in Iraq."

"Iraq," Kendall echoed. "This makes no sense."

"Maybe it does," Nathan said. "The page came from this." He held up the black book. "It's a journal I found on Thomas after he died."

"You found a journal on Thomas? My God, Nathan, what else are you hiding?" Kendall asked.

"I didn't want anyone to know about the curse. I wanted to find the relics and see if they cured me."

"How do you know the page came from the journal?" Jake asked.

"I matched it," Nathan said. He opened the journal and showed them the matching tears on the page. "It's exact." His light went out, leaving only Jake's.

"There's the Iraq connection," Kendall said. "Thomas had the journal and Jake saw Thomas in Iraq. It must have belonged to Thomas."

"Or the journal belongs to the Reaper. If it does, I'd bet he wants it back," Jake said, ever the pessimist. "It would make sense that the Reaper sketched them if he's been searching for them as long as Marco said."

"What's inside?" Kendall asked.

Nathan flipped through the pages while Jake shone his light. "There's writing in some kind of code, and these sketches. Four objects. They must be the Protettori's relics. This one," Nathan said, pointing to the one Kendall had thought was a knife, "must be the Spear of Destiny. Two others could either be cups or bowls. I figure one of them might be the Fountain of Youth." He tapped on the smallest of the cup sketches. "This one seems familiar."

Kendall looked closer at the drawing and thought that it looked familiar to her too. How was that possible?

"Do you want to hold the journal and see if you can pick up anything?" Nathan asked Kendall.

She stared at the journal, afraid to touch it. What if it proved her father was the Reaper? She swallowed and took the journal in her hands. She closed her eyes and felt the leather, opening her mind to the impressions seeping from the journal.

She expected greed, evil, but the strongest impressions were desperation, loss, and love. Family. She let go of the journal, breathing hard.

"What did you sense?" Nathan asked.

"Desperation." She didn't tell them everything, because she couldn't make sense of it herself. As far as she knew, her father died in a plane crash. Unless he was like Raphael and hadn't stayed dead.

"How the hell have you dreamed about the relics drawn on these pages?" Jake asked.

"I don't know."

If he was Adam, and if Marco was right about the vow causing a curse, that might be reason for Nathan to dream of the relics. The men he'd heard talking in his dream could be the Protettori discussing what to do with them. But she didn't voice her theory. It just seemed too ridiculous. Nathan's hair was darker than Adam's had been, though kids' hair usually darkened as they grew older and Adam's had always been bleached by the sun. Both of them had dark eyes, but lots of men had dark eyes. Jake did. As far as personalities went, neither Nathan nor Jake was like Adam. Adam had been outgoing, mischievous, full of laughter. Nathan and Jake were full of secrets. But they were both protective like Adam. "Tell us about the dreams," she said.

"I don't see the relics clearly, just enough to know that their shapes resemble these. And in the dream, I hear the men talking about a curse and that it must be removed. One of them is holding this journal."

"There's nothing in the journal to identify Thomas as the owner?" Kendall asked.

"No name that I could find, unless it's written in code too."

"Give Kendall some time with it. Maybe she can break the code with her voodoo stuff," Jake said.

"There's more," Nathan said.

"What else can there be?" Jake asked.

"I found another paper in the treasure room just before we left the first time. It has the same four sketches."

She thought she'd seen him put something in his pocket when they discovered the room.

Jake grunted. "I don't know about any curse, but you've got so many secrets I don't know how you keep them straight."

"No wonder you're so desperate to find these relics," Kendall said.

"I have to get rid of it," Nathan said. "I don't want to live like this. I don't know if there really is a Fountain of Youth, but if anything could cure a curse, I think the Fountain of Youth would do it. I want to be normal, do normal things."

"I'd feel a lot more comfortable if you were normal too," Jake said, flipping off his flashlight. "I don't like sleeping next to the

Hulk, but I'm so tired right now I'd sleep next to the devil himself."

"We'll help you find it," Kendall said. She shivered, and Jake took her hand and rubbed it between his. It felt so good she didn't pull away. "Did Raphael say anything that might explain a connection between you two?"

"I didn't get a chance to ask," Nathan said.

"I think you need to talk to him," Kendall said.

"Maybe Raphael's cursed too," Jake said.

Nathan didn't answer, and Kendall knew he was considering the possibility.

"That was a joke," Jake said. "Lighten up. We'll find the Fountain of Youth, if it exists, and see if it removes your curse. Then you can hide it wherever you've hidden the Spear of Destiny. . . . Where is it?"

"Safe."

"That's what I figured. I assume you tried the spear to see if it would cure you?"

"It didn't do anything."

She heard a rustling noise that she thought must be Nathan returning the journal to his pocket. "Maybe you need all four relics."

"That's what I'm afraid of," Nathan said. "Damn, it's cold in here."

The temperature had dropped several degrees. What she wouldn't give for her new thermal blanket, which was in her pack in the castle. "It is freezing."

"I'd give you my jacket if I had one." Jake relinquished her hand and leaned back. "I'd give my house for a pillow right now."

"I think I would too," Kendall said, trying to get comfortable. Were they going to sleep sitting up?

"I own a company that makes pillows," Nathan said dryly.

"You own half the companies in the world," Jake said. "Lot of good it'll do you in here."

"I've got to sleep," Kendall said. And she wasn't going to do it sitting up. She lay down on her back, staring at the blackness, awkwardly aware of Jake and Nathan sitting on either side of her like bookends. "Are you going to sleep sitting up?"

"Guess I'll be the one to state the obvious," Jake said. "We're going to have to sleep close enough to share body heat."

Nathan made a grunting sound that could have been an agreement or not. "It is bloody cold in here."

"Question is," Jake said, "who gets the girl?"

"Are you serious?" she asked.

"Damned if I'm going to cuddle with Nathan, and I doubt he wants to cuddle with me. I guess you're sleeping in the middle."

Kendall had spent enough time outdoors to understand the practicality of the situation. It was about staying warm. But when Jake and Nathan scooted close on either side of her, it gave her a tingle she wasn't comfortable with. They each lay stiffly on their back, not talking.

"This isn't working," Jake said. "I have to roll over." He did, facing her, and slipped a hand over her stomach. "Wanna spoon?"

Kendall felt her cheeks warm as she remembered how much she'd wanted to spoon with him earlier in the tower. It would be awkward facing him, so she rolled over and bumped into Nathan's shoulder. "Sorry." Her head was at an uncomfortable angle. She tried putting her arm underneath to cushion it.

"Lift your head," he said. Kendall did, and Nathan slipped his arm under her neck and pulled her into his chest. His arm circled her shoulders. "It's not a pillow, but it's better than a cave floor."

Much better. Kendall let her head settle against him. All sorts of strange sensations zinged through her as she felt his strength and the warmth of his skin. She'd never been this close to him, except when he'd hugged her in the inn, but this was more intimate. She could feel the muscles in the arm holding her, smell his scent. It felt awkward, but nice. The warmth of another human body was a beautiful thing. She didn't know what to do with her hands. Usually, in this position, a woman's hand would rest on the man's stomach or chest. It wouldn't be appropriate here, so she curled it in front of her, against his side. There was a nice hard line of muscle there too. She pulled her hands closer to her chest.

What was wrong with her? She'd almost made love to Jake earlier. She wasn't fast and loose. She'd known girls who slept with any guy they were attracted to. Both Jake and Nathan were good-looking, decent men, secrets and flirting aside. But Kendall didn't sleep with whatever guy she wanted. She hadn't slept with many at all.

"When I said cuddle, I was being sarcastic," Jake said.

Kendall felt a low rumble in Nathan's chest and knew he was laughing.

"Stop complaining," she said, feeling her lips brush Nathan's soft button-up shirt. He hadn't been wearing his usual suits lately. "I'm tired."

Jake muttered something and lay back down, tucking his body closer to hers. So close she could feel parts she shouldn't be feeling, but she couldn't move or she'd be on top of Nathan.

"Your arm's in my face," Jake said to Nathan.

"Move your face," Nathan said.

Jake grumbled and draped his arm over Kendall's hip, just below Nathan's, effectively covering her like a blanket. She lay there sandwiched between the two of them, warmth seeping in from both sides, and thought that if they couldn't find their way out, this might be a good way to die.

Of course she dreamed about Adam, and she woke once when she felt lips brush the top of her head. She didn't know whose, and she didn't care. She didn't even care that her hand was resting above Nathan's belt and that Jake's hand had found its way under her shirt and was against her stomach. Warmth. There was nothing better. Not food. Not even sex.

Her dreams continued, not of Adam, but of the cave, and the darkness she'd felt, and men on horses with swords. She felt them watching. Warning her. In the dream, she rose and followed them deeper into the cave. The markings on the wall were glowing. They led to a tiny opening in the wall. She immediately felt a stir of fresh air. When she woke next, she was still lying between Nathan and Jake, but they had all rolled. Now her cheek was pressed to Jake's back, her arm around his waist, hand over his stomach. Nathan was close behind her. Her head still rested in the crook of his arm, which was draped across her breasts. The other hand was on her stomach. She could feel his breath stirring her hair and his erection nudging her hip.

She lay there, feeling both men breathing—in unison, oddly enough—and wondered if she was turning into a floozy. Her feelings for each of them were strong. Not *love,* but something very real. They both irritated her. Jake and his male ego. Nathan and his secrets. The attraction between her and Jake was obvious. Whatever was between her and Nathan was subtle, seething beneath a surface neither of them was willing to crack.

She felt someone watching and thought it must be Nathan behind her. But a deep breath of sleep sounded at her ear. She snuggled deeper into the warmth, shifting her head slightly on Nathan's arm. She happened to glance up and saw a man poke Jake in the stomach with his sword. Not a man, a ghost. She jumped in alarm.

"That better be Kendall's hand on my stomach," Jake muttered. He sat up and turned on his light, scowling at Nathan who was untangling his arms from around her.

FOUNTAIN OF SECRETS

"I'm sorry, I . . ." She looked at the curious eyes watching them from faintly luminescent faces. Ghosts. No wonder it was so cold in here. There were dozens of them. The same ones from her dream. Some of them were on horseback; others on foot. They all carried swords. Warriors? Some wore chain mail. Knights?

It was unusual to see so many ghosts at once, and from their clothing, she would guess that they had been here for a very long time. Either they had died here or they were here for another reason other than to merely show them the way out. The one who had poked Jake with his sword stood back. He didn't look angry or violent. Just inquisitive. It might be best not to tell Jake and Nathan. She didn't want to alarm them. They were already distracted enough with worry over her and the tiredness they were all feeling.

"I must have had a dream," she said. The ghosts continued watching, but they backed off and stood near the opposite wall, heads bowed, as if in respect. Strange. "I think I know the way out."

But dreams and ghosts weren't always what they seemed. The opening in the wall wasn't where it should have been and the marks weren't glowing. They'd been walking for two hours with only Jake's flashlight since Nathan's and Kendall's were both dead. All three of them had recovered somewhat from the overwhelming tiredness, but their moods were worse. Getting more irritable by the minute, they were hungry, and probably dehydrated. She was not drinking urine, no matter how thirsty she got.

"There's no bloody end to this place. It feels like we're walking in circles. I thought you said you knew caves," Nathan said to Jake.

"You're the one who said you could write a book on bat droppings. You find the damned exit. Can't you *divine* something?" Jake asked Kendall.

"It doesn't—"

"We know," Jake said, frustrated. "I wish you'd figure out how the hell it does work." Jake's stomach rumbled. "I'm so hungry I could eat my socks."

"If you don't stop complaining, I'll hit you over the head with a rock. Then Nathan and I will eat your flesh."

"I'd give you indigestion and then haunt the hell out of you."

Kendall stopped as one of the ghosts materialized in front of Nathan. This one was a knight. He moved close, studying Nathan's face. His own features were transparent, but enough of his person remained that she could see surprise . . . and emotion. The ghost reached toward Nathan's chest where his cross hung.

Nathan hadn't felt the spirit's presence. He was still searching the walls. The ghost lifted the cross, and Nathan grabbed his chest and looked at Jake, who stood next to him. "What are you doing?"

"Nothing."

"You touched my chest."

"No I didn't."

"Someone did. You're the only one who could have," Nathan said.

"I didn't touch your chest. It must have been a rock. Hell, it was probably your cross hitting your chest."

Kendall could tell from the tension in Nathan's body that he didn't believe Jake. Kendall felt reluctant to explain that they were being poked by ghosts. They were already on edge. A few minutes later the same ghost moved closer to Jake. He stood off to the side, his head inches from Jake's, studying his face. The ghost reached for the chain holding Jake's cross. He appeared to be trying to pull the cross into view.

Jake turned to Nathan. "What do you want?"

"I don't want anything," Nathan said.

"You touched my neck."

"Not me."

"Not funny," Jake said. "You think this is payback."

"I'm not trying to be funny. I'm trying to get the hell out of this cave," Nathan said. He sounded irritated. "And I didn't touch your neck."

There was way too much testosterone for one cave. The men faced off for a moment before backing down, partly due to her cursing them both out. Nathan muttered to himself and kept examining one of the walls. Though how he could see without a light she didn't know. Where the heck was that opening? Jake and Nathan still fussed at each other as they searched the walls. Nathan cursed. Kendall turned and saw him rubbing his ear.

"Don't do that again," he said.

"What are you talking about?" Jake asked.

"You just hit me."

"No I didn't," Jake said. "I'm nowhere near you."

"Then you threw a rock."

Kendall saw the ghosts crowding around again. They were staring at all three of them, Kendall, Nathan, and Jake. They seemed more than curious, more than intrigued. Kendall turned and saw Nathan stalk toward Jake. She stepped between them just as Nathan shoved Jake. Nathan's hands caught her shoulders and she flew against the wall.

She heard voices calling her name and slowly opened her eyes. It was dark. Her first thought was that she was blind. Then she saw Nathan and Jake leaning over her.

"I'm sorry, Kendall." Nathan brushed back her hair, checking her head. "Did you hit your head?"

"No. I just lost my breath." She climbed to her feet. "But if you two don't stop bickering, I'm going to ditch both of you."

"I thought he shoved me," Nathan said. "I know it's no excuse—"

"It wasn't Jake. It was the ghosts."

"I think she's hallucinating," Nathan said.

"She probably has a damned concussion."

"I hit my backside, not my head. There are ghosts here, lots of them. That's why it's so cold. They were poking at you."

Jake and Nathan both turned, staring into the darkness of the cave. "Where are they?" Nathan asked.

"They're gone now," Kendall said.

"That's the shadow we saw?" Jake asked.

"No, that was different," Kendall said. "I think the shadow made them uneasy. They didn't want him here. That's why we felt the hostility."

"I think Nathan and I ran into the ghosts earlier," Jake said. "We thought it was bat shit or rocks falling from the ceiling. Must have been them poking at us."

"They're just curious about us now, I think. They seemed particularly interested in our crosses."

"That's strange," Nathan said. "So who are the ghosts? Why would they be interested in our crosses?"

"They seem to be warriors or knights. I think they've been here for a long time. They probably want to know what we're doing here."

"We're trying to leave," Jake said. "Tell them to show us the damned way out."

"They're the ones who showed me in the dream, but things don't look the same."

Nathan touched her shoulder, his eyes worried. "I'm sorry, Kendall. I don't know what to say."

"I'm fine. Let's just find the way out of here."

"You two go on," Nathan said. "I'll follow later. It's not safe for you to be with me—"

"It was my fault," Kendall said. "I got in the way. And your flashlight is dead. You can't stay here alone."

"I would rather you go with Jake. It's safer."

"He might be right," Jake said.

Kendall clenched her teeth and her fists. "I don't care what either of you want. We're all getting out of this cave and we're going together."

They looked at each other, but neither said a word. Using Jake's light, they continued searching the markings for the one she'd seen in her dream. A few minutes later, she saw two circles joined. "I think that's it." There was a ridge along the edge of the mark. She pushed it, and the sound of rocks scraping echoed in the cave as an opening appeared in the wall.

Jake put his arm in front of Kendall. "I don't trust these ghosts who showed you the exit. There's probably a rock slide waiting with our names on it."

Nathan sniffed. "I smell fresh air."

The opening in the wall didn't lead to a rock slide. It led to another wall with another mark. When they pushed on it, a door swung open, and they stepped into fresh air and trees.

"We were inside a mountain," Nathan said.

"Clever," Kendall said. The stone door was covered by grass, disguising it from sight. She looked down the hill at the lights from a nearby town. "I don't remember there being a town near the castle."

Jake was already looking toward the town. "There isn't."

"How bloody far did we walk?" Nathan asked.

"Farther than we thought." Jake looked up the hill. "There's something up there."

"Looks like a tower," Nathan said.

"I don't remember that either," Kendall said. Nothing about this place looked right. "I don't think we're near the castle. We would have seen a tower that high."

Jake looked up at the night sky. "Castle? Hell, this doesn't even look like Italy."

CHAPTER EIGHT

W E MUST BE IN ITALY," KENDALL SAID. "WHERE ELSE could we be?"

"Let's go higher so we can get a better view." Jake led the way up the steep incline. His flashlight died before they reached the top of the hill. He cursed and banged on it, but it was dead. When they reached the tower, they discovered that it was a lot taller than it had looked from below, but in the dark it was impossible to tell much more about it.

"Touch it," Jake said. "See if you can figure out where we are."

Kendall put her hands on one wall and closed her eyes, letting the sensations flow from the structure into her hands. Power, voices—chanting, prayers, battle cries—a fortress and ships.

"Getting anything?" Nathan asked.

"This structure is old. Many people have passed through here. Praying, fighting. And I saw ships."

"There's no ocean near the castle," Jake said. "You think this is one of those visions like when you touched Raphael?"

"I don't think so," she said.

"We can't figure it out tonight," Nathan said. "It's too dangerous to explore in the dark."

Jake agreed. "If this place is near the castle, we might end up impaled on spikes at the bottom of a pit."

"This is a good place to rest until morning," Nathan said. "We didn't sleep much in the cave, and we probably have a long hike ahead of us."

They found a stone ledge built against the wall, and Kendall sat. She didn't feel as weak now, but she still felt tired and chilled. It wasn't as cold out here as it was in the cave, but it wasn't warm, and she was dressed for bed, not camping. She shivered.

"Are you cold?" Nathan asked.

"Chilly."

He sat next to her, scooting close so that his shoulder touched hers. Jake sat on the other side, and immediately she felt warmth surrounding her. She stared at the stars and the lights of the mysterious town below as she listened to Nathan and Jake speculating about where they might be and arguing over logic and impossibilities. She closed her eyes and listened to their voices, searching for a hint of Adam. In spite of the situation, she felt a sense of contentment as she fell asleep.

Something hit Nathan on the arm, waking him. He squinted against the daylight, which was surprising after hours in a dark cave. He'd planned to start exploring at dawn, but underneath the tower, it was still shaded from the sun. Jake and Kendall were still sleeping too. Kendall's hand was clasped in Nathan's. He felt like gloating until he saw her head was on Jake's shoulder.

Nathan didn't feel as rested as he'd hoped. He had discovered that extra sleep helped him ward off the change. Ward off.

Made it sound like he was turning into a bloody werewolf. Hell, maybe he was.

A rock hit Jake on the head and fell near his feet. "Damned ghosts," he muttered, waking up. "They must have followed us out of the cave." He looked around and frowned. "We overslept."

Nathan heard a chuckle. He turned and saw a chubby little boy standing several feet away. He had red hair and a face full of freckles, and he wore medieval clothing. Maybe the question wasn't where they were, but when.

"I can see this one," Jake said. "He's been eating too much."

The boy's face screwed up. He opened his mouth and yelled, "Mother, he called me fat."

A woman appeared at the back opening of the tower. She had the same red hair and freckles and wore a flowing gown. "Some people just don't have manners. Really. Come along, Art. The garden will be opening soon." She took the boy's arm and pulled him away. He turned back and stuck out his tongue.

"That wasn't a ghost, was it?" Jake said.

"No," Kendall said.

"That's good news," Jake said. "At least we're still alive."

"You thought we were dead?" Kendall asked.

"I wondered," he said.

"If it weren't for the New England accents, I would wonder if we're in the right time," Kendall said. "When you fell through the maze, did you feel . . . weird, as if your body had come apart?"

"Pretty much," Nathan said.

"I think we found some kind of . . ." She shrugged. "I don't know what to call it."

"Are you trying to say we fell through a portal?" Jake asked.

"There aren't any towns near the castle," she said. "And this place obviously isn't Italy."

Jake scratched his head. "Portals are *Star Trek* shit, and that's impossible."

"You thought ghosts didn't exist a few days ago," Nathan said. "And centuries-old guardians from a secret order, and stone statues that once breathed. I think we're still in modern times."

A man walked past the tower. He too wore some kind of ancient robe.

"Excuse me, where we are?" Nathan asked him.

"What year is this?" Jake added.

The man's bushy brows rose in alarm and he hurried away.

Kendall turned and looked at the wall behind the ledge where they had slept. "Oh my."

"What's wrong?" Jake turned to look.

She pointed to the sign on a plaque above them: SAINT MICHAEL'S TOWER.

"Bloody hell," Nathan said. "We're in England."

"We can't be in England," Jake said.

"Saint Michael's Tower is in Glastonbury, England," Nathan said.

"How the hell did we get from Italy to England?" Jake asked.

"This is Glastonbury Tor." Kendall's eyes lit. "This is starting to make sense."

"Not to me," Jake said.

"Do you know what's in Glastonbury?" she asked.

Jake looked at the tower. "Saint Michael's Tower?"

"The Chalice Well," Nathan said.

"What's the Chalice Well?" Jake asked.

"An ancient well," Kendall said. "A sacred well."

"You're saying the Fountain of Youth is here?" Jake asked.

"Legend says the Chalice Well sprang up after a chalice holding the blood of Christ was buried here by Joseph of Arimathea. He was the man who gave his tomb for Jesus's burial. A fountain flows from the well, and people come from all over the world to drink from its waters, which are supposed to have the power to heal."

"How do you know so much about it?" Jake asked.

"Because I was going to bring Kendall here to see what she thought about the well." Nathan didn't trust psychics other than Kendall, if that was what she even was. "That was just before I found out about the Spear of Destiny." And that had taken precedence over everything.

Kendall smiled. "And the chalice that Joseph buried wasn't just any old chalice. It was the Holy Grail."

Jake looked surprised. "So the Fountain of Youth could have come from the Holy Grail? Damn."

Nathan felt a stir of excitement. Could he be getting close to the cure?

"There's no way the Fountain of Youth is gonna be out there for the whole world to see," Jake said. "Are you forgetting the booby traps and statues that protected the Spear of Destiny?"

"It should be hidden better than that," Nathan said, feeling disappointment crowding his hope. But still . . .

"But there must be a reason why we're here." Kendall still looked excited.

"There is," Jake said. "We fell through a maze."

"Exactly beside the site of two holy wells that are supposed to have healing powers?"

"Two?" Jake asked.

"There's another well here too," Kendall said. "The White Spring. It's supposedly powerful too. Two wells, one tinged red, the other white. And we find ourselves here right after Marco tells us we need to find the Fountain of Youth? Remember that fountain near the entrance of the maze? Maybe that was some kind of indicator."

Jake scoffed. "Like a damned street sign saying, 'This Way to the Fountain of Youth.'"

"Well, it's too much of a coincidence that we're here," Kendall said. "And we heard the statues humming in the cave. So something important must be here."

Jake looked down the hill toward town. "We thought we were underneath the castle then. The humming could've been something else. Sometimes you can hear strange sounds in old caves."

"We have to go back in there," Kendall said.

"We need to check the well first," Nathan said.

"You think it might cure you?" Kendall asked.

"No, but I have to try."

They started down the hill toward the town. Kendall was electric with excitement. "We went from Italy to England through a maze. Do you realize what this means?"

"We found a way to avoid airfare?" Jake said.

Jake's sarcasm almost made Nathan smile, but he hid it. It hadn't dampened Kendall's enthusiasm. Her spirit and excitement were two of the reasons he'd hired her. Not the most important ones, but they made Nathan feel alive.

"We traveled through . . . space. This is unbelievable. We just went from one country to another by walking through a maze. Aren't you excited about this?" she asked Jake.

"Excited isn't exactly how I'd describe it."

Jake couldn't stand not being in control. A trait that was both challenging and helpful for Nathan's purposes.

"First thing we need to do," Jake said, "is make sure we're even in the right century. Then we'll find these holy wells and see if it rids you of your curse."

They were in the right time, at least not in medieval times. There were several people on the hill, some sitting on the grass, others walking. A few were dressed in costume—which seemed to be normal around here—but most of them wore jeans or modern clothes. There were various accents, but most of them British.

Jake put a hand on Kendall's back and guided her around two men walking side by side.

"Can you tell us where to find the Chalice Well?" Nathan asked.

"At the bottom of the hill, just there," one of the men said, pointing.

"You must have walked right by it on the way up," the other said.

"We need to talk to Marco and see what he knows about this place," Nathan said as they walked down the hill.

"Marco seems to forget as much as he remembers," Jake said. "You'll probably learn more from that journal."

It took them twenty minutes to reach the Chalice Well Gardens. There were already people milling about, but the gardens weren't open yet. "Too bad we're broke," Kendall said. "There's a gift shop. I bet they have clothes. Mine feel like they could walk on their own."

"There's a public restroom and phones," Jake said. "We can clean up, wash off your wrist, and then we need food."

"We don't have any money," Kendall said. She had forgotten about her wrist.

"I have fifty bucks in my boot for emergencies," Jake said. "Like falling through portals."

"Dollars?" she asked. "You'll have to exchange it for pounds. You don't have ID."

"I could do it under the table."

"Don't bother," Nathan said. "I'll have Fergus send a car and arrange accommodations. Or we can go to the London hotel."

"Let's stay here," Kendall said. "I want to explore the area."

"And I need a decent meal before I starve. It'll take too long to get to London unless you bring in a helicopter."

"Then we'll find a local hotel. I'm going to the well while we wait for the car," Nathan said. "You get food and meet me back here."

"I don't think we should leave you," Kendall said. "We don't know what might happen at the well."

"Go with Jake. It might be best if I go alone," Nathan said.

Kendall looked uncertain, but she left with Jake. Nathan watched them walk away. He touched his chest where she had laid her head while she slept beside him in the cave. That was the closest he'd been to her. He watched as Jake reached over and touched her arm. He wanted to call her back to go with him, but it was best that he go to the well alone. He didn't know what to expect if it turned out to be the real fountain. Or what might happen if it wasn't. He found a phone and called Fergus.

"Where the devil are you?" Fergus asked. He sounded exasperated. "I've been trying to call you. The castle is in an uproar."

"We're in England."

"England." Nathan heard Fergus sniff. "You could have called, sir. People worry about you, you know?"

"We didn't plan to come to England. We . . . fell here. There's some kind of portal in the maze at the castle."

"Are you drunk, sir?" Fergus asked.

"You know I don't drink. There's a bloody portal in that maze at the castle. Kendall fell through it, and Jake and I did too when we went to find her."

"And you landed in England, sir?"

"Glastonbury, England. I need you to find accommodations for us and have a car sent to the Chalice Well. Something that won't draw attention, and have our luggage sent here."

"Are you OK?" Fergus sounded worried.

He wouldn't be OK until he got rid of this curse. "I'm fine."

"Do you have money?"

"Jake does for now, but have some money sent to the hotel." Nathan had more money than he knew what to do with, and now he was stuck without a dime to his name. He'd have to depend on Jake if he wanted to eat in the next hour.

"I see," Fergus said. "We'll come and bring your things with us. We're in Italy. We left as soon as they said the three of you had disappeared."

"We?"

"Marco insisted on coming with me."

"He's OK to travel?"

"He's doing remarkably well."

"How could you be in Italy? We've only been gone for a few hours."

Fergus was quiet for a moment. "Sir, you've been gone for well over a day."

"That's impossible." Nathan looked at his watch, forgetting that it had stopped. "It's Tuesday."

"It's Wednesday, sir. You vanished Monday night."

Nathan cursed. Somewhere along the way, they'd lost an entire day. "Fergus, don't come here. Just send our things." As much as Nathan wanted to talk to Marco face-to-face, he didn't want to put either of the men at risk. He was worried about that shadow in the cave. He didn't think it was Raphael. "Have you seen Raphael?"

"No."

"Tell the guards to be alert. He's going to be angry. Fergus, be careful."

"Don't worry, I have a gun."

Bloody hell. "Don't try to shoot him, Fergus." Everyone was in enough danger without Fergus carrying a gun.

———

Fergus hung up the phone and turned to Marco. "They're alive."

The old man nodded. "They must stay alive. They're in England. Where?"

"Glastonbury."

"Very good."

"I think we should go. I believe it's time to tell him the truth."

Marco stood. "Do we fly or take the maze?"

Nathan held a brochure in front of him and studied the entrance to the Chalice Gardens. He'd found the brochure on the ground where someone had dropped it. He was going to drink from the fountain until he couldn't drink any more. There was also a pool. He might just jump in it and roll around for good measure. The gardens had just opened, so they weren't busy now. He didn't have money, but it shouldn't be too hard to sneak inside. He waited until the woman at the gate was distracted with a group and slipped through. The woman turned and called out, but he kept going. He hurried up the path and darted behind a tree.

No one came after him, so he guessed he was safe. His mouth was dry as he followed the path to the fountain. Traditions varied on the actual source of the well, but he wasn't going to pass up the chance to drink. If his dreams were right, this could be his cure.

When he reached the fountain and saw a couple drinking, reality set in. If this was the Fountain of Youth, there should be millions of unnaturally youthful, cured people wandering the planet. Still, he rose and walked to the fountain. There was no one close by, but he could hear voices drawing near. He knelt on the stone and leaned over, putting his mouth under the stream of water flowing from the lion's head. The water tasted unusual. It must be the iron. That was what turned the water red. Some believed it was symbolic of Christ's blood. Nathan drank until his stomach felt like it would burst. He heard a voice behind him.

"Mom, he's drinking it all. There won't be any left for the rest of us."

"This well has been flowing for two thousand years, Art. Don't worry, it's not going to dry up now."

Nathan raised his head and looked at the boy. It was the redhead who had been throwing rocks.

"Make him stop drinking. It's my turn."

"He's almost finished, see. There'll be plenty of water for you."

Nathan started to move, but he caught sight of his hands gripping the stone and remembered knocking Kendall into the wall. He ducked his whole head underneath the flow, letting the cold water run down his neck and back.

"He's taking a bath in the fountain. Gross. Doesn't he know there's a pool?"

Nathan stood and wiped the water off his face. The woman and boy gaped at him as he walked past.

"See, it's your turn now, Art. Go on, darling, take a drink."

"Can I stick my head in like he did?"

"No, darling. Art. Be careful. Arthur, you're leaning too far. Arthur!"

Something nudged Nathan's memory, but before he could figure it out, there was a howl followed by the woman's cry. Nathan turned around and saw the boy's legs in the air as the mother attempted to pull him out of the basin. Served the little monster right, Nathan thought. Monster. That was a sobering thought.

He ignored the strange looks he got as he walked away and headed for the Vesica Piscis, where he found two circular pools intertwined. He dipped his head in these and then continued to the healing pool and walked down into the water. It was cold, but a couple of others were also wading. No one paid much attention until he sat down in the water and lay back, letting it wash over his head. Bloody hell, it was cold. He jumped up, shivering, and hurried away. He needed to find a place to dry off or he'd end up dying of exposure. He wouldn't need a curse to finish him off.

CHAPTER NINE

KENDALL AND JAKE USED THE PUBLIC RESTROOMS AND cleaned up the worst of the grime from the cave. While Jake waited for Kendall, he called Clint collect to check on things at the house.

"No sign of any more intruders," Clint said.

Clint was a good buddy. They'd known each other for years and had worked together on and off. Clint would have been with him in Iraq, but he'd been finishing up a job in Africa. If Clint had been there, he would have died with the rest of the team.

"You cool with hanging out at the house for a few more days?"

There was a pause. "No problem. You have any trouble sleeping here?" Clint asked.

"No." He wasn't home often to sleep. "Why? The neighbors being loud?" He couldn't imagine that. They were all retired.

"I keep waking up freezing cold."

"Did the temperature drop?" The weather had been mild for October when they left.

"No. But it's freezing in here at night."

"Turn up the heat."

"I did." Clint hesitated.

"What's wrong?"

"You ever feel like someone's watching you in here?"

"Never noticed it, but I'm not there much. Why? You think someone's got a camera inside?"

"I was thinking more along the line of a ghost. Thought maybe your grandma was still hanging around."

Last week, he would have laughed if anyone had said something like that. Not now. "If she is, I've never seen her."

Clint dropped the subject and Jake hung up just as Kendall appeared. She still looked beautiful in spite of falling through the maze and into a haunted cave. "You fixed the tear in your pj's?"

"I found a safety pin in the bathroom."

"How's your wrist?" Jake asked.

She turned it over. There was a thin line where it had been cut. "Better. I cleaned it up."

"You need a bandage."

"It'll be fine. I've lived with worse than this," she said. "Where do we find someone who can exchange your money under the table?"

"We're not going to," he said, looking across the street. "It'll take too long. By the time we walk to town and back, the car will be here. Come on." He took her hand and led her toward a gift shop.

"What are we doing?"

"Getting food."

"Without money? What are you going to do? Steal it? You're going to steal it?"

"Do you want to eat or not? It's just borrowing. We'll pay for it after we get money."

"I hope you have some shoplifting skills that I don't."

"I do. We're going inside that gift shop, and you're going to distract the person running it."

"How? Hit them, cuss them out?"

"Talk to them about the weather, or King Arthur."

Kendall opened the door and walked inside. The woman who worked in the shop was on the latter side of middle age and had a chunky, rectangular figure and gray hair caught up in a bun. "Excuse me. Could I ask a question?"

The woman turned a friendly smile on Kendall. "Sure, dear. What'll you be wanting to know?"

"I'm visiting the abbey and wondered what you might be able to tell me about the area, and about King Arthur, if you have a moment." From the corner of her eye, Kendall saw Jake easing toward a section with power bars and snacks.

"Of course. I used to be a tour guide, you know, but the old legs don't like so much walking at my age. We get scads of people coming here, everyone from history buffs to quacks. This was the site of the first Christian church in Britain. Joseph of Arimathea built it, him and Jesus when Jesus was just a boy. Joseph was Jesus's great-uncle, and he was a metal trader who did business here. They say young Jesus sometimes came with him.

"Anyway, the stories go that when Jesus was dying on the cross, Joseph took the cup from the Last Supper, the Holy Grail—oh, I get goose bumps just saying that—and he caught some of Jesus's blood. So after Jesus died, supposedly Joseph comes back here with some other men. They came ashore at Wearyall Hill, yonder," she said, pointing out one of the windows. "When Joseph put his staff in the ground, it took root. That became the Holy Thorn Tree. The one out there on Wearyall Hill was grown from the original tree that Joseph planted. It was vandalized in 2010. Black-hearted bastards."

"Why did they do that?"

"The man who owned the property had some legal issues. Maybe the vandals didn't like Christians. The town planted a new Holy Thorn, but it's still a sad thing. Anyway, when Joseph buried the Holy Grail in the hillside a well sprang up. The Chalice Well. Of course there are others who say the well is older, something to do with mother earth and goddesses and all that. I guess it depends on what you believe."

"So there's a lot of history here," Kendall said, looking over the woman's shoulder where Jake had moved on to a stack of clothing.

"Scads. Saint Patrick lived here and died here. Most people think he was Irish, but he wasn't. He was imprisoned in Ireland for a while. And then there was King Arthur. He and Guinevere were buried here. I'm sure you saw the site if you've been to the abbey."

Kendall shook her head no, but the woman continued on with her story. Kendall didn't interrupt since Jake was deftly shoplifting sweatshirts and pants.

"The graves were discovered back in the twelfth century. The abbey had burned down, and the monks needed money to rebuild. One of the monks had a dream about Arthur, and sure enough, when they started digging, there were Arthur and his queen buried sixteen feet down. Suddenly, people are flocking from all over to see where the great King Arthur was buried. And that brought money in. Later on, the bones were moved to a black marble tomb, but they disappeared when the abbey was closed."

The woman seemed to be winding down, but Jake was stuffing something into his boot, so Kendall asked another question to give him a little longer. "When did the abbey close?"

"In the sixteenth century. King Henry the Eighth was getting worried about the power and the wealth of the abbey. He asked for the relics and treasure, but the monks wouldn't give them up. The king accused the abbey of hiding them, so he closed them down. Richard Whiting, he was the last abbot. The king had him and two of his priors dragged up to the Tor, hanged, drawn and quartered. Lord, can you imagine? The abbey fell into ruins after that. The stones were carted off, and some of them were used to build houses and shops here."

Relics and treasure. That rang a familiar bell. "So the king got the treasure?"

"Not all of it. The monks had hidden some of it underneath the Tor. Legend says there are tunnels and caves underneath. Some run underneath the abbey."

Under the Tor, Kendall thought, her blood pumping faster. She knew for certain that there was at least one cave underneath the Tor. "It's such a magical place, isn't it?"

"Magical is a good word. There's all kinds of stories about the place, not just King Arthur and Joseph. Fairies, ghosts, magical lights. Some people say Glastonbury is Avalon, you know, and that the Tor is the entrance to Annwyn. The lord of the underworld lived there. The lord of the fairies, and not them little cute ones with wings, but tall, beautiful ones who were powerful. They lure men in and when they come out, they're raving lunatics and they've lost days, weeks, of their lives."

"Lost time?"

"Time is different for fairies, if you believe such things."

"You really think Arthur was real?"

"I say where there's smoke there's fire. There's too much legend not to have some truth. If only the bones were still here, King Arthur's and Guinevere's, they might be able to prove it was him. The king probably stole them, or one of the monks. Maybe even one of Arthur's knights. They say the ghost of a black knight haunts the abbey to keep people away."

"Why would he want to keep people away?"

"I don't know. Maybe the treasure is still hidden there. Or Arthur's bones. And the locals tell stories that the monks were more than monks, some secret group."

Kendall's thoughts started racing. "What kind of secret group?"

"Not sure really, probably like Templars. There are all kinds of stories here. There's some who say Arthur's bones are buried in a cave, waiting for the time when the world needs him, then he'll come back. I'm not sure if they're talking about resurrection or reincarnation. I'd buy the reincarnation thing, maybe. Wouldn't that be something if King Arthur and his knights were out there walking around? I wouldn't be surprised after some of the things I've seen around here."

Kendall felt a chill brush over her skin. Inadvertently, she looked at Jake, who was making his way to the door. "What sort of things?"

"Eerie things. Lights. Strange balls circling above the Tor."

"You've seen them?"

"I have. Gave me the shivers, I can tell you."

Kendall had the shivers now. She was tempted to touch the woman to see if she could sense anything more. But she didn't. "When was this?"

"About a month ago. I was here late because I'd left the key to my flat in the shop. I was coming out the door when I felt something strange through my shoulders. You ever get that feeling?"

Kendall nodded yes.

"So I look up at the mountain and I see these colored balls circling around like . . . like something out of one of them sci-fi movies. The lights circled around for a minute, then disappeared. Would have thought I'd lost my mind, except other people have seen them too. Next morning I had the darnedest headache. So bad I had a lie-in and was late to work."

124

Jake was out the door now, so Kendall thanked the woman and left the gift shop as chilled as if she'd been skiing an avalanche. She glanced up toward the Tor as she walked toward Jake, who was watching her with an impatient look on his face.

"Nice beer belly."

Jake had his arms over his stomach, trying to keep the clothes from sliding out. "I figured we might need extra clothes. It looks like it's gonna rain." Just as expertly as he had stuffed the things under his shirt, he removed them and put them under his arm.

"Your deftness at shoplifting is disturbing."

"It's survival. We'll pay them back. Consider it like buying on credit."

"We're going to owe Glastonbury a good bit of money," Kendall said.

"Nathan can afford it." He handed her a power bar and a bottle of water.

Kendall opened her power bar. "I can't believe we're eating stolen food." He'd taken several power bars and two bottles of water.

He pulled out a travel-sized package of tissues and presented them to her with a flourish.

"Where did you learn that kind of skill?"

"I hit a few rough patches in my life."

Kendall felt something simmering around him and she knew if she focused, she might see what kind of rough patches, but she didn't. Partly because she was so hungry, all she could think about was the next bite. "Did you get Nathan something to eat?"

"He's not worried about food. All he cares about is the well."

"He has to eat."

"I can't figure out if you're in love with him or think you're his mother."

"We work together, that's all."

"It's not like any working relationship I've seen."

"Does Nathan seem like the type to have a romantic relationship? He guards every part of his life, including his heart. So did you get him food?"

"I got him some damned food." Jake tensed, his body alert.

"What's wrong? You look like you saw a ghost." Kendall spun around but didn't see anything.

"A redheaded one."

"What?"

"She's gone now, but I swear it was Brandi."

"How could she be here?"

"Maybe she found the maze."

"We've got to find Nathan."

They didn't have money for the entrance fee. Jake scouted the place while she tried to look inconspicuous. He motioned to her from several yards away.

"I've found a place where we can slip inside."

"We're turning into criminals."

"Like I said, it's survival."

They climbed over a low fence and kept to the grassy areas to steer clear of people on the path. Kendall had never been here before, but she could immediately feel that there was something unusual about the place.

"You hanging in there?" Jake asked.

"This place is . . . unusual. I can feel some kind of energy here."

"I hope that's a good sign," Jake said.

The gardens were beautiful. Natural, not overly tended. There were several varieties of trees and plants, including yews and a Holy Thorn Tree. Some leaves had already turned beautiful shades of red and gold. There was a kind of serenity about the place that soothed her soul. "I could spend hours here," she said.

"Let's find this fountain first. That's where Nathan will be."

They walked along a serene path toward the Lion's Head Fountain. Kendall was so enchanted that she almost forgot their reason for being there. Then a whining voice approached and pulled her out of the moment.

"It was his fault. I just wanted to stick my head in the fountain like he did."

"Of course it was, darling, but you must be more careful."

"It's that brat that hit me with a rock," Jake said.

The boy and his mother walked by, dressed this time in normal clothing, but the boy's head was wet.

"Excuse me," Kendall said to the woman. "Did you say a man stuck his head in the fountain?"

The woman looked as unpleasant as her son. "He did. Very poor behavior in front of impressionable, innocent children."

"He drank all the water up and then stuck his head under," the boy said. "Hey, you're the man who called me fat."

The woman scowled and pulled the boy toward her. "Let's get you a dry shirt, Arthur, and then we'll go see the abbey and Camelot."

"Did you see which way he went?" Jake called.

The woman didn't answer, but the boy looked over his shoulder and stuck out his tongue.

Camelot. Kendall grabbed Jake's arm. "Remember Marco said to find Arthur? Well, Glastonbury isn't famous for just the Chalice Well. King Arthur was supposedly buried here."

"You think Marco meant King Arthur?" Jake asked. He sounded surprised. Almost hopeful. She sensed something coming from him, but his face went blank and she lost it. He'd blocked her. Just like Nathan. "Legend says he was buried at the abbey near here. I expected one of your sarcastic snorts, but you seem excited. Did you want to be a knight when you were young?"

Jake shrugged. "What boy doesn't dream of King Arthur and the Knights of the Round Table?"

"Adam was fascinated with King Arthur. He spent hours telling me stories." Some of them, so vivid she felt as if she were really there.

When they reached the fountain, a small group was just leaving. Kendall walked closer to study the spot. A stream of water flowed from a lion's head into a basin. The stone underneath had a reddish-orange tinge.

"Looks like an ordinary fountain to me," Jake said.

"This might not be the fountain Marco was talking about, but this is anything but ordinary. This well has been flowing for over two thousand years."

"There's no one here. Do your thing. See if it's the real deal."

"Why are you so anxious? You worried about Nathan?"

He scoffed but nudged her to the edge of the fountain. Kendall sat on the side. Jake put down the clothes he'd stolen and sat next to her, dipping his fingers in the stream of water. He touched his finger to his tongue. "Tastes like water. A little metallic. Come on, get your fingers wet."

Kendall touched the water, and she felt a rush of energy that jolted her so hard, she fell against Jake. He grabbed for her, but they both landed in the basin. Kendall gasped as the cold water ran over her head.

Cursing, Jake scrambled to his feet and pulled them both out of the fountain.

"That's cold," Kendall said, shivering.

Jake swiped water from his face. "Your gift sucks sometimes, Legs."

He hadn't called her Legs in a while. "I'm sorry." Kendall wiped her face with her hands. The day was nice for October, but for anyone wet and without a jacket, it felt like December.

"I think you have a gift of your own," Kendall said, pointing at the stack of dry clothing. "Good intuition. We're going to need those."

"Blimey, that's the fourth person to fall in the fountain today," a man exclaimed.

"This place has a strange effect on people," his female companion said.

Kendall turned around and saw a man and woman watching them curiously.

"Was one of the others a man?" Kendall asked.

"Yes," the man said.

"What did he look like?"

"Short hair, tall. Maybe thirty."

"Was he handsome?"

She heard Jake snort behind her as the man shrugged. "I don't know."

"Oh yeah," the woman answered. "He was a hottie."

The man gave her a startled glance.

"Well, you been looking at every pretty thing ye've seen. I've got eyes in me head too."

"Did you see which way he went when he left here?" Kendall asked.

"That way," he said. "Toward Little Saint Michael's."

"What's that?" Jake asked.

"It's lodging for people who support the well."

"What's he doing going that way?" Kendall asked.

"He probably made a phone call and bought the place." Jake took Kendall's arm and pulled her toward the entrance.

"Is she wearing pajamas?" the woman asked quietly as they walked away.

"Where are we going?" Kendall asked. "Nathan went this way."

"I don't care where Nathan went. We've got to get out of these wet clothes. People are staring. Don't give me that look. As much as I'd like to see you naked, I'm thinking about our well-being, not sex. We don't want to end up sick. We're a long way from home with nothing but the clothes on our back, my pocket-knife, and your sixth sense until the car gets here. And your sixth sense is quirky to say the least."

He handed her some dry clothing, and they went to the restrooms and changed. Kendall would have paid a hundred pounds for clean underwear. Her sweats were gray with GLASTONBURY, ENGLAND, emblazoned across the front of her shirt. It wasn't pretty, but it was better than pajamas and it was clean. She freshened up her face and finger-combed her hair. She got lucky and found a ponytail holder lying on the sink. She grimaced but pulled her hair back with it. "Ugh," she said to herself in the mirror, and then rolled up her old clothes, stuck them under her arm, and walked outside to meet Jake. He was wearing a matching outfit. His clothes fit better than hers, which were a little too snug.

"This getup does more for you than me," he said, looking her over. His old clothes were balled up in his hand. She didn't want to look twice, but she was pretty sure he was commando. Yep, there was his underwear sticking out from under his old jeans and shirt.

"We have to find Nathan. The car should be here soon," Jake said.

"I'm not sure if you're worried about Nathan or getting to a hotel for a warm meal."

"A steak sounds good."

"You're just too stubborn to admit that you care about him too."

"Nathan's all but holding me hostage. Work for him, or go back to prison. Does that sound like someone I should care about?"

"That sounds like someone who's desperate. And he has a good reason to be desperate. He needs you to help him get rid of this curse, what he thinks is a curse." There were times when she felt cursed, but she'd used her talents for good. She had helped people, protected relics, shed light on history. Maybe Nathan was looking at this the wrong way. It still left the question, where had he gotten this ability?

"You're the relic hunter. I'm just a bodyguard."

"You're more than that, and you know it. You've hunted plenty of treasure yourself. Where is he?"

"Probably avoiding us," Jake said. "He doesn't trust himself around you."

"You don't know that for sure."

"I know that's how I'd feel if I thought I had a monster trapped inside me and I'd accidentally knocked you down."

"It wasn't his fault. It was the ghosts playing tricks."

"As you keep reminding me. But if he had changed into whatever he changes into, he could have killed us both."

They found Nathan spying on a house near the entrance to the well. He was soaking wet, hiding in some trees. Kendall never would have spotted him, but Jake did.

"Decide to take a swim?" Jake asked.

Nathan turned around. He was shivering. "Why not?"

"You're turning blue. You're going to get sick," Kendall said.

"Here you go, billionaire boy. How about some warm clothes? And I have power bars." Jake tossed Nathan a set of sweats. "Money isn't everything."

Nathan took the sweats. "Thanks."

"Sorry, I couldn't find underwear."

Nathan went to the restroom to change.

"Now you're staring at the house," Jake said. "What do you see?"

"I don't know. There's something intriguing about it."

"You think it's something inside, or someone?"

"I don't know. There's some kind of energy there."

Nathan exited the restroom wearing his sweats. Kendall purposely didn't look to see if he was wearing underwear. "I think that's our ride," Nathan said, pointing to a shuttle van waiting on the street.

"No limo?" Jake asked.

"Too noticeable," Nathan said. "I'll make sure it's ours." He jogged across the street to the waiting van. After a conversation with the driver, Nathan motioned to Kendall and Jake to follow. Nathan opened the door for Kendall. "I told Fergus to send something that wouldn't draw attention. I don't want anyone to know we're here."

"I agree," Jake said. "I'm just surprised you thought of it."

Kendall nodded to the driver and took the seat all the way in the back, leaving the men the middle row. Nathan got in next. His hair was still wet. The red-haired kid and his mom walked past as Jake got in. The kid looked over and made a pig face.

"I'm going to scare the shit out of that kid if he's still here when we get back," Jake said, getting in.

"Ignore him," Kendall said. "All kids can be brats. I'm sure you were too. I bet you drove your mom crazy."

He didn't say anything.

"Where did you grow up?" Kendall asked.

"Here and there," Jake said.

"Army brat?"

"Orphanage. Foster care."

"Oh. I didn't realize. What happened to your parents?"

"I don't know."

"You didn't know them?"

"No." His face was tight.

"But you have a grandmother," Kendall said.

"She didn't know about me until I was older."

Kendall's curiosity was ramped. How could his grandmother not know about him? But she saw the set of his jaw and knew he wouldn't say more. Nathan was watching Jake with a thoughtful look on his face. Both Nathan and Jake had mysterious pasts. That was a bizarre coincidence. Both men had been there each time Marco mentioned Adam. Was it possible that Jake was the one Marco was referring to and not Nathan? She wouldn't use her abilities to pry. Not yet. But she was determined to find out if one of them was Adam.

"What happened at the well?" she asked Nathan.

He shrugged. "Nothing. At least not yet. I don't know what to expect."

"If Kendall wasn't here, I'd hit you and see if it worked," Jake said.

"Jackass. Give me a power bar."

Jake handed him a power bar and a bottle of water. "I borrowed them from the gift shop. We'll have to reimburse them." He glanced back at Kendall. "Are you cold? Your hair's still wet."

"I'm fine."

"How'd your hair get wet?" Nathan asked.

Jake gave a short laugh. "You're not the only one who went swimming. Kendall knocked both of us in the water."

Nathan stopped eating. "You touched the water?" He angled his body toward her. "Did you sense anything?"

"It shocked me."

"The water?"

She nodded. "There's something powerful about the fountain, but I don't know if it's just because it's so old or if there's something else there."

"There's no way in hell the Fountain of Youth is going to be right out there in the open," Jake said.

"He's right," Nathan said. "It doesn't make sense."

"Unless there's another part to it," Kendall said.

"What do you mean?" Nathan asked.

"Maybe you have to do something besides just drink from it."

"Bloody hell, I dunked my whole body," Nathan said, looking oddly vulnerable.

"I don't know, but I need to go back and study the place," Kendall said. "We only saw the fountain, not the actual well."

"Take a towel next time," Jake said.

Kendall thumped him on the head. "How's Marco?"

"Fergus said he's much better. They're in Italy."

"Marco is feeling well enough to travel?" Kendall asked.

Nathan nodded. "They wanted to come, but I said no. I don't want them in danger."

Jake pulled out the last two power bars and scowled.

"If you don't like them, why didn't you steal something else?" Kendall asked.

"They're practical, nutritious, and easy to swipe." He handed her one.

"No thanks. I'll wait until we get to the hotel and have a filet mignon." She leaned closer. "And maybe a cold beer or nice glass of wine." She smiled sweetly when she heard his stomach growl and then leaned back in her seat. She turned to Nathan. "You look tired."

"I am. The cave did something to me."

"That goes for all of us," Jake said. "I'd like to believe it was poor air quality, but I don't think it was."

"I think falling through the portal, or whatever that was, drained our energy." And maybe she wasn't the only one affected by that shadow she'd sensed. She would have to keep an eye on both of them.

"That cave isn't normal. I don't know how, but we lost a day in there," Nathan said.

"Come again?" Jake said.

"It's not Tuesday. It's Wednesday," Nathan said. "We lost time."

After Kendall and Jake had absorbed the shock, Kendall told them what the woman in the shop had said about fairies stealing time.

"This whole place is strange," Jake said. "Like the Protettori's castle."

"The castle and this place are obviously connected. Maybe the monks at Glastonbury Abbey weren't really monks," Kendall said.

CHAPTER TEN

F ERGUS HAD MADE RESERVATIONS FOR THEM AT THE NICEST
hotel in Glastonbury. Jake and Kendall were given adjoining
rooms for security. Nathan's room was on another floor.

The rooms were luxurious, but Kendall hardly paused to explore as she headed for the bedroom. She was going to take a bath as
long and as hot as she could stand it. She thought about Nathan and
Jake and the Fountain of Youth. She drifted off and woke up with
her chin touching the water. She climbed out and dried off before
putting on a plush robe and slippers provided by the hotel.

When she walked out, Jake was lying on her bed, sound
asleep with an open book beside him. Shaking her head, she
walked toward the bed. *Glastonbury Abbey* was the title of the
book. She considered pinching him, but he looked so peaceful,
she just stood and watched him for a minute. He was wearing his
stolen sweats, but his hair looked damp as if he'd showered. His
face was relaxed, mouth slightly open, jaw shadowed with a hint
of beard. His face was as incredible as his body. How could a
man look so good? she wondered as she picked up the small pillow from the foot of the bed. She smacked him on the stomach
with the pillow, and he bounded off the bed.

She jumped out of the way. "Why are you sleeping in my bed?"

"I brought you some books. Hell, don't ever startle me like that. I could have hurt you."

"And I'm not supposed to be startled to find you asleep on my bed in my locked bedroom?"

"I knocked. You didn't answer. I came in. Bodyguard, remember? That's how it works unless you want me to stay in here all the time."

"I'm surprised I was able to sneak up on you."

"I'm off my game from that damned cave. Nathan sent you some books." He pointed to the stack on the table, then picked up the one that had fallen on the bed. "There's some interesting stuff about the abbey in here. I was reading about the black knight who guards the abbey. Lots of people claim they've seen him."

"We need to explore the abbey," Kendall said. "We're wasting time here."

"We can't go anywhere without clothes, unless you want to wear your sweats. Nathan's having some things sent over until our bags arrive. Why don't you rest until then?"

"I'm tired, but I don't think I can sleep."

"Then we'll research." Jake plopped down on her bed again. "Grab a book."

"You can't research in your room?"

"Two heads are better than one."

Kendall took a seat on the bed opposite him. There were plenty of chairs in the room, but she preferred studying this way, and there was something comforting about having him here. They both read in silence, sharing interesting tidbits as they stumbled on them.

"This says Glastonbury is considered one of the most powerful energy centers in the world."

"Sounds like new-age stuff to me," Jake said.

"The area is crossed by ley lines. This says one line runs through Saint Michael's Tower on top of the Tor, and then straight through what would have been the high altar at Glastonbury Abbey. And another through the Chalice Well."

He stretched his legs and bumped his foot against hers. "Aren't ley lines like imaginary lines connecting sacred sites?"

She nodded. "Some people put a lot of faith in the lines. Many ancient sites are crossed by the lines, like Stonehenge. Even Celtic and Christian sites. Several of the great cathedrals are connected by the lines."

"Stonehenge isn't far from here," Jake said.

"No. And there's another stone circle at Avebury. It's the largest stone circle in Europe."

"Stone circles . . . Reminds me of statues that electrocute."

"I've never heard of Stonehenge electrocuting anyone. But it does make a person wonder if there's a connection. We've just learned of a secret order that protects powerful relics, and now we've *magically* traveled to a place full of mystical sites."

Jake looked like his wheels were spinning.

"What are you thinking?"

"That I wish I were on a fishing boat."

"But this is exciting," Kendall said.

"So is pulling in a trout. I don't like things I don't understand."

"You don't understand me."

He gave her a look that melted her midsection. "You're the exception."

She turned away and opened another book, this one about the Tor. At one time, the ocean's waters came right up to the base of the Tor. The bare, oblong mountain would have been visible from the sea. "This is interesting," Kendall said. "The Tor has been a sacred site for thousands of years. Even before Joseph of Arimathea brought the chalice here, ancient civilizations used the place for religious and learning purposes. I remember hearing that. Here's one I hadn't heard. King Arthur supposedly used the Tor as a stronghold. Glastonbury is thought to be the Isle of Avalon. And one of the Celtic legends is that it's the entrance to the underworld where fairy folk live, just like the woman at the gift shop said." Kendall didn't know about fairies, but she was pretty sure there had been knights there.

"Sounds like science fiction," Jake said.

"Might I remind you that we just fell through a portal?" Kendall said. "If you want more historical information, how about this? The lady at the gift shop was right about this too. The monks supposedly hid their treasure and relics in tunnels and caves under the Tor. Did you notice how one side of the Tor has terraces cut into the hill?"

Jake nodded.

"This says some experts believe the terraces are part of a maze of tunnels underneath the Tor. Some kind of labyrinth."

"A maze . . . That sounds disturbingly familiar," Jake said.

"If the monks hid their treasure in these tunnels, there must be some connection to the Protettori since their maze led to the Tor. Marco said they were in other places as well."

Several minutes later, she found something in the pages that made her head reel. There wasn't just a powerful well here. There was also a powerful chalice. The Blue Chalice, or the Blue Bowl it was sometimes called. Experts and psychics said it was from Christ's time. It was kept at Little Saint Michael's, the house that was used for accommodations for Well Companions, people who supported the Chalice Well Foundation.

Kendall looked up from the book to tell Jake about her discovery, but she saw he was asleep again. She thought about waking him, and instead she curled up on the bed near his legs and closed her eyes. She dreamed about Adam and the plane crash. When she woke up, she saw Jake sitting on the bed, watching her, his face thoughtful.

She sat up. "I guess I was sleepy."

"You were dreaming about Adam."

"Did I say something?" she asked.

"You were calling for him." Jake brushed her cheek with his thumb. It was damp. "You were crying."

"I dreamed about the plane crash. I dream about it a lot." Especially in the past few days.

"You said he was twelve when he died, and you were ten. I know you loved him. Still do."

"I did. He was . . ." her world. "He was my friend. I didn't have anyone else. Our fathers were always on some archaeological dig or looking for a new relic. Neither Adam nor I had a normal childhood. He looked out for me like you do." She smiled.

A strange look crossed Jake's face. She had touched on a nerve, but she wasn't sure what it was. There was a knock on the door and Jake went to answer it. A bellboy had two bags for Kendall from Nathan.

"I'm sorry, I thought this was her room," the bellboy said.

"It is. You got bags for me?"

He nodded and handed Jake two more bags. They contained clothing; jeans, shirts, underwear, shoes for Kendall and basic equipment.

"We need money," Kendall said.

"He gave me some when we first got here. I guess Fergus had it sent over. And we have new cell phones. Yours is on the table. It must be nice to pick up the phone and have the world at your feet."

"Then I guess we can leave," Kendall said.

"Sure you don't want to rest longer?" Jake asked. "That damned cave wore me out. How are you feeling?"

"Tired. I think that black shadow ghost thing did something to my head."

"If it wasn't a ghost, what could do something like that?"

"The Reaper?"

"Hell, you think it was the Reaper?"

"Maybe it was Raphael. I saw him in the maze, and he must be powerful if he can come back from the dead."

"I hope he's not here. Marco said he was looking for you. He wants his cross."

"That's why you're sticking so close?"

"It's my job."

"Let's go see Nathan and find out if the fountain worked."

Kendall quickly dressed in one of the outfits Nathan had sent, and they went to his room. He wasn't in.

"Should we wait for him?" Kendall asked.

"No. He said for us to go on and he'll meet us later."

"Did he seem OK?"

"I think he wants to be alone. He doesn't trust himself around you. He's afraid he'll get pissed at me and hit you again."

"We can't waste any more time. We have to get back." Kendall told him about the Blue Chalice. "I want to see it, but it'll be hard to get inside. The house is used for private guests who are supporters of the Chalice Well Gardens."

"Then we'll have to break in. You think it's one of the Protettori's relics?"

"Who's to say the Fountain of Youth is a well or a fountain? Maybe it's a chalice."

Nathan felt a tingling in his neck as he walked through the lobby. He looked back, expecting to see Kendall or Jake, but he didn't see anyone watching. He had sent a few items of clothing and money to their room so they could get by until their things arrived. He didn't like that her room was so close to Jake's, but he was worried about her safety. There had been attempts to kidnap her in Italy. It may have been Edward's plot, but if the Reaper was so desperate for these relics, he must realize how valuable she could be to him. Nathan had. And though he had some issues with Jake, he trusted him to protect her. He trusted Jake more than he trusted himself right now.

The change was happening more often, especially when Kendall was nearby. He was afraid if he didn't get rid of the curse soon, he'd end up killing someone. He had shoved her. What if he'd killed her? If he had gotten angrier and attacked Jake, he could have killed both of them.

He went into his suite and locked the door. His prison for the next day. If he didn't change in the next twenty-four hours, that should mean the fountain worked. He didn't know where it had come from—something from his past, the years he couldn't remember? Fergus said he'd been in an accident, the same accident that killed his family. His father had witnessed a crime, Fergus said, and the family had been put into a witness protection program. But they had been killed anyway, except for Nathan. He couldn't remember them. Not a trace of a father or mother. Because of the witness protection program, there weren't any pictures, any clue of what his life had been like before. Only one face was familiar to him, but it made no sense.

He pulled back the covers and stripped. He dropped his clothes on a chair and lay down on the silky sheets. He closed his eyes and remembered lying with Kendall in his arms. He blocked out the intruding image of Jake snuggled up to her back two feet away and remembered the feel of her, her scent. He would rather be sleeping next to her in a cave than without her in a luxurious bed. As sleep took its hold, he prayed that the curse would be gone when he woke.

The fire was hot. He could feel the flames, but he couldn't see them. He couldn't see anything. He held tight to the hand pulling him away from the heat. He tripped and fell, but the man helped him up.

"Hurry," the man said. "Hurry or we'll both die."

Nathan's eyes flew open. Someone was in the room. His muscles tensed and his eyes started to burn. He threw back the covers and leapt to his feet with a growl. He heard a gasp and someone ran for the door. A woman. Not Kendall. He got there first, planting his hand against the door so hard he heard the metal creak.

"Don't hurt me!" The woman held up her arm to protect her face. Nathan flipped on the light. It was Brandi. The redhead lowered her arm and scrambled away from him, eyes wide. Her gaze moved from his eyes to his crotch, and he remembered he was naked. He felt the adrenaline rush calming. He grabbed his pants and slipped them on.

"What the hell are you doing here?" he asked her.

"Following you. What's wrong with your eyes?"

His eyes. Damn. "It didn't work." He dropped onto the bed, his body heavy with disappointment.

Brandi stared at him. "What didn't work?"

Despair was sometimes like a living thing. Right now, it was clawing at his chest as if trying to remove his heart. He'd hoped, even knowing it was probably a false lead, still he'd hoped the fountain would work. He couldn't keep living like this. Now he was back to square one, searching for damned relics that might not even exist, and might not be his cure even if they did. He would never have a chance with Kendall. "Nothing. Why are you following me?" he asked, too disappointed to be angry.

"I want the Spear of Destiny."

"No." He rubbed his eyes, still hot, which he hoped was from the bloody curse and not unshed tears.

"It has to be destroyed," Brandi said.

"It's safe."

"Nothing's safe from him," Brandi said. "The only way to make sure he doesn't get it is to destroy it."

"I'm sorry, but I can't destroy it." Obviously the fountain hadn't worked, not that he'd really expected the Protettori to hide the Fountain of Youth where anyone could drink from it. His only hope was to collect all four relics. And there was no guarantee that would work. All his hopes were based on some damned dream that he didn't understand. "How did you get here?"

"I flew in this morning."

"How did you find me here?"

"I was at the Chalice Well when I saw you. How was the fountain?"

So she'd seen that. "Wet. Cold."

"What were you doing? Taking a bath?"

"I was thirsty. How do you keep turning up where we are?"

"I think we're following the same clues."

"Clues?" Nathan asked.

"For the relics. I know you must have some idea what you're searching for."

"How do you know what the relics are? What did Thomas tell you?" Thomas was the closest connection Nathan had to the Reaper. Nathan wondered if he should have been grilling Brandi along with Raphael.

"He knew the Reaper was looking for the Fountain of Youth, and he kept talking about England. I put two and two together. I'm not the only one who saw you at the well. There was a man watching all three of you."

"A man? What did he look like?"

"I couldn't see him well," Brandi said. "He was standing in the trees. When I saw him, he took off. He was tall. I know that much."

Raphael. What the hell had he done? Jake wasn't strong enough to protect her against Raphael. He had to find them before Raphael did.

Brandi moved a step closer. "Are you OK?" Her tone softened.

"No. I'm bloody cursed."

She shrugged. "Aren't we all?"

"I suppose. I would offer you something to drink, but I didn't invite you." And he was in a hurry to leave.

"I don't want a drink. I want the spear. I will find it. Where are Kendall and Jake?"

"Around."

"You're just like your image."

"What do you know about my image?"

"Dark, mysterious. Loves relics, hates people."

"I don't hate people."

"You don't like them."

Nathan stared at Brandi.

"I know because I've spent my whole life avoiding people too."

"I thought you were a nurse."

"I am. I was. Now I'm hunting the Reaper."

"That probably won't end well."

She gave a wry smile. "I know that. I have to try. He killed everyone I've ever loved."

At least she could remember everyone she'd ever loved, Nathan thought. "Jake's going to want to talk to you. He wants to know why Thomas shot him."

"He didn't. It only looked like he was firing at Jake. He was shooting at a man behind Jake. Thomas thought the man was trying to kill him."

"So Thomas saved Jake's life."

"The irony is that the guy wasn't shooting at Jake at all. He was shooting at Thomas. He'd found out Thomas was working undercover for the Reaper."

"What was the Reaper doing in Iraq?" Nathan asked. "Jake knows it wasn't really about the prince selling weapons to terrorists."

"That was just a cover. The Reaper wanted the prince's relic collection. Supposedly he had a fantastic collection, acquired illegally of course. The Reaper needed Jake and his team to get the relics. From what Thomas told me, the Reaper expected a fight. These relics were very valuable."

"Did he get them?"

"Yes. But the prince didn't have what the Reaper wanted."

"The Fountain of Youth?" Nathan asked.

"No. The Holy Grail."

"He's looking for the Holy Grail and the Fountain of Youth?"

"According to Thomas."

The Holy Grail and the Fountain of Youth. Two powerful things. Maybe that was the key. But he still had no idea where any of the relics were besides the spear. "Did Thomas see the Holy Grail?"

"He only saw sketches in a journal the Reaper carried with him. Thomas said the Reaper protected this journal like gold. Thomas assumed they were the relics the Reaper was desperate to find."

Nathan's heart pounded harder. "What did the journal look like?"

Brandi gave him an odd look at the question. "I think Thomas said it was leather. He took the page with the sketch of the relics, but he lost it. Sometime before he died, he stole the entire journal, but the page was missing."

That's because it was in Jake's bag. "Did Thomas have any idea why the Reaper insisted on hiring Jake?" Nathan asked.

"At first Thomas thought Jake was working with the Reaper."

So had Nathan. "Thomas changed his mind?"

"He found out that Jake tried to save those girls. That tormented Thomas. He didn't know about them until then. Neither did the Reaper. Thomas said he would have killed the prince himself if he'd known. He figured the Reaper would have too. Thomas said the Reaper has done some bad things, but he's very protective of children. Not that it would have mattered in the prince's case. The Reaper would have killed him anyway."

"For the relics?"

"For the relics," Brandi said. "Always the relics. I'm going to destroy the relics and kill the Reaper." Her lips thinned and she looked almost regretful. "I'll kill anyone who gets in my way."

"We're on the same side," Nathan said. "We're both trying to stop the Reaper."

"He might not be the only problem," Brandi said. "How much do you know about the Reaper?"

"As much as money can buy." Which wasn't that much when it came to someone as elusive as the Reaper.

Brandi shrugged. "There are some things money can't buy."

"Get to the point."

"Thomas found out something shocking when he was in Iraq. The Reaper has a child."

CHAPTER ELEVEN

A TAXI DROPPED KENDALL AND JAKE AT THE ENTRANCE OF Glastonbury Abbey. They'd left a message for Nathan, telling him what they had discovered about the Blue Chalice, the abbey, and the Tor. The area drew many tourists, nature lovers, and spiritual enthusiasts. As soon as they entered the grounds, Kendall knew why. She could feel the energy in the air. "This place is powerful."

"It's old," Jake said. "According to that book, there's at least two thousand years of history here, maybe more. Is that gonna make your senses go into overload?"

"There's only one way to find out." That it was so old made her think even more strongly that there could be a connection to an old secret order.

"Let's dive in, then. If it gets to be too much, let me know."

"You'll play knight in shining armor and rescue me?" She didn't know why she'd said it, and wished she hadn't as soon as the words left her mouth.

That odd look crossed his face again; then he grinned. "I'd make a damned fine knight. Rescue the damsel, earn a kiss as a reward, then dump her into the arms of a grateful father or lover, and off I'd go to the next damsel."

"Your concept of knighthood is whacked. Knights were selfless, honest, defenders of truth, and often chaste." Although many knights had been married, and some had committed adultery. Like Lancelot, one of the greatest knights. "I don't think you need to apply."

"I'm honest and true."

"You stole power bars."

"A selfless act so a damsel wouldn't starve."

"There's the chastity problem. It doesn't take a psychic to know you like sex."

"That doesn't mean I get much."

Was he kidding? With his looks? She gave him a look of disbelief.

"I'm not as nondiscriminating as you might think."

"You're no virgin."

"I might as well be," he muttered. "And you might want to remember who turned who down the last time."

That shut her up. She would have spent the night with him in the tower if he hadn't gallantly walked away.

"If that doesn't qualify me for knighthood, I don't know what does. I saved your virtue."

She hadn't wanted it spared then. Now she was glad, because she and Jake were just too complicated to get tangled up in bed.

"A true knight wouldn't remind a lady of such things."

He said something very unknightly, and they walked on. They passed several couples and families, and the occasional loner staring off into space, meditating or seeking some connection to the earth. The abbey grounds were beautiful and the ruins magnificent. They were in various stages of deterioration, only pieces of a foundation or wall in places, but others were remarkably intact, like the abbot's kitchen, a medieval kitchen, and the Lady Chapel.

As they made their way through the ruins, impressions flew at Kendall, bits and pieces of the past. And there was a lot of past here, as the lady at the gift shop had said. This was once the greatest abbey in Europe. Saint Patrick had lived and died here. King Arthur had been buried here, along with Guinevere, if the stories were accurate. And underneath the Lady Chapel was supposedly where Joseph of Arimathea built the first Christian structure in Britain, a wattle and daub church.

"You holding up?" Jake asked.

Kendall nodded. "I just feel . . . full." Sometimes she felt in colors and sensations that she didn't even know how to explain, sometimes visions, sounds, or smells. She could even hear snippets of conversation, but not enough to tell what was being said. There were conspiracies here. She could feel them in the air.

Occasionally they encountered someone in period clothing. Near one wall, four monks walked side by side, hands folded in front of them. "They look authentic."

Jake looked up from a marker he was studying. "Who?"

"Those monks by the wall."

"Uh . . . I think they might be."

Kendall frowned. "Real monks. Well, I guess monks would be interested in the ruins too. I mean, this was an abbey."

"Kendall . . . There aren't any monks."

"Right there, near the end of that wall—damn." The monks had vanished.

"Ghosts?" Jake asked.

"Or more memories of the past? Whatever they are, I seem to be seeing a lot of them."

"Sure you don't want to go on that fishing boat with me?"

She sighed. "Ask me in a week."

"The only ghost I'd like to see is King Arthur so I could ask him if he knows where the Fountain of Youth is. Think you could ask him?"

Kendall glanced at him in surprise, not sure whether he was joking. "I've never talked to a ghost."

"With all the encounters you've had?"

"I haven't had that many until recently. And they never talked."

"Let's go see if King Arthur's feeling chatty today," Jake said.

"The bodies aren't here anyway," Kendall said. "They were stolen."

"His spirit might be here."

A marker directed them to King Arthur's grave located near the Lady Chapel. Kendall sat beside the grave, overwhelmed with a sense of sadness. And oddly enough, guilt.

"Are you OK?" Jake asked, kneeling beside her. He put a hand on her shoulder but immediately pulled it away.

"Sorry, I just tapped into something," she said. "You felt it too, didn't you, when you touched me?"

He didn't answer, but he seemed disturbed. He put his hand on the grass, eyes dark, face tense, then suddenly stood. "I think it's this place. Let's get out of here," he said quietly. "If we're not going back to the hotel, we'll have to find a place to stay. We can come back here later."

Before she could stand, Kendall heard voices approaching. She turned and saw a group walking toward them led by a black-haired woman in a long blue dress.

"The grave of King Arthur and his queen, Guinevere," she announced in a somber, theatrical voice.

"Want me to scare them off?" Jake asked.

She had no doubt he could do it. Kendall shook her head and stood.

"Oh, there's someone here," the woman said. "We'll have to come back. We can go to the museum shop." She started to shoo the group away.

"Wait," one of the other women said. "They're leaving."

The woman turned back toward the grave. A look of frustration crossed her face as she walked closer. The rest of the group followed her like sheep.

Kendall stopped a few feet away, curious about the woman. Obviously she had, or was pretending to have, some paranormal abilities. Pretending, Kendall guessed, but she had always been intrigued by others with some unique abilities, wondering where they had gotten theirs. Most that she'd met were frauds. Occasionally she met someone with real abilities. She'd yet to meet anyone with her same gift, and she often wondered if that was what she searched for. Validation that she wasn't a complete freak.

"Do you think his spirit is here?" one of the women asked. She had brown hair, brown pants, and a brown shirt.

"I think this would be more effective in the moonlight," the black-haired woman said. "We could come back tonight."

"Let's try, please," the woman in brown said.

The leader walked close to the gravesite. She closed her eyes and held out her hands over the plaque. She started to sway slightly.

"You gotta be kidding me," Jake said too loud.

Kendall shushed him. "I want to see what she's doing."

"Arthur," the woman called. "Are you here, Arthur?"

"I think I feel something," the man in the group said.

"Like he's drowning in shit maybe," Jake suggested.

"I don't think so," Kendall said, looking at the figure that had materialized over the grave. "Oh my God." This last was said louder than she'd intended.

The woman in blue turned. She looked irritated, until she saw Kendall's face. Her eyes widened. "Everyone sit and hold hands. Close your eyes and think about King Arthur and Guinevere." As soon as the group was seated and eyes closed, the woman hurried over to Kendall with the grace of a linebacker. "You saw something, didn't you? I've seen that same look on Lizzie's face. Did you see Arthur?"

Jake had stepped closer to Kendall. The woman hadn't noticed him in her excitement.

"I'm not sure what I saw." Kendall had seen something, but it wasn't Arthur. She'd seen a woman with blood covering her face and clothes, standing next to the woman in a long blue dress.

"Tell me what it was. Please. If I don't give them something to keep them occupied until Lizzie gets here, this group is going to leave," she whispered harshly. "I have a fortune wrapped up in this trip. Half the group got a stomach virus and canceled. Then Lizzie didn't show up. That's my psychic. It's not easy to get into Little Saint Michael's. I'm desperate."

Before Kendall could attempt unraveling what the woman had said, Jake spoke up. "Little Saint Michael's?"

The woman looked at Jake and her expression changed. "Oh. I didn't see you," she said, appraising him. "That's where we're staying."

"We'll be glad to help out," Jake said. He stuck out his hand. "I'm Jake, her assistant."

Kendall stared at Jake. "Wait a minute—"

"I believe we should help out in time of need," Jake interrupted.

The woman raised an eyebrow at Jake. "You don't look like a psychic. You look more like a male stripper."

Jake's jaw clenched, but he folded his hands over his chest in an imitation of a spiritual man. "Physical appearance is of little worth."

The woman nodded and gave his physical appearance another appraising glance. "I'm Halle. I'm the tour guide. We're supposed to be on a three-day trip to discover King Arthur. We're planning to see as many King Arthur sites as possible. Tonight we're doing a moonlight meditation. Tomorrow's a big day. We're going to Camelot. Then later that evening we'll attend a moonlight tour of the abbey and a séance near King Arthur's grave. If we're not too tired, the next day we want to get in a hike to the Tor and visit Tintagel, King Arthur's birthplace, and Merlin's cave."

"Lots of moonlight events," Jake said.

"The moonlight gets people in the mood for magic. If you could meet me at the house in an hour, we'll make arrangements." She started to walk off but turned back. "Thank you," she whispered before rushing off to her followers who were peeking around with frowns on their faces.

"I'm sorry," Halle announced. "I'm feeling faint. I need to meditate to restore my strength. We'll have to come back tonight." She ushered the group off amidst complaints.

Kendall turned to Jake. "What are you doing?"

"Getting us in to see the Blue Chalice without breaking the law."

"I'm not a psychic. I'm not going to pretend to contact King Arthur for some unwitting group."

"Then we break in. Or we could demand the chalice at gunpoint."

"We don't even have extra clothes."

"At least they're clean. We can have Nathan send some more things," Jake said.

They did need to get inside the house, and this was the perfect excuse. "I'll do it, but just until we see the chalice."

They sat for a few minutes and planned their ruse. She was a psychic from America. Jake was her assistant. They would use their real names in case Nathan wanted to find them, especially since Jake had already blurted out his. It might be a mistake since the Reaper could find them too.

"This is . . . wrong. I feel like some kind of circus fortune-teller."

"It's survival."

Kendall rolled her eyes. "Is there anything you haven't done in the name of survival?"

"Not much."

Kendall and Jake had a little time to kill before they went to meet Halle, but not enough to go back to the hotel. They bought toiletries and extra clothes—the same damned sweatpants and shirts from the same store they had stolen from earlier today. Just in case it took them overnight to find the chalice, Jake said. He slipped an extra two hundred pounds under the register when the woman was bagging their items.

Carrying their things, they stopped by Wearyall Hill to see the place where Joseph had thrust his staff into the ground. Kendall's head was getting thick with impressions of the past, but she had a feeling that time was running out.

"Looks like someone got overenthusiastic with pruning," Jake said, looking at the trunk of a tree with shoots growing out in places.

"Vandals cut off the limbs of one of the trees. Such a shame. It came from a cutting that was grown from the tree Joseph planted two thousand years ago. If you believe the myth."

"Hell, I'd believe most anything at this point. You could try touching it."

She closed her eyes and touched the tree. Nothing.

"Not happening?"

"No. I think I've had enough impressions for one day."

They showed up at Little Saint Michael's, and Halle met them in the lobby. She took them into a quiet room where she fully explained her dilemma. She was a tour guide with a small group in Florida that specialized in enlightenment retreats. They were planning to visit many of the places where King Arthur roamed. Camelot, Tintagel, his grave, and Merlin's cave. The goal was to contact King Arthur, but her psychic hadn't shown up. "She's never done anything like this before. We need the money, especially with all those cancellations, but I don't know anything about spiritual stuff. I play tour guide, she contacts the dead."

Kendall had a bad feeling that Halle's psychic was the angry ghost she had seen at King Arthur's grave. "When did you hear from her last?"

Halle pursed her lips. "The day before we left. She was on her way to visit a client."

"What does she look like?"

Halle frowned. "Auburn hair. Slender."

That could have been the woman Kendall saw, but she didn't see her well because of the blood. It could have been someone connected to the abbey. The woman had been wearing a long gown, but that didn't mean she was from the past. Halle also wore a long gown. Kendall didn't say anything yet. She didn't want to alarm anyone needlessly, and if she was in fact dead, it was too late to help her.

Halle gave them a tour of the place. It was a cozy house. Lizzie was a long-standing companion, which entitled her to use Little Saint Michael's. There were several bedrooms and a sanctuary upstairs called the Upper Room. The house had access to the Chalice Well Gardens twenty-four hours a day.

"I'm afraid we only have one room left," Halle said. "The one Lizzie was going to stay in."

"Of course," Kendall muttered.

"It's OK," Jake said. "We're married."

"I'm sorry. The room has twin beds," Halle said.

"Damn," Jake said.

"Perfect," Kendall said.

Halle looked surprised.

Kendall sighed. "He steals the covers. We have to sleep in separate beds at home."

Halle grinned at Jake. "I wouldn't worry about covers with him in my bed."

Jake returned Halle's grin, looking a lot more like the male stripper than the spiritual-assistant/husband he was supposed to be.

Kendall poked him with her elbow.

"Dinner is at seven," Halle said. "You'll have time to rest or do some sightseeing before we meet in Arthur's garden at the Chalice Well at nine p.m. Will that work for you?"

"What is the group expecting from this meditation?" Kendall asked.

"It's just a quiet time, but they're really hoping to connect with Arthur, so the more the better. I really need this trip to be successful. Don't worry. If you don't feel anything at first, fake it. Sometimes Lizzie did until something real came through." Halle walked to the door. "If you need anything, let me know. I'm two doors down. Do you have luggage?"

"We'll pick it up later," Jake said.

Halle left them and Kendall looked at Jake. "Married, again?"

"We have to stick together. You want them to think we're living in sin?" He eyed the beds. "They look small. We could push them together."

"They're fine. I'm going to take a shower." She felt grungy after walking the abbey.

"Don't use all the hot water," he called after her.

The guests had to share bathrooms, but one was located just across the hall. When she got back to her room, dressed in an identical pair of the sweats she'd had before, Jake was shirtless, doing one-armed push-ups on the floor. Kendall gaped at his muscles for a minute. "Are you trying to impress me?"

"I'm trying to stay fit. Who knows what feat I'll face next in order to keep you safe." He rolled to his feet. There was a slight glisten of sweat across his chest. "I'm going to take a shower. There's a bandage for your wrist on the table. It's one of those with the antibacterial cream on it. Don't want you getting an infection on me."

"Thanks."

After he left, Kendall put the bandage on, dried her hair with a towel, and braided it. Jake was still in the bathroom, so she took out Nathan's journal. She couldn't make any sense of the coded entries. She was halfway to a headache, when Jake walked into the bedroom. He'd changed from his jeans into sweats. "I'm starting to get attached to these sweats," he said.

"I'm not."

He sat in the chair beside hers. She could smell him, clean and male. His hair was still damp from his shower. Tendrils softly curled below his ears, lying against his neck. Her fingers itched to brush the hair aside and replace it with her lips. She knew what his neck smelled like. What it tasted like. She looked up and met his eyes. Her breathing quickened and she knew his had too, but he didn't speak or move. He just stared at her, his eyes dark with something . . . regret. He looked away. "Any luck with the journal?"

"No. I think we need to start by exploring this place. The well, the abbey, and the Tor."

"Not tonight. We have an appointment with King Arthur."

"I can't believe we're going to trick these poor people."

"It's survival. We have to find the Blue Chalice and see if it's connected to the Fountain of Youth. You ready to go eat and meet our group?"

"You mean the people we're about to dupe? You go on. I'm going to try Nathan again. I'll meet you in a few minutes."

"Nathan knows where we are. He'll show up when he's ready."

Kendall tried Nathan via phone but couldn't get him. There was a knot in her chest that made her suspect he was in danger. Nathan was always in danger to some extent, but this felt more imminent. She didn't know if it was from Raphael or the Reaper, or perhaps Jake really had spotted Brandi. Times like these were the most frustrating, when she sensed something about the people she cared for but couldn't get a clear picture. She put her phone away and went to the dining room.

Several tables were scattered about and a buffet was set up on one side. She recognized some of the people from the abbey, and the back of one dark head was very familiar. Jake was sitting with Halle and two other women. All three ladies had rapt looks on their faces, making Kendall wonder if he was overwhelming them with his manliness or telling lies. Halle glanced up and waved, then motioned her over. She met Jake's gaze as she walked to the table, looking for some kind of prompt. Who knew what he'd been telling them.

"I was just about to come and get you," he said, standing to hold out her chair.

"Looks and manners," a redheaded woman said. "He's a keeper."

"He's handy to have around." Kendall gave him a fake smile. "What lies are you telling now?"

"He's telling us about all the historical figures you've contacted," said one of Jake's enthralled audience. "Oh, I'm Sandy. I'm from North Carolina. This is Alice, from Maryland." She pointed to a mousy-looking woman, the one wearing all brown. "And this is Rhonda from Florida." Rhonda was the redhead and was all eyes for Jake. "That's Larry over there. He's from DC." Larry was balding with glasses and reminded Kendall of a monk.

"We're all here to find King Arthur," Larry said. "I hope you can help."

"Jake said you've been in touch with many of our past presidents," Sandy said. She had gray hair and bright blue eyes.

"Yes," Rhonda said. "I'm especially interested in Thomas Jefferson." She fluttered her lashes at Jake. "I understand that he admitted to you that he had had an affair with his slave."

Kendall frowned at Jake. "You really shouldn't be telling such things."

"It isn't true?" Alice said. Her small voice matched her mousy appearance.

"It's just that . . . some things are told to me in confidence."

They looked impressed, and Kendall knew she had gone up in their estimation. Sandy asked her who was the most interesting spirit she'd contacted, and then everyone jumped in, peppering her with questions. "Who was your favorite spirit?" "Who was the most shocking?" "Have you had a spirit attack you?" "Climb in bed with you?" The last question was from Rhonda.

"Each time is different," Kendall said. "I never know what to expect." That wasn't a lie.

The time flew by, and Kendall began to enjoy herself more than she cared to admit. These people might be quacks by some standards, but they admired her, appreciated her. For once in her life since Adam, she fit in. Jake got her a plate from the buffet and watched her as she talked. He played the perfect husband, charming and gorgeous. She didn't realize he'd left until she saw him slip back into the room.

"When do we get to see the Blue Chalice?" Sandy asked.

"What's the Blue Chalice?" Jake asked, wearing a blank look as if he had never heard of it and hadn't most likely been searching for it as the group dined.

Alice's mousy appearance lit up. "It's Glastonbury's Holy Grail. They say it has power."

"Lizzie has been a supporter of the well for a long time, and the trust has agreed to let us view the chalice," Halle said. "It's quite an honor."

"Sounds interesting," Jake said. "When do we get to see it?"

"In a day or two, when the caretaker returns."

CHAPTER TWELVE

NATHAN PARKED HIS LAND ROVER IN THE GLASTONBURY Abbey parking lot. He locked the car and started walking toward the grounds. He'd gotten Kendall and Jake's message. He would join them at Little Saint Michael's, but first he wanted to check out the abbey grounds before it got too dark to see. Marco had said to find Arthur. King Arthur was supposed to have been buried here in Glastonbury Abbey. Maybe the fountain was near his grave. Maybe the fountain was inside his grave. He followed the signs, but someone else was there. A man stood with his back to Nathan. He was tall with dark hair pulled into a ponytail. He stretched out his hand and touched a marker that had been placed on the grave. Nathan could see sadness in the droop of his shoulders. In fact, he could feel it himself, a sense of anguish settling over him like fog. He didn't often sense things the way Kendall did, but this was strong. The man at the grave tensed as if realizing he was being watched. He turned, and Nathan saw it was Raphael.

He thought about running, then about fighting, and reasoned that both would end badly, so he decided to face things head-on. No one else was nearby. His heartbeat sped up as he walked toward Raphael. He felt almost ill, but not from fear. It was the grave that was troubling him. "I wouldn't have taken you if there had been any other way," Nathan said. "I apologize, but it was necessary. I would do it again if given the choice."

"You don't have the choice now, do you?" Raphael moved closer. "Where is my cross?"

Nathan pulled the cross from under his shirt and took it off. He handed it to Raphael.

"Where did you get it?"

Nathan wasn't going to name Kendall. "I took it off your body." His dead body.

"You must love her to lie for her."

Marco had probably told him Kendall found it. "She thought you were dead and wouldn't need the cross. Why aren't you dead?"

Raphael glanced at the grave, then glared at Nathan. "Who are you?"

Raphael was angry, but he also seemed puzzled. Nathan frowned. "You know who I am."

"Who are you really?" Raphael grabbed Nathan by the shirt and yanked him closer. Nathan felt the heat rushing through his veins. He tried to stop the change, but his insides felt like they were cooking and his eyes were on fire.

Raphael's eyes narrowed. "Damn Marco. That's what I was afraid of." Raphael slipped the cross over his head. "Now we can go."

That was the last thing Nathan remembered before he woke up on a stone floor. Raphael leaned over him and pulled out a dagger. He cut his own wrist and then he grabbed Nathan's. Nathan tried to pull away, but Raphael was too strong. The dagger sliced across his wrist and Nathan felt the sting. A line of blood welled up and Raphael touched their wrists together.

Nathan's head felt thick, as it had in the maze. Immediately, memories pounded at his brain like a jackhammer. An airplane, flames, someone grabbing him, dragging him out of the flames. Then an explosion and blackness.

"This way. We must hurry."

The voice beside him was weak. He didn't know where they were, but he could smell the earth and trees. A branch slapped his face, and he threw up his hands to protect it. "I need to rest." His head and legs ached, and fire flashed behind his eyes even though he couldn't see.

"We're almost there," the voice said. "He's meeting us at the rock." His breathing was ragged, and it sounded like he needed to rest too. After he had stumbled for a few more minutes, the hand guiding his arm dropped. "You'll have to go alone. I'm sorry, Adam," the voice rasped.

"Go where?" He didn't know where he was. He didn't know anything. Something cold was placed in his hands. He heard a harsh, rattling breath, then a thump. The forest was quiet except for his panting. "Where are you?" He stretched his hands in front of him, feeling blindly for the man. His foot hit something solid but soft, and he knelt, fear gripping him by the throat.

He put the cold object in his pocket—it was a cross—and patted awkwardly with his hands until he felt an arm. He followed it to a chest. It was still. No heartbeat. He felt a crushing sadness, even though he didn't know the man. He was sure he should. He sat down beside the dead man, surrounded by darkness, as lost inside as he was out.

He tried to remember . . . anything, but the only image he saw was a girl with blond hair. Her face wasn't clear, and the memory faded as quickly as it had come. His head burned, and he touched the rough bandage, trying to recall what had happened. He felt the stickiness of fresh blood; then his hands slid lower, touching nose, lips, jaw, searching for something familiar. Adam. That was the name the man had called him. He didn't know what to do, so he clutched the cross in his pocket, pulled his jacket around him, and waited for someone to find him.

Nathan opened his eyes and saw Raphael standing over him, frowning. He knelt and tied a cloth around Nathan's bloody wrist. "Leave this on for now." He turned and started walking out.

Nathan rose to his feet, but his head was spinning.

"Wait. Where are you going?"

Raphael kept walking. "I have something to do."

"Tell me where we are."

Raphael turned, giving him a look like one might give a flea. "A sanctuary."

"What sanctuary? Where?"

"I can't tell you."

"Are we in England? Italy?" And how the hell had they gotten there?

"We're where we need to be."

"Bloody hell, I want answers. You've kidnapped me, brought me to . . . I don't know where."

Nathan heard a rumbling sound and realized it came from Raphael. He was laughing, but it was a harsh laugh. "It isn't pleasant, is it?" Raphael asked.

"I told you, I didn't have any choice." Nathan was getting angrier by the second. His heart started to pound.

"Neither did I. You need to calm yourself. Your power is still out of control."

"What power?" Nathan asked.

"The change."

"You mean my curse?"

"Curse?"

"The fact that I'm not normal."

"You aren't supposed to be."

"I don't want this, whatever it is."

"You don't have a choice."

"There must be a way to get rid of it."

Raphael studied him. "There is, but it would be severe." He moved his hand toward Nathan, and Nathan felt his legs weaken and his eyes closing.

"Who am I?" Nathan asked, trying to fight sleep.

"I'm not sure. Sleep until I figure out what to do. You'll be safe here."

"Have you found them?" the Reaper asked the man on the other end of the phone.

"Yes, they're here."

"And the chalice?"

"They haven't gotten it . . . yet."

"You must get it before they do."

"They haven't made a move toward it. I'm not sure they even know of its existence."

"Then why are they there?"

"I haven't figured that out. Even if they do get the chalice, they might not have discovered where the fountain is hidden."

"If they haven't, Kendall soon will. Her talent is extraordinary." He felt a twinge of pride.

"Do you want me to bring her with the chalice?"

The Reaper hesitated. He had considered it. Kendall's gifts were so similar to ones he'd once had. He could put them to great use. He sighed. "Not yet."

"Are you certain this chalice is the Holy Grail?"

"No, but the only way to find out is to try it. Keep an eye on them in the meantime. And watch out for Raphael."

"I'll stay close."

"Not too close." He let the warning settle. "I know you're attracted to her."

"Who wouldn't be?" the man said. "She's a beauty."

"Don't let her beauty distract you. I can't take extra risks now. There are already enough obstacles."

Jake was quiet when they got to their room, not the fast talker she'd seen in the dining room. It was disconcerting how easily he put on an act. A handy talent for a mercenary.

"I don't like that look on your face. You're not planning to steal the chalice, are you?" she asked.

"Not if they show it to us soon enough."

"You could stay here and look for it while I do the meditation."

"I'm not leaving you alone, even with a group," Jake said. "We'll look for it later tonight when everyone's asleep. If that doesn't work, we'll wait until they're out of the house looking for Arthur."

"I'm worried about Nathan."

"You're always worried about Nathan," Jake said.

"Why hasn't he let us know if the fountain worked?"

"He's probably trying to find something else to try. If it had worked, I think he would have let us know."

"I think something's wrong. I don't know if it's Raphael or the Reaper, but I sense danger."

"I'm sure neither one of them is happy with him," Jake said. "Did you talk to him?"

"He didn't answer. What if the curse backfired or something?"

"If we don't hear from him soon, we'll go back to the hotel and make sure he's OK."

Kendall changed into the long dress Halle had provided—to put the group *in the mood*—and then she and Jake made their way to the Chalice Well Garden.

The meditation would be held in the part known as Arthur's garden. Appropriate, if one was trying to contact King Arthur. She felt guilty, knowing she would have to pretend to make contact.

"Do you want us to sit in a circle?" Sandy asked.

This felt more like a séance. She didn't like séances, and she hated deception even more, but as Jake said, this was survival. "Yes, in a circle and join hands." They all sat on the stones and linked hands. Rhonda hurried to sit beside Jake.

Kendall kept feeling as if someone were watching her. She turned but didn't see anything other than the Tor rising behind them. She hoped it was Nathan that she sensed, but it left her with an eerie feeling.

Kendall reached for Jake's hand. "OK, close your eyes, clear your minds, and focus on Arthur." Everyone closed their eyes. Moonlight-bathed faces turned up with expressions of reverence and anticipation. Then she turned to her side and saw Jake watching her. His look was not reverent. She nudged him with her knee and mouthed, "Close your eyes." It was going to be hard enough to fake this without him watching her.

He rolled his eyes and then closed them. In the spirit of camaraderie—or maybe guilt—she also cleared her mind and focused. She didn't know whether King Arthur was real, a legend, or a legend based on a real king, but she thought of what she knew from the stories of Arthur. She imagined Merlin, the sword Excalibur, the Knights of the Round Table, Camelot, and Arthur's quest for the Holy Grail.

A blast hit her so hard she at first thought there had been an explosion. She couldn't breathe. She stood outside a castle in the middle of a battlefield. Snow fell gracefully as horses taller than her head rushed past her, carrying men yelling out battle cries as they swung huge swords. One man sat taller than the others. At first she thought he was Nathan, that she was mixing dreams and reality, but she felt the bite of cold and the frozen ground beneath her feet. This was no ordinary vision.

The knight was King Arthur.

CHAPTER THIRTEEN

A HORSE GALLOPED PAST AND GRAZED HER SHOULDER. SHE fell on her back on the frozen ground. The stars shone above her. A massive black horse came into view, and the tall man looked down at her. He looked regal, and somehow familiar, though she had never seen him before. He spoke, but she couldn't hear him for the other voices calling her name. His face grew blurry. She blinked and saw it was Jake, not King Arthur.

Over his shoulder, she saw the others watching with wide eyes. "I've never seen anything like that," Rhonda said.

"Kendall, can you hear me?" Jake patted her face.

She grabbed his arm and sat up. No battlefield. No King Arthur. No snow.

Jake continued to frown. "That was a little too real," he whispered in her ear.

She couldn't yet speak.

"Was it Arthur?" Alice asked.

She nodded, and there was a gasp.

"What did he say?" Sandy asked.

Kendall tried to stand, but her legs felt numb. "Help me up," she said to Jake.

He put a hand under each arm and lifted her to her feet. "You're cold."

She was still unsteady, so she clutched his arm. "I need to leave," she whispered.

Jake took charge. "Kendall's encounter with Arthur has left her weak. She needs to restore her energy. Then she'll explain her vision."

There were disappointed groans as Jake led her away from the garden, finally carrying her after she stumbled twice. He carried her inside the house to their room, where he shut the door and set her on her feet. "Talk about starting off with a bang, but I thought you'd drag it out a little more. The whole thing didn't last a minute. They might feel cheated."

Kendall grabbed his arm for support. "It wasn't an act."

"That was real?"

She nodded and moved slowly toward the bed.

He helped her to the bed and took off her shoes. "Your feet are cold."

"It was snowing."

"Huh?"

"I was on the battlefield. It was snowing. There were horses and knights and swords."

Jake lifted that sexy brow.

"I saw him. I saw King Arthur."

The other brow rose.

"He said something to me."

"He talked to you?" Jake's surprised look turned a bit dubious. "Is this retaliation for the dead-presidents thing? I had to build up your reputation."

"No, I'll owe you for that. King Arthur rode his horse right up to me and looked into my eyes. He said something to me."

"What?"

"I don't know. I was yanked back into my body."

Jake stared at her. "How do you know it was King Arthur and not some other sword-toting knight on horseback in the middle of a battlefield?"

"I felt him. I know it was him."

"Damn. Has this happened before?"

"A few times, but more like what you saw when I touched Raphael. Like a vision. This time it felt like I was there. You didn't see anything?" He had been holding her hand.

"No. You flew backward like you'd been checked by a hockey player and lay there with your eyes open. At first I thought you'd hit your head on a rock and died."

"Then you wouldn't have to work with a *skirt* anymore."

Jake's eyes narrowed. "That's a dumb-assed thing to say. You know how I feel about you."

Did she?

"So when Marco said to find Arthur, he meant *the* Arthur," Jake said.

"It would seem so. He mentions Arthur, and then we end up here, where Arthur supposedly lived."

"And now you've had a vision of Arthur. What did he look like?"

That was an odd question to ask. "He's hard to describe. He reminded me of Nathan in knight garb."

Her answer seemed to trouble him. "We need to know what King Arthur said. Hell, I can't even believe I'm saying that."

She almost felt sorry for Jake. He had gone from being a complete skeptic to facing ghosts and things that even made her jaw drop in shock. "I can't just summon him. I didn't summon him this time."

"That's what those mediums on TV do. You're more real than they are."

"That's not the kind of gift I have."

He rolled his eyes. "*I* need a damned course in your gift."

"I think this is happening because of the place. It's strange here, just like the castle."

"Considering that we traveled from one to the other in a way that defies physics, then I'd say they're definitely connected. We need Marco. If we can unravel that tangled mess in his head, maybe he can explain this King Arthur connection."

"We should call Fergus and see if we can talk to Marco."

"I called Fergus's cell phone earlier," Jake said. "No one answered."

"There has to be a connection since he mentioned both Arthur and the Fountain of Youth," Kendall said.

"We don't even know what the Fountain of Youth is," Jake said. "It could be a well or a chalice or neither. The fountain in the Chalice Well Gardens can't be the real Fountain of Youth, or thousands of people would be eternally young. Hell, we don't even know if the fountain is the relic we need. Marco's not all there sometimes."

"His mind seemed clear," Kendall said.

"We need to ask Arthur what the hell he was saying."

"The group is planning to visit several King Arthur sites . . . Camelot, Tintagel, and Merlin's cave."

"Merlin . . . I've been thinking all this time that Marco reminds me of Moses. Maybe I've had the wrong white-haired guy."

Kendall had been thinking the same thing. She would have thought that was insane before now, but the bizarre was looking more and more credible. She rubbed her head. She did feel as if she'd smacked it on something hard.

"Let me see," Jake said. "Looks like you bumped it. You scared me. You sure you didn't get a concussion or something?"

"I'm fine, just drained from the vision. I get so tired of this."

"It has to be tiring having these . . . things . . . these visions mixing with reality."

"You have no idea."

"Can I get you anything? Water?"

"Rest. Thank you."

He pulled the covers over her.

"Where are you going?"

"To brush my teeth. Why? You want me to stay?"

"I was afraid you were going to steal the chalice."

He brushed back her hair. "Not yet. Sure I can't get you anything?"

"No thanks. But I would be eternally grateful if you would give the group an update for me. I know they're dying to know what happened. Tell them I'll let them know after I've rested."

"How grateful?"

"I won't kill you if you snore."

He chuckled and leaned closer, not touching her, but so near she could almost feel his skin. She expected him to go for something Jake-ish, but he just kissed her head. "I'll be back."

After he left, Kendall touched the spot on her forehead that still felt warm. She fell asleep with her fingers touching his kiss. And she dreamed not of Adam as she so often did, but of Jake and her and King Arthur.

She was in another time, another woman's body. Her heart beat quickly as she ran to where he was waiting behind the crofter's cottage. No one went there because the small stand of woods was said to be enchanted. She glanced back at the castle and saw a shadow disturb the light from the lantern in their bedchamber. He had returned early from the meeting with his knights. Feelings of guilt almost caused her to turn and run back to him. He would be look-ing for her as soon as he had bathed. She hurried on, planning to tell her lover that she could not stay. They must put an end to this madness, this betrayal. But when she saw him standing there, eyes dark with passion, her heart melted and resolve fled. She went to him, let him unlace her gown, let his lips touch her neck and, as her gown dropped, her breasts.

He made love to her with passion, leaving her heart and loins sated. "I love you," she said.

"And I you, my queen," he said, lips grazing her skin.

Jake stood at the back of the house, studying the window of the Upper Room. He'd told Kendall he wouldn't steal the chalice. He hadn't said he wouldn't try to find it. But it wasn't easy with so many people in the house. The chalice must be in the Upper Room or in the locked room at the end of the hall , where he'd heard a man's voice. He knew where everyone in the house was staying. He'd checked the rooms out earlier while everyone was eating dinner. Sandy and Alice were sharing a room. The odd couple, they were complete opposites. Alice, interestingly enough, was messy; Sandy, neat and tidy. Rhonda had her own room with stacks of romance novels and two bottles of wine. Halle was all business with her laptop and travel guides. She was breaking the rules. There weren't supposed to be any electronic devices used on the premises. Larry's room was filled with books on every subject from enlightenment to outer space.

Jake went back inside. Later tonight when everyone was asleep, he would search the two rooms.

Halle was still up, moving around the kitchen, her face flushed.

"Everything OK?" Jake asked.

"Jake, I didn't see you go out."

"Just getting some fresh air. I have a headache." He'd given the group a brief update on Kendall's vision but didn't answer too many questions since he was more concerned with finding out which room the Blue Chalice was kept in. He didn't want to wait until the caretaker returned.

"That's what I'm doing. My head's throbbing. Lizzie just called. She eloped with her boyfriend." Halle grabbed a bottle of Tylenol from the kitchen cabinet.

"Sucks that she didn't let you know ahead of time, but at least she's alive."

Halle gave Jake a puzzled look. "She claims she left a message at the house. I shouldn't be surprised. She was desperate to marry this guy. He's had cold feet because his first wife was an angry bitch." Halle sighed. "I guess I'm happy for them since I set them up. I might not be psychic, but I can spot a good match a mile away. Take you and Kendall. You two belong together. It's obvious you're in love."

"Really?"

"Yeah. The way she looks at you, the way you look at her." She sighed. "It's energizing . . . and depressing at the same time." She laughed. "I'm just jealous. It's hard to find love like that nowadays. Everyone's so busy and worried about their own interests."

Love? "She's definitely special," he said. It was alarming how special she was. He'd never felt this way about a woman, and it made him uneasy. "Can I have a couple of those?" Jake asked. He might need them after all.

Halle handed him the bottle, and he shook out two pills.

"Is Kendall OK?" she asked.

"She'll be fine after some rest."

"I've never seen any psychic experience so real."

"She's good," Jake added. Good enough to convince a complete skeptic. "Who's in the room at the end of the hall?"

"That's the caretaker's room."

"You said he isn't here?"

"He left to visit his sister in London right after we got here. He said he'll show us the Blue Chalice when he returns."

Then who was using his room? "I can't wait to see it. Well, good night. I'm going to turn in."

Jake went to the bathroom and waited until he heard Halle's door close again. Then he crept toward the last room. The caretaker might not be here, but someone was using his room. He tapped softly on the door and then heard a thump coming from his room. He hurried back and opened the door. A lamp had been knocked over on the bedside table. Kendall was tossing on the bed, moaning. Jake bent over her and touched her cheek to wake her.

Eyes closed, she grabbed his head and pulled him to her. Her lips were warm on his, feverish. "I love you." He froze, but she kept kissing him. She muttered something, but it was muffled against his lips.

"Kendall?"

She shot off the bed and he jumped back, only his quick reflexes saving his groin from her knee. She came at him again. He spun her against the wall, pinned her hands, and wedged her legs apart so she couldn't kick him in the balls.

"For God's sake, it's me."

"Jake." She stopped fighting. "I'm sorry. I woke up and saw you hovering over me . . ." Her chest was heaving against his.

"You were dreaming?" A hell of a dream from the looks of it. He released her arms.

The moonlight flickered in her eyes, and even in the dark he saw her flush. "I know," she said, staring at him.

There was a breathy tone to her voice that made him think things he shouldn't. God, she smelled good. What was it about her skin? He didn't try to move and she didn't either. "What was it about?"

"You . . . me."

It was a struggle to keep from pressing closer to her. "What were we doing?"

"I could show you."

His throat was as tight as his groin. "Show me."

Her face lifted and he met her mouth. Her lips were full and hot, giving as good as she got. He pushed her shirt up and cupped her breasts. But after days with her stuck in his head, he needed more. "Take your clothes off," he said, but he couldn't wait for her to start. His hands were quick as he stripped her down to the cross necklace nestled between her breasts. He stroked and nuzzled until he was ready to burst, but he couldn't stop touching her. He moved lower, and, when she gasped, he went back for another kiss, leaving enough space between them for his hands. Hers were busy too, all over him, under his shirt, touching his back and his stomach. She hooked her thumbs in his waistband and pushed his sweats down a couple of inches. Her fingers teased until he couldn't stand it anymore.

"Don't play games," he growled in her ear. He was too far gone. Too many dreams and imaginations and too little sex had his control shot.

She shoved his pants down and grabbed his ass with both hands. She was rubbing against him and making little moaning sounds. He kicked off his boots and clothes, put a hand under each thigh, and lifted her.

She wrapped her arms around his neck and sank down on him. Part way in, he couldn't stop now. He drove into her and then he did stop. He leaned his head against hers and closed his eyes, willing himself to last. But he'd never ever felt anything like it. His whole body was on fire. His head felt strange. An image flashed through his mind, a woman and a man in the forest. Her arms were open to him, long blond hair covering her breasts as her gown slid down her body and fell at her feet.

She wasn't moving, and he remembered how touching sometimes affected her. Hell, he wasn't sure it wasn't affecting him too. It felt as if he'd done this before. With her. "Are you OK?"

She nodded. "Intense," she said in a strangled voice. Her muscles clenched around him.

"Ah, damn." He couldn't stop. He pounded into her, fingers digging into her thighs, teeth grazing her neck, her ear. God, he could eat her alive. When the moment came, he felt like a bomb had gone off in his body. She dug her nails into his shoulders and gave a soft cry.

They stayed there, her back against the wall, heads together, bodies locked, for what seemed like minutes. It was as if time had stopped. He could have stayed here forever with her in his arms. When he felt himself softening, he pulled out. He grabbed a tissue on a nearby table and handed it to her.

She took it and held it between her legs. He took another tissue and cleaned himself off. "I'm sorry about your back." She probably had a wall burn. He should have carried her to the bed. "Sorry I didn't have a condom. I'm clean. I swear."

"I'm on birth control."

Hell, he hadn't even thought of pregnancy. That was how much she affected him. He tossed his tissue in the trash and pulled her into his arms. He wanted to carry her to the bed now and go to sleep in her arms, or maybe go for another round, but she felt rigid. "Are you OK?"

She nodded but didn't speak. There was still no light in the room. Just the moonlight coming in the window, but when he leaned back, he could see that she looked stunned.

"What's wrong?"

"I need to go to the bathroom."

"Sorry," he said again. Not for what happened. Sorry she was stuck with the mess. He would do it for her if she'd let him, but that would be damned awkward.

She pulled out of his arms and picked up her clothes. While she dressed, Jake pulled on his sweats. When she was finished, he moved closer and touched her arm. She looked at him like a startled rabbit and scampered toward the door. "Bathroom," she muttered, and disappeared into the hallway.

Jake sat on the bed, his mind and body blown. This was the closest thing he'd had to an out-of-body experience. It must be something to do with her abilities, but he'd never felt anything that even came close. He hoped Nathan didn't find out how incredible she was. Or did he already know? That might explain his obsession with her. Jake was still sitting there, staring at the door several minutes later when he realized what she'd muttered against his lips. She'd called him Lancelot. And then he realized she should have already gotten back.

Kendall sat on the toilet in shock. Holy crap, they'd finally done it. Her head and body were buzzing like a hive of bees. What was she going to say when she went back inside? *Wow, that was the most incredible thing I've ever experienced in my entire life.* Or *Let's try the other wall and see if it's as good.*

She leaned over, elbows resting on her legs, head in her hands, waiting for the buzzing to stop. It didn't. The dream must have triggered her emotion, killed her inhibitions. It had felt so real, like she was really there. This wasn't her first experience with sex, but the other times had been nothing like this. Most of them had been uncomfortable because of her sixth sense, all that skin rubbing together. And once when a condom broke, it had actually hurt her mind. But Jake . . . She'd felt his sensations along with hers, making it super intense, but in a good way. A really good way.

But they shouldn't have. What about condoms? It was stupid to have sex without one. She trusted Jake on some internal level, in some way she couldn't even explain, but he sometimes seemed callous about sex. And just because he thought he was clean wasn't a guarantee that he was. She was on birth control—she wasn't sure why since she so rarely had sex—but birth control failed lots of times. Orphanages were filled with kids as a result. Like Jake.

She decided to take a long shower, hoping to sort her thoughts before she faced him. She had dried off and dressed when she heard something outside the bathroom window. It had sounded like a curse. Surely he wasn't spying on her in the bathroom. Turning off the light, she opened the curtains a crack and peered out. The night was quiet, the moon soft. Saint Michael's Tower rose from the Tor like a scepter. Something moved in the bushes near the window, and she saw a figure moving along the wall. She couldn't tell who it was, or whether it was male or female. The figure moved to the far bedroom and appeared to be trying to look in the window. Jake snooping again?

Then the figure rose from its crouched position, and Kendall saw that it was a woman with red hair. Brandi. Kendall hurried from the bathroom and down the hall to the front door. She slipped outside as quietly as possible, keeping close to the side of the house. Easing around the corner, she saw Brandi, or whoever, hurrying away. From her movements, Kendall would have bet it was Brandi. Kendall was torn between going after her and going back to get Jake. Jake was better at tracking, but there wasn't time to spare.

Kendall heard a twig snap. She whirled as Jake stepped out of the shadows near the house.

"What are you doing here?" she asked.

"Chasing you. I'm not letting you run away from me."

"I wasn't. I heard something outside. Someone was looking in one of the bedroom windows. I thought it was you until I saw the red hair. I think it was Brandi."

"Damn, I knew that was her earlier. Which way did she go?"

"She ran into the garden. I think she went toward the fountain. Do you think you can pick up her tracks?" She knew he wanted to ask her more about Thomas and Iraq.

"I'll try, but you need to go back to the house."

"I'm staying."

"You're not wearing shoes."

"I'll manage."

He kicked off a boot and removed one sock, then did the same with the other foot and handed them to her. "Wear them. It's better than nothing. I don't need you getting sick on me."

"Do they stink?"

He scowled at her. "Haven't you heard it's rude to look a gift horse in the mouth?"

"Sorry. I was just . . ." being sarcastic to get them back on familiar territory after what they'd just done in the bedroom.

"I know. Come on." Jake entered the garden, eyes searching, body alert.

Kendall followed close behind him and looked at the trees and tall grass on the other side of the garden. "I don't know how you can see anything."

Jake touched a branch. "This way."

She followed and saw the branch had been broken.

"She's in a hurry," Jake said, studying signs in the branches and on the ground that she couldn't see.

They followed Brandi's trail—Jake followed the trail, Kendall followed Jake—to the road. She looked at the street. "This is Well House Lane."

"We'll never find her tracks here at night. Too many people and vehicles have been here. Let's head back. I'll come back tomorrow in the daylight and see if I can figure out where she headed."

"I think she was trying to look inside the bedroom at the end of the hall," Kendall said.

"Halle said that's the caretaker's room."

"You think Brandi is spying on the caretaker?" Kendall asked.

"According to Halle, he's in London."

"Brandi must know about the Blue Chalice and she's trying to sneak in."

"I think someone snuck in, but not Brandi. I heard a man talking in that room earlier."

"You sure it wasn't her?" Kendall asked.

"Yeah, it was a man's voice."

"Maybe you've got the rooms mixed up. It might be Larry's."

"No," Jake said. "It's not his room. I make it a point to know who's in which room."

"The caretaker could have returned," Kendall said.

"Halle said he hadn't. So who's in that room, and why is Brandi interested in it?"

"Nathan knew we were coming here to find the chalice. He might have gotten here first and started searching for the chalice."

"Then why didn't he answer when I knocked? We need to get inside that room," he said.

"We need to find Brandi too. She must be staying someplace nearby. I can't imagine her camping out in the woods."

"We'll check the local inns. See if someone has seen her."

They cut over to the road since it would be easier than walking through the trees and grass. Jake's socks were loose on her feet and they were getting damp from the dew, but she was grateful for the protection.

She felt more apprehensive as they neared the house. How could they sleep in the same room after this? When they reached the door, she stopped. "You go on. I'm going to check the area where I saw her and see if I can pick up anything."

Jake gave her a long look. "I'll wait."

"We need to wash your socks. I hope I haven't ruined them. If you want to throw them in the washer now, they'll be ready by morning." Kendall pulled off his socks and handed them to him, hoping he'd take the hint.

He stared her down. "I don't think Brandi is the only reason you ran away."

"Why would you say that?"

"We just had sex and you're acting as stiff as a damned statue."

"It's been a long time since I've . . ."

"Me too, but you don't see me running."

"Maybe you should," she said.

"Why would you say that?"

"Who wants to date someone who can look into his head?"

He hesitated for a split second. "Don't you think that should be my decision?"

"I'm not good with relationships." Or sex. Usually. She and Jake had been darned good. Better than good. Rocket-to-the-moon good.

"Neither am I, but there's something between us." He stepped closer, maneuvering them behind a bush. He touched her face then, a light stroke on her cheek with his thumb. "I know you feel it too." He pulled her into his arms, settling one leg between hers. Her body started tingling all the way to her toes. "I can't get you out of my head. You're there when I'm awake, when I'm asleep. I don't know what to do with you." He lowered his head and found her lips. Her lips parted and she kissed him back. The ground started to shake and she grabbed his shoulders. Wow, some kiss. Lights flashed and she was even more impressed.

He lifted his head, and she realized the lights were coming from the Tor. Balls of light circled above Saint Michael's Tower.

"What's that? A light show?"

CHAPTER FOURTEEN

I DON'T THINK SO," KENDALL SAID.

The front door banged open, and Alice and Halle came out. "Do you see them?" Alice gasped.

"I do," Halle whispered.

Kendall's skin felt icy as she watched the lights. There were several, all different colors, just as the woman at the gift shop had described. Blue, red, orange, and green. They danced in the sky for about thirty seconds, and just like that, they vanished.

Rhonda and Larry stood in the doorway, staring with their mouths open. "I've heard about the lights, but oh my," Rhonda said.

Jake and Kendall stepped out from behind the bush. Alice looked over and saw them. Her eyes were bright with awe. "First, you see King Arthur, and now the lights . . . It must be you causing these things to happen."

Kendall tried to deny it, but she knew they had made up their minds. After a few minutes, everyone but Kendall, Jake, and Halle hurried back inside, saying they needed to record the events and meditate.

Halle walked closer. "Are you sure you didn't have anything to do with that?"

"It wasn't me."

"Maybe it's because you summoned King Arthur."

She didn't tell Halle she hadn't summoned King Arthur. In fact, she suspected it was the other way around.

"I've got a good feeling about this," Halle said, looking at the Tor.

Kendall didn't. She felt the same cold she'd felt in the cave when the shadow hovered over her. She didn't know what the lights meant, but it wasn't good.

"You two are out late," Halle said, as if just realizing that they had already been outside.

"I felt like taking a walk."

"Barefoot?"

"Uh . . ."

"When she's barefoot," Jake said, "it helps her pick up sensations from the earth."

"Ooh, I never saw Lizzie do that. Maybe it was your meditation that drew the lights. If you've recovered from your vision, could you tell us more about it? Jake gave us a quick update earlier, but after seeing the lights, no one will be able to sleep."

Kendall didn't feel like talking, but if she spent some time with the group, she wouldn't be in the bedroom with Jake.

"Sure." She told them about the battle and her glimpse of King Arthur. She didn't tell them he had spoken to her. The group was ecstatic, and again, she felt a comfortable sense of belonging and acceptance. She didn't have to hide or pretend. Then the guilt set in. She was lying to them. Not about the visions. She wasn't telling them everything about the visions, but what troubled her was she was here under false pretenses, and these people believed in her. Kendall had always hated people who preyed on others' beliefs.

The group broke up. Kendall hung out till everyone had left. She dreaded going to the room. She wasn't sure how to act with Jake now. Or Nathan. Would he know what she and Jake had done? She felt as if it were written all over her face. She'd always been easy to read. Adam had tried to teach her a poker face. He said it came in handy at times. He was right. On the rare occasion when she shook someone's hand and knew they would be dead the next morning, it was best to keep a blank face. But she still hadn't mastered the art of hiding all her emotions. When she passed the bathroom, she heard the shower running. *Please let it be him.* She could get into bed and fall asleep first.

Halle had followed Kendall down the hall to the bedrooms. "Are you sure you're up to the events for the next couple of days? I can't tell you how much I appreciate what you've done so far. This is better than I expected."

She felt a sense of excitement and dread. "I'll be ready." Before now, she really believed he was just a myth, perhaps loosely based on some historical king or kings named Arthur, but after that glimpse on the battlefield, she was cutting to the front of the believer line.

Jake wasn't sure where he and Kendall would sleep since there were two beds. He didn't know whether she would expect him to sleep in another bed or be insulted if he did, since they'd just had incredible sex. Short, but mind blowing. Her bed, he decided, and turned off the shower.

He had considered going back to the hotel, but he wasn't ready to face Nathan. He wanted more time alone with Kendall so they could figure out where to go from here. It wasn't like picking up some girl in a bar. He worked with Kendall, respected her, admired her. He . . . He stopped there before his thoughts got him into quicksand.

After drying off, he put on his underwear and pants. The bedroom door was unlocked, which pissed him off. He was trying to protect her. If someone was sneaking around outside, she needed to be more cautious. She was too damned tough for her own good. Sure as hell too tough for his peace of mind.

She was in bed, but she wasn't asleep. He heard her breathing change when he walked in. She'd chosen the bed farthest away from the wall where they'd had sex. What did that mean? He didn't ask. He turned off the lamp and got into bed beside her.

"What are you doing?"

"Getting into bed?"

"You have your own."

"I like this one." He snuggled next to her, sharing her pillow.

She lay tense, staring at the ceiling. "You should have said something. I could have taken the other."

"Then I would have liked it better." He pulled her close. "Don't panic. I'm not going to try anything. I just want you next to me so I can make sure you don't sneak out to meet King Arthur"—or Lancelot—"or find the chalice by yourself. It's my job to keep you safe."

"This bed is small," she said.

He didn't mind. "I know. If you leave, I'll wake up. So what would you rather talk about first . . . sex, Lancelot, or those lights?"

His eyes had adjusted to the moonlight, and he saw her cheeks darken.

"We're going to have to talk about it sooner or later."

"Lancelot?"

"That ties in to the sex. Are you sure you want to start there?"

She looked alarmed. "The lights."

"What were they?" he asked.

"I don't know, but it's not good."

"You thinking aliens?"

"Aliens?"

"Circling lights in the sky . . . We have everything else weird and bizarre, might as well throw in some aliens. Now about Lancelot and the sex."

"What does Lancelot have to do with it?" she asked.

"You called me Lancelot."

Her green eyes widened, lit by the moonlight through the curtains. "I did."

"Yeah. Sounded like you were getting it on with him. Is that who you were having sex with? Him, not me?" That thought pissed him off.

"No. I don't know why I said his name. It was you." She frowned. "But we were dressed in strange clothes. Until . . . until we weren't dressed."

"Are you saying you were dreaming of us making love, but I was Lancelot? Like some kind of dream fantasy?"

She blushed again. "I guess it's because we're here where they once lived."

"Does that mean you were Guinevere?"

"That was just in the dream. After I woke up, I thought you were an intruder."

"I believe you. I've got a couple of bruises to prove it." He grinned. "You're good."

She looked startled, and he couldn't resist adding, "At both. And the second . . . way better than good."

She drew in a quick breath. "Back at you," she said, shocking him.

"Is that an invitation?" he asked, his body already taking it as a yes.

"That wouldn't be smart."

"But it would be fun."

"I'm sorry. This is awkward."

He leaned up on one elbow, looking down at her. "The fact that we had sex or that you want to do it again?"

"That's not what I said."

"You don't want it again?"

"I just meant it's hanging between us."

"I could put it someplace else, so it's not hanging between us."

"Would you stop?"

"Sorry," he said, grinning. "I love playing with you, and I mean that in every sense of the word." His grin faded. He stroked her cheek. "We had sex. I wanted it. You wanted it. I have no regrets, except I wish it had lasted longer. Next time it won't be so quick."

"Next time?"

"We can keep on . . . I don't know . . . seeing each other?"

"You mean naked?" she asked.

"I wouldn't complain, but other people might. I meant like"—he cleared his throat—"dating. I'm rusty. Not sure I remember how. 'Course I was rusty with sex too." He let his hand drift over her hip. "And I think that worked out."

"I don't know what to say."

"Yes would work." He lay down. The bed was so small they couldn't help but touch. "You feel like a statue again. You don't have to worry that I'll take advantage of you. Like I said in the tower, when you come to my bed, it'll be because you want to be there, not because you're running from something. And it doesn't just go for beds. That goes for walls, chairs, tables, sinks, showers, rocks, the ground, and anyplace else you can think of that we can do it."

She stared at him. "OK."

He didn't know what that meant, but he pulled her into his arms and settled her against his chest. "Night."

But his brain kept going, and it wasn't long before a disturbing thought occurred to him. If he was Lancelot in her dream and she was Guinevere, then who was Arthur? Nathan?

A voice woke Kendall in the night. She thought Jake was talking to her until she raised her head and saw that she was sprawled across his chest, one leg draped between his, and he was still asleep.

She tried to move away, but his arm tightened around her. "Lilly," he muttered.

Lilly? Kendall felt a rush of jealousy, followed by grief. Was Lilly one of the girls in Iraq? She remembered the vision of the grave she had seen when she touched Jake in the catacombs. Shallow, dark, with a swath of blond hair against the dirt. And the wooden doll he carried in his pack. She'd had the sensation of dirt filling her mouth and nose when she touched it. The doll and the grave had to be connected.

She looked at the clock. It was late. Everyone should be asleep. This would be a good time to look for the chalice. She tried moving again, but Jake put his other arm around her, effectively trapping her. A nice trap, she thought, relaxing against him, and gave up the notion of searching for the chalice tonight. She lay there for a few minutes, trying to go to sleep, but the feel of Jake underneath her, his arm wrapped around her, made her think about earlier, him and her, bodies hot with passion and desperation. She squirmed and considered waking him again. All it would take was to slide her hand lower and they would do it again, here in the bed.

No, Kendall. You work with him. It'll complicate things worse than they already are.

But her resolve didn't keep her from dropping a kiss on his chest.

When she finally met sleep, King Arthur was waiting for her on the battlefield. It was different this time. She didn't feel as if she was actually there, but she did see the same scene, the knights and the horses, and this time she heard what King Arthur said.

"Find the chalice. It's the key."

She shot up in bed and looked around the room. Jake was gone and the sun was shining through the window. She looked at the clock. Nine thirty a.m. She'd overslept. Kendall jumped up. She had just pulled one leg from her sweats when the door opened and Jake walked in. She did a one-footed dance and grabbed a pillow to put in front of her.

"Don't bother on my account. I've already seen it."

Kendall threw him a scowl. "Why didn't you wake me up?"

"When you didn't open your eyes after I peeled you off my chest, I figured you needed the sleep."

Kendall rolled her eyes. "About that knighthood application . . ."

"I behaved very knightly." He grinned. "I could have done a lot more than sleep."

"It wasn't my idea for you to share the bed."

"But you didn't kick me out. Actions speak louder than words." He dropped a kiss on her nose. "Breakfast is ready. I didn't want you to miss out."

"I thought we were meeting everyone at nine thirty."

"They postponed the trip until noon. Alice, Sandy, and Rhonda have headaches, and Halle has the mother of all headaches. Larry has a stomach thing. I'd wait a few minutes before you use the bathroom."

"I know what King Arthur said."

Jake frowned. "You saw him again?"

"I dreamed about the vision, but this time I read his lips."

"Read his lips in a dream? Your gift is damned strange."

"I know, but what can I do? I can't send it back."

"So what did Arthur say?"

"He said, 'Find the chalice. It's the key.'"

"Key to what?"

"I don't know, but we're in a house with a powerful chalice, so I'm going to find it."

"Now?" he asked.

"Why not?"

"That's not a good idea with everyone here. I planned to search last night, but I slept like the dead."

"I have to find it."

"You distract them. I'll look for it. Tell them about this latest dream. They're here to find Arthur, so give them Arthur."

Kendall nodded. "Good idea." She owed them that much.

"I'll go tell them you've had another experience to share over breakfast." Jake walked to the door. Kendall went to the bathroom and brushed her teeth and hair. She pulled it back with the ponytail holder she was still using. It irritated her that she knew more about the anorexic owner of the stupid hair tie than she knew about Nathan's location and safety. She saw a mark on her face and leaned closer. There was a cross imprinted on her cheek. She stared at it, and then realized it was from where she'd slept on Jake's chest. She rubbed at it, but it would be a while before it went away. Maybe no one would notice. She hurried to the dining room where everyone was anxious to hear about her new experience.

"Oh my God. There's a cross on your cheek." Alice hurried to Kendall's side, her expression as rapt as if she'd seen the Virgin Mary. "Everyone, come and look. Kendall has a cross imprinted on her cheek."

Everyone crowded around and Kendall opened her mouth to explain. Jake shook his head no and slipped out of the room. The mark was certainly a distraction. The group was electrified to hear she'd had another dream. She gave them more details about the battlefield and seeing Arthur and his knights fighting, but she didn't mention the chalice, though she wondered if she should. They might bring the Blue Chalice out sooner. But she needed to examine it in private, not with an audience. She dragged the story out as long as she could to give Jake more time to find the chalice, but it was disconcerting having everyone staring at the imprint of the cross that burned accusingly into her cheek. Jake showed up and rescued her as she was about to come clean and tell them the mark was from Jake's necklace. She left the group talking excitedly about the day's events.

"With a little encouragement, you might get them to start a fan club," Jake whispered as they walked back to the bedroom.

"They think the cross was some kind of sign. We'll probably burn in hell because of this. Did you find the chalice?" she asked when the door closed.

"No, but I think I know where it is. The Upper Room is locked."

"You didn't pick the lock?"

"I thought I heard someone in the hall."

"Everyone was with me. No one left the room."

"It must be whoever is in that last bedroom." Jake hurried toward the room and tried the door. Locked. "I'll pick it."

"You can't pick it with everyone here. If someone is using the room, he's getting in and out some way."

"He must be using the window. I'll see if I can pick up his trail outside."

"I'll nose around for the chalice. Maybe I can sense something."

After Jake left, Kendall asked Halle about the Blue Chalice, and she confirmed that the Chalice Trust kept it locked up in the Upper Room.

Jake came back a few minutes later. "I found footprints leading to the street. A man's. No way to track him on the road."

"Halle said the Blue Chalice is kept in the Upper Room, but we can't get in there with everyone here. And we can't ask her to show it to us. She doesn't even have the key."

"If we could get out of the Camelot trip, I can pick the lock or go through the window," Jake said.

"She thinks the caretaker will be back by tomorrow or the next day. We can wait that long. We can't abandon them," Kendall said. "They're counting on us."

"Counting on you. We need to find this chalice."

"You could stay and find it," she said.

"No. I'm not letting you go alone. And it wouldn't do me any good. You're the one that needs to touch it."

"Then let's wait for the caretaker. We have a lot of other stuff to explore. The Tor, the abbey, and the Chalice Well. I want to see the actual well. We only saw the fountain that the well flows into. And then I want to see the White Spring across the street."

"When we're finished, there are a couple of inns nearby. We can see if Brandi's been there."

Kendall would have preferred to go to the well alone, but she knew she would have a hard time convincing Jake. He was incredibly protective of her, just as Adam had been. As they left the house, she studied him . . . his build, his face, bone structure. Some kids were easily recognizable as adults. Some weren't. She couldn't tell with Jake. He could have been Adam, but there was nothing specific. Adam hadn't had any birthmarks or noticeable scars. He should have, as many times as they got bruised and scraped, but the scars always faded. Both of them had been amazingly healthy growing up.

Kendall and Jake slipped into the garden before it opened to the public. They followed the stone path to the Vesica Piscis pool, the fountain, and finally the Chalice Well. The well was in the middle of a recessed area paved with stone and surrounded by trees. The cover of the well was made of iron with two interlocking circles. Kendall immediately felt something calming here, but there was also power.

Jake seemed to sense that she needed solitude. He hung back a bit, exploring the trees, while she went to the well. She sat on the edge, as thousands must have done before her. At first she felt the calming presence, and then the images started to come. She saw a long table and heard men's voices speaking in . . . Hebrew? A long-fingered hand, gentle but calloused, picked up a cup and lifted it to his lips. A sense of peace filled her, love, and then terrible dread. Fear, followed by resolution, acceptance. *It must be done. There was no other way.*

The image changed, and she sensed pain, terrible pain, though she didn't feel it. She saw blood dripping from a foot, where a nail had been driven through the tissue. She heard a woman's soft cries and saw a man standing nearby, tired, weary, his soul torn with grief. If he had done more, could he have stopped them from killing him? Stopped the sacrifice? No. It was meant to be.

Kendall's head was starting to hurt, but she couldn't stop the images. She heard a loud agonized cry and a male hand held out a cup, which began to fill with blood. Not just any cup. The same cup the man had drunk from at the table.

The Holy Grail.

CHAPTER FIFTEEN

KENDALL LOOKED LIKE A STATUE SITTING ON THE EDGE OF the well. Her eyes were open, unblinking, and Jake knew she was someplace else. He was afraid to interrupt whatever was happening, and afraid not to. But when she gave a small cry, he couldn't wait any longer. He rushed over to her, knelt down, and touched her hand. "Kendall?"

She blinked several times and her gaze focused. "What?"

"What happened? What did you see?"

"Jesus."

"Huh?" Of all the things he'd expected her to say, that was the last.

Her fingers tightened on his hand. "I was there."

"Where?"

"The Last Supper. The Crucifixion. I saw it. I heard it."

"Holy—" Jake cut off the curse. "No wonder you're pale."

"It was incredible," she said, her voice breathless with awe. "The legends are right. Joseph did bring the Holy Grail here."

"The Holy Grail. So we're looking for the Holy Grail and the Fountain of Youth?" Jake almost cursed but stopped himself. He knew Kendall well enough to know she wasn't faking. But his scientific brain still balked at some of this stuff. But the other parts, the one that had seen Kendall's gift in action, and the boy in the orphanage dreaming that he was a secret knight on a mission for King Arthur so he didn't have to believe no one wanted him, those parts of him wanted to believe it was real.

Kendall's shoulders were drooping. She was tired. These visions sapped her strength.

"Can you walk?"

She nodded and started to stand. Her knees buckled and she sat down again. "Maybe not."

"Do you want me to carry you?"

"No. Just give me a minute. Let me close my eyes. Sit with me."

He sat beside her, slightly behind, and let her rest against him. He could feel some kind of energy coming off her. An aura . . . He didn't know what the hell it was, but it was so powerful it was frightening. He wasn't about to move and leave her to deal with it alone. His admiration for her grew, as if she weren't already on a damned pedestal. He closed his eyes and put his arms around her, pulling her against his chest. It was like getting a mild shock, but without the pain. He picked up flashes of something. Sensations maybe. He couldn't begin to describe or decipher them, but it felt as if they were wrapped in a soft cocoon of light. Just him and her. Nothing else existed. He couldn't have said how much time passed. It was as if time didn't exist. Then he felt Kendall stir in his arms. He didn't want to leave but he heard voices nearing. The gardens had opened.

"We should go," Kendall said, starting to stand.

Jake helped her up. She was still wobbly but able to walk. She seemed a little stronger when they got to their room, but he insisted she rest. "You know how these things affect you." He pulled off her shoes and made her lie down. "We have a lot of work to do here. We have to find that chalice and figure out why we're here.

I need you mentally and physically strong." He hesitated. "Nathan needs you to be strong. Curse or not, if he doesn't get rid of his condition, it'll kill him."

"You're worried about him too."

"I work for him. He's a paycheck."

"You don't believe that any more than I do. I do need to rest. The group is counting on me to find King Arthur."

"If anybody in the world can do it, you can."

She gave him a tired smile. "That's not what you used to say. You're really working on your knighthood status."

"I know I was . . . skeptical when we first met."

"You mean obnoxious?"

"Obnoxious then. Sorry, but I don't trust easily. I like what I can see and feel."

"Most people do. It's OK. You're being very supportive now."

"Well, a knight must do what he can. *'And always do to ladies, damsels, and gentlewomen succor, upon pain of death.'*"

"Where'd you learn that?" Kendall asked. "That's part of the knight's oath."

"Must have read it somewhere."

"What about the White Spring and the inns," she asked. "We need to find Brandi."

"I'll look for Brandi while you rest. Later, we'll go to the White Spring."

She nodded. "I am zonked. I get so tired of this."

"I know. But ninety-nine percent of the world would give their right hand to glimpse what you do. I don't understand it. I don't always like it, but it is a gift."

"Not a curse?" she asked, eyes closed.

Her hair was down, falling over her shoulders. Not a drop of makeup as far as he could tell, but she looked so beautiful it made his chest ache. Hell, what was wrong with him? He'd known her for only a few days, but it felt like it had been a lifetime.

He left her there and walked down the street to the closest two inns. At each, he told the innkeeper he was looking for his friend. He got lucky at the second one. A woman matching Brandi's description had been staying there. But his luck didn't last. She had checked out early that morning. Cold feet, he guessed, after they'd almost caught her. The owner said she'd asked about another inn in town.

Jake caught a taxi and went past the abbey into the main part of town. It was obvious from the storefronts that the town was immersed in the legends of King Arthur, the abbey, and the Tor. The area catered to everything from religion to paganism. He checked the inn where he'd hoped to find Brandi, but she wasn't there. He found a café with Internet service and searched for other nearby lodging. He made several calls with no luck. Then he tried Nathan at the hotel, but he didn't answer. Jake hadn't told Kendall, but he was getting concerned that Nathan hadn't contacted them. Sure he was worried that he'd hurt Kendall, but he could have left a message telling them he was either still cursed or cured.

It was a short taxi ride to the hotel, but Nathan wasn't in his room. Or he wasn't answering the door. Jake was about to get management to open the door, when a maid walked by. When questioned, she said she had seen Nathan leave his room yesterday. At least he was alive.

Jake walked out to hail a taxi and glimpsed a woman with red hair. Red hair, near their hotel? And she looked just like Brandi. Jake ran toward her, but when he reached the corner where he'd seen her, she wasn't there. He checked the shops nearby, but there was no sign of her. Maybe it was his imagination or another redhead.

He didn't want to leave Kendall any longer. He started to hail a taxi when one pulled up across the street. A woman got out. She looked at Jake as he approached, and her eyebrows rose in appreciation. He'd gotten used to the look. Sometimes he took what was offered. Sometimes he didn't. Lately, he'd been too caught up with the whole business with Nathan and Iraq to worry about women. Now, he was too caught up with a green-eyed blonde.

Ignoring the woman's interest, he grabbed the taxi and went back to the house. When he walked inside, Halle was planning the night's activities. "Good. You're back. I hope Kendall's feeling well enough for the moonlight tour and séance tonight."

"I think she'll be fine. She was tired. The visions take a toll."

"They did with Lizzie too, but Kendall's better than Lizzie. You think Kendall would be interested in doing another tour after this is over? I was thinking Stonehenge and Avebury. I haven't been since last year."

Jake didn't want to disappoint Halle, so he said something vague and then went to check on Kendall. She was still resting. He pulled off his pants and tossed them on the other bed, then climbed in beside her, moving close to her back.

"What are you doing?"

He draped his hand over her stomach. "Snuggling."

"You can't wear your pants while you snuggle?"

"You know me better than that."

"The least you could do is to warn me before you undress."

"And miss that look on your face?" He smiled. "How are you feeling?"

"Better. Still tired."

"I don't think we've recovered from that damned cave. I'm still groggy."

"I guess traveling through a portal will do that. And we lost a day, so we're behind on sleep." She started to get up.

He put his hand on her waist. "Where you going?"

"Bathroom. Is that OK?"

"Unless you need help."

"I'll manage."

She crawled over him, but he trapped her. "You have to pay the toll," he said, nuzzling her neck.

She kissed him hard and then jumped up. He watched her go, wondering what he was going to do about her. She was inside his head, and he was afraid there was no getting her out. He closed his eyes for a second. Yep. Still there. He must have nodded off, because when he opened them, she was there too, but this time she was standing on her head with her back against the wall.

"What the hell are you doing?"

She flopped back over onto her feet. "Trying to wake up, get my blood pumping."

"I can think of some better ways to get your blood flowing."

"I imagine you could."

"I was thinking of a foot massage," he said, smiling innocently.

"Really? Not something more . . . carnal?"

He leaned back against the pillow and watched her. "I'm working on my application for knighthood. But if you want something less chivalrous and more carnal, let me know."

"I'll be sure to do that. But right now, we need to check the White Spring. We should have time to go before dinner."

He groaned and got out of bed. He wanted to grab her and climb back in, spend the next twelve hours or so just lying in bed with her, but she was right. There was work to do. "Are you feeling up to this séance tonight?"

"I feel much better."

They grabbed bottles of water and started across the street. The White Spring didn't have a trust established to protect it, like the Chalice Well, but there was an attendant, a young man, who welcomed them. The spring was inside a building, dimly lit with candles. There were several flowers and gifts lying nearby.

"Why is it called the White Spring?" Jake asked.

"Because of the calcium," Kendall said. "It has a sweet taste. The Chalice Well has a lot of iron, which leaves a red stain on the rocks. It's interesting that the springs are so close but so different. Both of them are supposed to have powers to heal."

No one else was at the White Spring. Kendall bent down and touched the water, then cupped her hand and drank some. Jake stood nearby, wondering if it would have the same effect on her. She stood after a minute and shook her head. They looked around for a minute longer and then left.

"You get anything?" he asked.

"It's powerful and old, just like the Chalice Well, but no visions. I think my focus was off. Maybe because the attendant was watching. But I do think the two springs are connected."

"You think they're connected to the Fountain of Youth?"

"I know the Chalice Well is connected to the Holy Grail, and the two springs are certainly in close proximity. They've flowed steadily for over two thousand years, even in drought. That's pretty amazing. But I don't know if that means either of them is connected to the Fountain of Youth. I wish we could get up with Nathan to see if he's discovered anything."

"You mean if his curse is gone."

"I'm worried about him."

"You worry about him a lot. He'll find us when he's ready."

"I'm afraid he's in danger."

"Nathan's always in danger. He has enemies."

"This is different," Kendall said. "That shadow in the cave. I think it did something to my memories, but I believe it's after Nathan."

"He's a big boy," Jake said. "He can take care of himself."

"Is that why you're so worried about him?" Kendall asked.

When they arrived at the house, Halle's face was glowing. "We've just had a late addition to the group. A message was just · delivered."

"I thought the others were sick?" Larry asked.

"This guy's new."

"Someone new will be fun," Rhonda said.

Sandy agreed. "It brings more energy to the group. Look at how much has happened since Kendall and Jake joined us."

"I suppose you're right," Alice said. "Jake and Kendall are new, and they're fun."

"I think you'll be glad I allowed him to join." Halle looked like she might burst, and when she made the announcement, Kendall understood why Halle, with her worries over money, was so excited. "It's Nathan Larraby, the billionaire."

King Arthur, Jesus, and now Nathan. There was always some other man in her head. He grimaced. "Told you he'd find us."

There were exclamations of approval, and even Alice was agreeable. "I've heard of him."

"Nathan Larraby is the most eligible bachelor in America," Rhonda said with the authority of someone who was an expert on eligible bachelors. "They say he's drop-dead gorgeous."

"I bet he's the handsome man I saw outside the gardens earlier," Alice said. "When I went for a walk, he was looking right at the house."

Maybe he was the one sneaking in the window of the caretaker's room. Brandi had probably seen him and followed him here. Kendall was worried about what Brandi might do. The fact that she was here meant she had followed them, through the maze or by other means, and was more desperate to destroy the relics than they had thought. And after Kendall's vision at the well, she was convinced there was at least one relic here.

"I don't think I've ever seen his face," Halle said.

"With all that money and looks, he avoids the public," Rhonda said. "Every gold digger out there is probably after him."

"He must be shy," Alice said. "I like a shy man."

Jake stopped rolling his eyes and, grunting under his breath, stood. "Look at the time. We're going to be late for Camelot."

There was a rush for the bus.

"Did Halle say when Nathan was arriving?" Kendall asked when they were seated on the bus. She was anxious to tell him about her vision.

Jake did something to his boot. Probably checking to see if his knife was there. "Everyone was too busy drooling over him."

Cadbury Mound was about ten miles away. The bus driver gave them the background on Cadbury as they wove their way through the countryside. "Most people believe the hill fort is Camelot," he said. "There used to be a castle here, Cadbury Castle, and historians and archaeologists have found evidence of stones dating even farther back, the right time period to have been Camelot. Just like with Tintagel Castle where Arthur was born, just on the northern coast of Cornwall. Doubters say it couldn't have been Arthur's birthplace, since it was built later, but there are older ruins underneath, covered up by earth and time. There are some who swear that on Christmas Eve, King Arthur and his knights can be seen in a ghostly procession crossing from Cadbury Mound." The drive took them through rolling countryside and a charming village before dropping them off at a parking lot at the base of the mound.

"Camelot," Alice said, pulling in a deep breath, after she'd exited the bus. "Isn't it exciting? Too bad Mr. Larraby hasn't arrived yet. Where will he sleep?"

"He'll have to share a room with Larry," Halle said.

Larry nodded, looking intrigued. "I don't mind as long as he's neat."

The path led between two buildings. They started off, Larry and Halle in the lead.

"Have you been to Cadbury Mound before?" Kendall asked Alice.

"Twice," she said. "I'm certain it's Camelot. There's a presence here. I can just feel Arthur. Maybe he'll contact you again."

"Let's hope," Jake muttered.

"This is only my second time here," Halle said, falling back. The climb was getting steeper now. "It's one of Lizzie's favorite places."

Jake and Kendall quickly moved ahead of the group. He took her hand and guided her around a large rock. When they had passed it, he didn't let go. "Have you thought about my suggestion?"

"You mean the . . ."

"Dating."

"I'm not sure. I need to focus on Arthur." She could hear voices as the others approached. Jake gave her a sizzling look and lowered his head. His lips locked on hers, and he kissed her until her knees went weak. He leaned back just enough that she could catch her breath, then took her bottom lip between his teeth and gently bit. Kendall heard chuckling from behind them. Jake raised his head and gave her a cocky grin.

"Arthur might be a king, but he can't make you come."

Kendall's tongue was frozen, but by the time she could speak, they had reached the top of the hill and the tour group was catching up, so she was spared from having to comment.

There were a few other people here. Kendall put the kiss and her vision at the well out of her head. Like the Tor, Cadbury Mound was much higher than the surrounding countryside and offered a magnificent view. The top of the hill was level. Along the sides, the earth had been fortified to protect against an enemy attack. She could well believe it had once been Camelot. "It is beautiful," she said, imagining how it might have looked back then with a castle and knights on horses. As it had looked in her vision of King Arthur? Had she seen Camelot?

Everyone in the group had been here before, so they split up and explored.

"Are you getting anything?" Jake asked Kendall.

"No. I'll keep walking around and see if I pick anything up." After that kiss, she wasn't sure what he might do if they wandered out of sight. "I should go alone, focus my mind."

He nodded. "Alone? Here?"

"My God, Jake. We're on a hillside with grass and trees. It isn't likely that someone followed us here."

He frowned. "Don't go far. Stay in sight. Call out if you need me."

She looked at him—sexy, fierce, protective—and she dreadfully feared that she did need him.

She walked the place, sitting, touching the hill, trying to connect with Camelot. With Arthur. She needed to know more about the chalice, but she got nothing. She looked back as she walked down the side of the hill. Jake was watching her. Kendall heard a noise in the trees. A woman's laugh, her voice soft, and a man's deeper voice. Lovers, she thought. Something inside her ached. She didn't want to intrude, but the sound was so familiar she couldn't stop moving toward the laughter. Soon, she was running. She had to see him, one more time.

She passed the crofter's cottage and entered the enchanted woods. The trees were tall here, with springy moss underfoot. A small wooden bridge spanned a narrow stream. The water almost seemed to sing as it washed over the rocks, calling to her.

She found him waiting for her in their usual place. She stepped into his arms, and he kissed her as they undressed. When they were both naked, they lay on the ground and he made love to her. Her heart filled to bursting with love for him. Her Lancelot.

Kendall blinked and looked around. Where was she? What was she doing here? A shadow crept across the sky, and she felt the same sense of danger that she'd felt from the shadow in the cave. Something inside her head screamed at her to get out. She turned and started back the way she had come. The path didn't look the same. Nothing looked the same. Where was she? She couldn't be that far from the others. She felt something behind her and turned to look just as she hit a wall of air. "Jake!"

CHAPTER SIXTEEN

J AKE FELT A PRICKLE IN HIS SHOULDERS. HE OFTEN FELT IT when something was wrong, and something was sure as hell wrong now. Kendall was in his sight one moment, vanished the next. He ran after her. What the hell? Had she stepped into the trees to avoid him after the talk of dating?

A sense of urgency knotted his guts. He needed to get to Kendall now. He often had these gut feelings. They didn't make much sense, but they'd saved his life more than once. He hadn't thought of it until now, but his team used to tease him about being psychic. They knew he was skeptical of all things paranormal. If they could see him now, he guessed they would be having a good laugh.

He reached the spot where he'd lost sight of her. The trees were thicker here. He was surprised she would come this far unless she sensed something. His own sense of urgency grew stronger, but he also felt aroused, as if he'd been here. With her. An image shot through his head, a man and woman making love on the ground. What the hell? He pulled out his knife and started running as he called her name. "Kendall?"

Jake heard her voice then. He *felt* it. He locked on one spot ahead of him in the trees. It seemed to waver, like heat rising off pavement. He ran toward it, his heart pounding. He couldn't have said why, but he reached out, feeling for her, and in the midst of the air he felt her wrist. He grabbed it and pulled. Kendall burst out of nowhere. Her eyes were wide, her face pale. Where the hell had she come from?

"What happened?" she asked, holding on to him.

"I don't know. Where were you?" Because she sure as hell wasn't on the same hillside as he had been.

"I don't know. I was walking, and I found this beautiful forest. It was like a fairy tale. Like in my dream." She turned and looked back at the thick trees where Jake had found her. "That's not what I saw. Maybe it was a vision like the one with King Arthur."

"It wasn't a damned vision. I saw you the whole time in the King Arthur vision. This time you weren't even there. I had to pull you out of thin air. We're getting out of here. If Arthur wants to talk to you, he'll have to do it someplace else." He pulled her up the hill, and when they reached the top, the others were waiting for them, frowning.

"Are you OK?" Halle asked. "We were worried. We couldn't find you. Didn't you hear us calling?"

"We didn't hear you," Jake said.

"We felt something . . ." Sandy paused.

"Odd," Larry said.

"We didn't just feel it. We saw it," Rhonda said.

Alice looked nervous. "A cloud appeared right there in the sky, over the area where you had gone."

"It was more like a mist," Sandy said. "What happened to you?"

"I got lost." Kendall said. She still looked shaken.

"Here?" Larry said.

"I bet it was the enchanted forest," Alice said.

Sandy nodded. "There are rumors that an enchanted forest surrounded Camelot. Someone with your abilities could probably find it."

"Let's get out of here," Jake said. The others looked surprised to see his knife. "I'm her bodyguard as well as her assistant."

"And her husband," Sandy reminded him.

"Right." He put the knife away, and they all walked down Arthur's hill a lot faster than they had come up. But by the time they got to the bus, they were feeling more comfortable with the eerie experience. Relief gave a false sense of security. He'd often had a close call and afterward felt like he could take on an army. Or ten women. Not that he'd ever tried. For all his talk, he was a one-woman man. One at a time, that was. And now, just one.

"I've never felt anything like that," Alice said. "I wish I'd been there."

She would have died of fright, Jake thought. Kendall was tougher than most women, and the experience had shaken her.

"Another grand adventure," Halle said, playing up the event. "We should stop for tea."

"I'm not sure Kendall is up to it," Jake said. He wasn't sure he was. He didn't know what had happened, but he must have tapped into whatever Kendall was experiencing. Making love, it had felt like. Who had she been with? Him? Lancelot? Someone else?

"I'm fine," she said. "It might be nice to have a change of scenery."

The bus dropped them off in Glastonbury. It was Kendall's first glance at the town.

"We could go to the Abbey Tea Rooms," Rhonda said.

The group agreed that it sounded lovely. Jake would have preferred a hamburger and beer, but the others seemed enthused at the prospect of tea and scones. He found the tea shop and held the door as everyone entered. After everyone had finished, they decided to walk around the town for thirty minutes and meet back in front of the tea shop. Jake planned to sneak back to the house and look for the chalice. He didn't want to wait until tonight. They could make some excuse to the others later. He convinced Kendall, and they started toward the bus stop. A small group of people walked past, and he used the excuse to pull her close. It was troubling how much he wanted to feel her next to him.

Should he buy her something since they'd slept together? He wasn't sure of protocol. The women he'd slept with had been looking for the same thing he had. A night of distraction or fun, no strings attached. With Kendall, he felt tied up like a mummy.

"What the hell happened back there at Camelot?"

"I don't know. I felt as if I'd been there before, as if I were someone else. I had to see . . . him." Kendall frowned.

"Lancelot?"

"I think so. It's the same dream."

"It was damned odd. Like déjà vu."

"You felt it?"

"I felt something."

"The man and woman?"

He nodded.

"Then it changed. I felt something dark, like that shadow in the cave."

"You said there were supposed to be fairies under the Tor. If that was some kind of enchanted forest like Sandy said, maybe fairies lured you there."

Kendall stopped on the street, staring at him. "Jake Stone, are you saying you believe in fairies?"

He grunted. "Well, if you put it that way."

She laughed, and that made him smile. He was glad to see her mood lighten, even if it was at his expense.

"That fishing boat on the lake's looking better and better."

"Fishing isn't as exciting as this," Kendall said.

"I'd rather deal with fish. We're talking stuff that shouldn't exist."

"You don't like being out of control, do you?" Kendall asked.

"Does anyone?"

Kendall smiled. "I guess badass bodyguards have a harder time with it than most."

"Don't forget knights. If you're not well, I would be honored to tote you home if you feel faint." He wasn't sure why he chose that moment to look across the street. He saw a man watching them. He turned and disappeared into a small group. "Get inside that shop," Jake said, nudging her toward the door of a small shop behind them.

"Why?"

"Someone was watching us. I'm going to follow him."

"Maybe it's Nathan," she said hopefully.

"I can move faster alone. Go, please."

Surprisingly, she did as he asked, which would have pleased him if he hadn't been sure it was out of desperation to find Nathan. The man was tall and wore a hood, but he didn't move like Nathan. Still, something was familiar about the man. Jake hurried across the street, trying to catch a glimpse of him through the crowd. Both Jake and the man were taller than most of the people walking, but with everyone moving around, it was hard to keep him in sight. The group passed a street and the stranger disappeared. Jake hurried to the street. The man was running away. He looked back at Jake, but the hood made it impossible to identify him. Jake started running hard. He was catching up when the stranger darted down another street. Jake burst around the corner, but the street was empty. There were several shops. He could have gone into any one of them.

He jogged down the street, looking in windows, but didn't see him. On the next street, a car started and pulled out with a squeal. He must have run out the back door of one of the shops. "Damn."

What if there were two of them? Kendall was alone. Jake hurried back to the shop where he'd left her. She was watching out the window, green eyes narrowed. When she saw him, her face relaxed. She stepped out onto the street to meet him.

"No luck?"

"I lost him."

"Was it Nathan?"

"No. But he looked familiar. I've seen him somewhere."

"Here in Glastonbury?"

"I don't think so."

"If it wasn't Nathan, who could it be? Who knows we're here? It's not as if we flew here by plane. We fell through a maze." Her eyes widened. "Could it have been Raphael? Did he have long hair?"

"He was wearing a hood. Let's grab a bus before the others start back. I'd rather see the chalice now." They hurried toward the bus stop, but the others were waiting. Too late. They'd have to put off finding the chalice yet again.

Back on the bus, Halle moved to the seat in front of Kendall and Jake. She looked worried. "You aren't injured, are you?" she asked, her voice then dropping to a whisper. "We can't lose you now."

"I'll be fine," Kendall said.

As they got closer to the house, the talk on the bus turned to the magnificent Nathan Larraby. Alice was the only one who had actually seen him; at least she thought it was him since he was *so handsome,* but the others joined in his physical and financial praises until Jake felt like jumping off the bus. "If I hear another person say how amazing Nathan is, I'm going to walk the rest of the way."

"Jealous?" Kendall smiled. "You shouldn't be. The women are drooling over you every time you walk by."

By the time the doors of the bus opened, Jake had seriously considered using pressure points to put them all out. Larry wasn't much better. He seemed as intrigued with Nathan as the women were. "Finally," Jake exclaimed, getting off the bus.

"I hope he's here," Kendall said. That irked him even more than the women and Larry gushing over Nathan. But Nathan wasn't there. Everyone scattered to get ready for dinner and the moonlight tour at the abbey.

While Kendall showered, Jake tried to call Nathan. He still wasn't answering his cell phone, and the hotel said he wasn't in. Selfish bastard. Didn't he know Kendall was worried?

He left the room and heard a voice coming from the caretaker's bedroom. He hurried to the door. It was locked, but he heard a window opening. Jake ran out of the house and around to the window. He saw someone running toward the Chalice Well. A woman with red hair.

After Kendall showered and dressed, she went to find Jake. The hallway was quiet. She could hear everyone laughing in the kitchen. This might be the best time to at least touch the door to the Upper Room and see if she picked up anything. She climbed the stairs. The familiar buzzing filled her head, and her breath felt heavy in her lungs.

"What are you doing?"

Kendall turned around and saw Halle at the bottom of the stairs.

"I was just looking around. Is this the Upper Room?"

"Yes. As I mentioned, it stays locked. I was looking for you." Halle held up an envelope. "You have a message."

Finally! It must be from Nathan. She hurried down and took the envelope. *Kendall* was written across the front. "Thank you," she told Halle, and went to her room to read in private.

Kendall closed the door. She opened the letter and took out a folded piece of paper with the words, *Be careful. You're in danger.*

CHAPTER SEVENTEEN

S HE RAN BACK TO FIND HALLE. "WHO DELIVERED THE LETTER?" Kendall asked.

"A woman."

"What did she look like?"

Halle frowned. "She was young, maybe late twenties, kind of nervous. She just said, 'Could you please give this to Kendall Morgan,' and then she left. Like I said, she seemed jumpy. She kept looking over her shoulder. There was one thing I noticed. She had on a hat, but a few strands of hair had slipped out. Really pretty red hair."

Brandi.

"Is everything OK?"

"Yes. I need to find Jake."

"I saw him going toward the gardens about ten minutes ago."

"I think I'll take a walk too."

"Don't be too long. We're having fish and chips at seven, and then the bus will take us to the abbey."

"I'll be ready," Kendall said, edging toward the door. Clutching the letter, she hurried toward the garden. Jake would be pissed that she'd left the house, but it was daylight and she had to let him know about the letter. Alice walked in from the street. "Kendall, I see you're getting some fresh air too. I hope you're recovered from that incident at Camelot. I'm so excited about tonight. Maybe we'll even see King Arthur."

"If we're lucky," Kendall said. "Have you seen Jake?"

"I did. He went for a run."

A run? Kendall's alarm bells started ringing. Jake wouldn't go running away from her unless he was chasing something. "Which way did he go?"

"Toward the orchard across the road."

After Alice moved on, Kendall started running toward the orchard that joined the Tor. She cut between the trees, listening as she ran. She felt someone behind her and turned. Jake emerged from the trees, scowling at her. "I told you not to leave the house."

"I don't like orders any more than you do. I was looking for you. Halle said a woman just delivered this to the house." Kendall handed Jake the letter. "I think it was Brandi. Halle said she had on a hat, but some red hair had slipped out."

"It was Brandi. I just chased her here from the house." Jake opened the letter and read it. "I need to get you out of here. We're going back to the hotel."

"I'm not leaving until we get to see the chalice. I don't know if it's what we're looking for, but I think there's something powerful up there."

"You went up there?"

"I tried, but Halle interrupted me."

"I'll take you to the hotel. Then I'll come back and get the chalice. I'll bring it to you."

She took Jake's hands in hers. "We'll find out answers here, not back at the hotel. The abbey and the Protettori are somehow connected. I know you think it's a risk, but it's important."

Jake fussed and cussed and fussed some more, but he let the subject drop. "At least let them go without us. We'll look for the chalice while the house is empty."

"You stay and look for it. I'll go with the group. I might pick up something else from the abbey."

"You're not going anywhere without me. I'll make a deal with you. We go to the abbey for the first part of the tour. We'll slip away and come back here to find the chalice. Then we go to the hotel."

"Deal."

They went back to the house and had a quick dinner. The fish and chips were delicious, but neither of them ate much. Kendall knew from the look on Jake's face that he was in bodyguard mode. He showered and she changed into the dress that seemed to be a requirement for her role. The bus dropped them at the entrance to the abbey. Jake stuck to her side like Secret Service on a president. There were several men and women in costume. Monks, nuns, knights, and she got a glimpse of Henry VIII. A man who introduced himself as Richard Whiting gave them a tour.

"What about the treasure?" Alice asked. "Do you think it's still here?"

Staying in character, the guide replied, "Of course, my lady. We hid it well from yon thieving pagans." He pointed to Henry VIII. "The best still lies hidden in the tunnels."

"Where are the tunnels?" Kendall asked, thinking he might know more of local legend than she'd heard.

"Legend says there's a hidden entrance near the Lady Chapel, but the black knight guards it."

"The black knight?" Alice said. "You mean the ghost."

"Have you seen him?" Sandy asked.

A look of something, maybe fear, crossed the guide's face. "Once." He cleared his throat and stepped into character again. "Let us continue to the abbot's kitchen." The guide led them on, but Kendall's head was spinning.

They had reached the abbot's kitchen when she felt a prickle in her neck. She glanced around, thinking it might be Nathan or Raphael. Maybe even Brandi, but she didn't see anyone watching, just the group milling about. The feeling persisted. She was so busy looking for the culprit that she almost missed seeing her father.

He stood near the Lady Chapel, watching Kendall. That must have been what she sensed. His cowl was down and she saw him more clearly than she had at the castle. She started toward him, not blinking for fear he'd disappear. Someone called her name, but she didn't stop. She walked within two feet of him. He didn't move this time, as he had at the castle.

"Daddy?"

He wasn't looking at her, but at the Tor. He looked sad. And then he vanished. She grabbed for him, but he wasn't there. "No."

"Kendall." Jake stepped up to her. "They're coming."

She shook her head, disoriented for a moment, and saw the group rushing toward her.

"What did you see?" Sandy asked.

They looked at her with so much hope in their eyes, she wished she could give them her damned gift. "A monk," she said, keeping the emotion out of her voice. Probably not as successfully as she thought, since Jake was holding her arm and watching her with a worried frown. "An old monk."

"Did he speak to you?" Alice asked.

"No, but he seemed very interested in the Tor." The others turned to look. Larry thought he saw something, and it distracted the others long enough for Jake to pull her aside.

"What the hell are you doing? I don't care what kind of ghost you see, you stay with me."

"It was my father."

"Here? He gets around. He's probably here to help me. I'm sure he knows better than anyone how damned hard you are to keep an eye on."

"I don't think it was his ghost. I think it was another memory. He belongs here."

"I thought he belonged at the castle."

"I think he was here first."

"You realize this abbey was shut down in the sixteenth century?"

She nodded.

"That means he's . . ."

"Really old. I think my father is the Reaper."

CHAPTER EIGHTEEN

Jake said a word that made a woman with a young child scurry away. "You're shitting me?"

"No. When I felt that dark shadow in the cave, it felt familiar."

Jake's face was tense. "How long have you thought this?"

"For a while. I wasn't sure. I'm still not."

"Damn. We're out of here. I don't care what you say. I'll knock you out if I have to."

She knew he was serious. She had no intention of leaving, but in his frame of mind, it might be best not to tell him now. "What about the chalice?"

"I'll get the damned chalice first."

"Don't curse. That might be the Holy Grail you're talking about."

Kendall felt the ground start to vibrate under her feet. "Oh no." She turned and looked at the Tor. "The lights are back."

The abbey was completely silent as everyone watched with stunned expressions as the lights danced above the Tor.

"They're more powerful now," Kendall said.

"What are they?" Jake asked.

"I think it's the Reaper."

———

Nathan opened his eyes and sat up with a start. His head ached. What had Raphael done to him? He tried to stand, and on the second attempt, he succeeded. There was a sliver of light on the floor in front of him. He walked closer to the light and saw it was a door. The light and a humming sound came from the other side. He still didn't know where he was, or how he'd gotten here.

He had to get out of here and find Kendall. How? He wasn't so worried about Raphael finding her and killing her, but there were things he needed to know. He didn't know whether to tell her his suspicions or wait to find out for sure. It could be Raphael's past that he had seen, like Kendall and Jake had done when they touched Raphael's dead body. He didn't know how he could have forgotten her, but it would explain so many things. Like why he done as if he'd known her a lot longer than he had. And why the first time he saw her, he'd felt like a lightning bolt had struck him. And there were all the little things in the months since she'd been working for him. There were times he knew what she was thinking, and times he was afraid she knew what he was thinking. He'd learned to block her for fear that she would find out about his curse and that she would know how obsessed he was with her. Otherwise she'd have left for sure. And that would kill him.

Nathan walked toward the door. It was arched, wooden, an old door. He pulled it open and stepped into the golden glow. The light was soft, but after going from darkness, he needed a moment to see without squinting, and he was stunned at what he saw. The room was large. Cut stones covered the floors and walls, and columns stood along the edges, reminding Nathan of a Roman temple. The light seemed to come from the floor. He glanced at the ceiling and saw an elaborate painting resembling a da Vinci. He looked around and his breath caught. In one corner, there was a statue. Just like the ones at the castle.

He heard someone behind him and turned. Raphael stood in the doorway.

"I thought you'd sleep longer. You're more powerful than I thought." Raphael's amber eyes studied Nathan.

"What did you do to me?"

"Nothing that will hurt you."

"Are you going to explain anything?"

"In time."

"I want it explained now."

"You're used to ordering people around, but it doesn't work that way here."

"Where is here?"

"I can't tell you."

"Then tell me how to get out. I have to find Kendall."

"You love her?"

"No, she . . . works for me. I'm responsible for her. I got her into this mess."

"You didn't mean to hit her."

"Bloody hell. Did you just read my mind? What are you?"

A noise sounded above them, a whirring, and he felt a vibration in the floor. He looked up, thinking it might be an earthquake. The air seemed to waver over his head.

Raphael stared at the spot. "It can't be." Then he extended his arms toward the wavering air, stiffening them as if some force were coming from his fingertips, and his body pushed back, as if a force were being returned. After a minute, the whirring faded and Raphael lowered his arms.

"What the hell just happened?" Nathan asked.

"He figured it out," Raphael said, his face dark. "If he gets the chalice . . ." He didn't finish his sentence, but it wasn't comforting to hear the fear in Raphael's voice. He turned to Nathan, his face set like stone. "You must leave."

"I would have already been gone if I knew how to get out."

The next thing Nathan knew, he was lying in an orchard at the bottom of the Tor. There was no sign of Raphael. And Nathan still had no answers, except he was more powerful than Raphael realized. Had he dreamed the whole thing?

Frustrated, he stood and dusted off his pants. He was more lost and confused now than before. Raphael had opened up a lot of questions without offering any explanations. Nathan needed to contact Kendall and Jake. He still didn't trust himself to be around Kendall, but he had to tell them about Brandi's visit and about Raphael. And he still had to find a cure to his curse. Raphael had said there was a way, but it would be severe. He'd also mentioned a chalice. Could this be the same chalice Jake had mentioned in the message? Could the Blue Chalice be the Holy Grail?

"I'm going to get that chalice if I have to do it at gunpoint," Jake said as the bus took the group back to the house. After the lights, everyone decided to call it a night. There was excitement, but everyone complained of headaches.

"I'm starting to think that's the only way we'll see it before the caretaker returns," Kendall said.

"I'm not waiting for the caretaker to come back."

She didn't want to wait either. The sense of danger was stronger than ever. Nathan was in trouble.

As soon as they got inside, Kendall's pulse quickened. "Something's wrong."

"What do you mean?" Halle asked.

"Someone's been here," Kendall said. "Check the chalice."

"I don't have a key," Halle said.

Jake ran toward the stairs and the group followed. "You don't need the key," he said.

The door to the Upper Room was open and everything was in shambles. Chairs and a table were overturned with drawers emptied on the floor.

"Oh no," Halle wailed. "The Blue Chalice. Call the police."

"Do you think Nathan took it?" Kendall whispered as the others surveyed the damage in horror.

"You know how desperate he is to get rid of his curse," Jake said.

Desperate enough to steal? Probably. "Why didn't he let us know he was here?"

"My guess is he wants to try it to see if it works first."

"Brandi could have taken it," Kendall said. "She was here."

"I'm ruined," Halle moaned. "They'll think someone from our group did it."

"But we were all together," Larry said. "The thief must have broken in during the tour."

"I'm going to check the caretaker's room and see if he was there," Jake said. "Make sure no one comes that way."

The group lamented the loss of the chalice while waiting for the police. After a few minutes, Jake hadn't returned. Kendall said she would go watch for the police to arrive. She hurried down the steps to the caretaker's room. Jake stood by the bed. Kendall noticed the smell at the same time she saw the lump underneath the covers. Her legs went weak. "Nathan?"

"No." Jake moved away from the bed.

Kendall saw gray hair topping the bundle. "Who is it?"

"The caretaker, I'd guess."

Kendall looked at the body. The cause of death was obvious. His throat had been cut. Could Nathan have done this? Or

Brandi? Kendall walked closer to the bed. She had to know. The caretaker was staring at the ceiling with an expression of shock. His fists were clenched as if he'd woken to find someone over him. The smell of decay was more noticeable up close. She touched the sheet and focused. Nothing. Cringing, she touched the tip of one finger to his cold fist. She had a hard time with bodies and death, unless they were old. Old death was history. New death was just . . . death. She forced herself not to recoil. If she didn't pick up something from his skin, she would have to touch his blood. She shuddered at the thought and focused her mind.

The first thing she felt was fear. She knew he had in fact woken up and found someone standing over him. Surprise, shock. He hadn't known the man. A man. The murderer was a man. Part of her was hoping it had been Brandi in order to eliminate Nathan. She concentrated again and tried to see the man's face. Someone touched her shoulder and she jumped.

"We have to get back with the group." Jake bent and picked up a bloody knife that lay underneath the edge of the bed. He stuck it in his boot.

"What are you doing?"

"Do you want him arrested?" Jake asked.

"You think Nathan did it?"

"Not if he was in his right mind."

More than anything, that told Kendall how much Jake cared about Nathan. He believed Nathan was guilty, and he was still protecting him.

"It might not have been him. Nathan's not a murderer."

"But he's losing control. And we know he's desperate for a cure. If this chalice is the Holy Grail, this could be it." Jake took off his shirt and wiped their footprints as they walked toward the door. "They'll find out we know him. We don't want to connect any of us to this room. We'll already look suspicious since we're the newcomers." He locked the door and wiped off the knob. "Hurry."

They shut the door and wiped the other side of the knob. Jake slipped on his shirt, and they went back to join the group. The police arrived minutes later. They examined the room and took down everyone's information and location at the time of the accident.

"Are we going to tell them about the caretaker?" Kendall whispered.

Jake nodded. He told the officer about the strange noise coming from the caretaker's room. "The thief must have been searching for the chalice."

"While we were in the house." Alice clasped her hand over her mouth.

The officer went to the caretaker's room. "Locked," he said. He looked undecided. "Is there another key? I think we'd better take a look at this room."

"The caretaker told me there are extra keys to the bedrooms in the office," Halle said.

"It's not there," Jake whispered to Kendall. "I already checked."

Halle checked the office, but the key to that room wasn't there. "He must have taken it with him."

"I'm afraid I'm going to have to open the door," the officer said.

Halle's eyes were wide. "Whatever you need to do."

He kicked the door in and immediately stopped. "Everyone stay back."

Alice gasped. "Is that a dead body?" She started to faint and Jake lunged to catch her, then quickly handed her off to Larry.

"My God," Halle said. "This can't be happening. This place is supposed to be peaceful, a place where people rejuvenate their spirits."

The officer put them all in the living room. Within minutes, more police arrived. A detective questioned each of them. Alice told him about the man she had seen watching the house. "I really didn't think much about it, with so many tourists in the area and the proximity of the house to the Chalice Gardens. But he was"—she blushed—"very handsome. When I found out Nathan Larraby was joining us, I thought it must be him."

The detective frowned. "The billionaire?"

"He was supposed to be a guest," Alice said. "But he hadn't arrived yet."

The police were interested in Nathan Larraby and asked Halle about the missing guest.

"They're going to suspect him," Kendall whispered to Jake. "Should we tell them we work for him?" Either way, it wouldn't be good for Nathan.

Jake nodded and asked to speak to the detective. He told him who they were and about their relationship with Nathan.

Halle was standing within earshot. "You know Nathan Larraby?"

"I'm sorry," Kendall said. "We couldn't tell anyone. We have to protect him."

"So this was a setup?" she asked. At which point the detective's ears perked up, and Kendall and Jake had to spend several minutes explaining that they were here exploring the area so it didn't sound like a plan to steal the chalice. By the time they were finished, both of them had made Nathan sound like a saint.

"I apologize, Halle," Jake said. "It was my fault, but we needed a way inside to check the place out before he arrived. Kendall held up her end of the bargain well, don't you think?"

Halle nodded. "Yes, but . . . Nathan Larraby. I wish I had known." She sighed.

"Where is Mr. Larraby now?" the detective asked.

"I don't know. I haven't spoken to him today," Jake said.

The detective scribbled something in his notebook and asked them several more questions about Nathan and his business and activities. When the detective finished, he told them not to leave town and had them moved from Little Saint Michael's to the Abbey House, which was larger. The only good thing about the incident was that their new accommodations joined the abbey. Kendall knew there was a connection between the abbey and the Protettori in Italy. This would make it much easier to find. The convenience of the matter was overshadowed by worry that Nathan might have lost control and killed someone. Why? To get the chalice? He couldn't have done it. She knew Nathan. He wasn't a murderer. It must have been someone else. Maybe Raphael.

Since everyone still thought they were married, Kendall and Jake were given a room together. The manager, a woman with a soft voice and worried eyes, showed them to a large bedroom on the first floor overlooking the abbey ruins. She gave them a half-hearted description of the Abbey House, which dated back to the 1830s. Once a private residence, for decades now the place had been used for retreats. There were several bedrooms to accommodate large groups. "Some of the stones in the cellar came from the abbey when it closed. If you want to find solace after all this distress, you might go there."

Jake glanced at the bed. One. Was there even any point in discussing sleeping arrangements? They'd spent more nights in the same bed than not in the past week.

"I get the left side," Kendall said as Jake started his usual security check of the room.

He looked up, mildly surprised, and shrugged.

While he continued making sure there weren't any murderers or Reaper's henchmen hiding in the room, Kendall tried

Nathan's cell phone. He didn't answer. She called the hotel and was told that he wasn't in. Next she called Fergus's cell phone to see if he had heard from Nathan, but she got his voice mail. She left Fergus a message that they were trying to reach Nathan and that they were at the Abbey House in Glastonbury.

Kendall stood at the window, wondering where Nathan could be. If he was safe. If he was himself.

"At least we have our own bathroom," Jake said when he entered the room. He walked over and stood beside her. "You OK?"

She nodded. "I guess. Nathan's still not answering his phone."

"What did you see when you touched the caretaker's body?" They hadn't had a chance until now to discuss the murder.

"Someone standing over the bed. I didn't see his face."

"It was a man?"

Kendall nodded. "Maybe it was Raphael." And not Nathan.

"I don't know." Jake put an arm loosely around her shoulder. He was wearing his dirty T-shirt that they'd used to wipe the floor. Kendall leaned into him, then turned and put her arms around his waist, resting them above his belt, and laid her head against his chest. She didn't care about his dirty shirt. He was strong and clean underneath. He folded his arms around her, and they stood at the window in silence, looking out over the ruins. She closed her eyes, wishing she hadn't gone for a walk in the maze and wishing they were still in Italy. Or Virginia.

"Wait until the dust settles, then I'll find him for you. I'll go back to the hotel and see if he's there."

"If he's . . . out of control, I'm afraid for you."

He brushed a thumb over her chin. "You worry about me?"

"Of course. What would I do without my badass body-guard?"

"Is that all I am to you, a badass bodyguard?"

She felt the thump of his heart, his scent. No, that wasn't all. "You're sexy, smart, and you're strong." Strong enough to hold a girl in his arms while he made love to her. "You think fast on your feet. You care about people more than you think. Keep it up and you might qualify for knighthood after all."

"If you're looking for a knight or anything else, let me know." His voice was low, sending a tingle along her nether regions. The adrenaline was wearing off, and her body was looking for something else to replace the rush. To dull the worry. If she didn't step away, they might end up in bed.

She lightly caressed his back when what she wanted to do was lower her hands and pull him closer. She could feel him hard against her stomach. He wanted her, and she wanted him. "You could be my knight and my badass bodyguard?"

"Is that what you want?" he asked.

And suddenly she was tired of fighting with herself over him. She lifted her gaze and met his simmering dark eyes. "How about my lover?"

His eyes darkened and he lowered his head. He didn't kiss her lips. He kissed her cheek and then moved to her ear. It left her skin tingling, but she needed his mouth on hers. She turned her head and captured his lips.

"Are you sure it's me and not Lancelot?"

"It's you," she said, biting at his lip.

"You drive me insane," he said between kisses. He picked her up and carried her to the bed. He lowered her onto the covers and settled beside her. "This time, we'll slow down."

He moved over her, fully clothed, and kissed her lips, her neck, every exposed area of skin. Then he started undressing her, one piece at a time, kissing the new area until she wondered blissfully if someone could die from being undressed.

"Can you go a little faster?" she asked, trying to unbuckle his belt.

He captured her hands and kept kissing and touching her as she squirmed. "You've tormented me long enough," he said. "Now it's my turn."

"I haven't known you but a week," she said, trying to push his jeans down. But it was impossible with his belt still on.

"It feels like a lifetime." He finally got her undressed and he pulled off his shirt.

She attacked his neck like a starving vampire and grabbed for his belt. She yanked it out and shoved his pants down.

He grinned against her lips. "Slow down before you tear off a part we both need."

"Sorry, you're just moving too slow." She felt enflamed with desire. That gave her pause. What kind of phrase was that? She managed to get his pants off, but they got stuck. "Boots," she gasped. "Take off your boots."

He rolled to the side and kicked them off, and then his pants. Kendall pushed his underwear down and wrapped her legs around him. "I can't wait any longer. Please."

"Are you sure?" he asked again.

She shoved his shoulders and he rolled over. She straddled him. "I'm sure."

When he entered her, images flashed in her head like reflections on a broken mirror. She saw the forest again, and the couple making love. She stopped moving.

Jake gripped her hips. "God, don't stop now." Then he looked up at her. "What's wrong?"

"I'm sorry. I keep seeing the man and woman in the forest."

"It is us?"

She nodded.

He rolled over, putting her underneath him. "It must be one of your visions telling you that you belong with me." He started making love to her again, slow, and then fast, and then slow again until she didn't know what was present or what was past.

When it was over, and her senses and her mind and her body had come back together again, he stayed above her, fingers gently brushing back her hair. His eyes were dark, filled with things spoken and unspoken. "I don't usually do this."

"Have sex?"

He grinned. "Usually it's . . . well, you know."

"No. What?"

"Scratching an itch."

"Have you scratched a lot of itches?"

"More than I should have, but not for a long while. I've been too preoccupied."

"Are you scratching an itch now?"

"I don't know what the hell I'm doing. But it feels good." He frowned. "It feels like I've known you a lot longer than a few days."

"I know." More like a lifetime.

"I didn't tell you I saw your lovers in the forest the first time we made love."

"You did?"

He nodded. "I wasn't sure what to make of it."

"It's like being in someone else's body, but it's my body," Kendall said. "I know that doesn't make sense."

"Actually it does." He wound a strand of her hair around his finger. "Do you believe in fate?"

"Maybe." Was he saying they were fated? Was that why she felt this ingrained trust for him when on the surface he had seemed all wrong for her? Was it possible that she had known him before? She had never believed in past lives and reincarnation, but after all the things she'd experienced lately, she wouldn't rule anything out. "Do you?"

"Not until now." Someone knocked on the door. "You expecting anyone?" Jake asked.

"No. Maybe it's Nathan." Kendall jumped up and started throwing on her clothes.

"It'd be just like him to show up now." Jake pulled on his underwear and jeans and went to the door. It was Halle.

She looked at Jake's chest and blinked. "Uh, I wanted to see if you're all right," she said.

"Shaken," Kendall said. "That poor caretaker. Such a terrible thing. Has everyone gotten settled? Alice seemed troubled."

"They're fine now."

"I'm sorry we didn't tell you who we were," Kendall said.

"I understand. Someone with that kind of money has to be on guard. I hate to ask you this, after all the unpleasantness, but do you think you could make the séance tonight?"

"You're going ahead with it?"

"The group wants to, and I really need to keep them happy. I know death and all this negative energy has an effect on the psyche. . . ."

Kendall started to say no, but Halle looked so desperate, and they did need to explore the abbey. After seeing her father there, Kendall was certain there was a connection to the Protettori, and she was going to find it. "I'll be there."

After Halle had gushed her thanks, she left.

"Are you sure you're up to it?" Jake asked.

"Maybe I'll see King Arthur again. If this chalice is the Holy Grail, he might have the answers we're looking for."

"I thought you might want to go to the hotel."

"No. I want to stay here. There's a mystery to solve. I'll touch every stone in the place if I have to."

"Start with the ones in the cellar. The woman said some of the stones were from the abbey. I don't want you running around outside more than you have to. Don't frown at me. I'm trying to keep you safe. There's a killer out there."

And she was afraid it was Nathan.

"Even Brandi warned you," Jake said. "Did you try to pick up anything from the letter?"

"I didn't get anything from it before."

"We both know how fickle your gift is. How about we try again? I'd like to know where the threat's coming from."

Kendall picked up the letter and opened it. She rested her fingers on the paper and closed her eyes. She waited, but nothing came.

"Are you falling asleep on me?"

Kendall opened her eyes. "No. I'm not getting anything. Other than my apartment."

"What would your apartment have to do with the letter?" Jake rubbed the paper between his fingers. "Unless she stole the paper from you. Not that your apartment is easy to break into."

"That's not my paper. I don't see how there could be a connection."

"A psychic glitch?" he asked.

"They happen a lot," Kendall admitted.

"Or does it just appear to be a glitch because we don't have all the pieces to the puzzle?"

"I don't know." Kendall took the paper Jake had laid down. "I wish I knew what she was up to."

"Trying to find the relics before Nathan does," Jake said.

"How did she know about this place? We fell here," Kendall said. "We didn't come by choice."

"Maybe she fell through the maze too. If you remember, when she pulled that gun on us at the castle, we weren't far from the maze. She could have already discovered its secrets."

"She must know something that we don't, since she says I'm in danger." Kendall sighed. "I'm in danger. Nathan's in danger. Where the hell is he?"

"He could be anywhere. Paris, Africa, the room next door."

"Do you think he did it?"

"Nathan's not a killer, but . . ."

"But if he lost control, he could have hurt someone."

"If he did, he's going to need our help," Jake said softly. Kendall didn't think he realized he'd spoken aloud.

"Let's go explore the cellar," Kendall said. "I'd like to see the stones."

As soon as they stepped into the hall, Kendall heard a familiar whining voice. "But it's a cellar. Cellars are cool." The red-haired boy and his mother were walking up the hall.

"Arthur, we're not going to the cellar. The manager warned you not to go prowling around again. Do you want them to ask us to leave? Then you'll have to go back to your father in New Hampshire. Is that want you want?"

"Yes. I'm bored."

"Well, I'm not. I deserve this vacation. So march yourself right back to the room."

"I'd pay for the flight if she'd send him back," Jake said.

The stairs leading to the basement were narrow. The chapel was small, with a stained glass window and a stone table holding several candles.

Jake moved up behind her and slid his arms around her waist. "Ever made love in a cellar?" he asked.

"No."

"Want to give it a try?"

Kendall reached back and pinched his waist. "Behave. We're in a chapel."

The stones on the wall looked just like the ones in the abbey ruins. Jake poked at one. "If walls could talk, I bet these have some stories to tell."

She smiled and touched the wall near the stained glass window. The room faded. A cold fear settled over her skin as the scene before her unfolded. Four monks hurried across the abbey grounds to the Lady Chapel. It looked different. The buildings weren't ruins. One of the monks led the way and one brought up the rear, while the two in the middle carried a trunk between them. From their bowed backs, it appeared to be heavy. "Make haste," the one in front whispered. "The hour grows near." They hurried inside the church and made their way to the front. They set the trunk down and knelt on the floor. Were they praying? Then she saw a stone in the wall move, opening to a set of steps. The four monks carried the trunk to the steps. Kendall couldn't move. It was as if she were watching from above. They were hiding the treasure in the secret tunnels. As one of the monks moved, a cross swung at his neck. Just like the Protettori's crosses. Just like the one around her neck. He cast a worried glance over his shoulder, and Kendall recognized the angled cheekbones and the set of her father's mouth.

She let go of the wall with a gasp and the vision disappeared. "Oh my God." She stumbled and Jake put his arms around her. "I know where the entrance to the tunnel is."

"Here? This house isn't that old."

"No, it's in the Lady Chapel."

"And the wall told you where the secret tunnel is?"

"My father did."

There was a gasp from the stairs. Kendall and Jake looked over and saw a redhead with a freckled face staring back at them.

"It's that kid." Jake started toward the stairs.

Arthur yelped and ran away.

CHAPTER NINETEEN

I F WE DON'T STOP HIM, HE'LL TELL EVERYONE IN THE PLACE," Jake said, running after the kid.

Kendall followed him up the stairs.

"Where'd he go?" Jake looked around but didn't see the kid anywhere. "He must have gone back to his room."

"Let's just find the priest hole before he has a chance to tell anyone. We've got half an hour before the moonlight tour starts."

"You'd better wear your séance dress," Jake said as they hurried to their room. He opened the door and Kendall stepped inside. She came to a dead stop, staring at their uninvited guest.

Raphael sat in a chair, flipping through one of the books in the room. "Half this stuff is wrong," he said, putting the book down.

Jake pulled his knife from his boot and put Kendall behind him. "How did you get in here?"

Raphael glanced at the knife and shrugged one shoulder. He wore jeans and a dark shirt, not his ninja monk outfit, but he still looked deadly. "Does Nathan know you're sleeping together?"

Kendall glanced at the bed.

"It's none of Nathan's business where we sleep," Jake said.

"I doubt that Nathan would agree. Have you seen him? I need to find him."

"No, we're looking for him too," Jake said.

"He didn't mean to kidnap you, or at least not to hurt you," Kendall said, stepping around Jake. "He needed answers. And we'll return your cross. I'm sorry we took it, but we thought you were dead."

"You were dead," Jake said, putting Kendall behind him again.

"I already have my cross."

"You got it from Nathan?" Kendall's eyes widened. "Oh my God. Did you hurt him?"

"No. He's in danger, but not from me. From the Reaper."

"The Reaper is here?" Jake asked.

"He's trying to come through the gateway. His men are probably already here."

"You mean a portal?"

Raphael looked weary. "Our order has many secret places. There are gateways, or portals, between some of them."

"Is that what those lights on the Tor are, the Reaper coming through one of the gateways?" Kendall asked.

Raphael nodded. "I must stop him, or there will be catastrophic results."

Kendall stepped closer to Raphael, and Jake put out an arm to stop her. "Is the fountain inside the Tor?"

"I can't tell you that."

"Can you tell us how we fell through a maze in Italy and landed in England?" Jake asked.

"It's not for outsiders to understand."

"Kendall isn't an outsider. Her father was one of the Protettori," Jake said.

Raphael looked at Kendall. "How did you find out about your father?"

"I saw a vision of my birth in the tower room."

"I shouldn't have put you there," Raphael said.

"I didn't see the vision until later. You knew who I was?"

"Not at first. I started putting the pieces together after I saw the cross."

"Can you tell me anything about my father?"

"He broke our rules. Women aren't allowed. The order needs to be fully focused on their task. Women are distractions." Raphael looked at Jake as if he understood just how distracting Kendall was to him. "So he was forced to leave the group."

"Is there anything else you can tell me about him?" she asked. Her voice was level, but her eyes were afraid.

"Not now."

"What about the tunnel to the Tor. Is it in the abbey?"

"How did you know about that?"

"I had a vision," Kendall said.

"I can't speak of it."

"Then can you tell me about the chalice?" she asked.

His eyes narrowed, making him look almost reptilian. "What chalice?"

"I don't know. King Arthur told me to find the chalice."

Surprise replaced the harsh expression. "Arthur told you that?"

"In a vision. Do you know Arthur?"

"You have a lot of visions."

"Too many," Jake said.

Raphael stood, his relaxed demeanor gone. "Do you have your cross?"

"We each have one," Jake said.

"Wear them. You have to protect her," Raphael said to Jake. "I'll try to find Nathan. If he comes here, don't let him leave."

"You still haven't explained how you're not dead," Jake said.

"The fountain has restorative powers."

"Why didn't you turn into a sentinel?" Kendall asked.

Raphael frowned. "He told you that too? It's time for a new Keeper. I must go."

"Wait," Kendall said. "Did you know the treasure is missing?"

"Yes," Raphael said.

"Did you take it?" Jake asked.

"Yes."

"When?" Kendall said. "It was there when we left Italy. Nathan had you imprisoned in Virginia."

"I moved it after I left."

"How'd you get from Virginia to Italy and move a roomful of valuable treasure in a matter of hours? Nathan's Mercedes is nice, but not a magic carpet," Jake said.

"I can't tell you."

"You're like Nathan in more ways than one," Jake said.

"At least you talk a lot more now than you did at the castle," Kendall said.

"I didn't expect to see you there," Raphael said, and walked through the wall.

Jake and Kendall stared after him. "Did he just go through that wall?" Kendall asked.

"Either that or we're having a bizarre dream. I guess that's how he moved the treasure." What the hell?

"What do we do now?" Kendall asked.

"Keep you safe and hope he finds Nathan."

"Did you see how he looked when I mentioned King Arthur and the chalice?"

Jake nodded. "As if he knew him."

Kendall changed into the long dress for the coming séance. It was blue, fitted at the top, teasing with a hint of cleavage. She kept trying to pull it higher. The bottom was full, flowing. She looked like a queen. A sexy as hell queen. He'd known women who spent an hour getting ready for a date and didn't come out looking as good as Kendall did with no makeup, no curlers, or the contraptions women used on their hair.

They grabbed flashlights and hurried to the Abbey House's private entrance to the grounds. Their lights weren't necessary since lanterns had been set up for tonight's event, their soft glow making the ruins look haunted. Perfect for a séance.

"You think you can find it at night?"

"I saw it clearly in the vision. There were four of them. They took the trunk inside the Lady Chapel and opened a priest hole in the wall. But the chapel was intact, so it must have been no later than the sixteenth century. That's when the abbey was closed. The trunk is probably gone."

"But if there's a tunnel, it'll still be there. Did you see what was inside the trunk?"

"No, but it must have been something important. They were frightened. I could feel their fear."

"You're certain it was your father? Monks tend to look a lot alike."

"It was him. I saw the cross." She touched the cross around her neck. "Now I know for sure he was part of the Protettori."

"If these monks were part of the Protettori, where are the statues guarding the abbey?"

"It's possible that this was before the Reaper became greedy for the relics. They may have moved the group to Italy and put the statues up to keep him out."

"I still don't understand how the statues work," Jake said, "or why the cross keeps the person protected. I felt like I was in a bubble when I passed through them. It was one heck of a rush. Not to mention scary as hell."

"I felt the same way. And I assume he can't pass them even with a cross."

"That's the part I don't get," Jake said. "It's not logical." Not that any of this was. "I guess they took his cross when they kicked him out."

"I think so," Kendall said, touching her cross again. "I think I'm wearing it."

"Nathan's cross? It's crazy that he would end up with any of their crosses, but this one . . ."

"I know, but this looks just like the one my father wore."

"If your father is the Reaper, then he's probably long since stolen anything hidden near the abbey."

"Unless it's hidden deeper inside the tunnel, and there are statues guarding it. OK, let's hurry before the others get there."

But there were already a few people out. Lights flickered here and there as people walked the ruins. It was a beautiful night. The temperature was mild for October, the sky was clear, the stars brilliant—a perfect night for exploring ghostly ruins, which sucked when you were going on a covert mission. But most of the lights were nearer the house. The Lady Chapel was at the other end of the abbey.

The ruins looked like skeletons. Jake wanted to believe that was the reason for the knot in his gut, but he didn't think so. "Let's get this done."

Kendall paused every now and then, and tilted her head, as if listening. Jake couldn't hear anything but the sounds of night. It must be a burden to know things you shouldn't.

"I think it was here." She pointed to a section in the front of the chapel.

Jake grabbed a nearby lantern and placed it next to the wall. They searched the stones, but none seemed loose.

Kendall worked beside him. "I think it's here."

"You sensed something?"

"No. I see a crack. Give me your knife."

He handed her the knife, and she scraped the edge of a stone. "Look. There's a crack ."

He held the lantern closer. "That could be one side of an entrance. Let me try." He scraped at the edges of the large section of stone and found the outline of a door. "I don't see any way to open it without tearing up the stones. We need tools."

"There has to be a way to open it. The monks did it, and they didn't have tools. You work on clearing it, and I'll keep looking for a latch."

"Look for a circle," he said. He worked at the crevice. Centuries of dirt and footsteps had packed it tight. After a few minutes, he had it cleared.

"I think I've found something," Kendall said. "This stone feels different."

It was an ornate cornerstone. "It's round," Jake said. "That's a good sign."

"Kendall! Jake!"

"It's the group," Kendall said. They stood up as the others approached, each of them carrying a lantern.

"You're already here," Halle said, looking relieved. "We were going to walk around for a while before the séance. I have a good feeling about tonight."

Jake wished he did. "Good idea. We'll be here getting ready. I think with a little more meditation Kendall's senses will be more open to the spirits." He glanced at the stone behind Kendall. "Twenty minutes should have her in tiptop spiritual condition."

Everyone agreed, and the group hurried off.

"This stone moves," Kendall said, touching the ornate stone. "Should we give it a try?"

"We should probably wait until later tonight when no one is here. I doubt the hole has been disturbed in a few centuries. It might be noisy." And rigged with a booby trap.

"What if Art tells someone? He heard me say the secret tunnel was in the Lady Chapel."

Jake didn't think it was wise, but she was right about the kid. He checked to see if the area was clear. The closest group was near the abbot's kitchen. "Let's see what happens."

"I hope light doesn't shoot out like it did in the catacombs."

"I'll do it." Jake pushed the round stone and heard a soft rumbling sound.

"Something's happening," Kendall whispered.

"Move back in case it's a trap," Jake said. They both stepped back, and the wall started to slide. The creaking sounded loud in the quiet of night. "Damn. That's loud."

The wall slowed. "It's stuck," Kendall said.

"It's old." Jake pushed against the door, and it opened a little farther.

"I see steps," Kendall said, holding the lantern near the opening.

"Someone's coming," Jake said. They scrambled to close the wall. "Sit down and pretend we're meditating."

They dropped to the ground just as the group appeared.

"Is everything all right?" Sandy asked. "We heard the strangest groaning coming from over here."

"Kendall was meditating," Jake said. "Sometimes she's loud."

"Well, are we ready then?" Halle asked.

There would be no getting rid of them until they'd had their séance. He and Kendall would have to come back later tonight to check the priest hole anyway. It was too noisy to attempt with people around. "We're ready."

"Do we want to have the séance by King Arthur's grave?" Halle asked.

"Yes," Alice said, and Larry, Rhonda, and Sandy agreed.

Kendall seemed distracted as they walked to King Arthur's grave. Jake couldn't blame her. He wanted to know what was inside that priest hole too. Was it possible that they'd found something no one else had? If anyone knew about it, there would be some record.

The group got into position, sitting close to the gravesite. Once again, Jake sat next to Kendall and held her hand. Rhonda managed to get on his other side. Larry sat beside her, then Halle, and Alice sat on Kendall's left. "Join hands, everyone," Kendall said. "Close your eyes. Clear your minds of everything but King Arthur."

Jake closed his eyes this time. After that last séance he couldn't help but wonder if there was something more to his childhood dreams of King Arthur than just a kid's daydreams and wanting to feel like he was special. Most boys wanted to be superheroes or soldiers or knights, but there had been times when his dreams felt real. He hadn't told anyone except Lilly. She hadn't made fun of him. She understood. She was the one who woke him if the dream got too intense. Hell of a coincidence, he thought. He'd been obsessed with King Arthur and the Knights of the Round Table as a kid, and now he was on a real quest.

They sat in silence for a while, and then Kendall spoke. Jake had seen psychics on TV and movies, but there was something about Kendall's voice that was different. "King Arthur," she said so softly it was a whisper. "We're here."

Jake felt a shiver, and Rhonda squeezed his hand. He thought he felt a breeze at his ear. Kendall called softly again, and he felt as if he were leaving his body. Like he had when he had made love to Kendall the first time. He still didn't know if he'd imagined or sensed that couple making love in a forest, or if it was a spillover from Kendall's visions. Maybe everyone had some kind of sixth sense. People like Kendall were just more developed.

The feeling intensified. He couldn't hear anything except the sound of horses and men shouting. Then he was on a battlefield. A tall knight on horseback motioned to him, and they rode down the embankment toward the enemy. He felt a kinship with the man, as if they were brothers. And he felt a dreadful sense of betrayal, as if he had done him a great wrong.

A woman cried out, and Jake opened his eyes. He was back at the séance. His head felt thick. He saw Alice pointing at a ghostly figure near the ruins. "Merlin."

A white-haired old man stood near one wall a couple hundred yards away, staring at them. Everyone gasped.

"I see him too," Sandy said.

"Oh my God," Rhonda said. "Merlin."

"He's waving," Alice said. "He's waving at us."

Marco. What the hell was he doing here?

"There's another man," Halle said. "Oh my God."

"I think it's King Arthur," Alice said.

"He isn't dressed like a knight," Larry said.

That was because he was Fergus. "You need to faint or something," Jake whispered to Kendall, "so we can end this séance."

Kendall gave a dramatic groan and slumped against Jake. He announced to everyone that she'd used all her strength and needed to rest. The group was beside themselves with excitement. Even Jake felt bad for the deception. Nathan would have to send them on a trip to make it up. The rest of the group decided to stay in hopes of seeing something else.

Jake ushered Kendall back toward the Abbey House. "I thought Nathan said they weren't coming."

"I think Fergus does what he wants," Kendall said. They caught up to the two men just past King Edgar's Chapel. Fergus was fussing at Marco.

"I wanted to see the place again," Marco said. "It's been so long." He was wearing his dark monk's robes.

"Miss Kendall, Jake, very good to see you," Fergus said.

"When did you get here?" Kendall asked.

Fergus straightened his jacket. "About half an hour ago."

"I didn't know you were coming," she said.

"Neither did Nathan," Fergus said. "He won't be happy."

"Why are you here?" Kendall asked.

"I was worried," Fergus said.

Marco looked at Jake. "We need to talk to Adam."

"Adam?" Kendall looked at Jake.

Jake raised his brows and shrugged. "How did you find us?"

"A little boy told us that you were going to the abbey to find the secret tunnel," Fergus said.

"Damned kid," Jake said.

"Did you find the tunnel?" Marco asked.

"We found something," Jake said. "We didn't have time to explore."

"Do you know where the tunnel leads?" Kendall asked.

"To the Tor. To the fountain." Marco scratched his white beard. "He must not find it."

"You mean the Reaper?" Kendall asked.

"The Reaper. If he finds the fountain and the chalice, we're doomed."

"Raphael said he was trying to get to the fountain without passing the statues."

"You saw Raphael?" Fergus asked.

"He showed up earlier looking for Nathan."

"Where is Nathan?" Fergus asked.

"We haven't seen him since yesterday morning," Kendall said.

Fergus looked alarmed. "That long?"

Jake glanced at Kendall. Without words they agreed not to mention for the moment their suspicion that Nathan might have murdered someone.

"I don't think Raphael means to hurt him," Kendall said. "He seemed to be trying to protect him. He said Nathan is in danger from the Reaper."

"Let's get back to our room," Jake said. "We need to talk in private. You're staying at the hotel in town?"

"No," Fergus said. "We're staying here at the Abbey House. I thought Nathan would be here with you."

"No. We haven't heard from him."

"Most unusual," Fergus said.

"Did you bring our things?" Kendall asked.

"Yes. They're in our room." Fergus whispered to them that he didn't trust Marco on his own. "He's feeling much better, but he still wanders, mind and body. It's rather like babysitting."

"Has he mentioned Adam to you?" Kendall asked as they walked back to Fergus and Marco's room.

Fergus kept his voice low. "Marco mentions so many things. It's hard to keep track."

"Marco, Raphael said the Reaper mustn't get the chalice. What chalice?"

Marco turned. "The cup of Christ."

"The Holy Grail?" Jake asked.

"Yes, the Holy Grail," Marco said.

"You have it?" Jake asked.

"It was one of the first relics we protected, but we lost it many years ago," Marco said. "Raphael has been searching for it ever since. If the Reaper gets it, there will be little hope."

"Why?" Jake asked. "What can he do with the chalice?"

"The Fountain of Youth keeps us strong and healthy, so we can protect the relics. That's why we are so old. We must protect the relics. But we only drink from a ceremonial cup once a year. If someone were to take water from the Fountain of Youth and drink it from the chalice, then he would be eternal. And that is what the Reaper wants. To be eternal."

"That's just what we need. No offense," Jake said, "but why aren't you young like Raphael if you also drink from the fountain?"

"I stopped drinking years ago," the old man said.

Kendall looked at Marco. "May I ask why?"

"I lost the right to drink. That's all I can say."

"There was a chalice at the place where we were staying before," Kendall said. "It's supposed to have healing powers. It was stolen earlier today. Could that be your chalice?"

"It was here at the abbey once upon a time," Marco said. "I wasn't responsible for moving it, so I don't know. If the Reaper finds it and takes it to the fountain, we're doomed." He looked out the window toward the Tor. "The only way he could do that is if he's created another gateway, another portal."

"Like the one in the maze?" Jake asked.

"He can't use ours. They're protected by the statues, but if he has created another portal, it will be very bad. He and Raphael are very knowledgeable about such things. That's part of the reason they worked so well together."

"Raphael and the Reaper worked together?" she asked.

"At one time they were as close as brothers," Marco said. "When the Reaper betrayed us, he tried to persuade Raphael to join him. Raphael refused, but it broke his heart. A heart that had already been broken. That's why he avoids women. Raphael appears gruff, but he has a sensitive soul."

Jake frowned. "Are we talking about the same Raphael? The one with tattoos on his face and a wicked dagger?"

Marco frowned. "Pay me no mind, just the ramblings of an old man."

"Marco, do you know who the Reaper is?" Kendall asked.

Jake took a step closer in case she got the answer she expected.

"No one knows who the Reaper is now," Marco said.

"Now?" Jake asked.

"He will have changed his appearance." Marco rubbed his head.

"Plastic surgery?" Kendall asked.

"Perhaps," Marco said.

"What was his name then?" Kendall asked.

"Luke. He was Luke."

"I believe Marco needs his medication," Fergus said. "And he needs rest. He's still healing."

"Thank you again, Marco. You saved my life."

"It was necessary. We need you to save him."

Jake heard Kendall pull in a quick breath. She touched the old man's arm. "Save who?"

Marco frowned and looked around the room. "Where is my bed?"

Here we go, Jake thought.

"Your bed is here, Marco." Fergus pointed him to one of the two beds in the room.

"This place looks most strange," Marco said. "Where is Arthur? I always check on Arthur before he retires to bed. Troubles weigh heavily on his mind."

Kendall, Jake, and Fergus shared a glance. "He has spells like this," Fergus said. "Marco has quite the imagination. I believe he's very well-read."

And very old. Like Merlin-old.

CHAPTER TWENTY

B RANDI WATCHED AS A MAN STEPPED FROM THE SHADOWS OF a building across the street from the Chalice Well. Only one police car was left there. She'd heard that the caretaker had been murdered. At first, she'd worried that it might have been Kendall, that her note hadn't arrived in time. The man turned to glance at Little Saint Michael's, and she saw his face clearly for a second. It was Nathan. He must have stolen the chalice.

He walked toward the town, and she followed at a distance. She was going to destroy the chalice before the Reaper could get his hands on it. Nathan started moving faster, and she had to jog to keep up. God, he was fast, and he wasn't even running. He cut through Glastonbury Abbey. Brandi hurried to catch up. She heard a noise up ahead as if someone had fallen. She slowed when she got close, heart pounding wildly. It was crazy to consider trying to take the chalice from him, if he had it. She didn't know what was up with him, but whatever she'd seen back at the hotel wasn't quite . . . normal.

It was quiet now. She could see the ruins beyond her, but the sounds had disappeared. Where was he? She pulled out the knife Thomas had given her. There was a movement beside her, and a man rushed at her from the bushes. She tried to move aside, but he was coming too fast. Instinctively, she lifted the blade, and the knife sank into his chest. She gasped and jumped back.

He fell to his knees, clutching at the knife, then collapsed.

"Oh God." She hadn't meant to stab him. She just wanted the chalice. She knelt down to see if he was still alive. It was so dark underneath the trees, she couldn't see well enough to evaluate his injury. She grabbed his hand and took his pulse. None. Bile rose in her throat. Even though she had told Nathan she would kill him if he got in her way, she wasn't a killer.

Her knee hit something near his body. A bag lay on the ground. He must have dropped it. She felt the bag. There was something hard inside, the shape of a cup, a large cup.

She grabbed the bag. She couldn't leave the knife Thomas had given her, so she pulled it from the body and wiped it with the bottom of his shirt. Then cradling the bag in her arms, she ran.

Kendall's senses were still rattled after Raphael's unexpected visit. At least Raphael didn't appear intent on killing Nathan for kidnapping him. It was sad sometimes what had to pass for a ray of hope.

"We've got to go to the tunnel," Kendall said.

"We need to wait until everyone's asleep. There are too many people still wandering around. We should grab a few hours' sleep and plan on working all night."

"I need a shower," Jake said. He opened his duffel bag and took out a pair of underwear and his dopp kit. "My own deodorant. Life is good."

"What about pajamas," Kendall called after him, but the door was already closing. She smiled. Did it matter now? They had taken things to a new level. She wasn't sure how it would all work out, but for now, she would just let it ride. It felt good not to be on guard, worrying about a touch or a kiss killing a relationship. With Jake, her senses had a different effect. It was intense, but good.

Kendall went through her backpack and duffel bag. Seeing her clothes and brush and equipment was almost as good as finding a new relic. She hung the clothes that she hadn't even unpacked in Italy and heard the water turn off. She prepared herself for Jake to emerge in some form of undress. He shocked her by appearing in one of the robes from the bathroom.

"You all right?" he asked. "You look like you've seen a vision."

"You emerging from the bathroom in more than your underwear must be some kind of miracle."

"Sir Jake at your service," he said, bowing. "Shall I sleep in the hallway, m'lady, or perhaps you would allow me to rest upon the cold, hard floor. I can cushion my head upon my arms if you don't want to lend me a pillow from yon bed."

She smiled. "Shut up and get in bed. I'm going to shower and get changed."

He grinned and dropped the robe. He might as well have been naked.

Kendall slapped his butt. "Anyone ever tell you that you have a nice ass?"

"No one that matters."

Good answer.

He pulled back the covers that they had wrecked earlier and lay down, watching her. "I figure we'll sleep for three hours. That should be enough time for even the late-night wanderers to be in bed."

She hurried through her shower and joined him in the bed. He was staring at the ceiling. "What are you doing?"

"Thinking."

"About?"

"Life."

"Any part of it in particular?" she asked. "Or just life in general?"

"Parents. You and I and Nathan work together, and all three of us have screwed-up childhoods. Your mom died giving birth to you. Your dad's at least several hundred years old and part of a secret group." Jake shrugged. "And he may be the Reaper. Nathan can't remember anything about his childhood. It's all mystery."

"He told me some," Kendall said.

"When?"

"That morning in his bedroom when he changed."

Jake frowned. "What'd he say?"

"His mother died when he was a baby. His father died later. He was in a witness protection program or something."

"Hell, that's worse than I thought. No wonder finding anything out about him is nearly impossible."

"What about you?" Kendall asked, feeling a sense of anticipation. Would she find out he was Adam? Wouldn't he know if he was?

"I was orphaned when I was a toddler."

"A toddler?" Then he couldn't be Adam. But Nathan's father was in a witness protection program, and that didn't fit either.

"I never knew my mother or father or why they didn't want me."

"Oh, Jake."

"The only thing I had was Lilly."

"Lilly? You mentioned her in your sleep the first night at Little Saint Michael's."

"She was my friend when I was young. The only person I trusted for a long time."

"She was your Adam."

"What?"

"Your best friend. Like Adam was mine."

He nodded. "I could tell her things I didn't tell anyone else."

"Like?"

"My dreams."

"What kind of dreams?"

"King Arthur and knights. I've dreamed of King Arthur and the Knights of the Round Table for as long as I can remember."

Kendall's jaw dropped. "Why didn't you tell me before?"

"That's not something you advertise," Jake said.

"This is amazing. I thought you were a complete skeptic of anything unexplained."

"I was." He looked at her. "Until now. I thought the other stuff was just dreams. A boy wanting to feel important. Then I met you. I've seen other things since. Like the couple in the forest. And I didn't tell you this, but I saw King Arthur at the abbey when we had the séance. You were right. He looks like Nathan." Jake seemed disturbed by that statement.

"It must be this place."

"I guess. I don't know how you can deal with this stuff all the time."

"It gets old, but I don't have a choice. So what happened to Lilly?"

"She died."

"What happened?"

"I never knew. She just went away and they said she had died."

"I saw a grave once, when I touched you. Actually a couple of times. I saw blond hair. I wonder if that was her grave. But I had this feeling like I was suffocating."

Jake went completely still.

Damn, Kendall. She was his best friend. "I'm sorry, Jake. That was insensitive of me." He didn't speak, didn't even seem to be breathing. "Jake, what's wrong?"

Still he stared, unblinking. "Jake. You're scaring me." She shook him and he turned to face her. "What happened?"

"I remembered something."

"About Lilly's grave?"

"It wasn't Lilly's grave."

"One of the girls in Iraq?"

"No."

"Then whose?"

He looked at her, his forehead bunched into a frown. "I don't know."

"You remember a grave but don't know whose it was?"

Something flashed at the window. "What's that?" Kendall asked.

Jake got out of bed and walked to the window. He cracked the curtain, and Kendall saw lights.

"Is it the lights on the Tor?" she asked.

"No. Cops."

Kendall hurried over next to him. Two police cars were in the abbey parking lot. Several lanterns were moving across the abbey grounds. "I have a bad feeling."

"You wait here. I'll go see what's happening."

"I would rather be with you."

They dressed quickly and hurried outside to the ruins. "What's going on?" Jake asked a man who was walking close by.

"A little boy is missing. We're helping with the search. His mother said he kept talking about a hidden tunnel. After that murder at Little Saint Michael's, I guess the cops aren't taking any chances."

Jake cursed. "I knew that kid was trouble."

A minute later, they heard raised voices. "Art! Oh my God. Where were you?"

"There's a dead man. I saw a dead man."

"Art, stop that. I've had it with your lying. This won't get you out of trouble. I told you not to leave the room."

"But I saw him. There's blood all over his chest."

"Art! I'm going to send you home to your father."

A second later, a scream sounded farther away. Kendall and Jake started running toward the sound. A small group had already gathered.

"What happened?" Kendall asked.

"There's been another murder," someone said. "A woman fell over the body."

Kendall looked at Jake. Nathan couldn't have killed again. Kendall saw Halle near the front of the crowd. Alice stood next to her, face buried in Halle's shoulder. Halle turned and saw Kendall. Her face froze and Kendall knew. She stood, not breathing as Halle led Alice over to them.

"I'm so sorry, Kendall."

Kendall's heart felt like a chunk of wood. She asked the question anyway, holding her breath, hoping, praying for a different answer than the one she knew she would get. "Who is it?" she whispered, feeling the words scrape out of her mouth.

Halle touched Kendall's arm. "It's him, our missing guest. Nathan Larraby."

CHAPTER TWENTY-ONE

THE COLOR DRAINED FROM KENDALL'S FACE. HER KNEES buckled and Jake caught her. He felt her trembling against his side. "How do you know it's Nathan?" Jake asked.

"He's the man I saw watching the house, the handsome man." Alice collapsed into tears again.

"He can't be dead," Kendall whispered. "He can't be."

"I'm sorry," Alice said.

Kendall's face crumpled, but she didn't cry. "I have to see him." She turned desperate eyes toward Jake. "Help me, please."

"The police aren't going to let us near him," Jake said softly. Two officers held the group back, while three others stood some distance away, studying something on the ground. One of the officers stepped back to speak to someone, and Jake saw a man lying on the ground. It was too dark to tell more than the fact that the man was tall and he was wearing light-colored pants. Like khakis. Nathan often wore khakis. Then the light from a flashlight moved over him and Jake saw his bloody chest. He tried to turn Kendall away, but her breath hitched, and he knew she'd seen it too. "Kendall, we need to leave. It's not safe."

"But I have to know for sure."

"I'll come back. There might be some mistake."

She didn't argue but moved like a robot beside him. "We have to tell Fergus," she finally said.

"Let's wait until we know for sure." The first thing he had to do was get Kendall to her room. If Nathan was dead, Kendall might be next on the list.

Kendall didn't remember the walk to their room. She moved to the window and stared at the lights from the police cars.

"Stay away from the window," Jake said, shutting the curtains.

Kendall turned to him. "Why?"

"You might be next."

Kendall walked away from the window and sat on the bed. She had no feeling in her body. Even her head was numb. Jake locked the door and proceeded to check every inch of the room and bathroom. Kendall watched his movements, and the numbness inside her started to thaw. She didn't want Jake to see her cry. "I need to take a shower." She walked toward the bathroom on shaky legs. She closed the door and undressed with trembling fingers. She turned on the shower and stepped under, not feeling the cold spray. The water warmed, but she still felt numb. He was dead. If he was Adam, she'd lost him all over again.

Kendall leaned her head against the tile and let her heart break. She sobbed like she had the first time she found out Adam was dead, that they were all dead . . . Adam, her father, Uncle John. She didn't hear the bathroom door open, didn't hear Jake come in. He pulled the shower curtain back and reached for her, putting his arms gently around her. "I'm sorry," he whispered.

She knew he was hurting too. She had seen the grief on his face before he covered it. He cared for Nathan more than he admitted. Probably more than he knew. He turned off the water and helped her from the shower. He wrapped a towel around her. She held the towel as he got another one and blotted the water from her hair. He patted her face and shoulders dry, then bent and dried her legs.

"I'm OK. You don't have to do that," she said, but he didn't stop and she let him.

He removed her towel and dried the rest of her body. His hands didn't linger but moved perfunctorily as if he were her doctor and she his patient. He grabbed one of the robes and wrapped her in it. "I'm sorry. I know you loved him."

"I think he was Adam."

Jake's hands froze on her robe. His face fell. "Nathan is Adam?"

"I think so. I thought you might be until you told me about your past. Twice Marco mentioned Adam when he was looking at you and Nathan. He said he saw Adam."

"Marco isn't all there sometimes." But Jake looked shaken by her revelation.

"There's a connection between Nathan and me. You've seen it. I can't explain it. There's some kind of bond." Kendall's eyes burned. "I think I've lost Adam twice."

Jake's jaw clenched. He pulled her into his arms, trying to comfort her, but she could feel his own hurt. "I'll go and identify the body. Maybe there's some mistake."

Kendall held on to him, not wanting him to leave her, but she had to know.

"Do you want to put on your clothes?"

"No, I'm just going to sit on the couch. Sorry I got you wet."

"It's just a little water." Jake settled her on the couch and handed her a pillow. He knelt beside her and brushed her cheek. His eyes were sad. "I won't be long."

When the door shut behind him, she pulled the pillow close and let go. Tears rolled down her cheeks like melting ice as the numbness thawed. Twice, she had failed Adam. Her gifts never worked for the people she loved most. She felt someone enter the room. She didn't want to open her eyes. Didn't want to see the truth in his face. As long as she didn't know for sure, there was hope. Her lips quivered, and she knew she would cry again. She opened her eyes. It wasn't Jake standing there watching her.

It was Nathan.

Kendall lay still, staring at Nathan in shock. Had his spirit come to say good-bye? Her eyes teared up again. "I'm so sorry, Nathan. There's so much I should have told you. So much I needed to ask. But I didn't expect you to die. Not now."

"Die?"

Didn't he realize he was dead? She'd heard of this happening. "You don't remember being stabbed?" Oh God, how did she explain this? "You died. Someone killed you."

"I'm not dead."

"Nathan, I'm sorry, but the police told us."

"I'm not dead." Then he lowered his head. Kendall expected to feel a rush of air as she had when her father's ghost, or the memory of him, passed through her, but instead she felt warm lips settle over hers, and her senses went off like fireworks.

Jake looked up at the light burning in Kendall's window as he walked from the abbey. He hadn't learned anything more. The police had carried the body away just as he got there. He would go to ID the body tomorrow. He couldn't leave Kendall alone tonight. He would move her back to the hotel. He slapped his fist against a thigh. Dammit, Nathan couldn't be dead.

When he reached the door, he saw Art peeking around a corner. He looked so pale his freckles stood out like chicken pox. "There's a bloody man in there with her," Art said. "I think it's the dead guy."

Jake's heart dropped to his stomach. He grabbed the knob—unlocked, dammit—and opened the door. Kendall was on the sofa and a man was bent over her. Jake pulled out his knife and rushed across the room.

The man growled and stood, turning fiery eyes toward Jake.

Kendall jumped to her feet and grabbed the man's arm. "Nathan, no." She put her hands behind his head, stood on tiptoe and kissed him.

The bottom fell from Jake's stomach, letting his heart sink right down to his balls. "I thought you were dead."

Kendall released Nathan from the kiss and turned on a lamp. "He's not." She smiled. Her eyes were swollen, her face lit with joy. Nathan, on the other hand, looked dazed, lips still parted from Kendall's kiss. The fire had immediately faded from his eyes. He was shifting quicker now.

Nathan was alive. That was a relief. Jake wondered why he felt so sick inside. "If you're not dead, then who is?"

Nathan sat down on the sofa. "Must have been the guy who attacked me. I followed him to the abbey, and he caught me off guard."

"You killed him?" Kendall said.

"Not me. He hit me in the head with a bag that felt like it held a brick. I blacked out. I woke up when someone screamed. I found him a few feet away, dead."

"Sure you didn't do it and just don't remember?" Jake asked. "I can't see a bag knocking you out, with or without a brick."

"I remember when I kill someone," Nathan said.

"Did you recognize him?" Kendall asked.

"No. He was wearing a hooded sweatshirt. I didn't have time to check him out. I heard people coming."

"The guy who was watching us in town wore a hood," Jake said. "I chased him, but I lost him."

"I bet the chalice was in the bag he hit you with," Kendall said. "He must have stolen it."

"The Blue Chalice was stolen?" Nathan asked.

"Someone killed the caretaker at Little Saint Michael's and stole the chalice. We thought it was you," Jake said.

"Someone was using the caretaker's room, and you were registered here," Kendall said. "The group was expecting you."

"It wasn't me," Nathan said. "I was going to look for it, but I got sidetracked."

"Someone must have been impersonating you to get close to the Blue Chalice," Kendall said. "The only people who can get into the house are supporters of the trust that runs the place. I bet if you check, you'll find a fat donation to the trust in your name."

"I support the well," Nathan said. "I started months ago when I decided to investigate the place."

"I'd bet anything the same guy killed the caretaker and your attacker," Jake said.

"Maybe not a guy," Nathan said. "I smelled a woman just before I was attacked. It might have been Brandi. She said she'd kill anyone who got in her way. If he had the chalice, she probably killed him. I think she followed me from the hotel."

"She was at the hotel with you?" Kendall asked, sounding too possessive for Jake's comfort. Was she jealous?

"She saw us leave the well."

"What did she want?" Kendall asked.

"The Spear of Destiny."

"She keeps turning up like a bad penny," Jake said.

"She was already here searching for the Fountain of Youth. Thomas had told her that the Reaper was interested in England and the fountain. She did some research, found out about the Chalice Well, and came to check it out."

"Where is she now?" Jake asked.

"I don't know. I removed her from my room and came here to find you."

"Why haven't you contacted us?" Kendall asked. She kept looking at Nathan as if she'd seen a ghost. If Nathan was Adam, she had. A ghost that she had admitted she was in love with. How the hell could he compete with that?

"I was detained by Raphael."

"He kidnapped you?" Jake asked. "He didn't mention that."

"You've seen him?" Nathan asked.

"He was looking for you earlier," Jake said. "He seems to think he's your guardian angel."

"Where is he now?" Nathan asked.

"He walked through the wall and disappeared," Jake said. "Just like you said."

"He has some interesting tricks," Nathan said.

"Yeah," Jake said. "He admitted to hiding the treasure. And before you ask, no, he didn't say where. What does Raphael want with you?"

"I figured he thought turnabout was fair play, but he didn't hurt me," Nathan said. "He grabbed me in the abbey at King Arthur's grave. He did something and knocked me out. I woke up long enough to see him cut both our wrists and stick them together. Then I passed out again. I think he read my memories."

Kendall sat beside Nathan. "That's how I felt when the shadow leaned over me in the cave, like he was reading my mind, my memories."

"That might explain the cut on your wrist," Nathan said.

"Maybe it was Raphael in the cave, not the Reaper," Kendall said. "I wonder if there are side effects from mixing the blood." She glanced at her wrist with an uneasy expression.

"It sounds similar to what you do," Jake said. "Touch things, read them. You said blood and fluids are good conductors."

"Raphael has a dark side, but I don't think he's a monster. Though he's definitely got some odd abilities," Nathan said. "He can do this thing with his hands . . . like block stuff, make stuff happen. Something was happening in the room where we were. There was a whirring noise and he looked frightened. I saw some kind of misty thing. Raphael said 'he figured it out' and put his hands up like he was blocking something from coming through. Then I blacked out again and woke up at the base of the Tor."

"He told us the Reaper was trying to figure out a way to get to the fountain without crossing the statues," Kendall said. "So the fountain and the statues must be wherever he took you, and I would bet anything that it's under the Tor where we heard the humming."

"I saw a statue," Nathan said.

"You saw it?" Kendall asked, eyes wide.

"The room he left me in was just off another room. It looked like a Roman temple. There were columns, and the ceiling looked like a da Vinci painting. There was a golden glow coming from somewhere, but I didn't see a light. He refused to tell me where I was. He said 'in time.'"

"He didn't explain anything?" Kendall asked.

"Nothing that made sense. He said I was more powerful than he'd thought."

"Powerful? He was talking about your curse?" Kendall asked.

"I guess."

"Did he know where it came from?" Jake asked. "I mean it is odd that your eyes look like his when you go into adrenaline mode."

"He didn't say where it came from. He did say I wasn't supposed to be normal."

"That doesn't sound like a curse," Kendall said. "I've never thought it was a curse."

"On another note, Brandi had alarming information," Nathan said.

"She seems to be the bearer of bad news," Jake said. "What's it this time?"

Nathan looked grim. "The Reaper might have a child."

The color drained from Kendall's face. "I think it's me."

"What?"

"She thinks the Reaper may be her father," Jake said.

Nathan looked stunned. "Bloody hell."

"That's pretty much what I said," Jake said.

"Why would you think that?" Nathan asked.

"That shadow in the cave felt familiar. And dark. I think he recognized me."

"He probably knows everything about us," Jake said.

"You said your father took you to the castle. The Reaper can't pass the statues," Nathan said.

"He could have found a way past, or stolen someone's key. Marco said there was an attack after Adam and I left the castle and that many of the Protettori were destroyed. He must have found a way through."

"Or sent his minions to do his dirty work, like he did Edward," Jake said.

"Even if he is the Reaper," Nathan said, "it doesn't change who you are."

"We could speculate all day about who the Reaper is," Jake said. "We need to focus on stopping him. Let's wait a couple of hours. Then we'll go check out this priest hole."

"Priest hole?" Nathan asked.

They explained the hidden entrance to the Tor. "We might need equipment," Jake said, "but we can at least see if it's a tunnel or just a hiding place. Marco thinks it's a tunnel."

"Marco knows?" Nathan asked.

"Marco and Fergus are here."

"Bloody hell. I told them to stay away. Fergus takes orders as well as Jake."

"You'd better take a shower. Fergus might panic if he sees blood on you," Jake said.

"Fergus has seen me at my worst," Nathan said. "A little blood won't derail him."

"He knows about your condition?" Kendall asked.

Nathan nodded. "He's been trying to convince me to see a doctor. Lot of good that'll do. This isn't science or medicine. It's a freak show."

"Fergus brought our things from Italy. Jake, run down and get his bag," Kendall ordered.

And leave the two of them alone? Jake grunted and walked to the door.

"I'm glad you're here," Kendall said. "We were worried about you."

Nathan gave a humorless laugh. "I doubt Jake worried too much."

"A lot more than he lets on."

Nathan looked at the bed. "Is everything OK with you?"

Kendall was sure she was blushing. Nathan stared at her, his jaw tight, until she felt like she would burst with guilt. She nodded. "Nathan, we're . . ."

"I'm going to shower." Nathan got up and walked to the bathroom.

Kendall sat on the chair and felt like crying. She didn't want to hurt him or Jake. She cared for them both. She went to the kitchenette and heated up some soup in case he might be hungry.

The door opened and Jake stepped in, carrying Nathan's bag. Fergus was behind him.

"Isn't Marco with you?" Kendall asked.

"He's sleeping," Fergus said. "Forgive my appearance. I was in bed as well." His hair was perfectly groomed and his manner formal, even though he was in pajamas. "Where is Nathan?"

"He's in the shower," Kendall said. "I heated up some soup for him."

"You left the room?" Jake asked.

"Just to go down the hall for a can of soup. You know, Art is watching our room."

"I saw him earlier. He was worried about you. He thought you were in here with a dead man."

"Art did?" Kendall asked, surprised.

"Who is Art?" Fergus asked.

"The kid who told you where to find us before," Jake said. "He was the one who found the dead body."

Fergus's eyebrows shot up. "Dead body?"

"Someone was killed in the abbey earlier," Kendall said. "We thought it was Nathan."

Nathan walked out of the bathroom at that moment, wrapped in a towel.

"Obviously it wasn't," Jake said.

"Who was killed?" Fergus asked.

"We don't know," Nathan said. "But he attacked me. We think Brandi killed him."

"Oh my," Fergus said. "She does get around."

Nathan walked over and sat on the small sofa. He looked exhausted, but his eyes never left Kendall. It was an effort not to return the stare. Other than in his dark bedroom, she'd never seen him without a shirt.

"Are you all right, Nathan?" Fergus asked. "You don't look well."

"I'm confused and I'm hungry," he said, looking at Kendall. He'd been doing that a lot since their kiss.

Nathan had never kissed her. It must have been to prove that he wasn't a ghost, but the kiss had taken her by surprise. It had felt good. What was wrong with her? The bed was barely cold from making love with Jake.

"I heated up some soup," she said, pointing to the cup on the table. "It should still be hot. The drinkable kind is all they had. This one's pretty good."

He moved to the table. "Thank you." Usually, she couldn't read anything except his body language, and Kendall was certain he guarded even that. But this time she felt his hurt.

She looked away so he didn't see her eyes. "You have a cut on your neck. I'll get the first aid kit." It wasn't deep, but no telling where he'd gotten it. While he drank the soup and Fergus fussed over him, Kendall got the small kit she'd seen in the bathroom. She carried it to Nathan and pulled up a chair beside him.

"What are you doing?" Jake asked.

"Putting a bandage on his cut." And studying his tattoo. It looked like a circle with lines crisscrossing the middle. She was certain she'd seen that design somewhere before. After a moment, she realized why it was familiar.

"Can't he do that?" Jake muttered.

She clenched her jaw and touched Nathan's neck to examine the wound. She and Nathan both jumped. "Sorry, I'm jumpy."

"If you're jumpy, let Fergus take over," Jake said, still scowling.

"I'll manage," she said. The cut was small, but given the location, just above his jugular vein, she wondered if his attacker had been trying to slit his throat. He tilted his head so she could work on the cut. Jake stood by while she finished the job, brows drawn together like a disapproving chaperone. There was no denying that she was drawn to Nathan. Up close, his body was as sexy as Jake's. In fact, their bodies looked a lot alike. That sent her thoughts to places they didn't belong. She felt a blush flood her cheeks. *I am not a floozy. They just both happen to be very good-looking men.* Any woman would be attracted to them. Even if she was already halfway in love with Jake.

In love with Jake. That was the first time she had really admitted it to herself.

She jumped up as soon as she was finished and took the first aid kit back to the bathroom. She examined her reflection to see if she was as flushed as she felt. She was. She wet a cloth and pressed it to her cheeks. She walked back into the room, grabbing a bottle of water she'd brought from the kitchenette. She unscrewed the lid and took a long drink.

"You look overheated," Jake said, appearing at her side.

Kendall almost choked. "It's been an emotional hour," she said, wiping her mouth where the water had spilled down her chin.

"I know. I saw you kissing him."

"He was just proving that he wasn't dead. I thought he was dead. He kept saying he wasn't. Ghosts don't kiss."

Jake's jaw got even tighter. "They also don't shake hands. Guess that wasn't good enough." He picked up Nathan's bag by the door and walked across the room. "I'm sure you wanna get dressed," he said, dropping it on the table.

He and Nathan shared one of their testosterone-loaded looks. Nathan took the bag and went to the bathroom. Kendall glanced at Fergus and thought he rolled his eyes. He caught her looking and put on his butler face.

"I should get back and check on Marco," Fergus said. "I don't like leaving him alone for long."

"I'm surprised how well he's doing," Kendall said.

"He improved right after you left."

"Maybe he was faking," Jake said.

Fergus shook his head. "I don't think so. He seems to heal quickly."

"Something in the water, I guess," Jake said.

"He talked about drinking a lot after you left. I thought he was asking for water, but he didn't want water. Then he mentioned something about the fountain. I thought he was rambling."

"He didn't have anything unusual to drink, did he?" Kendall asked.

"I found a small vial under his bed. I asked the nurse about it. She hadn't seen it. It looked old, like something in one of Nathan's collections, but Marco hadn't left the bed."

"Where could it have come from?" Kendall asked.

"It was right after Raphael vanished," Fergus said. "Perhaps he gave it to Marco."

"Nathan said Raphael saw Marco," Jake said.

Kendall nodded. "And Raphael told us that the water from the fountain is how he recovered."

"You mean how he went from being dead to being alive," Jake said.

"You think it was water from *the* fountain?" Fergus asked.

"It could have been," Kendall said. "Marco is certainly doing better now. When I was in the room in the castle with the mural and the round table, I saw some vials and cups. That must have been water from the fountain."

"Oh my. There was a bit left in the bottom and I dumped it out."

"I wish you'd kept it," Kendall said.

"I wish I had drunk it," Fergus said.

Nathan came out of the bathroom dressed in jeans, a long-sleeved T-shirt, and boots. What was up with him? A tattoo? Jeans? She had thought for a while that he might be hiding behind his money, suits, and no-nonsense manner. Now she was even more suspicious.

Fergus stood. "Will I see you in the room later?" he asked Nathan.

Nathan shook his head. "No. I'm sleeping here."

Jake lifted a brow. "You are?"

"I am." Nathan sat down at the table.

Fergus frowned as he passed Kendall. "Will you keep an eye on him?" he whispered.

Kendall nodded. When the door closed behind Fergus, she sat at the table. "This has been a crazy, intense night, but we have work to do and not much time. Raphael said those lights over the Tor are the Reaper trying to come through. We have to stop him before he gets the chalice to the Fountain of Youth."

"Isn't this the Protettori's job?" Jake asked.

"I think the Protettori need help," Kendall said.

Jake leaned on the table, his brow furrowed. "We need a strategy and weapons."

"First, we need knowledge." She opened the journal.

"Did you make sense of it?" Nathan asked.

"It seems to be a mix of Latin, Italian, and Old English. I think I've found references to the Fountain of Life, hidden within sacred ground, and Beacon at Sea. Long ago, the Tor was surrounded by water. The mountain was referred to as a beacon. And it was considered a sacred place by ancient civilizations. I think we all agree that the Tor is probably where the fountain is hidden."

"We just have to figure out how to get inside," Nathan said.

"Easier said than done," Jake said.

"Not necessarily." She turned the journal to another page and pointed out a tiny sketch. A circle. "I think I've seen this symbol on the cave wall." She touched Nathan's shoulder. "And on your arm. Your tattoo."

CHAPTER TWENTY-TWO

D ON'T TELL ME YOU DREAMED ABOUT THE WHEEL TOO,"
Jake said.

Nathan looked almost embarrassed. "OK."

"Hell, is there anything about this stuff you haven't
dreamed?"

"You did dream about it, didn't you?" Kendall asked.

Nathan nodded. "A lot. In a . . . disturbed moment, I had it
tattooed on me."

"I'll translate that to a drunken moment," Jake said. "So
you're a walking map."

"I think if we can find that symbol again, we'll find the entrance to the Fountain of Youth," Kendall said. "The second part
is the chalice." Kendall turned to the sketches. "We know these
four sketches are probably the relics." She pointed to one that
resembled a bowl. "This one . . . I think this is the Holy Grail. In
fact, I saw it in a vision, and I'm almost certain that's what it is."

"You saw it?" Nathan asked.

She nodded. "It was amazing. I'll tell you all about it when
we have more time."

Jake looked so sullen she would have slapped him, but she was so glad they were both sitting at the table alive and well that she ignored his bad humor.

"Also, Raphael looked shocked when I told him King Arthur said to find the chalice. And we know what King Arthur's quest was."

"The Holy Grail," Nathan said. "Brandi said the Reaper was searching for it."

"I think that's proof. We're looking for the Holy Grail. What we don't know is whether the Blue Chalice is the grail. We haven't seen it. But people are dying over it, so we have to assume it is."

"We have to find the chalice before he does," Nathan said. "If it's not too late."

"Assuming your attacker stole it, I'm surprised it wasn't with the body," Kendall said.

"I didn't know it was missing, so I wasn't looking for it," Nathan said. "I didn't have much time to look at anything. As soon as I saw his body, I heard the police coming. I almost didn't get away in time."

"We need to go back and search the area," Kendall said. "If it's not there, then the cops found it, or the killer already gave it to the Reaper."

"Or Brandi accomplished her goal," Jake said. "After what Marco said, I think Brandi might be right about destroying the relics. If they're destroyed, there's no threat of some egotistical maniac trying to use them."

"We can't destroy them," Nathan said.

"We won't," Kendall said. "At least not until we see if they're your cure."

Nathan looked tired. "I don't think it will be. Raphael said there was a way to get rid of this thing, but it would be complicated. It's not likely I'll just drink from the fountain and be cured."

"But it keeps them young for . . . centuries," Kendall said. "And Fergus thinks Raphael gave Marco some to drink before he escaped the mansion. He found a strange vial under the bed. Maybe it'll cure you."

Nathan's face brightened. "Marco told me he hadn't had the drink in a long time. I asked if he needed water, and he said not that kind."

"You'll be taking a risk," Jake said. "We don't know what the side effects might be."

"Can they be any worse?" Nathan asked.

"Hell yeah. There are people who would kill to have what you have," Jake said. "You're like a superhero."

"Superheroes don't hurt people they . . ." He glanced at Kendall. "They don't hurt their friends."

"Maybe you need to control it. Like Kendall needs to control her gift."

"Don't look so self-righteous," Nathan said. "You have your own issues, your own secrets too."

"And we're back to fighting." She threw up her hands. "If you two don't stop this pissing contest, I'm going to walk out of here and let you find the damned Fountain of Youth by yourselves. I could be at home on a date right now with a really hot guy instead of listening to you poke at each other like kids."

Nathan and Jake turned their glares on her. "What hot date?" Nathan asked.

"The neighbor I told you about, the one who's trying to get in her pants. *Todd.*" Jake made it sound like a curse word. "You want to date him after what we. . ." Jake looked at Nathan and stopped speaking.

"I didn't say that—"

"You can't date him," Nathan said. "I haven't finished checking him out."

"My God. I don't need you to do background checks on my dates," Kendall said.

"Someone with your gift would be a target for crooks all over the world," Nathan said. "If they find out what you can do, you'll be on the run for the rest of your life."

"He's right," Jake said. "Dating isn't safe." They were both looking at her with identical frowns, and she'd noticed for the first time that they looked a lot alike when they were both scruffy and wearing jeans. Maybe that explained her attraction to both. That thought just made her more irritated.

"Are you actually sitting there telling me that I'm not allowed to date?"

"Why do you need to date?" Nathan asked. "You haven't been dating before."

Kendall shook her head in bewilderment. "I can't. You interrupt every date I try to go on."

"Me?" Nathan asked, looking blank.

"Yes, you do. I want to date for the same reason everyone in the world dates."

"Sex," Jake said, his face set like stone.

"Not sex." Not *just* sex. "Male companionship. Someone to talk to."

"You have *us* . . . *me,*" Jake corrected, frowning at Nathan.

"You two don't talk. You order," she said. "You demand. I don't like taking orders any more than you do, but I tolerate it because I lo . . . I respect you. I need more from a man than orders and demands disguised as protection." She turned and walked toward the bathroom.

"Well hell," Jake said as she closed the door. "She's cranky. If I didn't know better, I'd think it was that time of the month."

"How the bloody hell do you know it's not?" Nathan asked.

Kendall opened the door and stuck her head out. "If you're going to talk about someone behind her back, at least have the decency to whisper." She slammed the door. If there were a window in here, she'd climb out and find the priest hole herself. When she'd calmed down enough to realize her outburst came just as much from frustration with the situation as from frustration with Jake and Nathan for their bickering, she walked out of the bathroom.

Nathan grabbed her and pulled her against the wall. She gaped at him. "There's someone at the door," he whispered.

"It's probably Fergus," she whispered back.

"No, he knows to knock once, then twice. Stay here." Nathan eased toward the door, where Jake was already in place beside the door, gun drawn. On Jake's signal, Nathan turned the knob and yanked the door open. Moving fast, Jake whirled, gun pointed.

"Hell." He disappeared for two seconds and then appeared again, dragging Brandi with him, hand clamped over her mouth as she struggled. Then she saw Nathan, and her eyes widened with shock. She bit Jake's hand. He cursed and let go.

Brandi tried to get to the door, but Jake stopped her. She stared at Nathan. "You're dead."

"So I've heard," Nathan said.

"What are you?" She stepped behind Jake. "A vampire. Oh my God."

"He's strange," Jake said. "But he's not a vampire. I hope."

Brandi stopped struggling. "But I saw you dead."

"Were you dead?" Jake asked Nathan.

Nathan scowled. "Of course I wasn't dead."

"You never know. Raphael came back from the dead, and you both have the same eyes," Jake said.

"Then who did I kill?" Brandi asked.

"The guy who attacked me," Nathan said. "He hit me over the head with a bag."

"The neighbor. It must have been him," Brandi said. "He's tall. And I couldn't see his face in the dark."

"Whose neighbor?" Kendall asked.

"Yours," Brandi said. "Todd."

CHAPTER TWENTY-THREE

Todd's here? He's dead?"

"He works for the Reaper," Brandi said. "That's who I warned you about."

"Oh my God." Kendall was stunned.

"Why didn't you put that in the note?" Jake asked.

"I was in a hurry," Brandi said. "And I wasn't positive until afterward."

"How do you know Todd?" Jake asked.

"I saw him at her apartment. He was watching her. Then I saw him here watching the house where you were staying."

"I had no idea," Kendall said. Maybe she should have. With her usual luck in the romance department, she should have known that his persistence was more than attraction. "That's disappointing."

"We told you dating was dangerous," Nathan said.

Jake started to agree; then he frowned, probably recalling his request that she date him.

She'd never have a private life now. Heck, she wasn't sure she wanted one.

"Must have been his camera outside your apartment," Jake said.

"That means the Reaper is watching her," Nathan said, his brows knitted together.

"That's why I sensed something about my apartment when I touched Brandi's letter."

"Have you seen the Reaper?" Nathan asked.

Brandi shook her head. "No, but I heard Todd on the phone with him. He's coming here, and he's sending more men. He wants the chalice."

"Did Todd have it?" Nathan asked. "It was stolen earlier."

"I didn't see it," Brandi said.

"If he didn't have it, the Reaper must have it," Kendall said. "We've got to stop him. We'll have to go to the priest—" She stopped. She didn't trust Brandi yet.

"Exactly why did you come here?" Jake asked Brandi. "To confess to Nathan's murder?"

She brushed at a smudge of dirt on her shirt. "I don't have anywhere else to go. Someone broke into my room and took everything. I think it was Todd. I don't even have my wallet."

"You need a place to sleep?" Kendall asked. "You can sleep here."

"Here?" Brandi looked at Nathan and frowned.

"He's safe," Jake said, "if you don't startle him."

Nathan gave her a dry look. "I promise I won't kill you. Not tonight. I'm the one who should be worried. You said you'd kill anyone who gets in your way. I don't want to be your second victim tonight."

"I'm not going to kill you." She gave Nathan a sarcastic smile. "At least not tonight. Besides, what chance would I have against a man with Jake's skills and your and Kendall's abilities?"

"Well, we have an agreement," Kendall said. "No one kills anyone."

"If you do," Jake said to Brandi, "Raphael will hunt you down. He's grown protective of Nathan."

"Who's Raphael?" Brandi asked.

"You think Nathan's strange. Raphael's a hell of a lot scarier," Jake said. "How did you find us?"

"I knew they moved the guests from Little Saint Michael's to the Abbey House. I was in the hall when Fergus left your room."

"You can sleep on the sofa," Kendall said.

"Where will Nathan sleep?" Jake asked.

"You think you're sleeping in the bed?" Nathan asked.

"It's my room," Jake said. "And Kendall's."

"And where's she supposed to sleep?" Nathan asked, his eyes narrowed.

"In the bed, where she's been sleeping."

"Like hell."

"What's your idea?" Jake asked. "All four of us pile up in the bed?"

"We can worry about sleeping arrangements later," Kendall said. "Right now, we need to search the area for the chalice. Todd might have dropped it."

"We can't go until the cops leave," Jake said.

"That could be hours," Kendall said.

"We don't want them to catch us in the area," Jake said. "We'll try again in a few hours. They should be gone by then."

"I hope they didn't find it," Kendall said.

"We'd better get a couple hours' sleep," Jake said. "This might be our only chance." He glanced at the bed.

"Brandi and I will take the bed," Kendall said. "You two can share the sofa or go sleep with Fergus."

"Fergus and Marco are already sharing a bed," Jake said. "And I'm not leaving you alone, not with her." He glanced at Nathan. "Not with anyone."

"I'm not leaving either," Nathan said.

"I don't suppose I could borrow your shower . . . and some clean clothes?" Brandi asked Kendall.

They were about the same size, and Kendall didn't want her parading around in front of Nathan and Jake with only a bathrobe. "Sure."

While Brandi showered, Kendall, Nathan, and Jake discussed the priest hole. They agreed not to mention it to Brandi. They didn't know if they could trust her yet. The plan was to split up when the cops left the area. Nathan and Brandi were more familiar with the murder scene, so they would look for the chalice. Kendall and Jake knew where the priest hole was, so they would see where it led.

By the time Brandi exited the bathroom, dressed in Kendall's yoga pants and T-shirt, Nathan and Jake had made up a bed on the floor, having decided that the sofa wasn't long enough for either of them. Brandi got into bed—as far from the men as possible—and lay down. Kendall climbed in while Jake and Nathan were still sorting out pillows.

"You got anything to sleep in?" Nathan asked.

"I don't usually sleep in anything," Jake said.

"I'm not sleeping next to you if you're naked."

"I'm wearing my underwear," Jake said. "Why are you asking? You have your own clothes."

"I didn't bring anything to sleep in. I don't wear pajamas."

"You're sleeping in underwear tonight."

Both men stripped to their underwear after the lights were out. But they could still be seen by the light from the alarm clock. Kendall looked over at Brandi and saw her watching.

"You're one lucky girl," Brandi whispered. "I think."

"You don't have to live with them. Sometimes I'd trade them both for a good piece of fudge."

Jake and Nathan each lay as far to the edge of the blanket as they could, but the soft jabs continued.

"See what I mean," Kendall said. "They do this all the time." Kendall didn't expect to get any sleep. She wasn't completely comfortable next to Brandi, but she felt somewhat better knowing Jake and Nathan were a few feet away. Brandi was right about Nathan and Jake being handy in a fight. She'd put them up against almost anything. She drifted off, thinking about the chalice and the priest hole and woke in the middle of the night to an empty bed. Her first thought was that Jake was missing. Then she remembered Jake and Nathan were on the floor. Brandi was the one missing. Kendall got out of bed and walked toward the bathroom. A hand grabbed her ankle.

"Where you going?" Jake asked, leaning on one arm.

"I'm looking for Brandi."

Jake let go of her ankle and stood. "Is she in the bathroom?"

"I was going to check." They walked to the bathroom, but the door wasn't closed. Kendall opened it wider and flipped on the light. Brandi wasn't there.

"What's going on?" Nathan asked.

Kendall turned and blinked. She had gotten sort of used to seeing Jake in his underwear. Not Nathan. "Brandi's gone."

Jake turned on the lights in the room and walked to the bed. He touched the side where Brandi had slept. "It's cold. She's been gone for a while. Dammit. She's gone to find the chalice."

"I told you I didn't trust her," Nathan said.

"Could you both put on some clothes?" She needed to focus.

They picked up their clothes from the sofa and started getting dressed.

"We know where she's going," Kendall said, grabbing her things and heading to the bathroom.

"Between your sixth sense and Nathan's sense of smell, maybe we'll get lucky," Jake said.

Before they could leave, someone tapped on the door. "Maybe that's her," Kendall said.

"No, it's Fergus." Nathan opened the door and Fergus stepped inside. He looked disheveled. "Marco is gone. He was sleeping, and I woke up to go to the"—he glanced at Kendall—"restroom, and I saw he wasn't in his bed. He's probably wandering around the ruins. He kept talking about how long it had been since he's been here."

"Brandi's missing too," Nathan said.

"You don't think she would have . . ." Kendall stopped.

"Kidnapped him?" Jake finished.

"He's got all the knowledge she needs in his head," Kendall said.

"We have to find them," Nathan said. "We can't let Brandi find the chalice first. Fergus, you stay here just in case he's wandered off and comes back."

Jake stuck his gun under his shirt. He handed Kendall a knife. "You don't need a weapon," he said to Nathan.

Kendall, Nathan, and Jake hurried toward the door leading to the abbey grounds. Halle, Rhonda, and Art's mother were also there. Art's mother was in tears.

"What's happened?" Kendall asked.

"Her little boy is missing," Halle said, looking at Nathan.

"Again?" Jake muttered.

Art's mother wiped her eyes. "He disappeared from his bed. I'm afraid something bad has happened after those two murders."

Kendall looked at Nathan and Jake. Another person missing wasn't a good sign. If it was just Brandi and Marco, she would believe Brandi had taken the old man. "I'm sure he just went to explore."

"But he's scared of the dark. And after finding that dead body, he was terrified. What if the murderer came back to silence him? Oh, my poor baby."

"Don't panic," Kendall said. "I'm sure he's nearby. Little boys are braver than you might think." Adam was.

"He was really excited tonight. He kept talking about a hidden tunnel and treasure. Art's imagination has been even worse here. He was named after King Arthur, you know."

"Why don't you ladies let us look for him," Jake said. "We're experienced at this."

"You've helped the police find people?" Halle asked.

"Kendall is excellent at finding things," Jake said. "She'll be able to focus better with fewer people there."

"She is amazing," Halle said to Art's mother. "She contacted King Arthur, and we all saw a vision of Merlin. If anyone can find your son, she can."

Kendall was touched at Halle's faith in her, but she felt like a jerk knowing she'd deceived the group. "I promise I'll do my best to find him."

"What are you and Jake doing here?" Rhonda asked, her gaze drifting to Nathan.

"We were going for a walk," Jake said. "She felt drawn to the ruins tonight."

"Maybe it's because of Art," Halle suggested.

"Have we met?" Rhonda asked Nathan. "You look familiar."

"I don't believe so," Nathan said, already wearing his do-not-disturb face, but it didn't seem to have an effect on Rhonda.

"This is . . ." Kendall glanced at Nathan, unsure who he wanted to be.

"Kendall's brother Nick," Jake said, without giving Nathan a chance to speak.

Nathan frowned at Jake, but he looked relieved.

"We need to get moving so we can look for the boy," Jake said.

"Please hurry and find my baby," Art's mother urged.

"We will. You go back to the room and wait. He might be exploring and come back," Jake said.

It took a minute longer to convince Rhonda to stay at the house with the other women. Kendall hurried toward the ruins. Jake and Nathan stayed on each side of her.

"We should spread out," Kendall said.

Jake and Nathan both refused. "It's too dangerous," Jake said. "Move quietly. We don't want Brandi to know we're coming."

The ruins were quiet, and there was an odd feeling that Kendall couldn't put a finger on. "Let's check the murder scene first."

But they weren't there. Neither was the chalice. "We need to check the tunnel," Jake said.

"Do you feel that vibration?" Kendall asked.

"No," Jake said. Nathan shook his head.

"It's like the ground is vibrating. I have a really bad feeling."

Jake turned to look at the Tor. "The last time you said the ground was vibrating, we saw the lights—"

"What the devil is that?" Nathan asked.

The balls of light were circling above the Tor.

"The devil might be right," Jake said. "I think that's the Reaper trying to come through."

"We have to hurry," Kendall said.

They ran to the Lady Chapel and found the stone covering the priest hole. "Kendall, hold the flashlight. Nathan, you stand watch."

Nathan didn't listen. He leaned closer to the stone. "Do you hear that?"

"I don't hear anything," Jake said.

Kendall didn't hear anything either. "What do you hear?"

"A voice. I think someone is calling for help."

"Hurry," Kendall said.

Kendall pushed the round stone and the wall moved back, revealing the steps. A face appeared at the bottom. "Help!"

CHAPTER TWENTY-FOUR

A RT?" KENDALL LEANED INTO THE HOLE.
"No you don't." Jake grabbed her arm and pulled her back. He shone the light at the bottom where Art was scrambling up the steps. When he reached the top, Jake took his arm and helped him out. His face was white, freckles lost in a smear of dirt. "They took them. The bad men took them."

"Who?" Jake asked.

Art was panting. "Merlin and Guinevere."

"Who?" Kendall asked.

"I found them. I found Merlin and Guinevere." He wiped his face, leaving a big streak of dirt. "Well, they found me, but I saw them first."

"Where?"

"Over there." Art pointed to the abbot's kitchen. "I saw them sneaking into the abbot's kitchen. That's where she hid it."

"Who hid what?" Nathan asked.

"Guinevere hid the chalice. I saw her hide it earlier, before I found the dead man. I didn't know she was Guinevere until I saw her with Merlin. I thought she was just a redheaded lady."

"What happened to the chalice?" Nathan asked.

"I went to get it, but the bad men took it. They were going to kill Guinevere and Merlin if I didn't give it to them. Mom's never going to believe this."

"Excuse us a minute, Art." Jake pulled Kendall and Nathan aside. "What do we do about him? He'll tell everyone."

"What are you suggesting? That we . . . silence him?"

"We can't let him ruin this," Nathan said.

"We could take him with us," Kendall said.

"He'll slow us down," Jake said.

"I don't like how you're looking at him," Kendall said to Jake. "You are not going to hurt him."

"I never said I would hurt him," Jake said. "But we have to keep him quiet. Nathan, can you do your Hulk thing and scare him into keeping his mouth shut?"

"I don't know that I can do it on demand," Nathan said.

"I'll hit you," Jake offered.

"For God's sake, you're not going to turn Nathan loose on a little boy. I don't care how irritating he is. Stay here, both of you."

Kendall walked back to Art and knelt down in front of him. "You did a wise thing to give up the chalice, but we need to get it back and save Merlin and Guinevere. Can you keep a secret, Art? An important secret?"

He nodded.

"No one knows Merlin and Guinevere are here. And they can't find out. The secret must be protected. You'll be guarding King Arthur's kingdom, just like a knight."

"Are they knights?" Art asked, looking at Nathan and Jake.

"Sort of."

"Which one is King Arthur?"

"Uh . . . it's a secret."

"Is the other one Lancelot?"

"Uh . . . a secret, remember?"

"Maybe you're Guinevere, and not her."

"You have to keep the secret. You can't tell anyone what you found or what you've seen. Promise?"

Art nodded and put up his fingers in the scouts honor sign. "Can I just tell my friend Garrett?"

"No."

"Frankie?"

"Who's Frankie?"

"My pet snake."

"You can tell Frankie. No one else. Now run back to the house. We'll watch to make sure you get inside. Go straight to your mom and tell her you're sorry for scaring her. Tell her you wanted to see the ruins at night. Go."

Art started running.

"And knights never stick out their tongues at other knights," Jake called softly after him.

Art stopped and turned around. He thumped his fist against his chest and grinned. Kendall watched him until he was safely inside. Then she moved down the steps and joined Nathan and Jake, who had started checking the steps.

"The kid was excited. He should've been scared," Jake said.

"That was bloody brilliant," Nathan said. "You'll make a good mother."

Jake's jaw clenched. "I don't suppose we could get you to go back and stay with Fergus," he said to Kendall.

"No."

"If the Reaper is in there," Nathan said, "I don't want you here."

"You're wasting your breath," Jake said. "She won't leave."

"I appreciate your concern, but I have to see this through. I have my reasons."

"Because you think the Reaper is your father?" Nathan said to Kendall.

"Come on. We have to go," Jake said. "If the Reaper gets the chalice to the Fountain of Youth, it won't matter whose father he is. Watch out for booby traps."

The tunnel was in good shape for being so old. The stones that made up the walls and floor were hand cut. In other circumstances, Kendall would have loved to examine it. But now the place felt eerie, maybe because she was almost certain the Reaper was waiting for them on the other side. And she was dreadfully afraid that he was her father, no matter what Nathan said.

"This place could be filled with hiding places," Nathan said, directing his light at the walls. A few yards later, they came to a split in the tunnel. They stopped and looked at both passages.

"This gives me a bad feeling," Jake said. "Door number one or door number two? One of them is bound to be a trap."

"Kendall, you sense anything?" Nathan asked.

Kendall put her hand on the wall between the two tunnels. She closed her eyes and felt the air change. It was charged with electricity. Statues? Her eyes flew open, and she heard a wild yell, followed by a horse's snort. "Someone's coming."

"I don't hear anything," Jake said.

Nathan shook his head. "Nothing."

"You can't hear the yelling and the horse. The hooves are pounding—oh my God!"

A large black horse appeared out of the darkness of the tunnel. A knight dressed in black sat astride the horse, his sword raised. His eyes were glowing.

"What is it?" Jake asked.

"A black knight." He was probably another ghost, but Kendall grabbed both men by the arm and yanked them out of the way. Horse and rider turned toward them, coming fast. The black knight drew back his sword and swung. Kendall felt the rush of air and she screamed. The screaming continued even after she'd closed her mouth. She opened her eyes and saw she was lying on snow-covered ground.

"Nathan! Jake!" She tried to jump up, but her feet wouldn't move. She turned her head and saw both men lying near her, struggling to sit up.

"What the bloody hell?" Nathan looked at the ground. "Where'd the tunnel go?"

They turned and looked behind them. It was a battlefield, like the one where she'd seen King Arthur. Behind them a fort sat high on a hill—a hill fort, like Camelot had once been. There were men on horseback and some on foot, fighting as snow blanketed the ground, mixing with blood. "I think we're stuck in one of Kendall's visions," Jake said. "Look at that."

"You can see it too?" Kendall asked.

"Yeah," Nathan said.

"I think it's Camelot," Kendall said.

"Damn, it's him," Jake said. "There on the hill."

It was Arthur. The Arthur she'd seen in her vision. "It is him."

"Bloody hell," Nathan said, but he was looking farther down the battlefield. "If this is a vision, how come that knight is looking at us?"

"What?"

A knight tossed a decapitated head on the ground and urged his horse toward them.

"It's the black knight I saw in the tunnel," she said. And he didn't look any friendlier here than he had there.

"Vision or not, that sword looks real," Jake said. "I think we'd better head for the trees." They all got to their feet.

"We can't outrun that horse," Kendall yelled.

"Take Kendall," Nathan said. "I'll hold him off."

"No." Kendall saw Jake hesitate. Then Nathan turned, and she saw his eyes.

"Come on, Kendall." Jake gave her a nudge, and they started running toward the forest at the edge of the field.

"My legs feel like paper."

"Mine too, but we can't stop."

A roar sounded behind them and Kendall slowed. "Was that Nathan or the knight?" she yelled.

Jake grabbed her arm. "Keep moving."

Once they reached the forest, they turned to look back. Nathan was standing still as the black knight rode straight toward him. "What's he doing?" Kendall said. "He's going to get killed. We have to help him."

"I'll go." Before he could start back, Nathan let out a roar and started running toward the horse. It reared on its hind legs, pawing the air. The knight yelled something. He appeared to be trying to control the horse. It turned, throwing the knight on the ground, and ran off.

"It recognizes a more dangerous creature," Jake said.

The knight leapt to his feet and faced Nathan. The two men stared each other down. Then the knight backed away. Kendall watched to see what Nathan would do. "Don't kill him," she whispered. "Just run." He already believed he was dangerous. Killing someone else would just feed that fear. Then she saw the cross in her head. "Nathan! Show him your cross."

Nathan turned and looked at her. His eyes still glowed. He pulled the cross from under his shirt and held it up. The knight bowed his head and backed away.

Nathan ran toward her and Jake. He moved faster than anything humanly possible.

"How can anyone run like that?" she asked.

"Told you he was fast. I don't know what the hell he is, or how we got here, but I think he just saved our asses."

Nathan's eyes were almost normal by the time he got to Kendall and Jake. "You all right?" he asked Kendall.

She nodded. "We have to get out of here and back to the tunnel."

"How do we do that?" Jake asked. "We don't even know how we got here."

"I saw that black knight in the tunnel. He ran through us and I was touching you both. I think it . . . transported us."

"That's a hell of a thing," Jake said. "We see the ghost and then the real man. If that was the same knight."

"I think it was," Kendall said.

"The battlefield was the same as the one in the vision from the abbey."

"Wait a minute. You've both seen this before now?" Nathan asked.

"Jake has been dreaming of King Arthur since he was a kid," Kendall said.

"Bloody hell. I have too."

They all shared a look that must have been comical. "That's screwed up," Jake said.

"Maybe not," Kendall said. "I think we're meant to be here, to find this chalice."

"Fate," Jake said.

"I think so," Kendall said. "Let's hold hands. That seems to connect us. We've got to get back and stop the Reaper."

Nathan frowned and took their hands.

"Now what?" Jake asked.

"Focus. Think about the tunnel."

"How about we think about a fishing lake?" Jake said.

"If the Reaper has the chalice, he'll take it to the fountain. That has to be the room where I saw the statue," Nathan said. "We could concentrate on the room, skip the tunnel altogether."

"We don't know how this traveling thing works," Kendall said. "I think we need to think about something familiar to all of us or who knows where we'll end up. We were in the tunnel when this happened, so let's think about the tunnel."

As they held hands, Kendall tried to focus on the moment before she'd seen the black knight. "It's not working," she said.

"I could kiss you," Jake said.

"That won't be necessary." Just the mention of Jake kissing her and the resulting scowl on Nathan's face had done the trick. "Concentrate on the tunnel, the exact spot where we left." They closed their eyes and focused. It was difficult with the sounds of battle so close, but Kendall cleared her mind and tried again to recall the moment before the knight appeared. She felt something change in the air and a hollow feeling inside. It was happening. A moment later they were lying in the tunnel. It worked. She tried to move, but her muscles wouldn't cooperate. She turned her head and didn't see Nathan or Jake.

"Nathan? Jake?"

"Yeah," Jake said.

"Are you OK?"

"I'll let you know when my head reattaches itself to my body," Nathan said. He groaned and sat up.

"I don't know what the hell happened," Jake said, also sitting. "But I can live without it happening again."

Kendall slowly sat up, her head light and heavy at the same time. It took a minute before any of them could stand.

"Which tunnel do we take?" Jake asked, looking at the two tunnels.

"The one where I saw the knight," Kendall said. "He must be guarding something. Remember the legend of the ghost of a black knight guarding the abbey's treasures? And the ghosts I saw in the cave were knights. That's what they were doing, guarding the fountain."

They chose that tunnel and kept walking. The ground became more inclined as they went. "We've got to be getting close," Kendall said. "We've been walking for a mile."

A few minutes later they came to a wall.

"A dead end," Jake said. "Imagine that."

"The markings look like those on the cave wall," Kendall said. "Look, there's a nice fat circle."

"Circles are good," Jake said, shining his light on the mark.

"Try pushing it," Nathan said.

Kendall felt the warning, but it was too late.

CHAPTER TWENTY-FIVE

L OOK OUT!" SHE YELLED AS A RUMBLING NOISE FILLED THE tunnel. Something slammed into her. When the dust cleared, she saw Jake and Nathan both above her. They moved aside and she slowly sat up. "Next time you decide to knock me clear of danger, take turns. I think you broke my ribs." She regretted saying it, because they lost a full two minutes of valuable time with her trying to convince them she was being sarcastic.

"I knew we'd find booby traps sooner or later," Jake said. "Guess we shouldn't have pushed the circle."

The noise had come from a solid wall crashing down from the ceiling, blocking them in.

"This trap proves this is the right way," Kendall said.

"There must be a way to get out. We could push the circle again," Nathan said.

"The wall will probably start closing in and crush us," Jake said.

"Look for a keyhole," Kendall said.

"Is this one of your hunches?" Nathan asked.

"Hunches?" Kendall turned and looked at Nathan. "Why do you call them hunches?"

Nathan shrugged. "I don't know. Why?"

"Adam called them hunches."

Nathan's jaw clenched. Kendall saw something flash in his eyes before he looked away.

"Nathan, what did you remember when Raphael touched you?"

"A plane crash," Nathan said. "There was a fire. A man grabbed me and pulled me off the plane. Then it exploded."

"Who was the man? Did you recognize him?"

"No. I couldn't see."

"It was dark?"

"I was blind, I think. I couldn't remember anything. I don't think I knew who I was. He took me somewhere. I remember being in the woods. He pressed the cross into my hand, and then he fell. I think he died."

"I thought you found the cross," Kendall said.

"I've always had it. I never knew where it came from," Nathan said.

"How could you have gotten a Protettori cross?" Jake asked.

"From my father," Kendall said. "He must have given it to you. To Adam."

"You think I'm Adam?"

"I'm not sure, but I believe you might be," Kendall said.

Nathan seemed troubled by this.

"If your father died, he can't be the Reaper," Jake said.

"Raphael came back alive."

"We'll have to sort out Nathan's past later," Jake said, "or we're going to run out of air."

They examined the four walls, but it was taking too long and the air was getting thinner.

"If we don't get out of here soon, we're not gonna get out." He was looking at the wall where they'd found the circle. "There's a crack here on the side of the wall. It must be a door."

"A door isn't any good without a knob," Kendall said.

"We can break through it," Jake said.

"It's solid stone," she said.

"And Nathan has superhuman strength." Jake turned to Nathan. "You're the only one strong enough to move that wall. But you're gonna have to put some adrenaline behind it."

"No." Nathan looked at Kendall. "There has to be another way."

Jake shook his head. "There's no other way. We'll run out of air before we find the keyholes or whatever it takes to get out of here. You have to remember, they're guarding the Fountain of Youth. They're not going to make it easy to find."

"I can't just make it happen," Nathan said.

"I know. I'm going to hit you, get your adrenaline going. You have to focus your anger on that wall. We'll all die if you don't. Kendall will die."

"Then hit me and get the bloody hell out of the way."

"You can't hit him," Kendall said. "He'll kill you before you can get out of the way."

"You have a better idea?"

"Yes. Nathan, stand by the wall. Jake, come over here." She led him to the far corner of the closed-in space.

"What good is this going to do?" Jake asked.

"Nathan, focus on the wall." Kendall moved closer to Jake. Reaching up, she pulled his head down and kissed him.

"What the hell?" he mumbled against her mouth.

"Kiss me."

She opened her mouth against Jake's and nibbled at his lips, watching Nathan's reaction. His face was tight. He was getting upset, but she didn't know if it was enough.

Jake wrapped his arms around her and kissed her deeper. He lifted his head a little. "Is it working?"

"I don't know. He's upset, but he knows it's just an act."

Jake swiveled Kendall around so that he was facing Nathan. He moved his hands down to her butt and started pulling her against him.

Nathan's hands clenched. "Stop," he growled. His voice was different. Deeper.

"I'm sorry I had to do that," Jake whispered in Kendall's ear. "But I think it's working. His eyes are turning."

She glanced back and saw Nathan's body tense, his eyes fully changed now. They were amber but looked like a light was behind them, almost as if they were on fire as Brandi had said. He was magnificent.

He took a step toward them, fists clenched.

Kendall darted out of Jake's arms and stepped closer to Nathan, her eyes locked on his. She felt Jake grab for her, but she was too quick. "Nathan, please listen to me. You have to move the wall."

He stared at her for a moment longer, eyes bright as a flame, and Kendall understood the saying *like a moth to a flame*. Nathan could be dangerous in this condition, but she wanted to get closer to him.

He blinked once, then turned and slipped his hand in the crack along the edge of the door and started pulling. The door started to move, but it was slow. Nathan let out a roar that sounded deafeningly loud in the small space and pulled harder. It had only moved a few inches. Not enough for them to get through yet. They could get enough air to survive, but it wouldn't matter if they couldn't stop the Reaper from drinking from the chalice.

Jake slowly approached Nathan and knelt near the widening crack. Nathan turned and looked at Jake, and a shiver moved over Kendall's skin at Nathan's glowing eyes. What if he killed Jake?

"I'm going to help," Jake said. He sat down and put his back against the wall. He wedged a boot against the crack in the door, and he pushed while Nathan pulled.

"It's opening," Kendall said, starting toward them.

"Approach him slowly," Jake said softly.

"I can hear you," Nathan said. He turned and looked at Kendall. His eyes were still amber and he was panting.

"You're controlling it," she said.

He kept looking at her as the amber darkened until his eyes were their usual stormy gray.

"You did it, Nathan."

"Time for congratulations later," Jake said. "Let's get out of here."

They stepped through the doorway into the cave underneath the Tor. "I had hoped I wouldn't see this place again," Jake said. "Any idea how to get to the room Raphael kept you in?"

"No. He'd knocked me out," Nathan said.

"We need to find the mark on the wall like the one in the journal and on Nathan's arm," Kendall said. "I think it was closer to where we exited the cave."

"That should be this way," Jake said, pointing. "I can hear the statues humming. Everybody look for a wheel. And be quiet. He's probably got company."

His company found them sooner than Kendall expected. Several men rushed toward them. While Nathan and Jake fought them, two came around and grabbed Kendall, then dragged her off. She tried to dig in her heels, but it wasn't working. She bit the finger of the man who had his hand over her mouth. He yelled and let go. She whirled and kicked him in the crotch, then smashed the second man in the head with her flashlight.

She heard a roar as she ran back toward Nathan and Jake, but it was hard to tell what was happening in the dark. Flashlights cut haphazardly through the darkness as the men fought. Two bright orbs turned toward her. Nathan.

There were only two men left. Nathan threw one against the wall while Jake took on the other one. Kendall was close enough now to clearly see what was happening. Jake pinned the man on the ground, facedown with his arm twisted behind his back. He pressed his blade against his throat. "Where's the Reaper?"

The man laughed. "It doesn't matter what you do to me. He'll win."

Jake raked the blade lightly across the man's neck, and the laughter stopped. "I can cut your head off quick, or a little at a time. Where's the Reaper?"

"In there. Behind the wall."

"How do we get in?"

"You can't. It's those damned statues. He said to stay out here, keep everyone away. Except her. He wants her."

"Kendall?" Jake asked.

Nathan moved up beside them so quickly, he appeared to be gliding. With his glowing eyes, Kendall could almost believe he was a vampire or werewolf.

"What the hell is that?" the man asked, looking at Nathan.

"I'll let you find out if you don't tell us what you know," Jake said. "Why does the Reaper want Kendall?"

"He wants her gift. He needs to know if the chalice is the Holy Grail."

Nathan moved beside Kendall and looked at her with those fiery eyes. She could feel some kind of energy coming from him. Slowly, she reached for his hand. He jerked, but he didn't pull away.

"Don't let him near me," the man said.

Jake pressed the knife harder. "Don't worry about him. Worry about my knife. How did the Reaper know Kendall would be here?"

"He knows things. He said she'd come."

"How are you supposed to let him know she's here?"

"He said bang on the wall three times and he'll let her in, that she has a cross, whatever the hell that means."

"You'd better start knocking," Jake said, pulling the man to his feet. "One sound out of you to warn him and forget slitting your throat. I'll turn Nathan loose on you."

"The Reaper will kill me."

"You're already dead," Jake said. "You're just deciding whether it's fast or slow."

He shoved the man in the direction he pointed. The others were dead, lying behind them. They walked for a minute and the humming grew louder. "Hear that noise?" the man asked in a shaky voice. "The entrance is here somewhere. I have to look for a mark."

"Is this it?" Kendall asked, pointing to the circle that looked like a wheel, like the one in Nathan's journal and on his shoulder.

"Yeah. That's it."

"You sure?"

"Yeah. It looks like a wheel."

Jake did something really fast, and the man slumped to the floor.

Kendall jumped back. "Did you kill him?"

Jake didn't answer. "Nathan, get her out of here."

"No," Nathan said. "You take her. I'll go."

"Damn you both." Kendall picked up a rock and banged on the wall three times. "He wants me. He's probably my father. You two stay back."

There was a grinding noise, and a section of the wall began to open. A beautiful light emerged from the widening crack. A dark figure stood in the middle, shrouded by the glow.

CHAPTER TWENTY-SIX

THE STATUES HUMMED LOUDER AS THE SHADOW MOVED toward Kendall.

"You came." His voice was smooth, sharp, quiet, forceful. It was everything. It was nothing.

She touched the cross around her neck and stepped through the opening in the wall. She glanced back and saw Jake step through, then take off his cross and toss it to Nathan, who followed.

"That's not necessary," the Reaper said. "As long as you're touching someone who's wearing a cross, you're safe. Brandi came with Marco."

Brandi and Marco were pinned against a wall, but no constraints were visible. Brandi struggled, glaring at the Reaper with hatred. Marco just watched everything. It was impossible to tell if he was cognizant or not.

"Come in, please." He was still shadowed, with the compelling light behind him.

He turned, and Kendall saw his face for the first time. Maybe the second time, maybe the hundredth. She didn't know. He didn't look like her father or the man from the Italian inn or the historian he'd impersonated, but he did have on that red ring.

Kendall glanced quickly around the room. Nathan was right when he said it looked like a Roman temple. There were beautiful columns and a vaulted ceiling, beautifully painted as Nathan had described. The light in the room was warm. The source seemed to come from an opening in the floor. One statue stood a few feet away. Its presence might have been comforting if not for the Reaper standing in front of her. Obviously, he had found a way through the middle of the statues as Raphael feared he was trying to do. Where was Raphael? Had the Reaper killed him?

Nathan and Jake stood close beside Kendall. She could feel the tension radiating off them, but the Reaper seemed to be ignoring them for the moment. She knew from the power emanating from him that it was only an illusion. He was aware of everything happening in the room. She hoped he didn't know about Nathan. She could feel that he hadn't changed. Shocking, since even her adrenaline was surging, but she was glad he was controlling it, because she was certain it would be a very bad thing for the Reaper to see Nathan change.

"I'm sure you're here for the same reason I am. The chalice and the fountain. With your remarkable gift, I imagine you've discovered what happens when I combine the two."

"Eternal youth?" Kendall said.

"Yes." The Reaper studied her, his eyes roving over her face.

What color were they? She couldn't tell. She had been looking for some signs of her father, but she couldn't get anything from him. Not even the glimpse of familiarity she had gotten before. He was like a holographic image, appearing one way, but different from another angle.

"You must think me greedy. Evil."

"You've killed for this. What would you call it?" Kendall asked.

"Necessity," the Reaper said. "Sometimes terrible things are necessary for the better good."

"Whose better good? Not the men you've killed." Kendall glanced at Brandi, still pinned, her eyes burning with hatred. "Or the families you've destroyed."

The Reaper glanced at Brandi. "That is unfortunate. I wish I hadn't taken Brandi's father. I did not intend to destroy her family. I simply needed the relics he possessed." He held up his finger, showing the ruby ring. "This ring is powerful. It gives me health and strength."

"Why do you need them if it's not for greed? What is so necessary?"

"I don't know that I could explain my motives. You, of all people, might understand, but I won't go into detail now. I will ask a favor of you. I would like for you to touch the chalice and tell me if it's real."

"Why?"

"There are consequences that I would prefer to avoid if it isn't the Holy Grail."

"Why would I do this?"

"For your friends. If you do this for me, I will let them live. If you don't, I will kill them."

"Where is the chalice?"

"Nearby. Will you do this for me?"

Kendall nodded.

"Very good. I'm afraid Nathan and Jake will have to join Marco and Brandi while we work." The Reaper did something with his hands and Jake flew against the wall, pinned like he had been by her father in the chapel in Italy. Nathan wasn't so easily moved. His eyes instantly changed. He let out a roar and ran toward the Reaper.

The Reaper put up a hand as if to say hello, and Nathan stopped in midstride. He appeared to be blocked by some kind of wall. "What . . . is . . . this?" the Reaper asked, enunciating each word with awe. He stood with his hand raised, expression stunned, studying Nathan like a rare specimen at a zoo. "It can't be." He blinked and the shock faded from his face. His expression took on a look of delight, and Kendall started to pick up something familiar. Then he changed again.

While Nathan was stuck there, his eyes went back to normal. The Reaper raised his hand and sent him into the wall beside Jake. "For now," he said. He walked close and studied both men, staring at them for the longest time.

"Is it possible, Marco?"

Marco didn't answer. He watched the Reaper calmly, as if waiting for a hand of cards to be dealt. "Well now. That changes things." The Reaper appeared almost shaken as he walked over to a table near one of the statues. He looked up at the stone sentinel as he approached. A look crossed his face, perhaps arrogance, perhaps fear.

He removed a chalice from the box. It was wide, metal, bluish tinged, with engravings on the side.

"I envy your gift," he said. "I have many abilities, but not this." He handed the chalice to Kendall. "Tell me what you see and I'll release . . . your friends."

Kendall took the chalice in her hands. It was cold, but she felt energy coming from it. She closed her eyes. It was hard to focus, hard not to think about the others trapped against the wall. She had to do this for them. The Reaper might kill them all, but there was a chance he wouldn't if she cooperated. If she didn't, she was certain they were all dead.

She let the sensations move from her fingertips to her mind. The chalice was old. There was energy radiating from it, but it wasn't the chalice she'd seen at the well. This wasn't the Holy Grail. She dreaded to tell the Reaper for fear he would kill them in anger. Then she saw the Reaper drinking from the chalice. The image was so clear. If she hadn't held the chalice in her own hands, she would have believed she was seeing the Reaper drinking from it for real. She saw him cry out and fall to the ground, and when his face turned up to curse her, he looked older.

Kendall kept her eyes closed, pretending to examine the chalice while she decided what to do. The Reaper feared using the chalice if it wasn't the Holy Grail. He had said there were consequences if he used the chalice and it wasn't authentic. Would it kill him or just weaken him? If the Reaper could be weakened, perhaps Nathan could defeat him.

She opened her eyes. "It's very old and powerful. I can feel the energy coming from it."

"Is it the Holy Grail?"

"Yes. Please don't do this," she said, trying to make her lie seem authentic.

"There is no choice, really." He moved closer to her and touched his hands to each side of her face.

She heard Jake shouting curses at the Reaper, and growls that must have been coming from Nathan. She felt her mind slipping and knew he was searching her to see if she told the truth. She grabbed for something to think about, something that might block him or distract him. The first thing that came to her mind was Raphael. He had been close to the Reaper. She kept her eyes on the Reaper and her thoughts on Raphael. The Reaper frowned and lowered his hands. He took the chalice from her and held it in front of him. "Then I will drink. Finally."

He glanced at the wall where Nathan and Jake were still struggling to get free. Nathan's eyes were like flames again, and he seemed to be making some progress at pulling away from the wall.

Kendall shook her head. "Please," she mouthed to Nathan and Jake. "Don't." She moved her hand quickly over her heart. Anyone else would assume it was just a movement. For her and Adam it meant *trust me.*

Nathan stopped moving, watching her with those fiery eyes. He said something to Jake who was watching her as well. His eyes were full of anger, fear . . . and something else. Love.

The Reaper walked over to a stone on the wall that looked like a wheel, like the marking on the cave wall. He turned the wheel, and Kendall heard a grinding noise. "You should step back."

Kendall moved, and a large section of the floor began to open, revealing steps. The light grew brighter and she heard running water. She hadn't heard it before. The humming of the statues had disguised it. Kendall walked to the edge of the steps and looked down. The steps descended to a pool of water. A path divided the pool and led to two streams flowing side by side from the wall. One left a red stain; the other white. The water flowed into a stone bowl, like the one in the sketch from the black journal. A warm light emanated from the bowl. It should have been blinding since it was the source of light for the entire room, but it was soft, enchanting. The Fountain of Youth.

It was simple, not elaborate as she might have expected, other than the light. But she could feel its power from here.

"Would you like to touch it?" he asked.

She glanced at Nathan and Jake and nodded. She walked down the steps with the Reaper and sat beside him, wondering if he was her father, afraid to ask. She was torn between a desperate wish that he was, so she could see him again, and a prayer that he wasn't, because he was evil. He had hurt people. She dipped her fingers in the water. Her skin tingled, and she felt an urge to step inside the pool.

"Marvelous, isn't it?"

"Yes," she said.

"Do you want to taste it?"

She dipped her fingers in again and looked back at the wall where the others were still trapped. She shook her head.

"You are strong willed. And wise. The water is deadly unless drunk from a holy vessel." He patted the chalice, and Kendall hoped like hell that it wasn't holy.

"You were testing me?"

He smiled, his face changing without ever changing. It must be some kind of mind control, she thought.

"Perhaps." He stood and walked up the path to the bowl of light. "This is the strongest source. The light and the water." He dipped the chalice in the water and held it up.

Kendall wondered if it was possible to drown someone in the Fountain of Youth. He was too powerful for her. He would kill her and she knew, without vanity, that that would kill Nathan and Jake. So she waited, hoping her vision proved true.

The Reaper turned and looked at her. "I would ask you to join me, but I know you won't." He looked wistful, and she felt the sense of familiarity again.

She shook her head. "I can't."

He nodded and lifted the cup. "To the past and the future." He put the chalice to his mouth and drank.

Kendall quickly hurried up the steps. She didn't know exactly what would happen if her vision proved true.

The Reaper closed his eyes and took a deep breath. He frowned and touched his stomach. "What have you done?" He bent over and groaned. "No." His body twitched. "No!"

"Run, Kendall. Get away from him," Nathan yelled. He was struggling hard to get free, as was Jake.

"Get out of here," Jake yelled. "Run into the cave."

The Reaper came up the steps toward Kendall. "You've deceived me," he said, looking at his hands, which already looked older. He let out a terrible cry and lifted his hands toward Nathan, Jake, and Brandi.

"No!" Kendall threw out her hands, and the Reaper flew backward. He lay on his back, staring at her, stunned.

Kendall looked at her hands. What had just happened?

The Reaper sat up, his face almost recognizable in his shock. Then his features shifted again. "I didn't expect that. I think you didn't either." He looked older than he had when they arrived, but his eyes were still powerful. He glanced at the wall where Nathan and Jake yanked at their invisible bonds. He began moving slowly toward her.

Kendall wiggled her fingers, wondering if she could make the thing happen again. She didn't have to try. Before the Reaper reached her, something dark flew across the room and moved between them. Raphael.

He was dressed in his dark robes again. His hair was pulled back, and two braids hung on either side of his tense face. His eyes were glowing like Nathan's.

"My old friend," the Reaper said. "I wondered when you would show up." He took a slow step backward and studied Raphael. "I have missed you. I would hope that you've reconsidered my offer, but the anger in your eyes tells me no."

"The answer will always be no. You betrayed us all, especially me," Raphael said.

"I have made mistakes," the Reaper said. "Many mistakes. It would be useless to explain the reasons to you now."

"You've destroyed the order, forsaken sacred vows."

"I did not intend to destroy the order. I'm quite fond of it, in fact, and quite fond of you, my brother, but it was necessary."

"I don't want to kill you," Raphael said, "but you leave me no choice."

"Nor I you," the Reaper said, his eyes sad. He stretched out his hands, and Kendall felt a vibration under her feet as the air surrounding the Reaper thickened like a mist.

Raphael ran toward the Reaper and grabbed hold of him. Both of them disappeared.

Kendall heard thuds and saw Nathan, Jake, Marco, and Brandi getting up from the floor.

"Where did they go?" Kendall asked.

"I don't know," Marco said, looking at the spot from which the Reaper and Raphael had disappeared. "It could be good. Or very bad."

Nathan and Jake hurried over to Kendall. Jake pulled her into his arms. "You scared the hell out of me."

Kendall hugged him back. She'd almost lost him. And Nathan. Nathan stood beside them, his expression blank. She reached for his hand. Nathan took hers but kept his distance. Kendall stepped out of Jake's arms and faced Nathan. She studied his dark eyes, somber, not laughing, hair short, not wild and carefree as it had been then. Tears welled in her eyes. Nathan's jaw clenched, and for the first time since she had known him, she saw something in his mind. Herself . . . as a young girl.

She wrapped her arms around him. "I've missed you, Adam." Tears slid down her cheeks as he slowly put his arms around her. She laid her head against his chest and listened to his heart thumping. Alive. Adam was alive.

"I don't know if I am Adam," he said quietly, arms tightening around her shoulders.

"I do." She leaned back. "What does this mean?" She placed her open hand over her heart.

"Trust me," Nathan said.

"Only Adam would know that." She smiled and felt another rush of tears. "I can't believe I found you again. Or you found me." She wiped her tears and glanced over at Jake. "I found Adam."

Jake's face looked like a mask. She knew that in his mind Adam would be a threat to this thing between them. She didn't know how, but she was sure there was room for both men in her life. In fact, she couldn't imagine not having both of them around. The details would have to be sorted out later. For now, they were both alive. Kendall stepped out of Nathan's arms but held on to his hand. She reached for Jake's and squeezed it.

"So this isn't the Holy Grail," Brandi said, picking up the fallen chalice from the bottom of the steps.

"Trust her to go straight for the relic," Jake said.

Brandi's words brought them back to the present. Kendall wiped her eyes again. "No."

"You sensed it?" Brandi asked.

Kendall nodded. "I saw a vision of him aging."

"You're the real deal," Brandi said.

"You were very smart to trick him," Marco said. "Drinking from the wrong chalice has aged him, made him weaker, perhaps enough for Raphael to destroy him."

Brandi shook her head. "This is some seriously crazy crap. What are you? What is Nathan?" She looked at Jake and wiggled her fingers. "Do you have weird talents too?"

"No. Just guns."

"I think I'll get one myself. All I have is my brother's knife." A look of sadness crossed her face.

"You saved us," Nathan said to Kendall. "The Reaper would have killed us all if you hadn't stopped him."

"Arthur would be proud," Marco said.

"Who is Arthur?" Kendall asked.

"King Arthur. He was the first guardian."

"King Arthur was one of the Protettori?" Kendall asked.

"He was. As were many of his knights. That's why they searched for the Holy Grail. To protect it. And they still do."

"The black knight and the ghosts in the cave," Kendall said. "They *were* knights."

Nathan ran a hand over his head. "Bloody hell."

"I knew he must be connected when he told me to find the chalice. Obviously not this chalice."

"Not this one," Marco said. "But there is another one, the real chalice. We must keep it from the Reaper."

"Let's hope he's dead," Jake said.

"He'll be very difficult to kill," Marco said.

"Kendall knocked him on his ass," Jake said. "How did you do that?"

"I don't know," Kendall said. "It just happened."

Marco's eyes looked bright as he studied Kendall. "I knew you were strong, but I didn't expect this from you. Perhaps from Adam, since he's the one who took the vow."

"Adam didn't take the vow," Kendall said. "I did. Adam tried to stop me."

Marco looked puzzled. "He said he had done it."

"Adam was trying to keep me from getting in trouble. He always looked out for me." Kendall looked at Nathan. "Do you remember that?"

"I remember seeing the statues and the castle. I don't remember any vow."

Marco looked at Kendall and his face brightened. "If you took the vow, then you're the one."

"I'm the what?" Kendall asked.

"The new Keeper."

"Keeper?"

"Of the relics."

CHAPTER TWENTY-SEVEN

Y OU MEAN SHE'S ONE OF THE PROTETTORI?" JAKE ASKED.
"Yes. She took the vow to protect the relics. I knew the Keeper would come again, when it was time, but I thought it would be Adam."

"Adam was there too. He got caught in the light," Kendall said, looking at Nathan. "I thought I caused his death. You said the vow couldn't be taken lightly."

"The others were angry. He would have died, but I knew it was destined. That's why I sent Adam away to be protected."

"Does that mean I should have died too?" Kendall asked.

"Perhaps." Marco's blue eyes met Kendall's, and she knew he wasn't telling the truth. Not all of it anyway.

"Marco, am I Adam?" Nathan asked.

Marco smiled. "It's not for me to say." Claiming he needed rest, although he seemed to have more energy than Kendall had seen before, he asked Brandi to help him. His cross got them both safely past the statues.

Things were awkward with just Kendall, Nathan, and Jake there. They were quiet at first, each of them grappling with the events of the night and the discovery, or doubt, that Nathan was

Adam. Slowly, as in the way that the present always supersedes the past, their relationships fell back into place as they explored the temple. It was an astonishing place. They found seven statues, placed at intervals along the edges of the room. Kendall studied each one, wondering who was inside the stone, who the guardian had been before becoming a sentinel. She touched several of them and saw glimpses of lives lived and lost. The sensations were so strong they could have been overwhelming, but they weren't. She felt calm. Controlled. Then they made another astonishing discovery. In a small room behind an ornate, iron door they found three marble tombs.

"No names," Jake said, running his hand over the middle tomb. "Who do you think is in there?"

"I think we've found King Arthur and Guinevere," Kendall said.

"So the monks hid the bodies," Nathan said. "What about the third tomb?"

Kendall touched the cold marble and felt an ache in her heart. "One of the other knights? I don't know."

"Something about this place is eerie," Jake said. "Let's get back to the fountain."

Nathan frowned, his expression troubled. "Yeah. Let's leave them in peace."

Afterward, Kendall, Nathan, and Jake sat on the steps, staring at the Fountain of Youth.

"The red stream looks like the Chalice Well," Jake said.

"I think it's a combination of both the Chalice Well and the White Spring," Kendall said. "Two sources, both powerful."

Jake looked at Nathan. "You thinking about taking a swim?"

"Tempting," Nathan said.

"Don't risk it. We don't know how the fountain works," Kendall said. "The Reaper said it's deadly to drink from anything but a holy vessel. I saw a cup and a vial in the castle, in the room with the mural. The Protettori drink water from the fountain in a ceremony. I don't know if getting in the water would work."

"I guess the question is, would it hurt?" Jake said. "The Protettori do like traps. Look what happened when the Reaper drank from the wrong cup. He's going to be pissed."

"Pissed, or intrigued," Nathan said. "Neither one is a good prospect for Kendall."

"I don't like how he looked at her," Jake said. "If he isn't dead, he's going to come for her."

"You have to stay at the mansion where we can protect you," Nathan said.

"If I'm a Keeper, you two have to stop giving orders," Kendall said.

"Just because you're part of the Protettori doesn't mean someone can't hurt you," Jake said. "Even with that superpower thing you did to the Reaper. I doubt you have any control over it any more than Nathan does. Hell, I feel like the nerd here. I'm the only one without any superpowers."

Kendall patted Jake's leg. "You have guns and two of the best fists I've ever seen."

"That's not much compared to the Hulk here, and you, what are you, Wonder Woman?"

"Don't pout," Kendall said. "Who knows, you might have some kind of superpower too. I had no idea I could do anything like that. I think I'm going to have to try to read Marco. There are still a lot of loose ends to figure out. He isn't telling us everything. Raphael is hiding something too."

"What are we gonna do about Brandi? She's determined to destroy the relics, and now she knows where the Fountain of Youth is." Nathan scratched his chin, shadowed with two days' growth of beard. Kendall still couldn't grasp that he was Adam. After she had spent a lifetime being haunted by him, missing him every day, feeling like a piece of her soul was missing, that she had failed him, now he was here. Alive.

"She's probably plotting a way to blow up the temple as we speak," Jake said. "She knows too much."

"We're not killing her," Kendall said.

"I didn't say we should," Jake said. "But you know she'll try to destroy the relics. She's not going to care that you're the Keeper."

"If Raphael kills the Reaper, Brandi won't need the relics," Kendall said.

"I don't think the Reaper is dead," Nathan said. "I don't think it's going to be that easy."

"Then you could kidnap her," Jake said. "Make sure she doesn't interfere."

"I considered it at the hotel," Nathan said.

"You can't just go around kidnapping people," Kendall said.

"Nathan could buy her off," Jake said. "Give her a million dollars to go off to some resort."

"It wouldn't work," Nathan said. "She's determined to stop the Reaper. And now she has Thomas's death to avenge."

"Assuming the Reaper is still alive, we'll have to convince Brandi to work with us, not against us."

"And if she won't?" Jake asked.

"I'm not so worried about the temple," Kendall said. "She can't get in without a cross, and she can't blow it up without the whole world knowing. But I think she'll go for the chalice."

"We don't even know where to start looking for the real chalice," Jake said.

"That's why we have Kendall," Nathan said.

"Keeper of the relics," Jake said.

Keeper. "I can't believe this," Kendall said. She was part of the Protettori. It still didn't seem real, or even right. She was just Kendall. Just a woman. How could she be part of a secret order?

"I guess you'll have to tell her where you've hidden the Spear of Destiny," Jake said to Nathan.

"Will I?"

"If you don't, she might fling you around like she did the Reaper," Jake said.

"I'm not flinging anyone around . . . as long as you stop treating me like I'm helpless. So, what do we do with this place?"

"You're the Keeper," Jake said. "What do you think?"

"We guard it," she said.

"We?" Jake said.

"I can't do it alone. God knows where Raphael is. Marco comes and goes like the tide. We're it. Can you station guards throughout the tunnel?" Kendall asked Nathan.

He nodded. "We'll have to bring them in through the opening in the Tor. We can't let anyone know about the portal in the maze."

"And the entrance through the Tor," Jake said. "Although it's probably safe since it's been there for God knows how long and no one has found it."

"We'll put in a steel door with an access code," Nathan said.

"That might be hard to explain to the good folks of Glastonbury," Jake said.

"We'll have to bring it through the maze so no one sees," Nathan said. "That means you and I will have to do it. We'll leave the outside disguised as it is."

"And the priest hole will have to be sealed," Kendall said. "If someone did find it, they'd probably never get past that wall that fell. But we should seal the entrance up to be safe. We'll have to do it at night so no one sees."

"It's almost dawn. We should go back before Fergus comes with a search party."

They turned the wheel and watched as the floor covered the steps leading to the fountain.

"This isn't the end," Kendall said. "If the Reaper is still alive, he'll try to find the real Holy Grail."

"I guess that's our next relic," Jake said. "The Holy Grail. Sounds like a quest."

"Maybe that's why you dreamed of King Arthur when you were a kid," Kendall said. "Because one day you would have the same quest he did."

"It'd be nice if King Arthur would give us a hint where we can find it," Jake said as they walked back to the Abbey House. His words held their usual sarcasm, but also a bit of awe.

Fergus had already formed a search party of two—himself and Art. They were trying to get into the priest hole when Kendall, Nathan, and Jake found them. Fergus was dressed in his butler suit and was backing into the hole while Art directed him from below. When grilled, Art swore he hadn't told a soul about the great secret he had been entrusted with, that Fergus had forced him on pain of death to take him to the tunnel.

"That is an extreme exaggeration," Fergus said, glaring at Art.

After they got rid of Art, Fergus, Kendall, Nathan, and Jake went to the room. Nathan sat on the sofa. "Fergus, who am I?"

Fergus blinked. "What do you mean, sir?"

"You know bloody well what I mean. Who hired you?"

Fergus pulled in a breath that made the buttons on his shirt strain at the buttonholes. "Marco."

"How the bloody hell did that happen?"

"He contacted me through an employment service. He said he had an orphaned boy who needed to be looked after."

"You never told me this?"

"You never asked, sir. And Marco made me swear in writing that I would not tell you anything about your childhood. He said it was a matter of security."

"This is crazy," Nathan said. "Who was my father?"

"I don't know that, sir. Someone powerful with powerful enemies. Marco said you must be protected."

"Stop calling me sir. What about the money, the boarding schools . . . Where did it come from?" Nathan asked.

"The foundation, sir. The one you asked me to research."

"The one that owns the castle in Italy? Why didn't you tell me?"

"You already had so much on your mind. Then I saw Marco and I was shocked. I hadn't seen him since you were a boy. He and I talked, and we decided it best to wait a while to tell you."

"But you work for me," Nathan said.

"Not technically," Fergus said.

"I should fire you."

Fergus scowled at Nathan. "I was doing my job, sir. The job I was hired to do. I've done it very well. I've watched over you as I would my own son."

Nathan sighed. "I'm sorry, Fergus." He rubbed his chin. "I just wish you had told me."

"I couldn't. I was sworn to secrecy, and I thought your life depended on it. Are you planning to return to the hotel tonight? I think Marco will need to rest first, and I'm sure he would like to visit the abbey again before we go. It's been a long time since he was here."

"I'm not going anywhere tonight," Kendall said. Her brain was fried.

"We'll stay here until tomorrow," Nathan said. "I don't know about anyone else, but I'm too tired to move anyway."

Fergus fairly flew out of the room, leaving Kendall, Nathan, and Jake alone. She sat down across from the men. "Some night this has been. We found the Fountain of Youth, finally met the Reaper." She looked at Nathan. "Discovered that Adam is alive."

"I'm still not sure I'm Adam. There are some things that make me think I am. The man in my dream, or my memory, whatever it was, he called me Adam." He rubbed a hand through his hair. "The first time I saw you, I felt as if I knew you. That's one reason I hired you. I had to know why you looked familiar when nothing from my childhood was."

"I saw one of your memories in the fountain room," Kendall said. "I saw myself as a little girl. How could you have seen me back then if you're not Adam? And only Adam knew our secret sign for *trust me*. Do you want me to try to read you? Maybe it'll jog something."

"Maybe later."

"Why not now?" Kendall asked. "Then you'll know for sure." She wasn't positive she could read him, but there might be a chance if he wasn't blocking her.

"He's afraid," Jake said quietly, his lips tight. "He's afraid he's not Adam."

Nathan gave Jake an irritated look, but he didn't deny it.

"We need to go back to Great Falls and see if you remember anything," Kendall said.

"Great Falls?" Nathan asked.

"That's where you lived. Where Adam lived."

Nathan nodded. "That might help. I get these flashes of strange places. Strange faces."

"If you're Adam, and I think you are, I owe you an apology. You tried to stop me from leaving the room at the castle, but I didn't listen. I got you into this. I'm probably responsible for your father dying, for my father dying."

Nathan put his hand over hers. "I don't think you caused it. You said something was bothering your father, and mine, or Adam's. If he had money and a rare collection, I'm sure he had enemies. There were probably threats. Look at me. There are many people who would kill for my collection, not just the Reaper. It's not your fault." He shrugged. "I can't remember them anyway."

"Your . . . condition is also my fault. You were there when I took the vow, and you got caught in the light."

"I think you were right about it not being a curse. Not exactly. I don't understand it, but I feel like I've gained more control."

"You may be like Raphael. You have to learn to use it."

"Are you saying he's a damned guardian?" Jake asked.

"He's got the eyes and the speed," Kendall said. "And I didn't tell you that the black knight in the tunnel had glowing eyes."

Jake threw up his hands. "Now you're gonna tell me Nathan is Adam and some kind of modern knight?"

"I'm not saying that," Kendall said. "But it's kind of odd if you think about it. Marco said King Arthur and his knights were the first of the order. Raphael is really old. He could have been a knight, and his eyes glow like Nathan's."

"If Raphael gets back alive, he's got some questions to answer," Nathan said.

"I'm not calling you Adam," Jake said.

Nathan shrugged. "I've been Nathan for longer than I've been Adam, if I'm even him." Then he and Jake started arguing about sleeping arrangements. "Maybe there's another room available?"

"There's not," Jake said. "I checked for you."

"For me?" Nathan said, frowning.

"You two take the bed," Kendall said. "I'll sleep on the sofa."

"Let him take the sofa," Jake said.

"I'm going to take a shower. You two sort it out." She needed just a moment without having either of them around.

She walked into the bathroom and undressed. She pulled back the shower curtain to turn on the water and saw a man's legs stretched out in the bathtub. Kendall screamed and the man leapt at her, but he got tangled in the shower curtain and fell into her. They both landed on the floor. The bathroom door crashed open as Kendall realized who was on top of her.

Raphael.

ACKNOWLEDGMENTS

T HERE ARE ALWAYS SO MANY PEOPLE INVOLVED IN THE COMPLEX process of taking a book from that first glimmer of an idea to a published story. As always, I have to thank my husband and kids for their patience and love and inspiration. Austin, you have some great ideas! Thanks to my agent, Christine Witthohn, a true friend and champion. My critique partner, Dana Rodgers, for her wonderful editing and brainstorming. Thanks to Lori McDermeit, Tamie Holmes, and Fawn Johns for their insights into the book. Lori—if I'm ever out that way, I want one of your meals! To Clarence Haynes, my developmental editor, for his expert direction, and to Kelli Martin, my wonderful Montlake editor, and the Montlake team, thank you all!

ABOUT THE AUTHOR

N EW YORK TIMES AND USA TODAY bestselling author Anita Clenney writes mysteries and paranormal romantic suspense novels, including the bestselling Connor Clan series. Clenney grew up an avid reader, devouring Nancy Drew and Hardy Boys books before moving on to mysteries and romance. It was only after several successful but wildly different careers—including work as an executive assistant, a real estate agent, a teacher's assistant, and a brief stint in a pickle factory—that she discovered her untapped passion for writing. Clenney's first novel, *Awaken the Highland Warrior,* won the Single Title Reviewers' Choice Award. She lives with her husband and two children in suburban Virginia.

www.anitaclenney.com